DEATH KIT

SUSAN SONTAG DEATH KIT

FARRAR, STRAUS AND GIROUX • NEW YORK

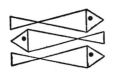

FOR DIANA KEMENY
with love,
gratefully

DEATH KIT

DIDDY the Good was taking a business trip. The Diddy, his family nickname, was used (now) only by his brother and a few friends left over from schooldays. "Hi, Diddy!" Paul sang out every time he came into town, dropping by the office without warning or turning up unannounced at Diddy's apartment at three in the morning. Diddy the Good is how he, Diddy, embellished the nickname, sometimes, in his mocking self-appraisals. Also: Good Diddy, Goody Did, and Done-Done. Himself and childhood friends apart, the right name was Dalton.

1

Dalton Harron, in full: a mild fellow, gently reared in a middle-sized city in Pennsylvania and expensively educated. A good-natured child, the older son of civilized parents who had quietly died. (Now) a rather handsome man of thirty-three. Quieter than he once was. A little fussy, perhaps; somewhat sententious. Used to getting an answer when he spoke politely to someone, and never reconciled to the brutal manners of the metropolis in which (now) he lived. But unresentful. The sort of man who doesn't mistreat women, never loses his credit cards or breaks a plate while washing up, works conscientiously at his job, lends money to friends graciously, walks his dog each midnight no matter how tired he feels. The sort of man it's hard to dislike, and whom disaster avoids.

Diddy, not really alive, had a life. Hardly the same. Some people are their lives. Others, like Diddy, merely inhabit their lives. Like insecure tenants, never knowing exactly the extent of their property or when the lease will expire. Like unskilled cartographers, drawing and redrawing erroneous maps of an exotic continent.

Eventually, for such a person, everything is bound to run down. The walls sag. Empty spaces bulge between objects. The surfaces of objects sweat, thin out, buckle. The hysterical fluids of fear deposited at the core of objects ooze out along the seams. Deploying things and navigating through space become laborious. Too much effort to amble from kitchen to living room, serving drinks, turning on the hi-fi, pretending to be cheerful. But Diddy's difficulties can't be solved by making a bigger effort. Stepped-up effort won't repair his ingenious sense of incapacity, which proceeds from a hallucinated erasure of the present as it becomes past. To supplement effort, Diddy needs faith. Which he lacks (now). Making everything unpredictable. Showing up promptly at ten o'clock at the Lexington Avenue offices of Watkins & Company must be accomplished five times a week in the face of Diddy's suspicion, each morning, that it's never been done before. Each morning he does it. That's a miracle. Yet, lacking faith, Diddy is unable to conclude that the occurrence of miracles guarantees a world in which such miracles take place. Concludes, instead, that to perform something one sets out to perform isn't really a miracle. More like a

2

gross rupture of the inert, fragile, sticky fabric of things. Or a silly accident; as when somebody carelessly brandishes a pair of scissors and makes an ugly rent in the fabric, or inadvertently burns holes in it with a cigarette.

Everything running down: suffusing the whole of Diddy's well-tended life. Like a house powered by one large generator in the basement. Diddy has an almost palpable sense of the decline of the generator's energy. Or, of the monstrous malfunctioning of that generator, gone amok. Sending forth a torrent of refuse that climbs up into Diddy's life, cluttering all his floor space and overwhelming his pleasant furnishings, so that he's forced to take refuge. Huddle in a narrow corner. But however small the space Diddy means to keep free for himself, it won't remain safe. If solid material can't invade it, then the offensive discharge of the failing or rebellious generator will liquefy; so that it can travel everywhere, spread like a skin. The generator will spew forth a stream of crude oil, grimy and malodorous, that coats all things and persons and objects, the vulgar as well as the precious, the ugly as well as what little still remains beautiful. Befouling Diddy's world and rendering it unusable. Uninhabitable.

This deliquescent running-down of everything becomes co-existent with Diddy's entire span of consciousness, undermines his most minimal acts. Getting out of bed is an agony unpromising as the struggles of a fish cast up on the beach, trying to extract life from the meaningless air. Persons who merely have-a-life customarily move in a dense fluid. That's how they're able to conduct their lives at all. Their living depends on not seeing. But when this fluid evaporates, an uncensored, fetid, appalling underlife is disclosed. Lost continents are brought to view, bearing the ruins of doomed cities, the sparsely fleshed skeletons of ancient creatures immobilized in their death throes, a landscape of unparalleled savagery. One can redeem skeletons and abandoned cities as human. But not a lost, dehumanized nature. Having been freed for so long from human regard, from the scrutiny and aspirations of people, the barren mountains of Tyrrhenia cannot resemble any known mountains on the planet. How they would shudder and sweat in the unsubstantial air.

3

So Diddy's life, since the customary opaque medium has begun leaking away. The soft interconnected tissuelike days are unstrung. The watery plenum is dehydrated, and what protrudes are jagged, inhuman units. The medium steadily evaporates; the teeming interlocked plenitude is drained of its sustenance. Dies. All that's left is arbitrary and incomprehensible. Including human speech, which declines into mere sound. Yet, Diddy observes, nobody has yet discovered, or at least dared to admit publicly, the gruesome fall of the water level, the drying up of vital lubricants, the erosion of the littoral of human-scale sense. Shall Diddy be the first to proclaim it? Presumptuous Diddy. Though he's always tried to be honest, he never claimed to be wise. Perhaps there's some wisdom embedded in the lie about life everybody mouths that Diddy doesn't understand (now), if perhaps he once did. So Diddy goes on speaking, just like everyone else. Words like acrid chalk-colored cubes spill out of a rotating cage. After scooping them up, Diddy lays out one implausible word after another, creating the plausible semblance of a line. Signifying ordinary intentions, promises, opinions, requests and denials, agreements and disagreements. Though he no longer understands why. And though it's hard enough just to exhale and inhale, without expending the little breath he retains on speech.

As the water line sinks, mere events loom up—monstrous, discontinuous. Diddy gasps for breath and, wherever he moves, bruises himself. Diddy, a failed amphibian. For whom all tasks have become senseless, all space inhospitable, virtually all people grotesque, all climates unseasonable, and all situations dangerous.

For whom all tasks have become senseless. Diddy's actions take longer and longer, and still never seem properly performed.

For whom all space appears inhospitable. And, more and more, untraversable. Having moved his body from one place to another, Diddy suffers from the knowledge that he hasn't taken a single step. And even if it could be established that some small displacement was effected, there's no telling how much. Suppose someone says, Go over there. Or, more amiably, Please, if you

4

don't mind, go over there. Where is over there? How would Diddy know when he'd reached the right place? His companion might say, That's right. Perfect! Stay where you are. But perhaps the person giving the directions is mistaken, or wishes to deceive him.

For whom virtually all people appear more grotesque and ugly. Each day it becomes worse. Diddy sees the surfaces of people, deformed and bloated and leaden and crammed with vile juices. Along with this Brobdingnagian eye, he's also cursed (now) with X-ray vision; he can see right through the flesh to the ghastly sorrow every two-legged upright creature conceals. Also, with unnaturally acute hearing. Whenever the volume of mute suppliant suffering in the world is turned up high, perhaps for the delectation of the more detached gods only, Diddy hears, too. The burden of sensing too much that arouses his sympathy is breaking Diddy's heart.

For whom all climates are unseasonable. Overheated during last winter's snows and generally restive in his heavy clothing, he felt chilled by the blaze of this past summer's sun and couldn't dress warmly enough. (Now) autumn has come. Another semi-artificial Manhattan winter about to claim its allotted duration. A too familiar sequence. As September threatens to break into October, Diddy knows what's coming. Something unpleasant. Perhaps he's preparing to defend himself. Is this why Diddy's hands are less under his guidance than usual? In the worst times (now) his hands seem to become ensouled, and want to do what they shouldn't do.

For whom all situations seem dangerous. It doesn't matter what Diddy does, and no situation is neutral. Depending upon the composition of his feelings, he's either paralyzed with fear or smothering a convulsive agitation. Those worst times, again.

One of the worst times is late at night, after he's walked Xan and bought the first edition of the *Times,* returned home, and gotten into bed with the newspaper. His fingertips keep insinuating themselves into his mouth. Unlike Paul, who's been a frantic nail-biter since childhood, Diddy never had the habit, and despises it, but (now), throughout his nightly reading, as well as in any movie, has to wrestle with an excruciating desire to offer his nails to his eager teeth. Worn out, he finally tosses the paper on the floor; sleeps; dreams. . . . The nervous raw music filters into Diddy's ears. He opens his eyes and it begins again, for early morning is the other worst time. At the open window, pulling down the blinds before he dresses. In front of the bathroom mirror minutes later, shaving. The lethal invitation of windows and mirrors.

Trying to control his strong hands. For both of these times have begun to present Diddy with a sinister, unnamable temptation.

Eventually, the temptation finds speech. Hands, innocent of language, need the consent of the mind, which is nourished by words. These words, a nomenclature of utmost seriousness. Meaning, seriously, to kill himself, Diddy swallowed half a bottle of sleeping pills one evening; after walking the dog, who sprawls (now) before the fireplace in the living room. It's twelve-thirty; in his bedroom, door closed, Diddy lies back and shuts his eyes. Begins to float down, softly, peaceably. Followed by an interval of undetermined length: some dark time, in which it's hard to breathe. He can hear the moaning, someone making sounds like a donkey braying. Stomach hurts. He falls out of bed, head first. Onto something painfully hard. And on the hard floor, something wet that smells foul. Xan is barking, and his neighbor in the apartment opposite— a pretty, off-Broadway actress—is shouting into his face. He's being shoveled into the rear of a truck. Then a youngish trim-looking Negro in white jacket and pants, reeking of vomit, massaged his stiffened limbs and wheeled a stomach pump to Diddy's new bed; Diddy's guts dried out with humiliation; in three days he was discharged from the hospital, minus twenty pounds of substance. For it's those who know themselves to be merely the custodians or lessors of their lives who make up the roster of prospective suicides. Knowing one has a life induces the temptation to give it up. One is dead. Therefore, one wants to die. Equally, one wants to be born.

In the hope of being born, fierce as the wish to die, Diddy had

6

always cherished the child in himself. Mary's boy has fallen and banged his head. Kiss it! There! A guileless lively schoolboy with a foolish nickname peered from behind Diddy's soft eyes, eyes that wept without tears over the diligent stoical grownup stationed at a desk: consulting reference books, writing copy, designing layouts, dictating letters, turning out interoffice memoranda. Yet it didn't seem that he could, honorably, discontinue what he'd been doing. Diddy the Done. Death had refused his hectic, inept petition. Anyway, Diddy was also afraid to die. Endowed with vast amounts of irony applied at his own expense, he vowed to go on placing one foot in front of the other. He has to feed his dog, to continue being a helpful older brother who is all the family left for Paul, and to pay Joan alimony. Diddy will meet the demands of the day.

Perhaps reprieved from death, and if that's the case, reprieved either by his own vitality or by the merest accident, Diddy acknowledges that he remains the tenant of his life; and that the lease to which he holds title has some time yet to run. Something of a natural gentleman, he aims to keep the property in decent repair. If only he could feel less, live less inside himself. Isn't that feasible? From this point onward. A posthumous person has certain new resources, new strengths. Isn't the force of Diddy's aversions and horrors somewhat reduced? Drained away, because he did have the courage to attempt, with all seriousness, to destroy himself, and because he's survived the attempt.

In the three weeks following his return to work, everything does seem less sharp and less painful. On weekends he stays in and reads and listens to music. Hardly eating at all. Taking naps, rather than aiming at a full night's sleep either Friday or Saturday. Though on Sunday night, trying to get in bed at a reasonable hour. On weekdays Diddy gets up at eight o'clock as he always has. Alarm clocks make too brutal a sound; he's awakened by a clock radio turned to WOR/FM, eternally ascending and descending among the Top Forty. Then performs morning tasks, which rarely include breakfast. Walks the dog; when he comes back, cleans up a little. He's got the apartment under control; none of the objects present themselves as too slimy or too repulsively dry, nor the space as too big to move in or too small. Arrival at the office. His jellied porous boss, Michael C. Duva, advances across the floor with a file of correspondence between Watkins & Company and *The Review of Scientific Instruments* that needs Diddy's attention. Why does Duva tilt his head to the left when he speaks, why does he smile, and why does he allow those drops of saliva to collect at the corners of his mouth? Riding out the tide of nausea, Diddy fingers the scuffed aluminum of his desk and stares urgently at the water cooler. His cardboard secretary is at her post, surreptitiously adjusting her stockings. Diddy doesn't mind handling papers. But, immaculate always, he dislikes changing a typewriter ribbon. Is frustrated to the point of tears while making a sketch for a new layout, when a narrow line drawn with India ink arbitrarily thickens or swells into a stain. Once Diddy had prided himself on being fastidious, and found it easy to be neat. These days, he suspects all that to be sham. Despises himself for being squeamish and thin-skinned. "He who despises himself esteems himself as a self-despiser." Diddy the Despicable. But he is, he is. Don't laugh.

And Diddy the Delicate, too. As a boy, Diddy had the normal amount of confidence in his body. At least, so he remembered. Paul, spending all his after-school hours at the piano, suffered more keenly than Diddy from the shameful anguish of early adolescence, envying his brother, only a year older, his precociously sinewy arms and stout chest. Paul never liked sports, while Diddy the Unmusical had gone out for athletics in high school, and made his mark. Because of his skills as an athlete, Diddy's manner of treating his younger brother was for a long time quite patronizing —despite his secret esteem for Paul's independence of character, which Diddy knew to be far more potent than physical strength. Still, Diddy was strong, too. And knew it. When had his physical confidence begun to wane? In the grim last years with Joan? But women liked him, always had. Their verdict counted for something. Yet Diddy didn't want to deceive. There was no reason for his body to go on being muscular and vigorous, while he only moves from taxis to the swivel chair in his office to chairs in restaurants to seats in theatres and concerts to the living-room couches to bed; his only exercise walking Xan. What's true should show.

Since it's felt anyway. And whether or not anyone can see it, he does feel less substantial. The bony skull under the slightly graying hair, which he kept short, felt vulnerable. So did the slender fingers with fine nails, the highly arched feet.

Until finally Diddy's appearance did begin to testify to the physically inert, becalmed life he led. Then came that irresistible vertigo which climaxed in the ordeal of September, the decision of September 30th, the stay in the hospital, and the four frightened days afterwards he spent alone, without going out of his apartment. (Now) he really is too thin. While keys, wallet, cigarettes, coins, pocket knife, pencil flashlight, the Phi Beta Kappa key have put on weight. He's sleeping only a few hours each night and, when he does sleep, waking exhausted from his strenuous dreams. Also, hardly eating. Extra flesh, fat on the soul, is difficult to restore. A visit to his tailor is necessary, since Diddy notices (now) the space between his clothes and his moist skin. Diddy shouldn't be continually aware of the loosely defined but ample space existing there from neck to ankles, except where the contents of his pockets slam against his ribs and thighs, should he? But something is dilating, a wall is opening out.

The firm has convened a week-long conference at the main plant, upstate. Rising competition from abroad had the New York office worried. An old established firm was not to be allowed to rest on its laurels. Seeking new ideas from the departments of research and development, production, advertising, and sales. Diddy, assistant director of advertising, was asked to go up for the entire week. Duva might or might not come up by Wednesday.

A flattering assignment, Diddy supposes. And something of a vacation. After packing his bag before he went to bed Saturday night, October 26th, Diddy's sleep, sounder than usual, was traversed by a dream. Paul and he are hiding in a forest, gathering logs, stacking them; when he stumbles or is pushed into a hole. What next? A foolish agony. Paul yells, "I can't help you." Goddamn it, I'm so fragile a hard wind can topple me, Diddy thinks as he falls. Paul is leaning over, looking down, screaming "Diddy! Diddy!" Frightened, crying. Diddy can't reassure Paul, or save himself. Joan is waiting at the bottom of the hole. Has she come back? But that part of the dream gets dark.

Diddy slept late. Brought his reluctant dog down to the basement and handed the super ten dollars to board him for a week. Xan was behaving the way he did when Diddy brought him to the vet. Whining, dragging his nails along the green linoleum that covers the entire floor of the super's tiny apartment, as Diddy, coaxing and threatening, led him into the kitchen. The super's small children want to start playing with Xan immediately. "It's all right, Mr. Torres," said Diddy to their father, who looked as if he already regretted the transaction. "He'll calm down as soon as I go." Would that Diddy were as confident as he sounded. The animal's whine nauseated him.

Then he caught a cab to the station, and boarded the third car from the end of the Sunday afternoon Privateer. Special new luxury express train, each car divided, European style, into compartments accommodating six people. One improves on the new by returning to the old.

On time. We left the city heading northwest. Diddy in a window seat, finding what comfort he could for his narrow haunches on the prickly upholstery, occupied himself for the first hour with the heavy *Times* he'd bought in the station. No obligation to look. Besides, he'd taken this trip often, was familiar with the strip of sights available from the window as we bolted through the outskirts of the city. If each factory has a smokestack, if all the housing projects are unadorned boxes built of brick, if a power station is a power station, and a prison always confines—what point is there in looking? To fabricate differences, discern nuances, is the job of those seeing for the first time. On other trips, Diddy's highly compromised desire for confrontation had permitted more looking at the houses seen through train windows—houses he could accept and refuse, as in a daydream, without ever inhabiting them. This time, Diddy refused the organized looking offered by the window.

What else? All the ideas he ought to be thinking, typed out on legal-size yellow paper and clipped together, were stored in his briefcase on the rack over his head. The rest were unthinkable. Diddy settled behind the newspaper, grateful to be able to wall himself off from his traveling companions. A compartment is public space, open to anybody. Yet it has a certain intimacy, too. A maximum of six persons are shut up together, temporarily sealed off from everyone else. A little cell of travel. Forced neighboring, which increases the reign of order.

Diddy bored (now). He's finished the newspaper. Hungry, which always happens on trains. Restless. A conductor comes to collect everyone's ticket. Whose tickets? Our tickets. In an express train which is rapidly passing many stations without stopping, each station identical with the last, Diddy is cooped up among interchangeable people. But being a fellow traveler of life, incorrigibly hopeful though sharply disillusioned, he will make the effort to tell one from the other. He casts a moderate, diffused look at the others in the compartment: to stare wouldn't be polite.

Occupying the window seat opposite, a woman in a faded woolen suit, with untidy gray hair and small sharp eyes, mistress of two bulging shopping bags at her feet. Perhaps the bags contain food. But the journey wasn't that long. Gifts for rowdy indifferent grandchildren? Whatever the contents of the bags, Diddy guessed, this was a woman who tried too hard and habitually gave what was not wanted.

She is whispering with congested urgency to an extremely pretty girl on her right. The girl seemed to be listening, but it was as if something, perhaps the large sunglasses she wore, exempted her from having to reply. The lenses were greenish-black; so dark the girl's eyes couldn't be seen, and Diddy wondered how well she could see through them. There's a wall for you!

Next to the girl, on the outside seat opposite Diddy, was a paunchy cleric whose plump face had been lowered toward his breviary since the train started; his underlip trembled systematically as he read. A breviary can't be used up like a newspaper; it's to read and re-read forever. What a system! Could Diddy the Good ever have been a priest, with something worthwhile and always the same to read? Not the right sort of goodness, maybe. Too much Done-Done.

Sharing Diddy's seat, on his left, was a ruddy, heavily built, ostentatiously clean-shaven man in a tweed suit, smelling of cheap after-shave lotion or eau-de-cologne. About Diddy's age. Who had spread a large magazine on his knees at the start of the journey, but instead of taking it up, plucked a handkerchief from his pocket, spat quietly at it; then remained quite still, looking into the handkerchief. The magazine didn't slip off his lap even when the train tilted, swooped round a curve.

The gray-haired woman was the first to speak, asking if anyone minded her opening the window. Not a bad day. Rather warm. Diddy the Good did it for her, dirtying the tips of his fingers. "Do not lean out of the window." We exchanged comments about the improved service on this line since the new trains had been installed, and about the refinement of traveling, six together, in a compartment, rather than being lined up and paired off in an open coach. The man in the tweed suit said he'd heard that the railroad, long rumored to be virtually bankrupt, was pulling itself out of the red. Diddy felt his mind getting gluey, his palate becoming furred. Conversation is always a trap for those who love the truth, isn't it? Yet common sense said Don't fret, Don't waste your integrity on a situation that isn't serious. A hard rule. Who cares about the condition of the railroad, its innovations, its finances? Does anyone here really care? Oh, but have pity upon people, poor soft-tongued creatures who should be kissing flowers but find, instead, that toads are leaping out of their mouths. Though irritated by the man's nervous way of speaking, Diddy has pity. Here's a toad, too. (Now) that the trains were punctual, Diddy remarked, they-ought-to-be-washed-down-more-often. He grimaced at the streaked windowpane, the dusty ledge, the trampled cigarette butts on the floor. The gray-haired woman found Diddy a paper napkin in one of her bags—a food bag, then—that he could use to clean his hands. Diddy thought the woman looked unwashed. Probably not dirty at all, but soiled by age.

The man in the tweed suit stuffed the handkerchief back in his pocket, cleared his throat, picked up his magazine. We could read the cover (now). *Philately Annual.*

"A collector, I assume." We hadn't seen the priest look up. The suave voice issued from a mouth that moved without rendering any more expressive the face surrounding it. A face such as psychoanalysts acquire early in their training. Veiled, nerveless, relatively immobile.

"Yes, I am. And a dealer, too." The man in the tweed suit seemed to need to cough or to spit again.

"Have you seen this issue?" said the priest. "Very rare, I believe." From his vest pocket, the priest produced a pair of tweezers; then from another black pocket on the inside of his jacket, withdrew a walletlike case, opened it, lifted up a flap with his thumb and forefinger, and cautiously extracted a block of blue stamps with the tweezers.

So the priest and the man in the tweed suit both turn out to be collectors of stamps, valuable paper miniatures of a country, a king, a building, a tree, a face; both took out and compared their latest acquisitions. At tweezers-length, the joys of common interests. Diddy, if he wanted to talk, was left to the gray-haired woman and, hopefully, to the pretty girl with whom she was traveling, silent so far. The woman needed little encouragement. She explained that she was accompanying the girl, her niece, who was going to have an eye operation at the renowned medical center upstate. Is the girl totally blind? Diddy wondered. Seemed rude to ask. The woman launched into a description of her niece's prospective surgery, how much it will cost, its hazards, its chances of success. She insisted on using, but kept mispronouncing, words like "corneal" and "ophthalmic" and "choroid." Diddy annoyed. He became restless when people spoke imprecisely, or didn't get things right.

"Hester, isn't that so? Isn't that what the doctor said?"

Thus far, the girl had refused to confirm anything. Perhaps she is embarrassed or angry. Or was she inured to her aunt's volubility? The aunt, as she babbled on, kept touching the girl's cheek, shoulder, and forearm in a proprietary dull way. Diddy wished he could tie up the aunt's hands. But didn't feel like silencing her, blocking off the stream of information. Since the events of a month ago, he had more patience with people addicted to recounting their illnesses and operations. No, not only that. Subjugated to some bolder desire he'd not yet acknowledged to himself, he floated down the old woman's river of discourse. Aimed his own words at the aunt, kept his eyes on the sightless girl. A blind person couldn't see Diddy, emaciated from his abortive closure with death and the hospital regimen. But the girl could talk, if she would; and Diddy felt sure it would be, unlike her aunt's talk, clean and unlittered. Diddy wanted to touch her, too.

Then, suddenly, the day failed. So did our conversation. Diddy remembered this tunnel, approximately two hours out of the city. But why didn't the lights in the compartment and the corridor go on? No? All right then. From the instant the compartment went dark, no one spoke. We wanted to wait, to be in silence as well as darkness. Then, after an endurable pause, resume our desultory conversations on the far side of the tunnel, at the exact point at which they'd broken off. The train charged through the darkness, it seemed to go faster, dangerously fast, its motion like a horizontal fall. But, just about when, according to Diddy's memory, we should have thrust the tunnel behind us, the train convulsed, shrieked, and came to a stop. Sighs, scrambling hands, exclamations. Anyone hurt? Instantly we all began to talk. If darkness had silenced us, darkness minus motion loosened our tongues. New situation, new behavior. Well, not *so* new. We weren't worried. Trains are reliable. Diddy consulted the luminous dial of his watch. We had been in the tunnel at least seven minutes. Then we saw a light jogging along the corridor, heard the neighboring compartment's door rattle open. A deep voice spoke briefly, words we couldn't make out. When the door was slammed shut, Diddy braces himself for a nearer, harsher sound. Officialdom calling has its distinctive noises and movements. And Diddy was something of an experienced traveler. What was happening (now) was just like a border control in funny old Europe, but this is a big country, too big; we weren't at a border, but in the middle of a tunnel. Sure enough, our compartment door was rolled back. A flashlight with a man vaguely outlined behind it on the threshold. "Apologies from the chief engineer, ladies and gentlemen."

"Is anything wrong?" asked the stamp dealer. When, obviously, something is.

"Young man, why aren't you in your caboose or wherever you're supposed to be, getting the train started?" said the aunt.

"I'm not the chief engineer, lady," said the man. A complacent toad. "I'm just bringing the apologies. Take 'em or leave 'em."

"What seems to be the difficulty?" asked the priest.

"We've had to make a stop in the tunnel."

"That we can see for ourselves!" said the aunt tartly.

The flashlight wobbled, then focused on the woman's face. "Lady, will you let me finish?" She gasped and threw up her arm; the light drooped. "We've had to stop because the track isn't clear. There's, uh, something in the way ahead."

"Is the track being repaired?" asks Diddy.

"No record of any work going on in this tunnel that we know of."

"I never heard of anything so stupid," said the woman. "Hester, do you hear?" Could she be deaf, too? Diddy wondered.

"Relax, lady. We'll get the train going."

"Crash right through," said the girl softly. Not deaf. Just quiet.

"Lovey, don't get upset. You see, young man, there's a sick person here."

"I'm not sick," said the girl. "I was only joking."

"What next?" said Diddy.

"Well," said the conductor or whoever he was, "as soon as they figure out whether this is the middle of the tunnel or close to the end . . . I mean, because it may be that we're in the wrong tunnel. . . ."

"Wrong tunnel!" exclaimed Diddy.

"But there's no doubt that the tunnel is blocked," concluded the conductor.

"Couldn't the right tunnel be blocked?" asked the priest.

"Look, folks, don't give me a hard time, will you? I'm just

15

passing on what I've been told to say, and that is, that right now the chief engineer and the head conductor are in conference—"

"Conference!" muttered the woman.

"Either they'll be able to remove the obstruction, which might not be all that solid, you know, just some prank. Or they'll back the train out."

Diddy could hear the stamp dealer's irregular, heavy breathing— indication, even before the man spoke (now), of his alarm. "What you're telling us is that we're in big trouble. Whether we just sit here, or try to plow through, or back out of the tunnel, we're likely to be rammed from the rear by the next train on this route."

More alarmed than Diddy? At this point, yes. Diddy was slow to panic. That's what he used his mind for. Good mind. Diddy remembered the stamp dealer gazing into his handkerchief. A hypochondriac, probably. Certainly the worrying type. And that collecting of little paper trophies. Obsessional, too.

"When's the next train due on this route?" asked Diddy, trying to be helpful. His shoulders ache with tension.

"Not for a long time. Close to an hour," replied the conductor, his voice dimming. He was backing off (now), his hand beginning to close the compartment door.

"Are you telling us the truth, young man?" asked the aunt.

"I'll be back soon," said the conductor. Slam. We heard the door of the compartment to our left roll open. People are cattle, thought Diddy. Why isn't anyone screaming? Or weeping or praying? Why, instead, so eager to believe everything's going to be all right?

We sat in silence, eavesdropping on the unintelligible discourse seeping through the partition behind Diddy and the stamp dealer. The same conversation? Diddy wondered if the occupants of that compartment were accepting trustfully the conductor's sloppy explanation. Or if, daring to feel alarm, they were pressing him with anxious questions. The stamp dealer struck a match. How shadowy and grim we all looked. The man already holds the cigarette between his lips. Diddy anticipated, then failed to detect, any trembling of the flame as it approached the man's jaw.

"I suppose no one has a flashlight," said the soft-voiced priest.

16

"I have a pencil flashlight." Diddy the Helpful. "If that's any use."

"Hardly," said the aunt, sulking.

Staring at the disembodied red tip of the stamp dealer's cigarette, Diddy was starting to come undone. The passably well-knit empire of his body yielding to secession and rebelliousness. His gut was a suitcase full of bricks, his chest a keg of eels. The blood thundered in his ears; whitish lines, like wilted lightning, went zigzagging from left to right. The door of the neighboring compartment slammed shut. Then a dim light went on in the corridor, probably an electric hand lamp, reserved for emergencies, lit by the evasive messenger before he passed into the car behind. Is this an emergency? At least the darkness wasn't total (now).

"How do you like them apples!" exclaimed the stamp dealer.

None of us seemed prepared to answer him.

"This is a hell of a mess!" he added. The stamp dealer sounded angry.

Diddy panicking (now). While others remain calm. Unbidden, the thought of his death settles like a flat stone on his chest.

"Do you think we're in real danger?" Diddy wondered to whom the girl's question was addressed. And whether, since she couldn't see anyway, she found the situation as oppressive as the others did.

"No," said the priest.

"No, darling," said the aunt.

Death, thought Diddy, is like a lithographer's stone. One stone, cool and smooth to the touch, can print many deaths, virtually identical except to the expert eye. One lightly inscribed stone can be used, reused indefinitely.

"I tell you, this is the last time I ride *this* railroad," said the stamp dealer. He cleared his throat.

Diddy, sliding down in his seat, trying to lift the stone off his chest. He has to move. "Look," he said, "I want to see what's going on. Maybe I can find someone with more information."

"Good," said the woman. Good Diddy.

What Diddy felt (now) could only be described as panic.

He got up and became dizzy, had to reach for the baggage rack and hang on in order to bypass pairs of dark shoes and the old woman's parcels and the cheap briefcase at the stamp dealer's feet without falling. Rolled the door back, stepped out. The corridor window as opaque and uninformative as the window in the compartment. Loosening his collar, he turned right and began to walk along the corridor, away from the emergency lantern. He tried to avert his glance from the dim shapes that slumped, tilted, leaned toward one another in each of the compartments. Why does everyone talk so softly? In one compartment a baby was crying. Ahead was the only other person who, like him, had fled to the corridor—a smoking person, Diddy could see at a distance; a fat woman wearing slacks, as he came closer. Turning sideways to pass her, Diddy drew in his chest, mouthed "Excuse me."

"Say, do you know the time?"

"Five-nineteen," said Diddy, more audibly. Jaw tightening, feeling the tentacles of her anxiety around his ankles. She seemed about to touch him.

"Boy, I hope they know what they're doing."

"So do I." Diddy moving on. No victim, he.

"Hey, wait a minute! Please!"

"I'm going to find out." If Diddy stopped, turned around, he'd feel sorry for her, have to carry her as well as the stone. Goody Did had given himself a different task, less chivalrous. But, hopefully, more useful.

When Diddy reaches the end of the car, he has a choice.

Either open the heavy door and pass over the coupling into the next car, also feebly lit by an electric hand lamp, also inhabited by quiet people docilely keeping to their travel cells—a car exactly like our own, except that no one is stationed in the corridor.

Or get off the train altogether, go exploring, find the obstruction and see, with his own eyes, what's being done about it. What if the emergency is already over? Even though the conductor hasn't come back with the good news. The train personnel just returning to their posts, the engineer about to pull the switch that starts up the Privateer?

Pauses indecisively. No, don't be afraid. Even if the train should get underway while he is outside, surely it would start up slowly. Allowing time to grab hold and clamber aboard. Reason expounded, Diddy was convinced. He wrenches open the exit door at the end of our car, the metal steps unfold.

He had left the train.

The tunnel is cool but humid, thick with the smell of oil and damp rock. At the first stroke of air, Diddy shivers. But at least he has room to move about in. Plunges his hands into the wet air, then cautiously extends one arm; the wall of the tunnel lies beyond his reach. How wide is it? He snaps on his pencil flashlight and discovers the wall still some ten feet away. The tunnel has two wide-gauge tracks; Diddy steps onto the empty track. Turning right. Using the dim light to illuminate a small spot ahead of his softly polished shoes, starts toward the front of the train. Tired, terribly tired. Keep going. No time to give in to fatigue. For a while, he hears only the slurred sound of his own steps on the firm tunnel ground. But after passing half a dozen cars, begins to hear something else: hard, evenly spaced sounds like the blows of an ax. It was toward that sound that Diddy was heading.

"Hey there!" he calls out.

Sounds in the tunnel are slightly deadened. An echo effect.

Though he's keeping to the center of the vacant track, Diddy senses that he is drifting to the right. Halts his march. He probes at the space between two coaches with his small light; discovers that the forward coach lies at a slight angle to the one behind. The same for the next space between two coaches. And the next. So the track isn't straight, the tunnel itself is curved; which means that the train's heavy body, stalled, lay arched within the tunnel's sheath, bent systematically at each of its iron joints. Does this make matters more difficult? The emergency more grave? As Diddy follows the curving track, the sounds become louder and he sees a source of light. Continuing. The tunnel brightens.

Destination achieved. Panting, Diddy stands alongside the vast greasy forward wheel of the engine. Just ahead of the train is a swarthy man wearing cleated boots, denim overalls, undershirt. And a light strapped to his brow, like a doctor or miner; which supplements the stronger lighting furnished by a row of five bulbs stuck in a short board and suspended from an iron hook in the tunnel wall. The man is indeed wielding an ax, slamming it into a barrier about four feet high that straddles the track. A kind of wall made of heavy boards nailed together. Braced by or anchored to several crossties set diagonally against the wall.

"Jesus, who the hell put that up?" Diddy the Companionable. Relieved. The barrier has a makeshift look. And it was wood, not stone.

The man stoops. Picks up another tool, a sledgehammer, from a large wooden box lying on the ground.

One of the ties is under attack. The tie jumps as the man hits it with the sledgehammer. Gradually it's coming loose. Strange sonorities. Then the man lays down the hammer, pulls a crowbar from the box of tools, and begins a different sound, continuous and higher pitched. "How's it coming?" Diddy asks. Appears to be going well. One by one, the thick diagonal supports are yielding.

The workman pauses. Perhaps he hasn't heard Diddy. A change of pace. Using the massive hammer (now), he's attacking the wall itself, sending up a haze of dust. Clearly the shuddering barrier isn't impregnable.

"Is that the obstruction? I mean, is that all there is?" Diddy almost alongside him (now), near enough to catch the familiar sweat smell that flows from the man's body, his faintly alcoholic breath. Just watches for another moment, tasting the grit in his own mouth.

"Wouldn't it go faster if you got someone to help you?" The workman either grunted or made no answer. Stolidly, efficiently, he just keeps slamming his hammer into the low wall. Not just neatly dismembering it, but breaking off ragged splintery hunks of wood. Whenever a big enough piece has come away, the workman adds it to an already sizable stack in a niche in the tunnel wall on his left.

Diddy troubled. "Listen, I'm talking to you."

The man goes on hammering. Then he shoves the hammer into the box, and takes up the ax again. Diddy has backed a few feet away from him, is trying to figure out what he's doing. Like a miner, he thinks. The damned train has barged into a mine. Something slides along the edge of Diddy's mind, a presentiment of awful danger. Maybe the workman is a saboteur, maybe he's undoing the tunnel, maybe. . . .

No, Diddy had to believe that what lies on the far side of the barrier is just more track. The rest of the tunnel. Not, say, a big hole.

"Hey, can you tell me where I can find the engineer?"

The workman looks up. "What the hell are you bothering me for? Can't you see I got a job to do? And what are you doing out here anyway?" Then resumes his work.

"Just tell me where the chief engineer is."

"Clear out, man," the workman barks over his shoulder, halting his labor again. "You're wasting my time."

"Listen," said Diddy, "I've a right to know what's going on. The rest of the passengers may be a bunch of sheep, but I'm not going to sit around trusting you guys to do the right thing."

"Man, are you going to get back on that train?"

"No."

The workman bringing his ax down on the wall, but his head is turned. "If you don't get out of here in five seconds, you'll be sorry." Whatever he's doing, it's almost done.

"*You'll* be sorry," shouts Diddy, taking a step forward. "Just who the hell do you think you are?"

A lull in the strokes of the ax. The workman lifts up the last two boards, hurls them onto the others. Then he rubs his face with his forearm, hitches up his pants, spits on the ground. He's looking at Diddy (now). Takes up the ax again. "You see what I've got here? Don't push me too far, mister."

"The ax?" says Diddy. "Oh, come off it! What's the matter with you? I'm asking a civil question and you can damn well take a moment to answer me."

The man advances toward him, the beam from his forehead drilling into Diddy's eyes. "I'll give you five seconds to get the fuck out of here. Move!"

"I'm staying," Diddy says. An outraged voice. "And I'm reporting you to the conductor." Glances at the engineer's cab: dark. Not

21

that he can't handle this pig all by himself. Still, where in God's name is the crew that operates this ultra-modern train? Off placating the passengers? Maybe some, sure. But all of them?

"Five seconds!" says the man, raising the ax. "One."

"You'd better watch your step," Diddy snarls. Clenched his fists. The man inches toward him. "Two."

"Really spoiling for a fight, aren't you?" Diddy says, bitterly.

"Three."

Diddy smelling his own sweat (now). He's mortally afraid; yet this is a more acceptable, cleaner fear than what he'd endured back on the train, cooped up with those zombies. Taking a deep breath; with twitching nostrils inhaling the unpleasant air. Stoops quickly and seizes the crowbar lying near his feet. Straightens up to see the startled look on the workman's face. The workman scratching his head in a satire of puzzlement, then grinning.

Four. It must be Four already.

Diddy tensing his arm muscles, hefting his cold weapon. "Go on, you bastard!"

"I guess you're gonna think I'm scared," the man says.

This is too easy. He's trying to trick me, to catch me off guard and grab the crowbar away from me. Then whack me with the ax.

"Come on, man! I don't wanna fight." The workman grinning again.

"Like hell you don't," Diddy says, panting.

"Hey, take it easy. I was just horsing around. Don't make a big deal out of it."

"I don't believe you." Diddy tightens his grip on the crowbar, licks his lips. Why doesn't he say Four?

The man laughs. "Okay, you win. Okay?" He winks at Diddy. "See?" Lowers the arm holding the ax. "I'm going back to work now, man. Right? You can do what you want." He turns, offering his back to Diddy. Takes a step, then pauses. A surprise is coming.

Diddy sees he's fiddling with the ax. Knows the man is about to wheel around and smash him with it. Five! "No you don't!" Diddy yells and brings the crowbar down on the back of the man's head. Diddy groans, the man groans. Diddy's hands tingle from the blow. Letting the crowbar drop, he flexes his cramped fingers. Which don't respond. Has to unlock the fingers of his right hand with his left, the fingers of his left hand with his right. Poor dry throbbing fingers. He would have wept, if it would have done any good.

The workman has fallen forward across the track, his neck resting on the far rail. Diddy kneels to look at what he's done. To see the black blood welling out of the man's hair into his ear, over his face. The light affixed to the man's forehead still shining. Diddy fumbles at the light, trying to turn it off. Several little knobs, but none of them makes something happen. Can't get at the damned thing! Maybe if he turned the workman over on his back.

A hard, heavy, uncooperative body. Diddy brought near to vomiting by the odd new smell the workman gave off (now)—a cold smell, like meat; flatulent. Stifling nausea and fear, Diddy is able to kneel and grip the body under the armpits. Is that wetness sweat or blood? Starting to roll the body on its right side. But it's still awkward, too big, hard to manage. What if Diddy drags the body a few steps back, where he can lean it in a sitting position against the front of the train? Done. Can't keep the upper torso, the part that's clothed in an undershirt, from slumping forward. Watch out! The body's about to keel over on its bare face. Diddy grabs hold just in time, props it up again more securely. Holding the lolling head by its loose jaw, pushes that part even farther back and to one side; so it lodges between the rim of the left forward wheel and the side of the engine.

(Now) he can figure out how to turn off this bitch of a light. Off! Diddy stands back. Without that third eye from the man's brow blighting his own vision, he can look. Make sure whether the workman is dead or alive. Since the moment he fell across the track, the man hasn't moved once or made another sound. Is he really dead (now)? One last test. As tentatively as if he had not yet touched him, Diddy gets close enough to poke the workman's bare shoulder. Wet. The man groans again, stirs slightly. Oh God, no! Diddy backs away, his throat aching with terror.

Terror gives way to fake toughness. You asked for it, you bastard! But Diddy's attempt to feel brutal and self-righteous doesn't convince even him.

Fake toughness gives way to the pangs of exile. Heartsick Diddy

23

considers the time before he struck the workman: his whole life. The life he'd found bitter and uninhabitable. But thinks of (now), in the new perspective just opened up, as incredibly fortunate. How lucky he'd always been. And didn't know it. Never, never could he have imagined he'd been racing toward this moment. (Now) he was cast on the far side of the appalling moment—looking back with something much stronger than nostalgia; looking back with anguished longing at the years behind, receding. Done, like a slice. Never to be undone.

The pangs of exile give way to fear. Will I have to go to jail? Diddy thinks sadly. For this moment? No mitigating circumstances? This one moment? Don't the others count for more?

Fear gives way to guilt. I've got a murderer inside me, thinks Diddy the Mortified. Why did I think I was such an amiable fellow? All along, I thought it was my own death I carried within myself. Like an interminable pregnancy which would nevertheless end one day, quite unpredictably. But it wasn't my death coming, it was someone else's. That's the Done-Done I always dreaded.

Guilt gives way to more fear. I'm closed in. Trapped. I was brought here to do this. Diddy has killed a dark man in a dark tunnel. Diddy the Stupefied has never felt more alive.

Looks up at the darkened engine of the train. Has no one seen him; isn't anyone at this moment hurrying forward to apprehend him? Where are the watchers, where are the witnesses? Asleep? Drunk? Drugged? Bewitched? Get rid of all that light. Diddy pulls down the brace of naked lightbulbs and smashes it against the wall. True darkness (now). Still Diddy stands.

How long can Diddy stand there by the body of the slain workman? Not long enough to feel all that he has to feel. He might as well return to the train.

Dried blood on his hands or clothing? A close check with the pocket flashlight turns up only some chalky stains on his trousers.

Having dusted off his trousers, Diddy the Neat has started back without the aid of his flashlight; hopes not to be noticed by someone gazing out of a corridor window. Isn't hard to walk in the dark as the blind have to do, if one knows the way. And Diddy has traversed this space before. On the return trip, sensation is reversed. Feels the proximity of the enclosing tunnel wall on his right, the great iron body of the train with its dirty, softly lit windows on his left.

He has retraced his steps; when he reaches the third car from the end, mounted the train; passed along the corridor; regained the compartment. His compartment. Our compartment. As he takes his seat, hears the priest and the girl talking quietly. But Diddy can't, for the hammering of his heart and the air hissing in his ears, grasp what the suave male voice and the lighter voice of the girl actually say.

For the others, nothing in our situation has changed. Only for Diddy. Who locks his arms against his chest. Waits for the aunt, someone, to say "Well?" Someone to ask if he's found out anything more about our predicament. Diddy is readying his lies, prepared to explain that he found no one, that he never got off the train. But nobody asks.

What are the priest and the girl discussing? Him? Do they know? No, that's absurd; they can't know anything. What's their conversation about then? Stamp collecting may be safely ruled out, since the girl is blind. Perhaps the priest is offering, the girl receiving, a dose of consolation. For the condition of blindness. Or, for the fact that she—along with all of us—is marooned on this dark immobile train.

The train lurched forward. "At last!" exclaims the aunt. "We're starting."

"No," whimpers Diddy. The train hadn't started, really. Just testing. First, the giant takes a small brazen step. All the obstacles cleared away?

"About time, too!" says the stamp dealer.

Another convulsive movement, in which the creaking train seems to hurl itself backward a few feet.

"Oh!" the girl exclaims. She must be confused.

Diddy is confused. He wants the barrier to be impassable, wants a motionless memory. The skull of the workman, broken open. Man, the upright animal, fallen.

The train is really starting (now). Unevenly, shuddering and jerking. But in earnest. The overhead fluorescent lights in the compartment go on, first sputtering, then locking into a continuous flow. A collective "Ah . . ." Diddy's eyes hurt, he covers them with his hands. He is a stone without eyes. Anything to shut out the image of the bleeding heavy animal he'd left sprawled against the train. Though still enclosed within the tunnel, the train is (now) moving along smoothly. It can only go forward, dangerously metallic and earth-bound. Diddy encapsuled in the train crushing the workman's body. Foolish of Diddy to have expected to feel a telltale bump when the front wheels of the train passed over the body. Matched against the weight and velocity of the train, flesh and bone yield like water.

If that's what happened. The final disposition of the workman's body beyond Diddy's control. The body might have fallen between the rails and escaped being pulverized or dismembered by the wheels.

Is the train fleeing the body left behind? Is that why we're picking up so much speed?

"That's better!" Which one of us has spoken, groaning with relief? Could have been anyone—though least likely to be the girl. The train has broken out of the tunnel, is careening through the countryside. Crimson birds fly alongside the window, the air has a purplish neon glow, a great blue silo rises from a distant hill, strange groupings of trees throw animal shadows to the ground. Telephone wires swoop and sag like roller-coaster tracks, signs and billboards are undecipherable. A fantastic landscape? Or is Diddy hallucinated, already poisoned by remorse? The stone, the stone. Diddy is choking. He puts his face into his hands again, afraid to look. The train is going very fast (now). Diddy wonders if the iron-black wheels are bright with blood. If they are, some farm boy idling on the slope beside the track, watching trains go by, will' sound the alarm.

When Diddy looks up again, the stamp dealer is jotting something down in a small notebook; the priest is mumbling over his breviary; the aunt, a brown pear in her hand, has fallen asleep propped against her niece. The girl looking straight ahead. It might be at Diddy, he doesn't know.

Diddy must talk to someone. It can only be this girl with the inhuman, leaden vision. But he doesn't want to be overheard. Leaning forward, he covers her stockinged knee with his hand. "What is it?" she whispers. Already a conspiratorial tone.

"I have something to tell you," Diddy says hoarsely. "Will you come outside?"

The priest glanced up, then sank back in his breviary. Diddy beckons to the girl, as if she could see. The girl gently eases her shoulder away from her aunt's heavy head; the gray-haired woman, her eyes closed, stirs about until she finds the adjustable headrest, grimaces, is still again. The girl stands up, removes her washable suède gloves, and lays them on the seat. She's almost as tall as Diddy. Who takes her warm hand and guides her over the feet of the priest and the stamp dealer, past the stamp dealer's briefcase and the aunt's shopping bags. Having pulled back the compartment door and then shut it behind them, now what? Diddy stares at the girl in perplexity, releases her hand. Though no one else is standing in the corridor, he still feels unsafe, exposed.

"Come to the end of the car." She hesitates. "Come!"

The girl again extends her hand for Diddy to lead her. His eyes smart with gratitude for that gesture of trust. Of course, when one is blind one is compelled to trust everyone. Or no one. Diddy wished he had fewer alternatives, like the blind girl.

They stand next to the lavatory at the near end of the car, round a corner and out of sight of anyone who might come out into the corridor. Swaying with the movement of the train.

"Tell me," the girl says.

"Something . . . has happened."

"Is it the train? I was frightened before."

"No, no," says Diddy. "It happened off the train. It's me. I've done something terrible."

"When?"

"After I left the compartment."

"You mean just now?"

"No, before."

"When did you leave the compartment before?"

"When? How can you say that?" Diddy shouts softly. "I know you can't . . . didn't see me. But you must have heard me say I was going. To see why we were stalled, remember? I was . . . I was frightened, too."

"No."

"You must have heard me get up and leave!"

"I didn't hear you leave."

"But you weren't asleep," pleads Diddy, more and more alarmed. "I was watching you all the time. Don't you remember? Try to think. Please! I said I was going for more information. For all of us. To find someone on the train who knew what was going on."

"I don't remember that. I'm sorry."

"But if you don't believe me," Diddy says, almost in tears, "how can I tell you what happened outside the train?"

"I didn't say I don't *believe* you left the compartment," says the girl, soothingly. Her hand tightened on Diddy's. "I just said that I don't remember your leaving."

"That isn't good enough," groaned Diddy.

"Please tell me," she says, reaching out to touch his face. "Please don't cry."

"Oh, don't pity me!" Diddy pushes her hand away, but it comes back. "I can't stand pity. If you only knew how sick I am of feeling sorry for myself."

"I'm not sorry for you. I swear it. Tell me what happened."

"All right." Diddy takes a deep breath, pulling his face slightly away from her fingers. Even the air felt guilty. "I—" He can't. Why won't it come out? "I was going to kill myself. That's why I went outside. I intended to lie down on the tracks and wait for the train to start up again." The girl is silent, her palm resting on Diddy's cheek. He gazes imploringly at her. It wasn't the truth, but it felt like the truth.

"Why do you want me to know this?" says the girl quietly. "Do you think I can help you?"

"I don't know." Diddy, closing his eyes for a moment. "I suppose I just had to tell someone. Otherwise, it's so unreal."

"But it's equally unreal to me," says the girl in a still quieter voice. "Since you didn't do it. Since you're here. With me."

"Am I real to you?" Diddy's eyeballs ache.

"Very." She continues caressing his face.

"But you can't . . . You can't . . . see me."

In reply, she leans against his chest. For a moment Diddy thinks she's been thrown there by the motion of the train; then realizes she wants to kiss him. Eagerly, gratefully he folds his arms around her, strokes the girl's plump liquid body, curiously soft, boneless. As if she were naked. The brown print dress of some cheap synthetic material feels like another skin, to which his hands seem to adhere. There is suction in the tips of his fingers, desire warming his belly. "I want to make love to you," he whispers. Has she understood? "There's something I haven't told you. I mean, something you didn't ask me."

"What?"

"Why I didn't go through with it. Outside."

"Because you were afraid?"

"Well, that too. But it was also because I thought—I thought of you," says Diddy, one hand on the girl's breast. Diddy the Seducer. "I'd been staring at you ever since the train started. I wanted to touch you, to make love to you. That's why I came back."

"I'm glad."

Is it wrong, what Diddy the Seducer is doing? Another wrong? A crime, an insult to trust?

"I want to make love to you," he repeats stonily. A tryst, a truce.

She nods, drops her hands to his waist and rubs her face against his cheek. For a moment they stand there immobile, a tableau of desire. Graven on stone.

Then the dry, withering grief breaks over Diddy, and he sags under its weight. The girl seemed to vanish; there's only the whistling train, and Diddy trying helplessly to remain standing, allowing himself to be propped up. "What am I doing?" he groans. Feels the train under his feet, furiously eating up the track. Its obscene velocity mocking the languor that now invades his frail body. "I think I'm lying to myself." What he feels isn't simply the languor of desire. It was a craving for rest, or for something even stronger. To which Diddy wished to surrender himself alone. He felt that tiredness on entering the tunnel, but had refused the feeling. Diddy grasps the girl. "Maybe I don't want to make love. Maybe I just want to sleep."

"Come," she said, and tugged at his hand.

"Maybe I want to die."

"Come."

The girl extends her hand, feeling along the wall until she finds a door handle. "What's this?"

"The washroom."

"It's empty, isn't it?"

"Yes," Diddy says.

"Shall we go in here?"

Diddy follows the girl. Inside; the lavatory door locked. It was done. It was about to be done. In the lavatory, smelling of disinfectant and urine. A secret place, a hiding place: lowly yet secure. Diddy glances into the mirror above the metal sink. Then, expectantly, at the girl. "Take off your glasses," he whispers. She removes them, holds them out for him to put somewhere safe; he lays them in the sink. Takes her in his arms, pressing her against his chest very tightly. Kisses her long and at the end brutally on the mouth.

Diddy's face (now) a few inches from the girl's. Her eyes are a grainy imperfect blue, like milk glass. Diddy stares into them, searching for some modulation of expression. But although they move and blink, they have the monotony of ornaments. Could one infer a look, it would be a sad useless look. Innocent of utility, unable to achieve dominion by staring.

> Bleached eyes.
> Tiffany glass eyes.
> Eyes like teeth.
> Eyes like cooked white of egg.
> Eyes like a specimen of dried white of egg, prepared for the microscope.
> Eyes like tulip bulbs.
> Eyes like an electric drill.

Prehensile eyes.

Guilty eyes.

Metal eyes.

Meteor eyes.

Lima-bean eyes.

Paper eyes.

Carrion eyes.

Annealed eyes.

Damp eyes.

Wet eyes: the intricate vial of liquid.

Crisp eyes, soggy eyes.

Tattered eyes, elegant eyes.

Stained eyes, clean eyes.

Creased eyes, smooth eyes.

Rotten eyes, fresh eyes.

Sharp-focus eyes, soft-focus eyes.

Concave eyes, convex eyes.

Bespoke eyes, ready-to-wear eyes.

Stiff eyes, flexible eyes.

Univalve eyes, bivalve eyes.

Single eyes, multiple eyes.

Eyes with and without their outer shell.

Empty eye sockets.

The white hymen of the eyeball.

"Can you see at all?" he asks softly. One never knows. An eye within an eye, perhaps. The fabled sight of the blind. She shakes her head. But as sight isn't only in seeing, eyes aren't only to see with; eyes, like mouths and hands, are organs of suffering. "Do you ever cry?" he whispers.

The girl has unzipped the back of her dress. Diddy helps her pull it over her head.

"Why do my eyes interest you so much?" She stands (now) in her bra and half slip.

Her aunt had called her Hester. "It's not your eyes. It's you, Hester," says Diddy. Not exactly the truth. "Do you ever cry?"

The girl pulls down her slip, extends it to Diddy to take from her. (Now) she's wearing only the low-heeled suède shoes, her stockings held up by a tiny garter belt around her hips, and the bra. No underpants. Diddy astonished and excited by her sudden virtual nakedness. Is it so easy for her to be naked with a stranger because she can't see herself being seen? Because exposure of her body to the eyes of a stranger seems no different than exposure of her face to all invisible strangers?

Something cool and experienced about Hester's undressing. Still, Diddy is almost afraid to acknowledge his erection. Undoubtedly, she's not a virgin. But does the girl really know what she's doing? In some way, she's as opaque to him as he's invisible to her. "*Do* you cry?" Diddy persists, stalling.

"Are you asking me if I've worn out my eyes weeping?" says the girl.

Could one really weep oneself blind? Or will oneself blind? Maybe Diddy had been thinking of that. "I don't know," he says. "I guess I am curious about how it happened. Though maybe you don't like to talk about it. But . . . is that how . . . I mean, why you're—"

"Maybe," the girl says. She puts her hands to his belt. "Why aren't you taking your clothes off?"

No more stalling. The girl is taking off her bra. Diddy feels his body weaken again, his sex cringe. "Do you really want to, Hester? You can't see me. You don't know me." The humiliation of the Done-Done knotted his groin.

"I know you." The girl puts her arms around his neck. She smells of salt water, the sea. Diddy holds her at the waist, licks her closed eyes and ears. Is she forgiving him? By accepting his touch, does she prove that it can be a caress and not just a murderous blow? One can't forgive oneself. There must be two: forgiver and forgiven.

He unknots his tie; takes off his shirt, T-shirt, shoes, and trousers. Then his shorts. Diddy piles their clothes on the sink. She reaches for his sex, he for hers. The gestures are all too easy, weightless. A clandestine festivity with nothing to celebrate. Diddy feels unmanned. With his skinny body, he holds her gently in place against the wall but, for a moment, does little. Then, he can do more. Begins weakly, gathering strength as he goes along. His sex is taut again. The cadence of the train assisted him; and when it swerved and their bodies collided more roughly than he intended, he received the train's impetus into his own body, accepted its directives gratefully, and shared his augmented energy with her. Bowing his head to kiss her breasts, Diddy imagines he is in the cold tunnel. With the distances different, smaller, more intimate. But the lavatory floor seems very far away, as if seen in exaggerated perspective. Towering above the floor, giants are entangled in the act of life.

Diddy will have to give over his image, and does so gladly. As he enters the girl's body, the space shrinks. Intimate space, warm instead of cold, known instead of unknown. He was outside, (now) he is inside. They are both inside.

Diddy's blind body is happily housed in the girl's body, moving without constraint. Surely she knows (now) what really happened. But does the act of life annul his crime? Don't look, don't listen— not even to the rattling windowpane. The girl guides Diddy's body in and out of hers, moves toward and away from him. She comes softly, quietly. It's hard for her to stand; Diddy has to hold her up. Hooking his bent arms under her armpits, bracing his forearms and palms against the wall, as he drives his last sightless thrust deep into her and surrenders to his body's need to weep. A stream which flows; not a chain, which is jointed. He rests his head on her shoulder. They lean together in a stupor of self-forgetfulness. Diddy, his eyes tightly closed, stands in the darkness as though at the bottom of a pool of water. Opens his eyes. The sounds of the train instantly acquire a different, harsher tonality. Time to wake up. He sighs.

Reaching for his T-shirt among the clothes stacked on the sink. Stooping down in front of the girl, and gently wiping her thighs. For the first time Diddy notices a number of yellow and blue bruises on the girl's hips and thighs; no doubt, from falling or bumping into things. Then wipes himself, and stuffs the damp shirt into the disposal slot under the sink. When he turns around, kisses her. "Are you all right?" Diddy murmurs. She makes a purring sound, smiles. Diddy begins to hand the girl her clothing item by item, helping with her dressing when he can. Then hastily dresses himself. Washes his hands. Asks her if she wants to wash hers. She does; and to comb her hair.

"Where are my glasses?" Diddy sets her glasses on her face, sighing.

"What's the matter?" whispers the girl.

"It's no good!" (Now) Diddy's going to botch everything.

"What?"

"It's not you." He puts one arm around her. "It's me. I was lying to you before."

"About the train?"

"No, about what happened. While I was out on the tracks." Touch had not burned away the need to confess with words. Diddy didn't feel absolved.

"It isn't true that you wanted to kill yourself?"

"Yes. That's true. But four weeks ago." He paused, dreading the next sentence. It was speeding along, right behind the one before. Crash. "That isn't what happened now. In the tunnel."

"Tell me. I like the truth." Brave words, upholding a standard that Diddy wanted to honor. But did she really want his confession? As she had really wanted him physically? Flesh doesn't lie. Still clasping the girl, he stepped backward, sat down on the cover of the toilet, drawing her onto his lap. Her soft body was trusting. Diddy took a deep breath, effortful with the weight of the girl leaning on his chest.

"I had a fight with someone outside, on the tracks. I was just trying to find out what was going on. . . . No, I shouldn't try to excuse myself." He struggles to find a straight line of words. "And I think I killed him."

The girl gasps, a kind of interruption, but Diddy pretends not to notice. The truth was falling like bricks.

"If I didn't actually kill him, he's dead anyway, and I'm responsible. I hit him with a crowbar and he fell in front of the train, so that when the train started up again—"

"But," the girl, interrupting, "you never left the train." She loosens herself from his embrace. "I was trying to tell you that before. You were never out of the compartment, believe me. I have excellent hearing." Is the counsel of the senses to be trusted? No.

"Listen, you must understand. . . ." Diddy doesn't explain anything (now), of course. He just repeats himself. She shakes her head. Interrupts him again and again.

How far apart they are (now), even in the tiny space of the lavatory. The gluey touch is forgotten, the damp hair, and the sweet rubbing and melting. Diddy has let that go, as a common thing, and stands behind his tray of words.

"We should go back," the girl says gently. "My aunt might worry."

Diddy sighs. Of course. Unlocks the door. Hand in hand, they turn right, then right again into the corridor. A few steps. Diddy waits while Hester smooths down her hair once more. And without telling her, scans her clothing for any telltale disarray or stains; his clothing, also. Pressing his face against the girl's cheek once more, feeling the hard frame of her glasses between them. Then Diddy slides open the compartment door. Her aunt is still asleep, snoring slightly, mouth askew; the priest and the stamp dealer still reading.

Seated in the compartment, Diddy gazes at Hester, who seems different (now) than she did either in the corridor or in the lavatory. She's leaning her head against the back of the seat; he can't tell if her eyes are shut.

Diddy shuts his own eyes. Why is the girl so obstinate? She must remember! Suppose she doesn't? Does Diddy dare ask the priest or the stamp dealer if he had left the compartment before? Could the girl be right? Perhaps he conjured up the coarse workman; dreamed the broken male body hugging the track. Maybe he's transposing back into the vast, humid, uterine, dusky world of the tunnel the adventure that's just occurred in the cramped space of the washroom. An adventure hardly less expected than what he thinks took place earlier in the tunnel. Is Diddy capable of such a bizarre error? Confusing the transaction of desire with the transaction of violence, trust with fear. Mixing up different domains of blindness and enclosure.

Diddy is beginning, just beginning, to doubt his memory. But that always happens, doesn't it? All past events, both real and imaginary, are consigned to the trusteeship of the imagination.

35

Whether the killing of the workman was fantasy or fact, Diddy has no access to it (now) except through his imagination. The past must be reimagined; memories aren't like furniture, something solid that you can own.

How to remember. The task of remembering supersedes even the task of getting himself forgiven. Or does it? Diddy worries that he's taking the easy way out, letting himself off the hook.

Nothing he can do for the moment, except try to remain calm. When he reaches his destination, he can investigate. Oh, there will probably be no need for that. If indeed a workman has been killed in the tunnel, the news will be carried on the radio, on television, and in the papers. Most of the time Diddy does believe that he's killed someone. But the size has changed. The ruthless velocity of the train is carrying Diddy away, somewhere farther. Elongating perspective, establishing the past as past in an all too purely material way of altered distance and scale. As the train charges forward, the formidable workman has become diminutive, although all the more precious for his small size. Diddy must strain to see him still. It's as if Diddy needs glasses (now). The workman has become a little figure in a little tunnel, a toy object, almost a hobby of Diddy's wandering will. Like a rare postage stamp, much sought after by collectors, picturing the miniature flag of a defunct country since absorbed into a newly created larger nation, or the small pompous profile of a king who had abdicated or been dethroned long ago.

Diddy sitting in the compartment, pondering the curious size of things. A grayish twilight is coming down. Looking inadvertently out of the window, Diddy catches the moment when a light goes on in a distant farmhouse. A vigil light, perhaps. Saying to the weary husband and father still astride his tractor, finishing a day of strenuous labor: Come home for your hot supper, to your children who will scramble into your lap, to your wife's ample bed. Though himself without the safety of home, Diddy responds to the signal. Longs to get out (now), into this plenitude; off the train while space is still open and empty. For soon the ground will be filling up, the houses coming closer, crowding to the edge of the tracks, multiplying and eventually congealing into large buildings.

Soon the train will bisect a town. Then, after a shorter interval, plunge through another town. And finally to the city where we all have to haul down our luggage from the racks overhead, and get off.

Then, marooned in the city to come, Diddy will have to face what he's done. Or not done. All of which has been thrown into question. He blames this on the girl, but it's not her fault, really. The confusion, and the need to complicate matters, must lie in him. For the coarse menace of detection and punishment, Diddy has substituted the subtler menace of uncertainty. He has given his anxiety the form of an enigma.

The untidy aunt has awakened, and gone back to sleep again. Diddy and Hester in the glass-roofed club car (now), the last car in the train. Diddy sits with his back to the rear door of the car. Doesn't want to watch the tracks narrowing so hastily behind the train, or be distracted by the two couples at another table playing bridge. Hester is having a daiquiri, Diddy a rye and water.

"I have to ask you about what happened back there . . . between us." Diddy is uneasy, embarrassed. "What do you feel? Now."

"I'm fine," she says tonelessly.

"You're not sorry about it?"

"Why should I be? I enjoy making love." Something bitter in her voice that pains Diddy. She could be angry at his story about the workman, which she apparently finds preposterous, and at the fact that he had first lied to her. Or she could be angry at his present line of questioning, find it presumptuous or in bad taste. Diddy chooses to think it is the latter, and becomes offended himself.

"Do you often make love with strangers?" Diddy the Jealous. "Do you?"

Diddy sighed. "That was a stupid thing to say. Forgive me."

"There's no point in not doing what you want, is there?" said Hester. "I mean, if nobody's stopping you."

Diddy sighed again, and took the girl's hand. How complicated everyone is! "Tell me something about yourself, besides that you're having an operation."

"There isn't much to tell. When you're blind, it's all inside."

"Have you always been blind?"

Hester didn't answer that question, but went on haltingly with the one before. "How can I describe my life to you? People wait on me, they have to. And I think a lot, listen to music. I'm fond of flowers. I'm—"

"Do you cry sometimes?"

"You asked me that before."

"I know. And you didn't give me the answer, remember? . . . Please answer. Maybe I want to know because I cry a lot myself, and I'm not ashamed of it."

"The answer is yes. Often."

"Why?"

"Probably not for the same reason you do."

"How do you know? Anyway, how many reasons are there?"

"Well, I don't think it's because I'm unhappy. If that's what you're imagining. Maybe I cry because I'm bored."

"I'll bet anything that's not true," said Diddy. "Why do you say that? Is the truth too private? Am I prying?"

"No, I would like to tell you. But all I can think of is that I cry because there are tears."

Diddy didn't like that answer. He wanted her to be unhappy, to be like him. "Are you very lonely?"

"Not exactly. But I don't have enough things to touch."

"Things? You mean people?"

"Yes. People, too."

"Do you love anyone?" Diddy the Possessive.

"I don't think so. At least, not the way I think you mean. When you're blind, people are changing all the time. The same person is never the same person. He's new every time he speaks or moves or touches me."

"Do you love your aunt?"

"Oh, no. Not love. But I like things she does. Her constant talking is awful, but I like her touching me. And reading to me. She's a coordinator of children's services in the public library."

Diddy, relieved, felt bold enough to approach what he really wanted to know. "Do you love me? I mean now." Diddy, an old adept at unrequited love.

"I did. Back there." Hester paused. "I don't know about now. You're not as real to me as you were."

Nettled. Well, what did Diddy expect? "At least you're honest."

"I try to be. Don't you?"

"Yes, I do! But it hardly matters, does it? Back there, I told you what happened in the tunnel. I told you the truth. But you don't believe me."

"How can I? I have to believe what I heard. I didn't hear you say you were going outside. And I didn't hear you leave the compartment."

The girl is adamant. And Diddy doesn't want to quarrel. He wants to be united with her, to be clear as she is clear. And to be blind, too. Still, he needs to talk; and senses that he can address her sympathy if not her credulity. She must be drawn to him, feel for him, or she wouldn't have made love, wouldn't consent to be with him (now).

"I want to tell you the whole story anyway," he says. "Even though you think I'm making it all up."

"I didn't say that. Tell me." She tightens her hand on his. "You're awfully thin. Don't you like to eat?"

Diddy fights to keep from getting wet-eyed at her gift of sympathy. Think of the workman! He begins from the beginning. The walk through the tunnel, the curious obstacle and the solitary workman, outsized and brutish, like an armed angel. Then the monstrous unnecessary battle, and the unhinged body falling across the track. Propping the body against the train. . . .

"You were daydreaming," said the girl firmly. "That's why the man seemed so big."

"Daydreaming in a tunnel?"

"Why not?"

"But I know it happened! I was there."

"Then ask the others."

"I don't want to," Diddy said. "*You're* my witness."

The girl was silent. Diddy longed to rip her glasses off, to slap her face. As if that way he could make her see.

"You're always sighing," said the girl. "Do you know that?"

"Sure. That's because I'm angry. But I don't know what to do with my anger."

"Angry at me?" said Hester.

"Yes. Very angry."

"Why?"

"For being stubborn," said Diddy.

"You mean, for being blind."

"No, I don't mean that." Diddy sat with half-shut eyelids, unable to look at the girl. Feels imprisoned with her. The adventure is over. Time was dragging. Perhaps the trip will last forever, the train go on speeding through endless twilight. The train has acquired the physical and moral energy of a human body; it judged Diddy. And there was to be no absolution from the girl. So be it.

There was nothing but to return to the compartment, and stare out of the window at the metaphor of nature. In the landscape's farthest recesses, in the very experience of seeing in perspective, to find a model for the depths of what had happened.

The compartment again. Hester's aunt, thoroughly awake, obviously entranced to discover that her niece has been spending so much of the train journey in the company of the personable young man sitting across from them.

Introductions are made. Mrs. Nayburn. My niece, Miss Hester Nayburn. But, of course, by now you two young people must be long past the introduction stage.

Diddy, not remembering that Hester still knew neither his first name nor his last, addressed her aunt. "Dalton Harron."

"Well, isn't this nice. . . . What do you do, Mr. Harron? If it's not too forward of me to ask."

Diddy sent a despairing glance to Hester, who was leaning back in her seat. "I work for a company that manufactures micro-scopes."

"One of the big companies?" asked the aunt.

"How interesting," said the priest, looking up from his breviary. "What a privilege to gaze so closely upon the wonders of nature."

"Oh," said Diddy hastily, "I don't do any of the looking through the microscopes." Wanted to bury this insinuation, awkward in the presence of the girl, that he lived through his eyes. "They're made at the plant upstate and shipped from there. I'm in the New York office. I design brochures for mailing campaigns and work on the advertising placed in scientific and trade journals."

> An Elementary Lesson in the Naming and Use of the Microscope:
>
> Place your microscope on a firm support facing the window.
>
> The lens through which you look is called the eye-piece; the lens at the other end is the objective.
>
> The support on which the slide rests is the stage.
>
> Below the stage is the diaphragm which controls the amount of light that the mirror throws through the circular hole in the center of the stage.
>
> The mirror is used for gathering light to illuminate transparent objects on the stage.
>
> When a solid object, such as the head of a fly, is examined, the light must come from above and from the front of the stage, since the light from the mirror cannot penetrate solids.

"Have you had your job long?" asked the aunt.

"Yes," said Diddy.

The aunt subsided, perhaps unable for the moment to think of another question. Diddy looked, questioningly, at the girl. The optical microscope was an ancient and noble instrument, essentially unchanged over the centuries. But useless without eyes, a far nobler instrument and infinitely more ancient. Was the girl born blind? One elementary piece of information her aunt hadn't volunteered. Hester hadn't answered him either, when he asked if she'd always been like this. Diddy wants to know. Yet hardly something he could ask (now).

> Corneal opacities usually date from birth. But not necessarily. Hester could have gone blind during childhood; her eyes badly scarred from, say, severe conjunctivitis. She might once have seen everything in the usual way: flesh, flowers, the sky. Even looked through a microscope in her eighth-grade science class.

"What kind of microscope?" said the stamp dealer. Was he interested, too?

Diddy's company manufactured several of the standard varieties. Some of the less familiar types, too.

> Toolmakers microscopes.
>
> Metallurgical microscopes.
>
> Comparison microscopes.
>
> Projection microscopes.
>
> Ophthalmoscopes.
>
> Retinoscopes.
>
> Otoscopes.

These last three, medical tools, used by eye and ear specialists.

The aunt perked up. "Maybe they use your company's microscopes at the Warren Institute. Your company might make something that the doctors really need, that's going to help my Hester."

"I'd like to think that," said Diddy, feeling still more uncomfortable at this tactless turn of the conversation. The girl, being blind, had become a thing; discussed as if she weren't even present in our compartment.

"If I could see through an instrument," said the girl suddenly, "the one I'd choose would be a telescope. I'd like to see the stars. Especially to see the light coming from a dead star. One that died a million years ago, but goes on as if it didn't know it was dead."

"Lovey, you're being morbid again!" The aunt, nestling into Hester's unresponsive shoulder. "I want my little girl to continue to be brave."

"It's not morbid to be more interested in big things than in little things," said the girl sharply.

And, feeling anew the wave of kinship that flowed between them and the magical synchronicity of their thoughts, it occurred to Diddy: Then perhaps it's not morbid to be more interested in what is dead than what is alive.

He, at least, no longer had a choice. The workman was like one of the dead stars that Hester longed to see. Already extinguished, but still sending forth over long distances a beam of light as life-like and convincing as that issuing from the most vibrant and contemporary star. Diddy had to remind himself that the workman existed in the past. Not be led astray by appearances. However strong the light which the workman cast on Diddy's mind, the man was really dead. Diddy had killed a black sun, which now burned in his head. Surely the girl could see the black sun, if she tried. Even being blind. Or perhaps because of that. Was she testing him? He must hold fast to the difference between dead stars and living stars, however the evidence of his senses confuses him.

Hold fast as well to the difference between large and small, far and near. Every moment the train bore him farther away. And night was falling, when all light becomes false. An artifice: a brave lie to stave off fear of the dark; a trick. Like all sighted people, Diddy needs to be able to tell the difference. While the girl, forced to live consistently in the dark, is exempt from that perilous task of discrimination. But perhaps she was different from most people. So different that even if she weren't blind or her sight were (now) to be restored, she wouldn't become confused. All light, all that she could see, would be true. Diddy no longer angry. She'd told him the truth as she knew it. And though Hester was mistaken about some of the facts, and though she might never be persuaded she was in error, there was a prodigious truth she did know. And that truth Diddy the Incomplete wanted to learn; to possess it alongside his own truth. No one should venture into the dark alone.

Upon arriving at our common destination, feverish Diddy carried his own light suitcase and the suitcases and parcels belonging to Hester and her aunt off the train. Pushed ahead of some other

43

passengers waiting to engage a redcap, and half bullied the man into taking their things first. Then escorted the two women through the old-fashioned station. With its extravagantly high-ceilinged main waiting room. Walls surfaced in marble. Neo-Roman columns. World War I memorial statue of the frail wounded doughboy caught up, just as he went limp and was about to fall, in the robust arms of the Republic: a large stern woman who gazes resolutely over the head of the dying youth. A railroad station is public space, open to anybody. Though promiscuous meeting and transit may be difficult for Diddy at this time, that lofty ceiling he especially approved of; the more space, the better. But as on every trip upstate to the plant in recent years, Diddy can't help marking the steady deterioration of the surfaces and furniture of this station. On each arrival the floor, walls, columns, bronze statue, information booth, clock, ticket windows, newspaper stand, wooden benches look more indelibly stained and grimier and more thickly littered. Not only mere negligence is at work here, surely. A question of policy or principle. Only a matter of time before the wrecker's ball gets around to undoing this generous space, so that something smaller can be put up in its stead. But isn't there a good deal to be said for keeping a doomed place clean and in decent repair? The claims of dignity, for instance. Especially since nemesis is proving to be somewhat dilatory in paying its anticipated call.

Following some twenty feet behind the redcap taking their luggage on a dolly; Diddy and the aunt on either side of Hester, steering through the crowd. Between the neo-Roman columns flanking the main entrance out to the sidewalk. Diddy tips the man, then stands off the curb trying to estimate their chances of getting two taxis in the next few minutes if they remain where they are. But these services didn't seem enough, and he dreaded letting the girl vanish from his life. Standing on the sidewalk, well back from the curb; patiently allowing—or so it seemed to Diddy—one arm to be held in her aunt's protective, unnecessary, unrelenting embrace. Diddy looking for some signal from the girl, not finding one. And not knowing what to look for.

He was startled, too, by the depressing look of the city. Heavy, gray, uncoordinated. And terribly noisy. A furious bluster of noise, hard to sort out. Not at all like the insistent, demanding, authoritative sounds of the train. Did the girl mind noises when she couldn't interpret them?

Longish wait. When a taxi pulled up, Diddy, who hadn't known that's what he intended to do, got in with the two women and accompanied them to the Warren Institute. "But it's out of your way, Mr. Harron. We don't want to put you to any trouble." Doesn't matter, doesn't matter. All the street lights were on, but the buildings looked like two-dimensional drawings of themselves. The hospital no different. "Hold the flag, driver. I'll be right with you. Now, Mrs. Nayburn, Hester, please tell me. . . ." After being assured that the girl's room was waiting for her and that the aunt had a reservation at a boarding house three blocks away, Diddy carried their suitcases into the hospital as far as the admissions desk. Shy good nights. Then went back downtown to the Rushland, where out-of-town executives and salesmen always stayed at the company's expense when visiting the home office. Luckily, no one else from New York coming up for the conference was in the hotel lobby when he registered.

Nearly ten-thirty when Diddy was shown to his room. Unpacked, showered, then called down to the desk to inquire about the first edition of the local morning paper. It came out around 2 a.m. He asked to be phoned at that hour. (Now) eleven o'clock: Diddy turned on the television and found the program he wanted. From behind a desk a bland balding man offered an allotment of communiqués from the front—large enemy losses exactly counted, our casualties light—and politicians' tautologies; items about someone shooting his mother-in-law, a penitentiary riot, the impending divorce of a celebrated Hollywood couple; a condescending account of how the heavyweight champion smashed a young pretender in two rounds in Mexico City; and something about the weather: fair and colder, winds from the northeast. But no fatality on the railroad that afternoon. Perhaps such a death wasn't important or picturesque enough to rate inclusion in the "News." Diddy turned off the set, and decided to try turning himself off as well. Although the hour is early, too agitated to entrust himself to the open spaces of the city streets, with their possibilities of haphazard, impersonal

45

encounters. But something seems almost as threatening, in a coy way, about the anonymous surfaces and the carefully neutralized smell of this room. He will have to go further into himself, away from all coherent rational spaces. Perhaps he can sleep. Of the twin beds in the room, Diddy chose the one near the window, though he didn't open the window or switch on the air-conditioner.

But he can't sleep; he can barely manage to keep his eyes closed for more than a few moments. A wide-angle photograph of the workman fallen across the track projecting itself on the inside of his eyelids, though this is (now) a stop-action shot repeatedly interpolated into a sequence of moving images, filmed with a shaky hand-held camera, that Diddy just watched on the "News": a dead GI, a large body on a stretcher covered from head to foot with a coarse blanket or tarpaulin, being loaded into the maw of a waiting helicopter which has alighted, blades flashing, motor roaring, body shuddering, in some alien rice field. Terrible to die, terrible to have life revoked before one is willing to give it up. And Diddy has done that to someone. Panicked, played the terrible landlord, foreclosed a life. Over and over, this time without picturing, he reimagines the encounter with the workman. Yet, it might be argued that what Diddy has done was excusable, even legitimate. The workman had, for no reason, provoked him. Was inexplicably menacing; was armed. Still, Diddy wasn't convinced that he'd acted simply in self-defense. Were Diddy his own judge, at a real trial, he would never have accepted that plea. The workman was uncouth, insolent. Yes. But insolence couldn't be assumed to augur more, more than just further insolence. And hadn't the man shrugged off his own behavior and, as if to prove the harmlessness of his intentions, turned his back to Diddy? To be sure, some suspicious movements had then followed. But maybe the man was just preparing to toss the ax in with his other tools, gather them all together, and go off. Where? To board the train? Unless he was too anarchic, too much of a loner, to have been one of the train's crew, submitting to group discipline. In that case, his destination was probably wherever the solitary laborer on duty was lodged, like a sentry, ready for any emergency or breakdown—perhaps in some chamber branching off the main space of the tunnel. . . . At this moment, Diddy inclined to give to the workman the benefit of the doubt. The only certainty: that Diddy the Good will never be able to establish, to his own satisfaction, what the man had actually intended. Nor could he know then, in the tunnel. Either astutely observing or blindly assuming that a sneak attack was imminent, Diddy struck first. His opponent either a murderous bully who had dropped his guard or a defenseless human being. But either way, a cowardly assault; since the workman, formidable as he was, never had a chance.

Diddy has left on the small night-table lamp. He doesn't want the dark. He's been in the dark enough today to last a lifetime. No darkness! He must remain alert and perceptive, to fend off the bloody ghosts, to repel the creatures who thrive on the absence of light. Even if it means banishing all creatures. Even if it means being alone. Diddy is alone. Which is almost bearable. He's been much alone the last three years, since Joan walked out. But "alone" seems undignified, pitiable, weak. Again, as he has so often, he tries to convert loneliness into something noble, when freely elected: solitude. Solitude is strong. Yet there is a great difference between solitude in a space with an immense horizon and solitude in a small space. Diddy cornered. Cooped up in a small antiseptic space with pastel walls and maple furniture; and on the wall, daintily framed, "O beauteous land, O gracious land." Solitary, with no lines out to the world. He thrashes about in the narrow bed, sweating, each purposeless turning of his naked body further loosening the sheets and creasing them. Thinks of phoning his brother. But Paul's out on tour; and Diddy left behind in his apartment Paul's letter containing the schedule of concerts. Paul's agent in New York, from whom he could find out where the great virtuoso is tonight, probably wouldn't be home at this hour. And Paul, wherever he is out there in the beauteous gracious land, has the fans and musicians and celebrity-collectors who crowd backstage to look over for possible pleasures, sexual or professional, as well as the after-concert parties to reconnoiter. Is unlikely to return to his hotel until long after midnight. Anyway, having reached Paul, what would Diddy say? Such a call would be an evasion of manhood's responsibilities, a childish bid for sympathy from someone close who had never been genuinely sympathetic or close. If there is a telephone call to be made, Diddy thinks, shouldn't he just get it over with? Diddy considers calling the police.

Still, there's no hurry. If Diddy even suspects a little that the murder of the trackman was just a nightmare or, as Hester Nayburn suggested, a daydream, then he ought to make sure. He can wait at least until he checks the papers. Nothing served by making a fool of himself. Something he's done a good deal this past month. If he contacted the police at this late hour, they'd rush over in a squad car to arrest him, stick him for the rest of the night in a cold cell, an even smaller space than this. And if it turned out in the morning that the murder Diddy claimed as his was a phantom-murder, it would not be easy just to walk out of the jail. The police would undoubtedly insist that Diddy undergo psychiatric tests. He'd be taken from jail and deposited at the local Bellevue, missing the ten o'clock opening of the conference tomorrow morning, and probably the whole day's session. His absence would be remarked, inquiries made, and when the company discovered where he was being detained and for what reason, he'd be fired. Needless to say, no one at Watkins & Company knew why Diddy took a week's leave last month. He'd told Duva an old virus infection had flared up, requiring hospitalization.

Diddy resolved not to panic again. He's decided not to call the police, to be patient, and to await the newspaper's verdict. Still, he can't sleep. But (now) doesn't really expect to.

At two o'clock the phone rings. The bell's sound sears his nerves. "Is it here? Yes! Thanks very much." Diddy has ordered the paper to be brought to him immediately. He hurries out of bed, puts on his trousers, opens the door, and peers down the hall. A teenager in a red suit is ambling along the carpeted corridor, bearing the precious document.

"Here! Here!" Diddy calls out hoarsely. He gives the boy a quarter, grabs the paper, and steps back into the room, bolting the door behind him. Where shall he settle to examine this bundle, smelling of wet ink, that will decide his fate?

Sitting cross-legged on the white pompon spread covering the bed near the door, Diddy resolutely begins to read. Nothing on the first page. Or on the second. Or the third. He doesn't allow himself, in his impatience, to scatter the disappointing pages as he finishes with them; each page, once thoroughly perused, is neatly aligned with its predecessors.

International disasters!

Department store ads!

National electioneering!

Newest model home appliances!

Local bond issues, the municipal council debates over the new cultural center, a scandal in the sanitation department!

A sale on sheets and towels!

Editorial on air pollution and syndicated columns on genocide!

Society page!

Ads for movies and road-show theatre!

Woman's page!

TV and radio listings!

Sports!

Comics!

Real estate!

At Obituaries, his heart jumps. But nothing there, either. Stock market averages, and the paper is done. Nothing. Nothing! Hands trembling, Diddy folds it all up. Wants to hurl the paper into the wastebasket, but. . . . Maybe he ought to do it again, from first page to last. The mind is a malicious sovereign. Can arrange matters so you simply don't see what's right in front of you; if it's what you most fear to see. Even with the aid of a magnifying glass or a microscope.

But Diddy knows he can look over the paper later. And doesn't want to dispirit himself excessively. Better (now) to find a new goal. He phones down again to the lobby. "This is room 414." Hang on! The night clerk mustn't notice how distraught Diddy is, mustn't hear the rabidly demanding edge to his voice. Slowly! "Could you tell me when the next edition of the *Courier-Gazette* comes out?" The words emerge rather skillfully.

"There's only one more edition, sir. Usually delivered to the hotel around 7 a.m., and I don't think you'll find it on the streets any earlier. The truck comes straight from the printing plant."

Diddy is grateful, painfully grateful, for the innocence of facts. "You've been extremely helpful. Thanks. Good night. Oh, and I want to be awakened at six-fifty."

Diddy trying to fill the unresponsive room with his attention. There's nothing to do but wait. Unless. . . . He tries the television again. On one channel, the Late Show. On another, the nightly sermonette that closes the broadcasting day. A bespectacled priest in an arm chair looks straight out of the screen at Diddy the Guilty. Does he sit in a studio set or the parish library of a real church? The priest earnestly invokes blessings upon this great land of freedom, and on our boys fighting overseas to extend those freedoms to the entire world. Slow dissolve at that point: the vanishing priest was replaced by pounding seas, and in the background organ music began to rise faintly. But the voice went on without its body, as confident and cheerful as before. "Bless those who are strong, that they employ their strength wisely." Was this for the President, or for America? "Bless those who are weak, that they receive succor and care from their more fortunate brothers." The sea continued to thrash against the beach, the invisible priest intoning: "Life? you ask. Life is a journey that each of us must make. . . ." A journey! "If in the day's journey, differences occur between neighbors, try to remember that your neighbor is your brother." Differences! And the final anticlimax: "Peace be with you." To which was appended the celebrated name of the sponsoring firm, a family firm consisting of stern father, compassionate son, and the principle of unpredictability. Mere nature could not decorate so grand a signature. The sea was succeeded by a silhouetted cross—an image sustained for about a minute while church bells tolled.

Diddy couldn't take his eyes from the set. Why was he looking? What fascinated the veteran atheist, who'd long outgrown the secret, incoherent asceticisms of his childhood? Diddy's secret conversion to the Catholic faith at the age of twelve had left him exhausted at fifteen, drained of all energy for such glamorous, deceiving exaltations. A relapse (now)? Had the wounds of this

50

day so unnerved him that he could be consoled, or in any way inspirited, by inane pieties? Unlikely.

Suddenly, Diddy understood. He'd connected this priest with the paunchy one on the Privateer, who was another witness to his first absence from the compartment. Why hadn't he confided in him when he came back from the tunnel, instead of in that girl? A priest is accustomed to receiving lurid confessions, and pledged to keeping them absolutely secret. And a priest can instruct the sinner on how to become innocent again, can tell him, Go, and sin no more. Not that Diddy could ever really believe in the literal validity of a priest's absolution. But it was at least more shapely, more definite than the vague informal quittance or release from his crime which he had sought in carnal intimacy with the girl. What a fool he'd been. Crawling back for the familiar tender indulgence of women.

A sentimental fool, lacking all tough-mindedness or proper self-respect. He'd been put off by the priest's impersonal voice, his lifeless fleshy face. Why, it was just those qualities that accredited the man and should have given a sinner confidence in the impartiality and scrupulous fairness of any judgment he might render.

As this fretful thought was subsiding, Diddy noticed with a start that he'd lost track of what was on the screen. For how long? The cross had been replaced by a disk, partly shaded in and branded with the channel's number and network affiliation; and the church bells by an unpleasant buzz. Both were unchanging, unmodulated. Diddy twirled the dial to the Late Show. Mid-plot, a familiar story:

> Peaceful cattle ranchers being done out of their land by brutal railroad men. Good versus bad? Yes and no. The coming of the railroad signified progress, the brutes had on their side the ultimate justification of history. At this moment, most of the gunslingers hired by the railroad to terrorize the ranchers are shooting up the saloon. Cross-cut. At the same moment, two of them are setting fire to the house of the most intransigent of the ranchers. A kid gallops up the dusty street, flings himself from his pony, bursts into the saloon to shout the news. "Paw! They're burning down the ranch!" The brawlers instantly break apart; the bad guys grip their sides with

51

laughter, as ranchers and loyal hired hands stream out of the saloon like water plunging headlong down a drain, leap on their horses. . . .

Diddy has switched off the TV. No more about wicked railroads, please. (Now) everything conspires to speak to Diddy. If only the world of the tunnel had been so eloquent. If only the swarthy laborer on the track had replied to Diddy's questions right away, in any tone he liked. But he hadn't. And the priest on the train hardly spoke to Diddy, either.

There was something wrong with that priest, something besides his flabby body and odd voice and dead face that put Diddy off. What was it? Diddy, straining to remember, remembered. The stamp collecting. It had bothered him strongly, he realized (now). But why it had bothered him wasn't clear. The hobby hadn't seemed objectionable in the man in the tweed suit. But he, after all, was a stamp dealer. Those arbitrarily valued little colored paper rectangles were his business, trade in them his means of livelihood. Whereas, in the possession of the suave priest, they indicated the presence of whim, frivolity, an indulgence of self. A priest's business was his priestly office; all his energies should be employed in healing, consoling, remonstrating, forgiving.

The television is off, dead. Just about (now), Diddy guesses, the Western's plot has galloped to its conciliatory conclusion, all virtues triumphing. No reason to turn the set on again, since there's nothing on the other channels. Well, Diddy's done what he could. Done all that an ingenious mind might propose short of flinging himself straight to destruction, without even allowing for the chance of reprieve, a saving error, or delusion. (Now) will simply have to be patient. He is pledged to wait for the morning edition of the *Courier-Gazette*. If the story isn't there, then Diddy will have to acknowledge that his own urgent, unambiguous memory stands in serious question. Still, later in the morning, he can visit the offices of the railroad and make inquiries. He will. And, if that doesn't turn up any confirmation of the workman's death, he can also. . . .

But no use in thinking that far ahead. The story is bound to be in the paper. Must be. At this point, Diddy would rather discover that he is sane and guilty than innocent and mad.

Diddy undresses and wearily reenters the rumpled bed, kicks off the blanket and pulls the sheets up under his chin. The night-table lamp kept on. Again, unable to stop tossing, sweating, sighing. Another light begins to attract, and ends by distressing him. The sulphur-yellow neon sign flashing on and off outside his window. Somehow Diddy's heart has gotten locked in step with it, and Diddy begins to propose to himself the mad conceit—he knows it's mad —that when the sign is turned off, say, at dawn, his heart will stop, too.

This fancy reminds him of the way in which the sexual rhythm of his body that afternoon had meshed with the plunging effortless rhythm of the train's wheels. The difference was that the train's rhythm was not merely accurate, marking time; it was supportive, aiding Diddy, buoying him up. What bewilders Diddy is that it was the same train whose heavy brutish structure must have mauled the workman's body, finishing off Diddy's treacherous assault. The same train whose weight and ponderous velocity, when it first started up again and burst out of the tunnel into the air, Diddy had sensed so keenly and painfully he could almost feel it scraping his flesh, treading on his viscera, grinding his bones. Yet that same train, when he and Hester were embracing in the lavatory, had seemed almost freed from gravity, producing a voluptuous speed that resembled flying more than racing earthbound along iron tracks. His body, his and the girl's, had flown, too. The train had made it possible.

(Now) Diddy didn't want his heartbeat to be guaranteed by the pulsing of that insensate yellow sign. Call it a sick fancy, if you will. Diddy the Daft is taking no chances. He throws off the bunched damp sheets and gets up, dresses again; goes downstairs. Maybe for something to eat. From his last stay at the Rushland, months ago, already in his insomniac period, he recalls an all-night place several blocks down the street, the Café Miami, patronized by truck drivers and college students. Once there, however, seated in a booth, hungry Diddy finds everything proposed on the menu disgusting. If he allows himself even to picture a real egg

53

salad sandwich or a real hamburger or real bacon and eggs, his stomach begins to heave. But he's thirsty, and that can be dealt with innocuously. Diddy orders a whole pot of coffee. Since he obviously isn't going to sleep, might as well get more awake; so he can move through tomorrow without collapsing. After drinking two cups of the hot, watery coffee, Diddy feeling calmer, less anxious. Also, curiously enough, starting to feel really tired. Tired enough to sleep. It isn't only the coffee that's making him feel better. He's begun thinking of the girl, moving her about in his mind with irrepressible tenderness. If he is very attentive and inward, he can still smell the musky flavor of her body, taste her slightly salty flesh in his mouth, find the odor of her sex on his fingers. At this moment she must be warm with sleep, lying on her back, clad in an ungainly cotton hospital smock, secured under the coarse unwrinkled sheets of a tightly made hospital bed, her milky eyes shielded by the delicate skin of her eyelids, her mouth slightly open, a few strands of blondish hair strewn across her face. Diddy sure this is exactly how she's lying (now) miles away in that bleak, streamlined fortress of healing and dying. He can see the table by her bed, and on the table her dark glasses folded in a leather case, perhaps a plastic jug of water and some paper cups. And a lamp for the convenience of the nurse who might begin the day's first ministrations as early as 6 a.m.

Diddy aches to hold the girl. He finishes the coffee, and has returned to his hotel. Another question to put to the helpful night clerk, who looks up from *Introductory Sociology* when Diddy leans over the desk. Is there an all-night florist in the vicinity? "At this hour? Gee, I doubt it, sir. It's four o'clock. But there is one three blocks down the street. He opens early, I think, because there's a big funeral parlor on the side street there. Around seven-thirty."

Diddy smiled, said good night. He appreciated the man's courtesy, a welcome contrast with New York. Refused to discount it as behavior untypical of night clerks, which he might well have done since the young man—boy really—was obviously a college student, working in the hotel only part-time.

At the elevator door, he called back, "Don't forget to wake me at six-fifty."

"No, sir, I won't."

Diddy let himself out of the self-service elevator at his floor. Down the quiet hall. Gaining his room, locked his door behind him; sat down heavily on the bed, (now) extremely messy, that he has claimed as his. Could he sleep? That seems unlikely. But the room is too small and underfurnished for him comfortably to wait out the balance of the night's vigil anywhere except in bed. Though not expecting to sleep, undressed once more and crawled between the (now) familiar sheets. Once more, he tossed. Stretched out on his stomach and sank his head in the pillow. Lay on his side, knees bent, seized the pillow and hugged it to his chest. About dawn he may have dropped off. Asleep, he may have dreamed of a doll that he was given by his nurse when he was a small child.

Raggedy Andy with a pink open face, topped by long, carrot red hair;

button eyes, thick and smooth as raw lima beans;

flat red triangle nose and black-and-red crescent mouth;

a wide rigid neck and no shoulders;

a pink cotton torso—Diddy had instantly undone the clothes to examine him—seamless, sexless;

pink cotton hands sticking out of his blue-and-red print shirt;

red striped legs hanging loosely from his royal blue trousers.

For a long time Diddy couldn't fall asleep without the doll. Nor would he, at first, consent to go to kindergarten without taking Andy with him. Andy sat propped up on Diddy's lap at the dinner table, and was offered tribute from Diddy's plate. Andy accompanied him to the toilet. Andy perched on the rim of the tub when Mary was bathing Diddy. Andy came along on the rather solemn occasions when his mother and father took the boys for an outing, and they on their best behavior, cautioned by Mary "not to be acting like silly kids and go on upsetting your folks, who want to enjoy themselves." Not only had Diddy loved that doll more than any present he'd ever been given; Andy was dearer than anyone. Dearer to Diddy than his parents. But that was easy, he was afraid of them. Dearer than Paul. Dearer than Mary. Yet in the end the doll deteriorated into an almost unrecognizable state, virtually dismembered. A fistful of Andy's bright wool hair had been torn out minutes after Diddy was punished for stealing five dollars from Mary's purse to buy a birthday present for his father. Then there were Andy's lima-bean eyes, which Diddy clawed off after he came home from school and found Paul, who was down with the measles, playing with Andy in his bed, making him tumble down onto his chest from the summit of his bent knees. There were, in fact, two kinds of provocations. Some were insults to Diddy, that he transmitted to or registered upon the docile stuffed body of his familiar. Others were insults to Andy himself, which included any infringement upon Diddy's exclusive ownership of the doll; these were just as inexorably certified through a violence. For each provocation, Andy bore a scar or mutilation on his clothes or person. But it never occurred to Diddy that he was "ruining" the doll, as Mary and sometimes his mother remarked irritably. Diddy knew what he was doing. With each added injury, Andy became an even more precious historical totem, an album of Diddy's hopeless sorrow. Sightless, bald, maimed, soiled, in tatters, his integument ripped in a dozen places, Andy grew in glory. It was precisely destroying the doll that made it precious to Diddy.

Anyway, it was of this doll, long since discarded into a Halloween bonfire when Diddy was eleven, that the man Diddy dreamed; if indeed Diddy did sleep. In the dream, he had Andy back, considerably less battered than he remembered the doll having been in the final stages of its career. Of course, the lima-bean eyes were still missing. But that didn't matter, because (now) Andy could talk. Talk through the printed slit of a mouth that hardly moved. And said something that started with "For—"; it was either "Forgive" or "Forget." Either way Diddy heard it, he wasn't too far submerged in his dream to fail to appreciate that he was also watching a movie, perhaps projected in a theatre, perhaps miniaturized and coarsened on TV. This was a movie about Andy, a documentary record; priceless because Andy no longer existed, had long ago been consigned to the Halloween flames by Diddy's shameful wish to ingratiate himself with the other boys, to be one with the prankish neighborhood kids with whom he played softball but never talked. Who could hardly imagine that their surly able shortstop played in secret with a doll.

He had to invent Diddy the Mischievous. In order to make plausible the bringing of the sacrifice out of his own house to the bonfire, Diddy had told the boys that this was the favorite doll of a cousin who was staying with them. An imaginary cousin, of course—Diddy had neither sister nor girl cousins—but complete with name, physical traits, and a whiny helpless all-girl character quite her own. The boys seemed to admire the brutality of the prank, to relish the thought of his imaginary cousin's sorrow upon discovering that her favorite doll had been burnt. They told stories about what Ann would say, improvised a fantasy about the stream of tears she would shed. The tears were endless. Cousin Ann would be lying in bed late at night, sleepless with grief. Tears would pour out of her head, drenching the front of her cotton nightgown, down onto the sheets, thoroughly soaking them, and you know what the grownups would make of that in the morning. Still flowing, gathering, the tears would tumble off her bed; a pool of tears would slither across the floor of the guest room where she was supposed to be staying. Then out the door, along the corridor and, with a thunderous rush, down the staircase, a waterfall of irresistible force, a torrent of tears that would force open the front door, surge down the walk and pour into the street, filling Drachman Street, sweeping along the rubbish that lay in the gutters so that the drains became clogged, and when Drachman reached Main, thundering down Main Street, turning right on Sixth Street, flooding the junior high, the church, the library, the drugstore. Via Speedway on out of town, inundating the farmers' fall crops, bulldozing the neat cones of hay already placed about the fields, and ruining the unharvested hay by making it wet. Hurtling on and on, a Niagara of tears, toppling silos, drowning cows, overturning Greyhound buses and cars speeding along country roads, washing away the stucco motels on the highway, felling telegraph poles and power stations, making bridges buckle and trains tip over into ravines. Until, finally, the liquid avalanche plunged into the raw formless sea.

Diddy elated by this vision of stanchless grief conjured up by the

57

other boys. He saw in it only the beauties of enthusiasm, nothing that was cruel. Nor did he see himself as the accomplice of even an imaginary cruelty. Birdlike, he soared over the saline tidal wave as it lacerated and engulfed town, land, and people. As in a dream, he stepped forward; crept nearer and nearer the fire. It had begun to scorch his cheeks but he didn't mind. At a distance, the other boys watched. Diddy flung the doll into the flames, which hardly flared up at all on receiving their new fuel. Then the boys began to laugh and jump up and down. Chant "Diddy burnt Andy! Diddy burnt Andy!" Diddy felt his horrified heart turn into an iron safe. Understanding (now). They'd known all along he still secretly cherished a doll from his early childhood; Paul must have told on him. Wait! Stop! Andy's blackened corpse clearly visible, his limbs flung about awkwardly, aslant one of the burning boards. But it was too late. The doll was irretrievable. "Forgive," whispered Diddy, his eyes smarting only from smoke. Though he ached for the relief of tears. And "Forget," too, he must have muttered to himself as he stumbled back to his house, without yelling a word of insult or reproach at his friends. The offense of their callousness and Paul's treachery was too great to be requited. Diddy could conceive of neither revenge nor reparation.

Anyway, it was of this Andy—uselessly sacrificed familiar, diminished double—that Diddy (now) dreamed, Sunday night, in the hotel room. If he did dream. Certainly, this memory of the doll and its immolation was accurate enough to be no dream at all. Just the amplified and extra-vivid remembering that flourishes in the transit between being asleep and being awake.

One piece of evidence for it being a dream was that his memories seemed to be a movie. And Diddy in some solitary projection room to which he had sentenced himself to watch over and over again his gullible child-self perform, all unknowing, the dreadful, unnecessary deed. Watch it and try to cull some lessons for future behavior from this awful error.

More evidence: the fitful presence of something or someone else, that couldn't be part of his memory. While the Andy-bonfire repeated itself. While the Andy-bonfire, distanced by being seen on film, was being rerun. Over many showings of the ellipitically edited film, a new character gradually emerged; as if a supplementary reel soaking in the emulsion in the photographer's darkroom was being developed piecemeal and then awkwardly spliced in. At first, the cast consisted only of Diddy and the other boys. The way it really had been. Then Diddy could perceive another figure, somewhat out of focus, a stranger, but—he guessed—the one who truly presided over the scene. An adult, indeed an elderly woman with untidy gray hair and sharp features, in burlap tunic and hood, munching a brown pear with her pointy teeth. A terrible old woman. A witch for Halloween. In the dream, Diddy tried not to look at her. And found this possible to do. Though always hovering at Diddy's eye level somewhere near the tumultuous fire, she never fully alighted on the ground. But whenever Diddy managed to shut the witch out of his vision, by staring past her at the noisy flames or down at his own feet, some clarity was lost. Everything in his mind wobbled and bent; the way Billy and Ira and Chris and Mark did, viewed through the fiercely heated air surrounding the fire.

What he (now) suspected couldn't be so. Would make everything come out wrong. Yet he couldn't banish the insidious thought, presenting itself as a realization, that Andy wasn't his doll after all, never had been. That, envious of his young cousin's treasure, he'd only been pretending to be Andy's rightful owner. So it was true that poor Ann had a miserable time awaiting her. Would sob pitifully to discover Diddy the Treacherous has murdered her beloved, helpless Andy. Not Niagaras and Red Seas inundating the world. But still, copious salty tears; too strong for her eyes to bear. When she discovered Diddy's theft and learned that Andy had been cremated, she would weep herself blind.

What to do about this confusion? Diddy paralyzed before his dream, if it was a dream. He'd already told the boys what might be, what he prayed would still turn out to be, what must be—a lie. The lie about the doll's ownership. So he couldn't ask them (now) to tell him whether his lie was true. Could he? Neither could he ask the witch, drifting all too near him, throbbing in the scorched air, Who please, who, himself or his cousin, owned Andy. She was ugly, and he was afraid of her. Only a fool would expect such a loathsome creature to be generous. Why should a witch be kind enough to unravel a riddle, to grant him the surcease of truth? Diddy must decide for himself to whom Andy belonged. To assist him, he had the advice offered by Andy, an Andy miraculously resurrected, to Diddy's unspeakable joy, and (now) cradled in Diddy's arms; an Andy who could speak, with printed mouth, almost distinctly. Forgive. Forget. Diddy unaware of any contradiction in the course of events. He lets Andy's sibylline advice, blurred, overlapping, brusque, tentative, fill his mind.

Or maybe Diddy didn't dream about the doll. Maybe only remembered it. For it did happen: the discarding of Andy into a Halloween bonfire when Diddy was eleven. An act of senseless bravado which Diddy had recently come to regard as his first suicide attempt.

At ten minutes to seven, he was prized from somewhere inside himself by the phone. Inexact to call it awakening. Diddy got up; as he rapidly showered, shaved, and dressed, listened to the TV. A few minutes of Mickey Mouse; then the seven o'clock news came on, still lacking an item about the death of a railroad workman yesterday afternoon. Only the same war, floods in Italy, famine in India, exposure of high-school narcotics ring, local et cetera. Diddy deciding to give the media one more chance. Went down to the lobby; picked a copy of the fresh edition of the *Courier-Gazette* off the top of the stack of newspapers on the desk. The courteous student night clerk had been replaced by a stout bespectacled woman in her forties, wearing an orange cable-stitch cardigan and knitting something green. Paper in hand, Diddy scanned the apparently vacant lobby, hoping not to see anyone from the firm emerge from behind a pillar, or discover a colleague dozing in a deep chair on the far side of one of the potted plants. But seven-fifteen must be too early for anyone to be down yet. Except for himself and a porter steering a carpet sweeper around, and the desk clerk, the lobby was empty. Diddy sank into an upholstered lounge chair against the right wall, under an ornately framed seascape in oils; lit a cigarette. Laid the paper on his knees and avidly began to read it through, starting with page 1. Is Diddy's talent for thoroughness being wasted? "Late Final" seemed identical with

"City," the edition he'd pored over upstairs in the middle of the night. Two identical editions? Was this a bad joke or an affectation? A provincial newspaper aping the scale of big city enterprises, insinuating urgency, claiming that there's more news than there actually is or than it's able to provide. Diddy enraged. Scornfully turning page after page. Wait! Diddy is wrong. On page 16, second column, the following headline:

WORKER HIT BY EXPRESS TRAIN
RAILROAD INVESTIGATING

and a four-paragraph story under it. Amazing how calm Diddy feels as he begins to read:

> A trackman employed by the New York, Boston & Standard Railroad for thirteen years was killed yesterday afternoon. Angelo Incardona, age 37, of 1863 Maplewood Boulevard, who was engaged in minor repairs of the track running through the Hudson Hills Tunnel 430 miles south of here, was apparently struck by the Privateer, the new ultra-modern express train making its daily run from New York to Buffalo. The body was discovered by the engineer of the Summerton local, the next train to pass through the tunnel.
>
> The Privateer left New York City from Grand Central Station at 3:10 p.m., as scheduled, railroad officials report. The trip was without incident, and the train arrived here at 9:15, and reached Buffalo at 10:05 on time. When questioned, the Privateer's chief engineer, Martin Pelty, of Albany, said that neither he nor any member of his crew saw Mr. Incardona as they passed through the Hudson Hills Tunnel, and at the Privateer's speed they could not have felt any impact had the train struck someone. Railroad officials have emphasized that laborers working on the track are briefed on train schedules. Officials cannot explain why Mr. Incardona did not get out of the way of the Privateer. Like all tunnels on this route, the Hudson Hills Tunnel is equipped with an electronic warning system. Approaching trains trigger a loud siren in the tunnel that gives ample time for anyone on the track to move off it and stand safely in one of the numerous shelters, seven feet high, five feet deep, and seven feet wide, in both walls of

61

the tunnel. Railroad safety rules require that workmen stand well within these shelters while trains are passing through.

One railroad official, who asked to remain anonymous, said that the circumstances of Mr. Incardona's death did not rule out the possibility of suicide. Local police are discounting the suicide theory but declare they have no intention of closing the case immediately. The newly reorganized Accident Investigation Squad, headed by Capt. Arthur G. Mallory, has opened a file on the case and expects to determine whether any responsibility belongs to the railroad. "I'm not saying there are, but there just might be some loophole in the precautions laid down by the railroad for the safety of men working on the tracks," Capt. Mallory said last night when reached at his home by the Courier-Gazette. Capt. Mallory said he plans to inspect the lighting available in the tunnel, the system of shelters and storage areas, and the functioning of the electronic warning system. Representatives of the New York, Boston & Standard have already pointed out that their safety regulations are far stricter than the minimums established by federal and state law. But they have assured the police of their continued and full cooperation with every phase of the investigation.

Hasn't the anonymous author of the story been carried away by the faint prospect of a larger story, an investigation leading to a negligence suit that might put the state's second wealthiest railroad on trial? Forgetting his original subject, mere Angelo Incardona. But eventually the zealous reporter had to descend to the commonplaces of an obituary; summarizing a life that had only the most schematic existence as far as public records show. Perhaps his rewrite man had to cut away a good deal more pyramiding of supposition about the railroad, to bring the reader smack up against Incardona, as he existed before his abruptly accomplished removal from this world. A few facts, anyway. Not much to tell in this fourth, and last, paragraph.

Mr. Incardona was born in Utica but moved to this city at the age of fourteen. He graduated from William McKinley High School, where he was a star quarterback in his senior year. After graduation, he enlisted in the army and served in Korea during the Korean War. He was a

member of American Legion Post #701 and the Brotherhood of Maintenance of Way, AFL-CIO. He is survived
by his wife, Myra, and a son, Thomas Francis, 11. Services
will be held tomorrow at 2:00 at the Floral Gardens Funeral Home, 303 Schuyler Avenue.

Diddy sat, hands twitching, the coarse sheets of the newspaper
agitated beyond his control.

All doubts resolved: a man had died yesterday. Whose home, by
an unspeakable coincidence, was here. The city where Diddy was
obliged to remain for a week.

(Now) Diddy has his sad triumph over Hester. The messy,
mortifying uncertainty was over, quelled by the dreary but precise
screed of newspaper prose. Undeniable relief to know he was sane.
If anyone suffered from absences of mind, it was Hester. And also,
he recalls irritably, the man who wrote headlines at the *Courier-
Gazette*. Can't people read? That headline not merely inaccurate. It
contradicted the story. Wasn't the railroad who was investigating,
or proposing to investigate, the incident in the tunnel; it was the
police.

So, everything was certain (now) with respect to the past. But
what's Diddy to do, at this moment? This morning? Present himself to Capt. Mallory, informing the conscientious cop that his
suspected case of negligence is actually a murder? Well, perhaps
not a true murder in the technical sense. It occurs to Diddy that
if he confesses promptly, he might be tried on a reduced charge.
Hadn't he been overdramatizing his crime? From a legal point of
view, it wasn't murder straight and simple. What he'd done to
Incardona sounds to Diddy the Layman more like manslaughter,
in which the assailant isn't acquainted with his victim; so that the
crime is not premeditated. Than murder, where the killer knows
his victim and can plot the crime in advance.

Could Diddy's lawyer make that argument stick? So that, at
worst, he'd be tried for manslaughter or for murder in the second
degree?

But wait. Diddy is going too fast. Already bargaining with Capt.
Mallory, with the sergeant at the station, with the D.A. Somewhat

premature, when he has yet to decide bluntly, once and for all, whether he intends to give himself up.

One ordeal he means to spare himself. That of mockery and derision. It's possible the police won't believe him. Diddy the Demented, one of the horde of guilt-stricken folk longing to be punished who stride by the hundreds into police stations each year, to confess loudly to crimes they read about in the papers, perhaps wish they'd committed; but surely didn't commit. No, his confession must be supported by evidence. Witnesses. His fellow passengers will testify that he was absent from the compartment long enough to commit his crime. Can't be that the others share Hester's inexplicable lapse of memory. God, why hadn't he taken down their names and addresses! Surely they can be traced. And don't forget that his fingerprints must be smeared all over the crowbar he used on Incardona—unless some idiotic foreman has already assigned the dead man's tools to another laborer, who's wielding them right (now), dissolving Diddy's prints with fresh sweat and grime. Lastly, an autopsy; which might disclose that the train that may have crushed Incardona's torso couldn't also have broken open his skull. No time to waste. Before the priest and the stamp dealer, candy effigies, melt, vanish into oblivion; before Incardona's corpse is retouched by the mortician's lying skills, stuck underground, and begins to rot.

But wait. No, no. Something wrong. The newspaper would have it that the Privateer's run was without incident, that the train passed through the tunnel without stopping at all. Diddy knows the world is built on lies. But why would they tell such a stupid lie, one so easily exposed? The railroad must be desperate to conceal its fallibility, to deny that breakdowns and unforeseen accidents ever occur. Those buck-passing bastard bureaucrats won't be allowed to get away with such tricks. Everyone aboard the Privateer can testify that the train stopped for about forty minutes. Even Hester remembers that.

Quick, then. To work. Either that, or don't move at all. Diddy the Dilatory doesn't rise from the deep upholstered chair in the hotel lobby. He can't help thinking, why should I? Why was Diddy bent on confessing to a crime no one suspected him of committing, the penalties for which he could, if he chose, escape entirely? The justification for that impulse, once plain to Diddy, had dissolved a mere moment ago into a murky elusive blur of inner speech, tuned down so as to be unaudible. But it's not as if Diddy isn't permitted to think any more, once he's reached a decision. No. Then think. Thinking some more. Maybe it wasn't judgment or punishment he desired, only clarity and certainty. These he'd yearned for with such passion, and with so little hope of attaining them, that he could easily have misread his desire as a craving for judgment and punishment.

But (now) he had them both, clarity and certainty, clenched in his fist. Like splinters of glass which, miraculously, fail to lacerate the hand. Why go any further? Did he want to die? Diddy the Done. No, he wanted to live. But was that enough of a reason to remain sitting in this chair?

And what about the lovely girl sequestered in the hospital? Hadn't Diddy set himself two projects to carry out this Monday morning? Discover if he were a murderer, and send Hester some flowers. He's seen through one project. Before turning himself in, he'd take care of the other. Diddy tore the story on page 16 out of the *Courier-Gazette* and tucked it in his wallet. Then left the hotel and strolled down the street, unexpectedly lighthearted, inhaling the damp fresh morning air, lightly pricked with sensations from the miniature rush hour getting underway, like a toy imitation of Manhattan. The buses crammed with sleepy-eyed office workers and compulsive shoppers. He crosses the street. The florist, a small brown paper bag clamped between his elbow and right side, was just pulling up the iron shutters and unlocking the door when Diddy arrived, his first customer. Diddy, pacing about the dark, humid, fragrant interior of the store. All dark places should smell like this. The man watched him patiently, permissively, while sipping coffee from a cardboard cup.

Real nice morning.

Yes, very nice.

It was a challenge to choose flowers for someone who can't see them. For whom flowers must be legible and pleasurable in all ways except the ordinary one, sight. Diddy selected lilacs for their scent.

Pussy willows for their texture. Six anthurium stalks for their keenly erotic shape. "They're awful expensive, I have to tell you. Get them flown in all the way from Hawaii." Diddy said he knew and that it didn't matter.

Making out a card to accompany the flowers. "I hope to see you today. Dalton." After that, Diddy started back for the hotel. He's walking more slowly (now). Away from life, back to death. True, he's all but convinced himself that no good would be served by turning himself in to the police. Yet the final step is not in place. Hence, conviction doesn't arrive. And all his reasoning is sterile. Diddy on the way to confession, humiliation, and imprisonment. He will enter the Rushland, go to his room, and telephone the police. It's done by taking one step at a time, putting one foot in front of the other. But Diddy has yet to cross the whole of the lobby, he's still twenty feet short of the elevator door, when someone calls "Hey! Hey, Dalton!" Jim Allen of the sales department hailing him. Diddy knew Jim was among the group from New York picked to attend the conference. But how long has he been here? Was it possible that Jim, unperceived by Diddy, had been about the lobby earlier; watching Diddy feverishly scanning the newspaper, finding what he sought, tearing it out, and secreting it in his wallet? "When d'you get in, Dalt?"

"Early yesterday evening," replied Diddy, anxiously wheeling around. He was startled to find Jim just behind him. Close enough to be stretching out his arm for a handshake. Diddy managed it. "I took the Privateer," he continued slowly, not sure whether that was a prudent admission. Hastily, before Jim thinks of an item he may have read in his morning's paper, adding, "When did you arrive, Jim?"

"A few minutes ago. I caught an Earlybird. I just don't have the patience for trains any more."

What reply could Diddy make to that?

"Say, is Duva coming up for any of this? I can't ever get a straight word out of that guy. What a cold fish. It beats me how you can work with him."

Duva would be up on Wednesday if he came at all, Diddy said.

Hardly believing that these were the words coming out of his mouth. In this casual tone.

Jim grunted. Looked distractedly around the lobby, then at Diddy. "Have you had breakfast?"

Diddy said he hadn't.

"Come on then! Neither have I, and we're due at the plant by ten. They're sending a car by the hotel at nine forty-five for us and the two other guys . . . you know, Bill Katz and Fred What's-his-name."

Diddy, drifting from his firm purpose, knew it. What he's set out to do, what he had to do, was not getting done. Diddy the Delayer. But what could he reply to Jim? "Excuse me, but I must go upstairs to call the police." "Yeah? Why?" "It's to turn myself in for a murder I committed yesterday afternoon." "What! Come off it!" Diddy shakes his head gravely. "C'mon, Dalton, don't try to put me on." Until, eventually, in another voice: "For God's sake. Where?" Diddy's reply: "On the Privateer. No, off it." Then a wry joke. "Pity I *do* have the patience for trains." Diddy the Comedian.

Diddy could not perform so clumsy and predictable a scene. Something else, then. Taking a step away from the elevator, hesitating. There, alongside affable gelatinous Jim Allen, was the track of his life stretching out before him. He had only to keep going, not look back. Even though the track curved sharply. But curves are natural. Nobody would know. Only Hester knew Diddy's truth, without believing it. Why should she (now)? Hardly likely that she was having the local newspaper read aloud to her, cover to cover, at the hospital this morning. And sooner or later the paper would drop the story, if no lunatic with a wild tale jumped forward to make it more interesting. Capt. Mallory's zeal might flag, or the railroad make it worth his while to abandon the investigation. Then, once the story disappeared from the *Courier-Gazette,* no chance the girl would ever hear of it. There wouldn't be anyone to connect Diddy with the accidental death of a railroad laborer named Incardona.

Was this Diddy's mandate? Striding across the lobby with Jim Allen, Diddy took it to be the mandate of life. Giving himself up

67

to the police would not resurrect Incardona. That was just a way for Diddy to commit suicide, this time successfully. And he didn't want to die (now). Diddy mellowing toward himself. Loving himself, even his lean body, turned very pale since that sad decision last month. The heat of increased consciousness relayed into an unaccustomed sense of bodily vigor. (Now) Diddy consented to breathe even noxious city air; could imagine himself walking briskly, running, and swimming; was eager to work. Xan's matted hair needs combing out. He wanted to continue sending Joan the money so she could finish law school. He wanted Jim Allen to feel easy with him, he wanted to be close to Hester.

"I'm hungry," says Diddy, smiling. "I didn't have any dinner last night."

Diddy found his appetite with Jim. Both men put away a big breakfast. Speculating on the conference, wondering whether anything useful would be accomplished.

It was possible that everything the company had built up was about to be washed away. The firm was unprepared; they'd been accustomed for so long to being secure from serious competition. Manufacturers of the Micro-Recorderscope, known familiarly in memos and on charts as Scope 21. Cornerstone of the company's reputation and financial solidity; the item that accounted for fifty percent of its profits. An apparatus about eight inches high which combined the features of a rigorous, high-powered magnifying instrument with the resources of an excellent camera. An apparatus no one could rival.

But (now) all that was changing.

Four years ago, there appeared on the market a Swedish microscope-camera that was every bit as good as the Micro-Recorderscope. Why shouldn't it be? It was constructed on almost identical principles. The availability of the Swedish apparatus had halved the European sales of Scope 21. But because the instrument was priced higher than Scope 21, the Swedes hadn't tried to invade the American market.

This year the big trouble arrived. A company in Belgrade, believed to be French-financed, had come up with a powerful instrument built on principles different from those of Scope 21, but equally small, sensitive, and efficient. And cheaper, too, even after allowing for the duties. Since the Yugoslavs had set up an office in New York, their photomicrographic outfit had already been adopted by several of the company's best customers. A big hospital in Philadelphia, a biological institute in Chicago, the laboratories of one of the highest-ranking medical schools in the Northeast.

(Now) coming up, something worse. The Japanese model.

Rumors had been flying about the New York office for months. Some people said it didn't exist. Diddy wondered if perhaps the top echelon of the firm mightn't be spreading the rumor themselves to goad the junior executives to work harder, or to prepare some of them for a salary cut or for dismissal.

"I wonder," said Jim. "It's not that I think they're too honest to pull a stunt like that. I doubt if they're clever enough. No, I believe in that Japanese boogeyman."

Diddy wasn't sure. Not easy to lay a suspicion to rest, to decide conclusively whether something dangerous is true or false. But what did it matter? Wasn't it best to believe the worst?

"I'm with you there, Dalt," Jim said. "Especially since it usually turns out that right behind the worst jam you can imagine is something even worse. So bring on the disasters," he concluded cheerfully. "We'll still be ahead of the game."

Diddy said he doubted things looked that grim for Watkins & Company.

"Grim! They're dead on their feet and don't know it," exclaimed Jim. "You know what's wrong with this company? The goddamn company philosophy. They make me puke with their phony dignity. You know? All that stuff about science and public service. A bunch of fat lazy ostriches is what they are. Soft sell and lots of prestige is okay. But business is still business. And this one is going down the drain."

Is the company that badly off? Diddy hadn't noticed. Nor ever imagined Jim to be so disaffected.

The question is, can anything be done about it. "Honestly," Jim went on, "I don't think Watkins or Reager has any idea what the company is up against. When they see sales drop off, they always assume there's something guys like you and me can do, like selling louder, to make the figures go up again."

Diddy mentioned his ideas for a new advertising campaign. The material typed, lettered, and drawn on the sheets of yellow legal-sized paper, clipped together in his briefcase.

"Dalton, come on! Do you really think you're going to turn the tide that way?"

No.

From sarcastic speculating on whether anything useful would be accomplished at the conference, Jim passed to more griping about the firm's old-fashioned business practices and lamenting the pack of useless relatives and untalented descendants of the founder that filled the top executive positions.

"I don't know, boy," said Jim. "I figure I'm really stuck, labeled, you know, good member of a team. Right now in the Bolivian foot-hills some poor slob is mining the gold that's going into the watch Reager will present me with on my thirtieth year with the firm. Well, I'm not sticking around for that. Life's too short. Don't repeat this, but between us, if things don't look different in eighteen months, a hell of a lot different, I'm putting myself on the job market. Now that I got the M.A., it shouldn't be hard. It better not be! I've got a wife and three kids."

"Lucky you," said Diddy. "I wish I had a wife and three kids."

"Sure, I'm lucky. I know that. But sometimes, don't I wish it were different! Do I ever! Look at your setup, Dalton. Assuming the whole company doesn't fold up, you could survive a retrench-ment. Or maybe I'm exaggerating, and it's not that bad. But if they are about to tell us to pull in our belts, you're not too squeezed. And if it's just a matter of their not promoting you pretty soon, you can afford to wait. Unless you get the chance to jump to something better."

Diddy shrugged his shoulders.

"Anyway," Jim grinned, "you might end up marrying Reager's daughter or one of those other broads in the direct line of succession. Then you'd be sitting pretty, and no sweat."

"I hope to marry again," said Diddy pensively. "But Evie Reager isn't exactly what I have in mind."

"Got someone in mind?"

"Maybe."

"Don't want to talk about her, huh? Okay, I won't pry."

Diddy does feel lucky (now). Even Jim's well-meaning inanities don't gall him as they usually do.

"Anyway, Dalton, you know I'm not sounding off just because I think I've had a rough deal. It makes me mad to see how things are run."

"Well, they have had practically a monopoly. And now they're going to have to give it up."

Jim didn't answer.

"Let's show them how to compete, Jim," said Diddy, laughing. "Young business geniuses from Manhattan in vinyl space suits invade dull upstate city, tweaking the noses of the old fuddy-duddies, climbing right over their rocking chairs. After taking over the foundering genteel business of their choice, they reorganize from top to bottom, offering a new—"

"You making fun of me, boss?" said Jim good-humoredly.

"Yes, if you want to know. And of myself."

"Look!" Jim shouted, waved. "Over here, you guys!" Katz and What's-his-name, two other delegates from the New York office, had just walked into the hotel restaurant. They came over to the table and joined Diddy and Jim for coffee. Diddy excused himself for a minute. Hurried upstairs to get his briefcase. At nine forty-five, all four men were in front of the Rushland, where a black limousine driven by an elderly Oriental wearing a dark blue uniform waited for us. The front door on the driver's side has a small dome-shaped insignia, painted blue and gold. Otherwise, all black. Like a hearse, Diddy thought. But it didn't bother him.

"What's your name, son?" said Jim, putting his hand on the chauffeur's shoulder.

"Chang," said the man. Jim winked at the others, then settled back in his seat.

Diddy claimed the jump seat. Not altogether comfortable. Because of an ache in his spine, it took time to search out the good position. Turning sideways, to face the rear door of the limousine. He couldn't cross his long legs. But because his seat was different, almost an afterthought, Diddy felt himself to be under a different dispensation than the others. Exempted from tacking on to those indigestible strips of words being exchanged by the three men seated in a row to his left more strips of words; his words, which were bound to be sticky as taffy or tough like overchewed bubble gum. Allen, Katz, and What's-his-name, sitting side by side, sunk deep in the gray felt upholstery. Jim not perceptibly different from and no more human than the rest of the trio; and Diddy no fonder of him than of the others. Nothing remained. Mr. Dalton Harron in the jump seat maintains, always has maintained, exacting standards for personal relations, though life has promised him nothing. Knows that idle conversation of one with three cannot be, fully, the word- and paper-clogged plenum of business, unswallowable but at least necessary or anyway justifiable. But is already too many for real talk. One with three is a middle condition, serving nobody. The number precludes genuine nourishment, which is possible, when it's possible, with one. Only one other.

On time. We left the city by the northwest. In a few minutes the car had cleared the disheveled downtown area, the streets scarred with trolley tracks and bloated with traffic; the views disfigured by clashing buildings and punctured with construction sites.

Monday has bloomed into a sunny soft late October morning. (Now) we were cruising along the expensive smooth asphalt of quiet residential streets; no irregularities in the surface or unreasonable gaps in the views. Streets lined with long sloping lawns and widely spaced houses sixty to eighty years old, all well cared for and in pretty much the same pleasing style, but whose original symmetry had been violated with the addition to each house of a garage in which two cars were tucked away.

72

"Here's where the local Four Hundred hold the fort," sneered Katz.

"Wonder where the local Chinatown is," said Jim in a stage whisper.

Diddy, rendered almost nerveless by contradictory feelings, doesn't mind Jim's abrasive coarseness. And finds it easier (now) to stomach Katz, whom he made a point of having little to do with in the New York office. By sneering, Katz exposed himself, made himself understandable. But why did Katz move about restlessly in his third of the comfortable seat? Could all that fidgeting be provoked by the spectacle of such commonplace, modest luxury? Katz probably grew up in a Bronx slum apartment with nowhere to play except P. S. Number Something's cement recreation yard, shut in by a high Cyclone fence. Or on the sidewalk of his dingy block where he'd had to worry about the ball shattering a window, calling down the curses of screaming tenement housewives, among them his own mother. Don't be too hard on the envious. Be glad you have, or had in the past, something enviable. Diddy will be generous. He had been lucky, sheltered. Enough space, green space, in which to play. For Diddy had grown up in just such a spacious house, entrammeled with ivy, as those they were passing (now), on such a mild tree-lined street, and in a smallish city not unlike this one. Before the war. Before all such prosperous old neighborhoods concealed, beneath their complacent regard, an anxious insecure look which came from learning what was to be their eventual destiny: demolition. And faceless apartment buildings and housing projects, filing cabinets for living away one's life, put up in their stead.

But maybe they wouldn't be torn down. To Diddy today the bastions of the small-city bourgeois family looked virtually impregnable. The car glided along the wide, sparsely traveled asphalt that separated the facing houses. Houses that are quiet (now), emptied of father-breadwinner and school-age children. Being cared for and stocked with provisions by mother-wife and her domestics. It was five minutes to ten. In two hours, the children would rush, trudge, and dawdle home. Someone like Mary would have the table set and lunch ready. Some of the fathers probably came home, too.

73

"Mind if I open the window," said Diddy. Not a bad day. Rather warm. Diddy was accepting the ride, able to gaze out of the car window at the complacent houses and the livid red and brown foliage of autumn's trees.

He did not refuse these houses. How could he? That would be to refuse himself. Nor did Diddy feel ironic about their inhabitants. The businessman and the businessman's wife. The lawyer and his wife. The minister and his wife. The doctor, who was like his father, and the doctor's wife, who was like his mother. The principal of the local high school, like Uncle John, and his wife, like Aunt Alice. Nor did he, even in imagination, condescend to their pampered well-fed children; equipped with shiny English bicycles that moved on thin hard tires, tended by garrulous devoted Irish nursemaids, packed off for their weekly piano lessons. Why should Diddy mock himself?

We paused at a railroad junction, then crossed over with a rude bump into the less prosperous belt of two- and three-story frame houses and narrow front yards, small grocery stores, used-car lots, and warehouses that girded the edge of the city. The surface of the streets became rutted and uneven; all the available curb space for parking was occupied. Diddy catches a glimpse of blue and gold profile, which vanishes after a moment. No vistas here. Besides cars, the street was crowded with slow-moving trucks; some, double parked in order to make deliveries, nearly blocked our passage through the street. The black limousine moves slower (now), but there's less for Diddy to look at. The long low-lying factory was just ahead. Jim gave a mock groan. "Here we go! Ready or not." The car went through the gate; without needing to stop, or anyway not stopping, to be cleared by the guard, who stands still as an effigy in his tiny booth. We go by too fast for Diddy to see his face. But time enough to notice that he wore a uniform different from our chauffeur's. Wrinkled, less smart. Hadn't the company driver who picked up Diddy at the Rushland on his last trip worn a tan uniform similar to the guard's, rather than the navy blue worn by today's chauffeur? Diddy would concede that about this his memory might be mistaken. But he's positive the other chauffeur wasn't an Oriental.

74

Up the long landscaped driveway. We halted before the main door of the plant. No farther to go. "Thanks, Chang," said Jim, still insisting on finding a joke in the man's name or simply in his own effort to be familiar with him. No jokes for Diddy. There aren't many Orientals who drive hearses, are there? But the man would be good at that job, too. An alert careful driver. One couldn't imagine him running anyone over; or even, through no fault of his own, being involved in an accident.

And stepped out of the limousine. Before a building that had not been a harmonious whole for three decades.

Once there was one structure built of brick. A pungent, dusky red color. Four stories; perforated by high, narrow, deeply recessed windows with heavy wood frames. And surmounted by a sloping, gray-slate roof.

In the late 1940's, two long wings or annexes were added, over whose basic building material, reinforced concrete, a thin skin of stucco had been applied; and on that a relentless decoration of crescent lines had been incised. The stucco once white; a stained, coarse off-white (now), the color of a vanilla ice defiled by mud and urine. Three stories. A thin continuous belt of window glass on each floor. Flat-roofed.

Diddy winced. The original edifice had been enclosed by two huge parentheses of ugliness. The building spoiled. But perhaps not entirely. All depends on the viewer. To see beauty under most circumstances, one had to look discreetly. Wasn't it like that always? Narrowing the aperture of vision, bestowing the fraction of a look. The better to discriminate between beauty and ugliness, life and death.

Diddy could narrow his look and see just the central portion of the building, a rather handsome example of Victorian factory architecture, where the firm's offices, laboratories, and demonstration rooms were located (now). The factory proper having been moved into the wings. The ugliest construction of all, a building dating from the 1950's which served as warehouse and shipping office, is located in the rear and mercifully hidden from Diddy's present view.

75

Jim was greeting some men who were getting out of the limousine which had pulled up behind us. Diddy standing apart. Waiting for Jim, looking up. And not simply at the cloudless azure sky.

The blue and gold dome which topped the old brick structure had been the founder's pet idea. After the architect brought from Boston had drawn up his plans, Amos Watkins (1834–1909) had insisted on his redoing them in order to work in a chapel. At noon and in the late afternoon, all factory employees from the lowliest janitor to the heads of the firm were convoked for prayer meetings.

His son Hubert (d. 1931) had dismantled the chapel at the turn of the century. After ripping out the pews and the altar, but leaving the stained-glass windows depicting an allegory of the Triumph of Industry, Amos' son installed desks and files and personnel, mostly women, of the expanding firm's bookkeeping department. In 1928, someone convinced Hubert that the huge vaulted space could be used still more wisely. Bookkeeping cleared out, the main laboratory of the company's department of research and technological development moved in. But the dome remained, forever hinting at, while quite properly lacking, a cross. Presiding over the chapel that (now) no longer existed.

The present Watkins, Hubert's son (1914–   ), knew only the laboratory. His grandfather's chapel was a quaint ancestral folly. Not real at all. The old flooring still exposed in the narrow aisles, between the squarish bulky machines and the long worktables of the technicians, was worn quite smooth; holes made by the bolts that fastened down the pews had long been filled in. The stained-glass windows were taped on the inside and then covered by heavy tan drapes, to prepare for the advent of reliable, uniform, artificial light.

Diddy, alongside his three New York colleagues, crossing the carpeted lobby of the old building. Waving to some men he knows from the Los Angeles office, nodding to the resident personnel. The four men identify themselves to the receptionist, receive a smile in return, and head for the elevators. To the left of the elevators are the high wide wooden doors that once admitted all employees to the old chapel. More restricted (now). "Research and Development." Later, Diddy will step in, as usual, for a look.

We are standing in front of the elevator, which Diddy thinks of as a vertical bore through the center of the building. A bore which might exit into the dome itself. Could one go up there (now)? In all these years Diddy had never inquired about that. It's about time. Here's a tiny idea, a pretext. Diddy will propose that a visit to the dome be added to the tour of the plant offered to the public each Wednesday at eleven o'clock. Entirely suitable. For this is what the dome had become: an asset for public relations. This third-generation Watkins, noting that the dome was (now) just a head missing a body, an idle, spiritually pretentious ornament atop a busy profane building, was unwilling to leave it at that. The wrong head for this body. Hubert's son considered decapitating the building, then decided upon a reprieve. Invested the useless dome with a new function, one that was strictly secular. The dome, re-gilded for the first time in forty years, was designated as the company's emblem. Henceforth, a colored image of the dome was stamped on all microscopes turned out by Watkins & Company, inscribed at the top of the company's stationery and business forms, painted on the side of all vehicles owned by the company, stenciled on retail packaging and on the crates in which the instruments were shipped to dealers, and featured prominently in advertising. Look, the woman elevator operator has the outline of the dome sewn on her blouse pocket. And on the Oriental chauffeur's uniform? Diddy hadn't noticed.

The elevator doors close. Moving up. The conference room is on the third floor.

But maybe it was an insult to revive the dome on these terms? Let the dead rest, leave what is superseded to its natural repose. The adoption of the dome as the firm's insignia took place in the mid-1940's, when wartime government contracts had tripled the company's profits. Just before a portion of these soaring profits was allocated for constructing the outsized wings that (now) flanked the old building; whose bulk and ugliness had the effect of making the dome seem so much smaller and less imposing than it had been. A miniature dome (now), shrunken vestige of its former glory. A kind of toy.

Even though its colors were, by constant repainting, kept brilliant. Visible at a considerable distance.

But for Diddy, the tiny figure on the letterhead, on the microscopes, and on full-page ads was one thing; the massive original, with its curious history, quite another. During the ten years he'd been with the company, Diddy, a chronic if erratic connoisseur of spiritual independence, had developed his own view of the dome.

It was the fantasy expressed in Amos Watkins' addition to the architect's original plan that Diddy appreciated. Like the fantasy that produced the original sketch of what became the Micro-Recorderscope.

To think of uniting two such different devices in one compact, high-powered, easily manipulable tool. A bold thought when Amos Watkins had it, around 1900. Cameras then were large, cumbersome, bulky, relatively new contraptions: hoisted and precariously maintained aloft on tripods. While microscopes, in existence since the late sixteenth century, were, had always been, small and delicate: ready for use as soon as they were set down, secure on their horse-shoe base, upon any table, or even a window ledge. Watkins had insisted that it was feasible to combine the aristocrat and the upstart. The big and the small. A bizarre marriage was being planned.

That sparkling playful dome that incongruously topped the austere brick building was the embodiment of old Amos' energies. More than the compulsive godliness of a typical old-style Protestant. In Diddy's imagination, Watkins was a truly pious man. Not the piety that's illustrated by his having been a pillar of the church who never defaulted on his tithes, who contributed generously to the mission in China, who wanted all his employees to pray as well as work. Not even the inane but convenient piety which persuades greedy men that becoming rich is a duty, gratifying to the deity; for which God must be thanked, on the very site of one's labor.

Pious in a larger sense. Old Amos must have been pious about himself. Must have felt lucky, fortunate, blessed. That's what the dome proclaimed. Obstinate, shameless pleasure in making useful machines and in raking in profits. Pleasure in being himself: not only shrewd Yankee businessman, ardent Methodist and Republican, but also successful eccentric. One who had had his way.

It was that energy of self-approval commemorated in the sturdy dome which had always charmed Diddy. Who didn't find it easy to love himself. And felt no greater admiration than for those who could. Those who could affirm their lives. Diddy, not pious toward himself, revered the relics and clues of innocent well-being. The vision of a man who does not inhabit, but simply is, his life. Amos Watkins the Pious had his acolyte. In this mediated sense: Diddy the Pious.

There are six people in the crowded elevator, (now) passing the second floor. For someone from the Chicago office has gotten on with Harron and Allen and Katz and What's-his-name. We're chatting loudly, but Diddy is silent. Reassuring and yet also numbing to Diddy's mind: to be cooped up in a small space. Without alternatives. Focused mainly on the task of maintaining himself in an upright position, without getting in the way of the other bodies or allowing them to get in the way of his.

Diddy wishes the elevator could go straight up, into the dome. And nestle there. He could get out first, then rudely close the others in. Less rudely, he could simply send the elevator down to the third floor, without him. Another possibility: the elevator might stall between floors. The lights go out, and there's no explanation. Some of his fellow passengers are bound to panic, but Diddy will remain calm. Offering to go for help, he will get a boost from Jim and force open the trap door in the roof of the elevator cage. Climbing up the cable, hand over hand, is messy work; cables in elevator shafts are covered with thick grease. But, if necessary, Diddy the Clean would do it. Until he reaches the top. Leaving below him in the shaft the small dark cube of the elevator, immobile, filled with nervous passengers . . . Any of these situations would do, as long as he can gain the dome by himself.

Once left to explore the dome alone, who knows what Diddy

might find? Is it a great cool place, heavily timbered and sheathed with planks? Or claustrophobically hot, humid, soaking up the sun through its thin outer shell?

Perhaps Diddy will find he is not alone. Perhaps he'll come across a workman repairing the inner face of the dome; removing broken planks and decaying timbers, nailing up fresh supports. Or the workman may not be visible at first. Diddy will think he has the whole dome to himself. Until he notices a small exit, hardly big enough for a large man to squeeze through; and, peering out of the dome, sees the workman precariously stationed on a flimsy scaffold, buckets and brushes at his feet, applying to the outer face the necessary fresh coats of blue and gold. Diddy just wants to see what he's doing, to watch him work. He wouldn't intrude, or ask questions, or make any sudden movement that might startle the workman and cause him to lose his balance and fall. A long fall, the equivalent of six stories. Certain death. The body of the workman sprawled on the grass below. Limp, broken, bleeding.

Diddy knows what's possessing him. And that these are not the right thoughts for him to be entertaining while on the job. While sharing this small space with four other delegates to the conference; in an elevator that's stopping (now) at the third floor. Diddy has promised himself not to dwell on the gory anecdote about the railroad worker. Not here.

Time for us to get out. "Here we are."

But suppose Diddy can't keep his mind reined in tightly? Suppose, having vowed not to resurrect Incardona in his mind, he does do just that? Diddy knows a remedy. There's something else, rather someone else, to think about. When the spectre looms up before his retrograde vision, she comes to caress his face and to kiss his eyes. To banish the workman, to heal Diddy.

She never fails to come. But always after. The workman arrives first. Diddy driven and counter-driven.

Upon leaving the elevator on the third floor, meeting and greeting. Considering what heals. Who heals. But Diddy was already thinking of her before.

When he and his colleagues first clambered into the black limousine, it instantly occurred to Diddy that, on the way to the factory, we might have to pass the Warren Institute.

Impatient. Looking out of the car window; insisting that the window be rolled down. About to ask. Then, within minutes after so-called Chang drove the car away from the Rushland, Diddy figured out it wasn't going to happen. Diddy, since childhood, gifted with an excellent sense of direction. On the overnight hikes in the woods his brother and he took, during the summers spent at their grandfather Edward Dalton's farm in Ohio, Paul was always getting lost; but Diddy's gift for spatial orientation brought them safely home. Dad had acknowledged Diddy's talent, too. Before starting first grade, he'd sometimes been allowed to come along when his father went out on house calls in the afternoon. His father would start the motor of the Buick, recite the patient's address while backing out of the driveway; then let the child tell him how to go. That acute memory for place, even places visited just once, allowed Diddy the Navigator to figure out rapidly that the factory lay in the same general direction as the hospital. But that to reach the factory we ought to take a slightly different route out of the center of town.

Becoming patient. Diddy could dispense with that quick scanning look at the hospital building he would have managed, had we been carried past it in the black limousine. Could forgo the satisfaction of being able for a brief moment to throw his gaze, let it adhere to the wall: an instantaneous, motorized replica of the gaze of a bashful suitor prowling for hours before his beloved's darkened house.

No matter. Diddy intended to phone Hester during the day and tell her he would come by during the evening visiting hours.

The first day's session at the plant.

On time. We're in a spacious, high-ceilinged, wood-paneled room. High windows with maroon drapes. Portraits of past presidents of the company. Nineteen men seated around the long oval table; each man's place supplied with an ashtray, a pad of paper, and two finely sharpened pencils. A stenographer at the far wall, taking the minutes.

Diddy in harness, eager to prove that he can function on the surface of life without slipping into a dark hole. A pompous speech of welcome by Reager. A longer speech by Watkins extolling the company's democratic structure of decision-making, and not so subtly reminding those present of the profit-sharing scheme enjoyed by all employees in managerial posts. Coffee and sandwiches served; everyone settled down to work. Memoranda and charts passed around the long table, figures scrawled on the blackboard. Whispering and exchanging of notes. Factions were being grouped and battle lines were drawn up. We were jovial. But there is a tacit signal known to everyone that starts the arguing. Bad feelings spill from people's mouths, like cold greasy coffee.

When little is at stake, Diddy likes to argue. And what can be at stake when the room is so clean, the space so generously conceived? When everything is so neatly ordered?

Think, for instance, how much simpler it is for all of us that the conference was divided into exactly two factions. Just two.

> On one side, those who insisted that the new competition could be beaten back by, one, more advertising and, two, a drastic reorganization of distribution and selling procedures. Inefficient personnel had to be weeded out; dealers made to work harder to retain their franchises; and salesmen's territories reapportioned to conform to shifts in population and buying power, for instance, by doubling the sales force in California. Diddy guessed this was the line that the top brass was backing.
>
> On the other side, a group of younger executives, advised by some of the scientists and technicians, argued that the basic model of Scope 21 had to be overhauled, to compete favorably with the comparable prod-

uct being offered at a lower price by the Yugoslavs, and perhaps by the Japanese.

Had the Japanese really produced something to rival the company's instrument? Diddy would wait to see it before he fully believed in it. But wait, there it is. The Japanese model. Perched in the center of the oval table. Its caretaker, a balding young scientist, explains that what we're looking at may be only a provisional version of their photomicrographic outfit. The apparatus, still undergoing tests, hasn't yet been released by the factory, even for sale in Japan. But, already, a superb instrument. Bound to be available in the States soon.

Diddy wondered how, if they were as inept as Jim claimed, the company officials had gotten hold of it. Perhaps through orthodox means. Perhaps not. Spirited out of the factory in Nagasaki by a defecting employee or disgruntled junior executive. Someone like Jim, only with yellow skin and slant eyes and straight black hair. Maybe that person was "Chang," who was then paid off with American citizenship, a handsome uniform, and a sinecure which requires him to act occasionally as a chauffeur for the company. Chang, whose real name was something like Mayamoto.

Let's not kid ourselves, someone three chairs away from Diddy was saying, about the superiority of the new Japanese instrument to ours.

Not what the bosses wanted to hear. "Draw those curtains, Goldberg, will you? The light's in my eyes," said Reager irritably. (Now) Reager took the floor. Saying that the problem could and ought to be solved in Washington. What about the government's obligation to use the tariff to protect domestic industries, which couldn't possibly compete with the prices set by foreign manufacturers supplied with endless cheap labor? Yugoslavs and Japs, indeed! And as for improvements, you gentlemen know that no expense in that sphere has ever been spared. Eighty years of pioneering research stands behind this company. It is unstinting research that made the Micro-Recorderscope the outstanding instrument of its type in the world today.

Diddy tired of boasting and lies. Tired of having his faith tested. If Reager made the realistic challenge to the company's position into a crisis of faith among his employees, he was a fool. No one wanted to believe what couldn't be believed. Even though everyone wants to believe something.

Reager had probably not wanted the conference at all. His idea: to have as little as possible happen. Business was good. Who can imagine things to be different from the way they are today?

But times are changing. The junior men leap back with their arguments as soon as the old man stops.

Who is right? Everybody. Diddy found the arguments of both sides sound. Which policy, then, should be adopted? Both. But that's not likely to happen, is it? Most unlikely that in a single week of meetings the company would embark on two major and mutually exclusive programs of development. We'll be able to choose only one. Which will Diddy choose? His own recommendations, which he's to present this afternoon and which took most of his evenings in the last two weeks to prepare, were the outline of a new advertising campaign. Quite properly. Diddy minds his own business. Wishes other people would mind theirs. And he knows that, in the larger dispute, he's expected to stand behind Reager and the old guard. An easily assembled majority—even though Watkins, sucking on his pipe at the far end of the oval table, had said nothing yet. But of the other eighteen, Diddy estimated, five would line up with Comensky and Goldberg of R&D. Leaving ten behind Reager, if Diddy counted himself.

But shouldn't count himself in yet. Today he feels like doing the unexpected. He'd been impressed by the minority faction, who came equipped with elaborate diagrams drawn with India ink and models, twice the actual size, of the revamped Micro-Recorderscope, and with long opaque words that spilled from their mouths. Still hadn't decided which faction to support. But suspected (now) it would be that of the scientists and technicians. Let Reager blow his top. I'm tired of humoring him.

When the meeting broke for lunch, it was already one-thirty. Today we were eating here; uniformed waitresses were already wheeling in carts with food. Diddy went out to the phone booth in the hall, called the Warren Institute. Finding that Hester didn't have a phone in her room yet, he left his message with the floor nurse.

When he returned to the conference room, the work materials had already been cleared from the table and nineteen place settings laid out over a mammoth white plastic tablecloth. Diddy hadn't realized how the room stank of tobacco. Before sitting down to his meal, got the pole and pulled the top half of one of the high windows halfway down. Maybe he wasn't just oppressed by the smoke but stalling, too. Not believing he could manage another meal after that heroic breakfast. Certainly not overdone slices of roast beef with lumpy succotash. But Diddy did eat. More than he thought he could.

The rest of the afternoon dragged by, painfully. Diddy got up to make his presentation of the new advertising campaign, then concluded by expressing doubts that this tactic would indeed reverse the tide of competition running against the company. Suppose a choice has to be made—between allocating funds for more advertising or putting more money into the hands of the scientists. "In such a case, I'd advocate pouring every last cent into research." When Diddy sat down, Jim gave him a toy salute from across the table.

It may very well be that this speech hasn't pleased either faction. But at this point, Diddy couldn't care less. Is Diddy pleased with himself? That's what's important. Does the old anodyne of work still deaden the pain, still take him out of himself? Transform him into nothing more than a function of his situation? Perhaps too much has happened in the last twenty-four hours. Can't be as opaque as he'd like. Not any more. Diddy becoming vitrified, like paper soaked in grease.

Diddy tuned out of most of the ensuing discussion. Words are starting to thicken again, and acquire that curious muffled edge, something like an echo, that renders them almost material and makes their meaning easier to ignore. Diddy wants to ignore whatever he can. Doesn't notice that, by four o'clock, his back has begun to ache from slouching so long. In a roomy chair that's mainly wood, with only a token skin of leather on the seat. For better or for worse, Diddy not very observant this afternoon. Diddy, inside himself. Which, for Diddy, doesn't necessarily mean being in his body. In his mind, then?

Pass over the failure of words, their hypermaterialization. Other ways that Diddy has of understanding the world are failing, too. A lapse in sensation itself.

Except for registering changes in the temperature and amount of tobacco pollution in the high-ceilinged room.

Except for being annoyed by the fidgeting and chain-smoking of Ambergate, the company's treasurer, sitting to Diddy's left.

Except for watching Pete La Salle, head of Export, Watkins' nephew, skillfully dozing without the others noticing.

Except for noticing with mild revulsion that Buchanan of the Production Department, sitting to his right, chews his cuticles savagely.

Except for following the subtle waning of the afternoon light streaming through the high windows of the conference room.

A random suite of prickly impressions. Apart from which, Diddy is hardly present. Being somewhere inside himself, anticipating this evening. Repeatedly, Diddy the Romantic cautioned himself to have sensible thoughts about Hester. Making love with a girl once often means nothing these days: no more to her than to you. And even if their encounter was truly audacious and sexually stirring, don't expect its special quality to live on in this evening's meeting. With another room, another demon of place. Expect nothing. Yesterday was unique. Diddy transfixed with bewilderment, guilt, fear, and the longing for a healing touch. Hester in her endless darkness, frightened by the train's unexplained stop in the tunnel. Their encounter on the Privateer was too charged and urgent. Its searing flavor bound to be diluted in the milky atmosphere of ordinary circumstances.

A good thing that he has thus prepared himself. For the hospital visit, both rich and empty, was a strain. It starts badly. With Hester thanking Diddy for the flowers, in words that sound lifeless and dutiful. Again, they're sharing the same enclosed space. (Now) a medium-sized room on the seventh floor of the principal building of the Warren Institute. Generous dimensions for a private room. And with a handsome view of Monroe Park. Diddy wishes she could see out the window. Unnerved by the blind girl's infinite enclosure in herself. As he hadn't been, really, yesterday. But Hester seems diminished, less absolute in this room than in the train compartment, or in the corridor, or in the washroom, or in the club car. Or even when she materialized sporadically in Diddy's head during last night's excoriating vigil.

Wait. Probably, it's not some change in Hester herself. Not her fault, any more than his. Her aunt's? For Hester and Diddy weren't alone. Mrs. Nayburn was in the room when Diddy arrived; and she stayed, she stayed. From the beginning, heaping attention on him; virtually ignoring her niece. As the woman becomes more flattering, loquacious, overbearing, Hester lapses deeper into the same inert passivity Diddy noticed, and was frustrated by, in the early part of the train journey.

Consider the only other time the three of them were alone in the same space: when they rode out to the hospital in a taxi last night. Had they been as uncomfortable as (now)? Diddy tried to recall. Blank, at least about this. All he remembers is wanting to break away from them for a second in the waiting room. To buy a newspaper. In case, by some miracle of printing technology, a late afternoon's violent death can be processed so swiftly into words, afterwards into type face, that the story appears in the evening paper. Then realizing that was absurd . . . Except for continuing sporadically to wish he had gone for a newspaper before getting into the taxi and feeling more of the same indigestible anxiety and numbness he'd been enduring for hours, he could remember nothing of the taxi ride.

In the hospital room. The aunt is firing questions at Diddy about his family background, his college, his job. The size of his apartment and its location. "Oh, how nice! From what I read in the papers, you can't be too careful about getting into a good neighborhood in New York these days. It's getting to be that a white person is hardly safe anywhere now. . . ." Since Diddy's apartment isn't in a "good neighborhood," he can't decide whether Mrs. Nayburn, besides being compulsively ugly-hearted, is ignorant about New York, devious, or merely inattentive. More questions. When Diddy said she might have heard of his brother, who was a concert pianist, she went up an octave, shrilling: "My goodness! Don't tell me your brother is Paul Harron. Really? How exciting!" Not only has she heard of Paul, she owns his recording of the Tchaikovsky Piano Concerto. Was she going to ask Diddy to get an autograph for her? This wasn't the first time Diddy regretted mentioning Paul to a new friend or acquaintance. Paul's name doesn't fly out of Diddy's mouth horizontally, light; it falls to the floor with a thump. To mention his brother can't help but sound weighted, like bragging. Diddy worried that's what the girl may think: her silence distresses him. But knew better than to suspect her aunt may also decide he was boasting. Modesty or reticence wasn't within Mrs. Nayburn's range. The only delicacy with such a woman: to be absolutely mute. Since everything he discloses seems to please her.

The all too predictable climax arrives when she nervously ventures to inquire whether Diddy is married. Diddy, angry, tries to expel the word "Divorced" from his mouth in a casual tone. Damn the woman's prying! She must have fixed on him as a prospective husband for her handicapped niece not later than the very moment that extravagant batch of flowers was delivered this morning to Hester's room. Maybe she's not counting on the success of the forthcoming operation. And the immoderate warmth of Mrs. Nayburn's attentions to Diddy suggests that Hester has no other suiters; at least none that her aunt approves of—or knows about.

Diddy unused to having what he wants, or might want, handed to him without heavy effort. Though women liked him, Diddy never altogether trusted their approval. A precarious sense of his own manhood. The self-contempt that began to infect his will when Paul overtook, then outstripped him in vitality and achievement. A shameful envy of the blind, uncompassionate vitality of men who looked like Incardona; men of the sort Diddy's always disapproved of and disliked, been disliked by, feared. It follows then that should Diddy want Hester, he should have to overcome almost insurmountable barriers. And just this normal state of affairs, her aunt was suggesting, wasn't true (now); as if Hester was hers to dispose of. Mrs. Nayburn was promising wordlessly that the girl might be his without a struggle.

No competition? Despite the girl's beauty?

Long fine blond hair, hidden eyes, delicate hooked nose, wide mouth, slim neck, fleshy shoulders, full bosom, thickish supple waist . . . Hester is beautiful, isn't she? Diddy trying to be fair, to see the girl (now) as extraordinary and compelling as she appeared to him yesterday. But her aunt's indiscriminate chatter and his necessarily mechanical responses have muted Diddy's energies for perceiving, silenced his feelings, frozen the nerves that animate his flesh. Diddy the Stupefied. About to stand up, say good night to both of them. When Mrs. Nayburn, sensing perhaps that she wasn't furthering what she took to be her niece's interests by staying around, gets up quicker. "Lovey, I just remembered I have to buy some things." To him: "You'll keep Hester company for the rest of the hour, won't you . . . Dalton? May I call you Dalton?"

"Of course," Diddy says.

Laden with one parcel and a bulging shopping bag like those of yesterday, Mrs. Nayburn leaves the room. Almost immediately, the air lightens. Breathing itself less oppressive. Diddy started feeling looser, more whole. His blood starts to flow, his nerves begin to pulse, his vision clears. Can (now) really look at the girl.

Smothered in nightgown, sheets, and a blanket, the shapeless body extending the length of the bed gives little hint of what Diddy knows to be its subtle contours. What's unchanged is Hester's face, a fourth of which is masked by the dark glasses.

Hester seems to be looking at him.

As she did yesterday, she can direct toward him an intelligent facsimile-look with movements of her head. But never real looking: an exiting from the head by means of sight, an exchange of looks, complicity with the eyes. The faces of the blind are not in dialogue with other faces as faces. Only with other faces as flesh. Touch, the sole complicity.

Her expression not perceptibly altered since Mrs. Nayburn's departure.

Had Hester's face been equally inexpressive yesterday? With Diddy hardly noticing, so profound and urgent was the need he'd felt for union with the body below the face. But isn't that very idea, "a face" atop "the body," one only sighted people can entertain of themselves and of other people? Among blind people, the face is just another part of the body.

The independent life of faces depends on sight. If sight goes, the face largely dies. Or becomes tentative, provisional. A representation—maybe skillful—of a face; not a real face. An object-face.

The faces of the blind are set above their bodies like lanterns that have been turned down, or extinguished. A face with dead eyes, lacking the visual clues for learning expressiveness from other faces, will never invent that whole vocabulary by itself. Haphazard or approximate signals of feeling may be attempted, out of the longing to conform to an imaginary uniform ideal. But were it true to its own condition, the face without sight has neither reason nor means to become any more expressive than a hand or a foot or a breast.

How does an inexpressive face age? More slowly, one would suppose. A sightless face, one that's never learned to be consistently expressive by watching other faces, probably remains unlined many years after the exertions of expression have creased and wrinkled seeing faces of the same chronological age. Maybe Hester isn't as young as she looks. With another rhythm of use, another rhythm of aging.

Is Diddy looking too intently? The wrong power microscope. Step back to get the unassisted view. Perhaps Hester is just being quiet, waiting for him to speak first. Something stirs in her face. Around the mouth, that's where he must look. If for ordinary people the eyes rule the face, with blind people it must be the mouth. There was the complicity he sought. Not of eyes and looks. But of mouths and touch.

Yet Diddy doesn't feel like kissing Hester at this moment. Something too passive about her, too willful in him. The hospital room is inert, dead. How different from the compartment on yesterday's train, a space that was buoyant, that became an independent vehicle equipped for vast stretches of travel. Or from the close, droning space of the washroom in which they both stood; clinging and mingling with each other.

Diddy slouched in the chair near the foot of the bed, faintly reviving the hurt in his spine that had begun in the conference room about four o'clock. "Already started your tests?" he says stiffly.

"They took some blood this morning. An ECG. A urine sample. That's all."

"Those are just routine pre-operative tests. Has anyone been around to look at your eyes?"

"Not yet."

Diddy doesn't know what words to bring up next. He's far away. Looking out the window, enjoying what Hester cannot—a view. Colors. Moving shapes. The recurring distribution and thinning out of things into "near" and "far."

"Want some chocolates? Aunt Jessie brought me a box, but I don't like them."

Where are the chocolates? On the night table. "No thanks."

Diddy inspecting Hester's room, as if it might serve as a mnemonic device. A memory room, a series of places to which Diddy might return in imagination at some future time; as he moves through the room, extracting from the memorized places the images he had stored in them. But the featureless room seems to resist such a use.

All the hospital has supplied converges on a single color. The walls are off-white, and so are the muslin curtains. The wooden chest of drawers is painted a flat white, as is the iron bed, which has a white blanket over the usual white sheets. The white metal table beside the bed has a white Formica top; the shiny white porcelain base of the table lamp offers the faintest contrast with the dull sheen of the white plastic shade. And the two chairs—indicating an official maximum of two visitors?—are covered in grainy white Leatherette. Had he not known better, Diddy might have surmised that ophthalmologists find white to be easier than any other color on ailing eyes.

The maroon and gilt cardboard box containing the chocolates, a yellow bathrobe across the foot of Hester's bed, the tan leather sandals on the floor beside her bed, and Diddy's flowers are the only things in the room that aren't white.

"I like your flowers," Hester says. As if she could read his mind. "You didn't believe me, did you, when I thanked you before? And I know why. My aunt was in the way. But you should have, you know. I'm not polite. If I say something, I mean it." She smiles radiantly. And Diddy is there to see what he partly longs to see. A new face, delicate and alive.

Diddy pulled back from the wide space into which he has wandered: cold, harshly lit, stony. Drawn back, gladly, to the smaller space of tenderness surrounding the girl. Melting. A sudden rush of sensual, weary happiness. He springs from his chair to the one nearer Hester that her aunt had vacated; draws it alongside her bed. Presses his face against the girl's arm. But not to bare flesh or to any texture that felt naked. She's wearing a long-sleeved flannel nightgown whose rough texture denies yesterday's memory of flesh. Withholds any further knowledge Diddy's left cheek might gain of the shape of Hester's smooth firm arm. She, too, must dislike the feel of such material on her skin. Wouldn't it be depressing if the nightgown weren't even hospital issue, but some bargain-basement treasure imposed on the girl by Mrs. Nayburn? He sighs. "Well . . . How are you? Really?"

"Sad."

As if startled, Diddy looks up. She begins stroking his close-cropped hair, and he bends his head again. "Why?"

"I'm not hopeful about the operation. And I've been worrying

about you, remembering what you wanted to do to yourself yesterday. I was afraid that today you'd regret not having gone through
with it."

What effort of will for Diddy not to pull away brusquely from
Hester's body and sit upright. "Hester, listen! Once more, that
wasn't what happened yesterday on the train. I committed that
folly a month ago." An effort to remain stilled, huddled under her
caress. To continue accepting her touch: placid, but imperious.
"Please believe me! Can you forgive me for have lied to you at
first? Because what really happened yesterday was something else,
something completely different. It's what I told you about . . . after.
The fight with the workman. . . ."

Diddy wondering if he should go further. He has no intention
of producing the newspaper clipping and reading it aloud to Hester.
After summoning a nurse on the floor to stand by, someone who
can look over his shoulder and verify for Hester's benefit that he's
reading what's actually printed there.

Since that's Diddy decision, should he have gone even this far?
Remember that Hester is the deluded one, not he; that it's her
faculties which, at least briefly, lapsed. But proving her error to
her, so easy to do (now), would be a dangerous triumph. More
prudent for Diddy to let the girl continue thinking he's had a hal-
lucination. "Hell, I know you don't believe any of this," he adds.
"Do you? You don't believe I was ever out of the compartment,
much less off the train."

Diddy hoping he's covered his tracks (now). Not that it matters
much what he says at this moment. However long he goes on urg-
ing Hester to believe in yesterday's murder, she won't be convinced
—if Diddy doesn't display the irrefutable printed evidence in his
possession since this morning. Why should she be?

But even if Hester doesn't credit his confession, doesn't become
the sharer of his secret, she still may have reactions that spell heart-
ache or trouble. Believing in Diddy the Innocent, she may become
afraid of Diddy the Deluded. A natural, self-protective reaction:
for the relatively sane to fear the mentally damaged. But Diddy
would hate that. Or if she isn't afraid, worried. Then, when worry

becomes too painful, she may relay his tale to someone else; maybe one of her doctors. Not to betray Diddy, since Hester believes he hasn't done anything, but just to get professional advice on how best to answer a lunatic friend whenever he starts insisting again on the literal truth of his fantasy. And that third person might connect Diddy's so-called delusion with the item in today's *Courier-Gazette*. And call the police.

Hester has been silent for a long time.

"What are you thinking?" Diddy asks. All right to move his head (now). Not angry, not running away. Sits up straight, then leans over to rub his lips on Hester's warm cheek. A kiss she doesn't overtly welcome. "What's the matter, Hester?"

"I'm thinking. You know, this is something we shouldn't talk about. At least not now. About what happened in the tunnel . . . I'm no help to you with that, Dalton. I may even be doing you some harm."

"Harm?" echoes Diddy, astonished.

"Yes. Believe me, it's not that I *want* to injure you. But I have the feeling, it's hard to put into words, that something bad for you might come from me. Don't ask me what. I've only a very dim idea. But you'll have to trust my judgment anyway. I may know very little, but you don't know anything about it at all."

Diddy is mystified, balked. How could Hester determine anything important about the two of them so soon? Shouldn't he insist (now) that she explain? Then frustrated, because he can't. Further questions seemed like bullying. And also relieved. Yet if they have made a pact to steer clear of that inexhaustible topic, the world of the tunnel, not much is left to discuss. Hester isn't easy to talk to. But he wants to talk. Diddy the Tongue-Tied, for all his revulsion at wasting words, once more condemned to flabby conversation. To the volley of insensate questions, gathering useless information. Well, he might as well plunge in.

> Are you comfortable?
> Are the nurses pleasant?
> Do you like your doctor?
> How's the food?
> How soon is the operation?

"Don't," she says sharply, shaking her head. "You know you don't want to talk to me that way. And I don't want you to. Please!"

Diddy astonished. Does she know this, too? But unable just to be grateful for Hester's intervention, passing on without comment to better words. "God knows, I don't want to ask you a lot of empty questions." Diddy has to explain. "But I feel awkward. I don't know what to say, or what to do here."

She touches his hair. "What you should do is get up and go. Without saying anything." Takes her hand away.

Diddy gazes at Hester for a long time without replying. She's right, of course. Clearer and braver than he. But there's one question he has to ask, foolish as it may seem. "If I go . . . I mean, when I go, you will hear me, won't you? You won't think this time I'm still in the room with you?"

Hester sits up a little higher in the bed, propped against the pillows; folds her hands in her lap; turned in Diddy's direction. She nods. But doesn't say anything.

Diddy doesn't want to get up. The silence between them has become very thick—full of magical, distressing, electric, paralyzed feelings. Diddy feels magnetized, then dizzy. A kind of metallic vertigo. With a thin narrow lining of panic. The footsteps of nurses and visitors in the corridor seem especially loud. Perhaps Diddy will sit here, enthralled forever. Despite the vertigo, a part of his feeling is peaceful. Unutterably tranquil.

"I think I understand for the first time what it's like to be blind," he says.

"Do you?"

"I know how imprisoning it must be, don't misunderstand. And what a cruel deprivation of ordinary freedom it is. But still, I imagine, there's something good in it. It makes easy—necessary— a certain experience that's rare and enviable. It's the experience of paying attention all the time, with that attention never slackening, so that everything is at once very distinct and very complicated."

"That's part of it." She seems to be smiling.

"And I've thought of something else, that's harder to describe." Diddy closed his eyes. "The world of blind people . . . I mean the world you see, the world I sometimes inhabit in my imagination, too . . . it's terribly unstable. There's always a hole just in front of your feet. You know about the hole, yet you have to keep on walking. But you feel dizzy all the time . . . And very free, too. It doesn't really matter, matter in the old way, I mean, if you . . . if you fall."

"Yes. That, too."

Diddy wrenched his eyes open. Ashamed. Insensitive, self-absorbed Diddy. "I wish I could stop talking," he says wistfully.

Hester didn't answer. Perhaps she was going to help him. A breeze had come up and was ruffling the curtains. Although already night, it seemed to get darker. Diddy sat a while longer, sometimes looking at the girl, sometimes comparing shades of whiteness, sometimes gazing at nothing in particular. After a time he stood up, threw his coat over his arm, and went out the door without saying a word.

Diddy took a taxi straight back to the Rushland, and found Jim disconsolately hanging about the lobby, pretending to be waiting for someone. Almost eight-thirty. Meeting Jim (now) not what Diddy would have chosen. He would have preferred to be alone for the rest of the evening. Feared to feel himself, by ordinary contact with people, repudiating or blunting the subtle connection with Hester.

Still, he wasn't too sorry. Perhaps running into Jim was for the best, since Diddy didn't altogether trust himself to be alone. Judged that he didn't yet merit that noble condition. Once safe upstairs in Room 414, isn't he likely to give way to renewed brooding and to morbid indecision? His resolve to stay away from the police, at least not to go (now), was shaky; too new to be truly binding. This resolve was no mere whim—but it was as boneless, feathery, and contingent as a whim. It lacked the weight that a genuine decision ought to have, and does eventually put on. With time. Like a premature baby that must be stored in the incubator until it reaches a normal bulk. Diddy's newly fledged hankering for life needed coddling. A special diet. Only the fit survive, and the fit are fat.

He would eat dinner in the hotel with Jim. He would nourish his decision, he would feed himself. Proper self-feeding apparently requires the company of another person. Diddy has discovered something about his habits of the last four weeks. Particularly why and how he has virtually stopped eating.

Until this time he'd allowed two hypotheses about his not eating. An unconscious penance imposed by his body for the fiasco of a month ago; or a dismal sequel to his humiliating regimen in the hospital. Both true enough, perhaps. But he's neglected a crucial detail. It was after Diddy came out of the hospital that he'd begun to take all his meals alone. Refusing any dinner invitations. And, as an excuse to get out of business lunches, inventing a daily appointment at noon with a doctor who was giving Diddy shots to prevent a recurrence of his illness.

Call it queasiness, call it a fast. It was something of both. Whatever it was, Diddy resolved, it must stop. Diddy who has already put away two meals today. Will have another. Had Jim eaten dinner yet? No. Fine. Jim seemed relieved by the invitation. Diddy flushed with good intentions. Using words, he will go along with what interests Jim; and he will just breathe. Breathing in, breathing out. He mustn't be alone.

Diddy found that the appetite for food that he'd prayerfully ordered with the lobster dinner arrived. But what about fattening up the soul? Putting muscle into the weightless bald will? Growing a skin around the rickety frame of the feelings that won't bruise at the mildest touch? Ah, these are harder tasks. It wasn't so easy: breathing in, breathing out. Jim's banter, an asylum of inane, cranky wholesomeness at breakfast this morning, was driving a nail into Diddy's brain tonight. Could barely listen to Jim, and his own share of the conversation was humorless, forced. Even Jim notices, and several times inquired if he were ill. Diddy kept saying no, he felt fine. But then Jim would go at it again. "You know, you really have been looking pretty run down lately, Dalton." And advise him to ski this winter, or take up tennis, or work out several times a week at a gym.

Diddy didn't understand what had misfired. Kept trying to make the meal work. Which is why he dawdled over his hearty portion; not because he had trouble finishing everything on his plate. And why he ordered extra cups of coffee, and then a brandy he didn't want. Diddy stalling, hoping to find out how it's done.

Later Diddy gave up. Ashamed to be exploiting this decent enough guy whom he didn't like but didn't not like either. He was bad company for Jim, who'd been perking up as the sulky units of clock-time slid by. Diddy aware that (now) Jim has gotten his second wind, is feeling full-blooded enough to go out and, as he'd say, paint the town red; is lingering out of considerateness, aware that sallow, listless Diddy isn't up to any night life, and reluctant to leave him in the almost deserted hotel restaurant. "The Pine Room." Clearly Diddy's responsibility: to dissolve the bond of politeness, throw open the doors for Jim. Which he did, first yawning and then mock-confessing to a revived Jim that he was tired and heading for bed.

"I guess you haven't really kicked that virus you came down with last month," Jim said, scarcely concealing his delight at being released from Diddy's company.

The two men stood in the lobby. Jim slapped Diddy awkwardly on the shoulder. "Good night, Dalt," he said. "Get some shut-eye, you hear. I mean, don't do anything I wouldn't do, huh?" At the revolving door, he waved. Diddy at the elevator waved back; went upstairs.

Staring resentfully in the bathroom mirror at his morose face. Trying, by sheer will, to thaw himself out. What a burden Diddy the Disaffected is to himself, as well as to others.

After showering, he immediately got into bed. Although Diddy hardly expects to sleep before first enduring the usual lengthy ordeal, there's no place comfortable enough to settle in besides bed in this small, meagerly furnished room. But Diddy doesn't know himself as well as he thinks. Hadn't even time to start devoting attention to the flashing yellow sign outside his window. Diddy the

Done-In was indeed terribly tired, and fell into sleep with all the lights on before realizing what he was doing.

Diddy dreamed that night. Not as unpleasant a drama as he might have invented. No stark images of the slain workman or of the ambiguous sexual catharsis with Hester. It was a verbose dream, the dream of an exhausted man. Two persons from the train on Sunday, the stamp dealer in the tweed suit and the priest, are discussing the hobby they have in common. But it isn't stamp collecting. In opposite seats of the compartment, leaning intently toward each other, they were passing a handsome shell back and forth between them. A fine, rosy specimen of a shell that Diddy recognizes: *Conus gloriamaris,* the Glory of the Sea. The two men are lavishing praise upon the shell, calling each other's attention to its intricate whorls and markings. Not clear to Diddy who owns the Glory of the Sea. If it belongs to only one of the men, the other shows no signs of envy or covetousness. And if the precious object is their joint possession, it doesn't seem to cause any dispute or friction between them.

Diddy, both a spectator within the dream, sitting in the compartment next to the man in the tweed suit, and outside, somewhere, nowhere. Electrified with envy. He wants the shell for himself, though aware that he's succumbed to an ugly feeling. For Diddy neither admires the shell nor finds it beautiful. Were he, while strolling alone along some empty beach, to come upon the Glory of the Sea resting on top of the damp brown bubble-studded sand, he wouldn't honor it with a glance. Unless he stubbed his toe on the shell, in which case he'd kick it or, better yet, grind it under his heel. Diddy the Bad covets the shell (now) solely because he observes the value set on it by the man in the tweed suit and the priest.

But he has no qualifications for ownership. Unlikely that these men would consider surrendering their prize to Diddy, who collects stamps.

Thus permanently excluded from the indefinitely renewable joy that passes back and forth between the two collectors, Diddy grows more and more frustrated. Must do something. He doesn't wrench the shell from their hands. For some unclarified reason knows he

99

can't take physical possession of the shell; at least not (now). But he can diminish their pleasure in it. Taking moral possession of it, so to speak.

In an instant, act. Before the claims of conscience begin to whimper; materializing their rusty, familiar fetters. Diddy intervenes brutally. Merely by giving a lecture, one which distills all the rage and disappointment choking him. In order to deliver his discourse, he leaps gracefully from his seat up to the baggage rack. Sits leaning forward, for there's not enough room to straighten his back; with his feet dangling. Looks down at the two men and begins to harangue them.

First point: the great era of conchology is definitely over. There's no point in trying to return to the past, is there? He looks below to check the impact his words are having on the two men. Already, they seem less elated. This hobby, Diddy continues, flourished in the nineteenth century, when there were still genuine discoveries to be made. (Now) everything is known and has been catalogued, these objects are no longer worthy of attracting the fancy of a truly serious person. Shell collecting, as one might expect, has passed into the hands of sentimental amateurs, who are content with arbitrary samplings and arrangements. And amateurs are notoriously credulous, easily taken in by fakes, forgeries, and misattributions. With no one to uphold the old standards of conchology, the market has been glutted with sanded-down, glazed, and tinted objects claiming to be shells. Which are really the beautified corpses of shells. One result of their being too numerous was that shells ceased to be treated with the respect properly owing to a wholly natural object, and taste in shells was irrevocably corrupted. In fact, Diddy raises his voice, eager to drive his point home, good taste in *all* domains fell into decline. An esoteric bit of information: the ruinous desire to improve on nature began with the first man who set about to convert a shell into a work of art. That, said Diddy the Capricious, spitting at the priest, is the true account of original sin.

The priest is quietly wiping saliva off the front of his jacket, as Diddy goes on. If Mrs. Nayburn were here, she'd be thrusting her handkerchief at him before he'd time to reach for his own.

Second point: the poor shells themselves, defenseless as the soft molluscs they once housed, could do nothing to halt this degrading metamorphosis. Most gave up right away; a few struggled, in vain. How could they resist, much less hope to prevail, having no eyes? So not only their quantity but their very substance altered. Shells became coarse, brutish. Look closely, Diddy says, at that shell you've been fondling. It's true that once the Glory of the Sea was the rarest, costliest, the most coveted of shells. In the early 1800's, there were only two known specimens in the entire world; both found in the waters east of New Guinea. But by the end of the century the shell was being found in indecently profuse numbers. The price plummeted. (Now) anyone can send away for one of the debased, modern specimens. Not to mention the carefully crafted imitations being turned out by several factories in Japan.

"Now, let's have a look at this particular specimen . . ." Diddy snaps his fingers brusquely. The man in the tweed suit clambers to his feet and reverently passes the shell up to Diddy on his perch. No need for Diddy to bother with the stethoscope or the reflex hammer. What's wrong with this shell, he declares, is plain enough to the unaided senses. With a negligent thrust of his right index finger, Diddy calls attention to the fact that the body whorl is tilted in the reverse direction of the true Glory of the Sea, and that the reticulations of the whorl run transversely to those of authentic specimens. Shows the abashed connoisseurs below him that the shell has a badly chipped lip, too, and a thickened margin in exactly the wrong place. They react to this denunciation of their prize with appropriate dismay. Diddy, unpitying, persisting. "You've been cheated. A worthless trinket!" Callously tosses it down for them to catch, if they can. "In short, gentlemen," Diddy concludes triumphantly, "what you are holding in your hands is a murdered and broken shell."

Diddy stares down at the two men contemptuously, as they frantically handle the shell and peer into it, in the hope of refuting his superbly ordered attack. Diddy has sized up what kind of people he's up against. The priest and the dealer are large, fat men; and therefore partial to small things. Stamps, shells, dolls, key rings, matchboxes, little magazines, recorders, small cars, miniature dogs, minor paintings, little virtues. Diddy likes big virtues; and large, strong things. Nothing exquisite or fragile suits his tastes. A slug of gin any day for him, in preference to a bowl of jasmine tea from Peking. Still, he can feel protective toward what is delicate or vulnerable. Right (now), for instance, Diddy worries that the fat priest is taking up far too much room, more than his third of the seat; squeezing Mrs. Nayburn and Hester. Diddy's concern is needed to rectify the priest's gross conduct. They're probably too polite to complain.

But the blond girl and her aunt aren't in the compartment any more. Probably disturbed by so much arguing. An affair of men only. In the ensuing debate, Diddy, having boldly taken an unpopular position, will have to stand his ground.

The silken-voiced priest asks Diddy, who has admitted to not being a conchologist, the source of his information. Diddy knowing that his whole lecture is a pack of lies. And delivered with such a clear conscience. Diddy the Dauntless or Diddy the Depraved? But wait, maybe what he's been saying is true. Without his knowing it. A lucky break, that perhaps he once saved a newspaper article on the Glory of the Sea which set forth everything one might want to know about it.

Triumphant Diddy replies to the priest, citing that definitive unchallengeable article. Adding that, needless to say, he always carries the clipping in his wallet. For just such emergencies of credibility as this. The two men ask to be allowed to examine the clipping. Isn't that suspicious? Clever Diddy smells danger in their reasonable request. Suppose they intend to confiscate his clipping —either tear it up or pocket it themselves. Should he lose the clipping, which is irreplaceable, Diddy has lost the only hard evidence he possesses for his fraudulent case against the shell. So Diddy tells them he'll bring out the clipping some other time; they'll have to take his word for it right (now). Then begins his whole speech over again.

As he is hectoring the two men from above their heads, Diddy fears he's overdoing it. A thesis utterly remote from the truth doesn't, in the end, convince or deceive anyone. So his destructive intention won't appear too blatant, clever Diddy decides that it's

102

time to call attention to some of the shell's virtues. The fine granulations on the outer valve, the delicate tones with which the shell is ringed or banded. But just as he's getting his eulogy underway, Diddy observes that these good features no longer exist. The shell is (now) as unequivocally ugly as he had maliciously pronounced it to be. The two collectors see that just as clearly as Diddy does. In disgust, they hurl the shell from them. Out the window. "Do not throw anything from the train window."

Suddenly Diddy feels contrite. Reviles himself for having been mean-spirited, dishonest. Has slandered something beautiful. Thereby, ignorant that he had such powers, turning it into something ugly. At this point in the dream, Diddy is reminded of blackened Andy twitching on his funeral pyre while the neighborhood kids stand by, jeering. He wants to retrieve the shell, hoping that he can restore it, resurrect something of its former beauty and reawaken the esteem of its disgruntled, gullible ex-owners. "Wait," he shouts to the two men, "I'll be right back." What Diddy does is to jump from his high perch, eyes tightly closed, off the rapidly moving train. Do not throw oneself from the train window?

Falling is simple, if you don't think about it. Landing, Diddy has scraped some skin off his knees and palms; like a kid, Diddy himself when a kid, sliding into first base. Pain flickers, subsides. Getting to his feet, dusting himself off, he sees he's in a dark tunnel. Although the train, maintaining its high speed, has already flashed out of Diddy's sight, he isn't worried about being able to catch up with it eventually, far ahead (now) along the track, and climb aboard again. After he's found the shell.

If there were light, Diddy could use a microscope. Purpose: seeing the unseen. Method: enlarging small objects. But without proper external light, optical microscopes are useless. Diddy mustn't underestimate the difficulty of what he aims to do. It's no easy task to locate so small an object as a conical shell about five inches long, unassisted, in the dark. Diddy's task almost as hard as these fiendishly difficult assignments passed out to ingenuous young princes in fairy tales, as a test of their courage and innocence. But the young prince, long before he collapses in despair, is invariably accosted by a benevolent old crone with untidy gray hair and small sharp eyes, who donates a first-class item of magic gear to his cause, or by some helpful little animal gifted with human speech, who volunteers a secret password or gives some necessary directions. No one is helping Diddy.

Diddy wanders through the damp tunnel, and doubles back. Then makes the same round trip again. Always fearful, because he can't see well, that he may inadvertently tread on the shell and shatter it. Would the light, bony, inanimate structure bleed? Could a tiny, frightened mollusc still be hiding inside? What seems like hours limp by, without Diddy having any success. Diddy the Discouraged. But then something changes in the topography of his quest that wipes out failure; makes everything come out right. Another victory for Diddy's unshowy, methodical mind. Good mind. Abruptly though unclearly, Diddy understands the reason why, despite all his hard thorough scanning of the dark tunnel ground as he marches back and forth, he's been unable to find the pink and white Glory of the Sea. It's because he's already inside it (now). The discarded shell, no longer small, is as vast and capacious as the tunnel. Tunnel and shell can substitute for each other, so Diddy can wander in either as he sees fit.

That for this moment he half walks and half climbs along the slippery, whorled inner face of the shell relieves some of the alarm Diddy felt over a fact noted early in his fruitless walking, when in the tunnel. What was alarming was how much sharper the curve of the track seemed (now) than it did before. Diddy leaves that "before" unexamined, feeling himself excused by the well-known rule that there's no time in dreams, only space. But rules of thought are made to be thought through, surpassed. If that hasn't occured to Diddy, is it because he's lazy? or evasive? or merely not very bright? Doesn't he know there is not only time but times; many times; some continuous, others intermittent, running simultaneously or concurrently or disjunctively? Somewhere he does know, surely. And Diddy is anything but eager to think of the other time he was in the tunnel.

As instructed, the desk clerk phoned Room 414 Tuesday morning at six-fifty. Diddy, already awake, requested the *Courier-*

Gazette to be brought to his room immediately. Today he will be able to take a better sounding of this deep business. First, by whether there's a follow-up on yesterday's story on page 16. Second, for he assumes there is, by the length and position of the new story. Is it longer or shorter than yesterday's four chunky paragraphs? Has it been moved further front or to the back of the paper? And what's the second article's theme? More about Incardona? Or developments in the inquiry the police are making into possible negligence on the part of the railroad?

Diddy in suspense, let down. Today's paper, just as scrupulously read as the two yesterday, contained nothing about the workman's death. Not even a paragraph on the obituary page. Nor so much as a line about investigating the railroad. Could people's interest be that short-lived, so that the furor is really over? Reducing an arbitrary and violent death to something just as slight and unrecurring as a half-column of newsprint?

Of course, Diddy hadn't forgotten Incardona's funeral, which, according to yesterday's "Final," takes place this afternoon at two o'clock. If he goes, it won't be in order to view Incardona's mangled corpse. Diddy the Ghoul has not yet been dreamed of. A corpse which it's unlikely Diddy could see even if he wanted to; usually, when the body is mutilated, the coffin is sealed immediately. Nor, if he attends, will it be to mourn Incardona. Doesn't honestly feel grief over the workman's death. Horror still, though more remotely. Little apart from that.

What mainly prompted Diddy to consider attending the services at the funeral home—at the cemetery he'd be too conspicuous— is the wish to set eyes on Incardona's widow and son. Their reality had to become welded to his experience. Perhaps seeing them in the flesh would lay to rest forever his cramping residual doubt, despite the incontrovertible evidence of the *Courier-Gazette* story, whether he'd ever had the encounter with the swarthy workman. Especially wanted to see Thomas Francis, age 11. In whom, if this is the son of the man Diddy killed, he'd surely see at least a trace of resemblance to his father. Then Diddy would be certain that he'd gotten off the Privateer when it stalled in the tunnel. Had assaulted someone. And that the someone was Angelo Incardona, who was dead.

The other decision awaiting Diddy's attention: whether or not to visit Hester today. He'd awakened feeling he doesn't want to go. Yesterday Hester virtually sent him away. Faulty in knowledge; awkward in conduct. He shouldn't return until he understands more about the barriers that separate them. Further, Diddy doesn't want to suggest to either of the women, by paying two consecutive visits, that Hester could count on a visit every night during the week he's here.

At least that's settled. Not a hard decision to make. Just a post-ponement, since he could see Hester any time this week; tomorrow night, if he likes. But Incardona's funeral would take place only once.

All Diddy has to come up with is a plain Yes or No. Should he go this afternoon? No answer. Diddy repeats the question. Should he? Still no answer. How complicated everything seems. And is. Something morbid in this plan. Diddy the Peeping Tom. Spying on people's grief for his own splintered motives. Not to mention the bad taste: a murderer piously, rather than gloatingly, in attendance at his victim's funeral. Something merely self-destructive in it, too. Perhaps Diddy just wants to put himself in a situation where he could suddenly find himself at the feet of the widow and orphan, sobbing out his confession. Maybe the desire for a quick confes-sion is drawing Diddy, balked by the thought of the complex mediations of police and judiciary, to the Floral Gardens Funeral Home at two o'clock. And yet. . . .

The phone rings. A telegram from Duva saying he won't be up for the conference at all. Special delivery letter follows.

What was Diddy thinking before the phone rang? Well, he couldn't decide (now). And meanwhile he was neglecting the non-controversial order of the day. Let's get in step with that for a time. Make his appearance downstairs, breakfast with Jim and the others, go out to the plant, take part in the morning meetings. One foot in front of the other. The decision could be made just before lunch. Diddy put on his jacket, checked his briefcase to see he had everything he needed. Went downstairs.

In the elevator, Jim saying in a low voice to Katz, "Hey, this town is wide open. Things have sure changed around here in the last couple a months. You could have knocked me over with a feather. Plenty of after-hour clubs. And all those places on Parker Street."

"Where?" said Katz.

"About fifteen blocks from the Rush-Me." Jim always grinned at his own jokes.

Reager reaching the door of the conference room at the same time as Diddy. A chilly "Good morning, Harron," as he passes into the room first. I'm going to be spared an evening with the family this trip, Diddy thought; perhaps dinner at the club as well. Reager's disfavor acted like a tonic on Diddy, crystallizing the muddle inside his head.

Unlike yesterday, when sitting at the oval table was a continual eerie struggle. Today Diddy able to keep his mind on his work. So much so that after a heated argument on discount policies in which Diddy eloquently championed the unpopular position and finally brought a majority around to his view, he passed on to lunch in the cafeteria on the second floor without looking at his watch. Not until he was spooning out a second helping of creamed chicken did Diddy notice the time. Already ten minutes to two.

So there hadn't been a real decision. Instead Diddy had let the funeral fall out of his head. Before Diddy can get from here to the funeral home, Mrs. Incardona and son will be on their way to the cemetery; or already there, flinging earth on the coffin. Diddy horrified reviles himself for his absence of mind. (Now) he can't eat another mouthful. The chicken looks like boiled mucus. The morning's performance of bright, hard-headed, friendly, energetic, slightly priggish Dalton Harron before his colleagues seems grotesque (now); inexcusable even as a performance, even as the skillful play-acting of a man with better concerns to occupy his mind. Who is he to be detached at this moment? Immediately he thinks of Hester. Diddy won't alter his decision not to visit her to-night. That, added to his failure even to remember the funeral, would complete the exhibit of his enfeebled will. But before the coffee comes, he will phone the hospital to inquire how she is.

That evening, he sets himself a small penance. An evening alone. No distracting dinner with Jim or any of his other colleagues. He will take some sandwiches to his room, and use his mind for a change. Make unadulterated contact with the inner man. A task he's been neglecting; for which he's (now) paying the price. Nothing seems to have the right weight any more. He's being light-hearted about the serious, solemn about the casual. Diddy the Dunce. He must try to think. Not worry, fret, or castigate himself. But think.

Even though it's not easy to be alone. He worries that Hester may be expecting him although he'd spoken with her at two o'clock —they've installed the phone in her room—and told her he wasn't coming this evening. Without making any excuses. But it pains him to imagine her there, swathed in her homely nightgown, sightless and unable to move, pinned down under the barrage of her aunt's endless chatter. He'd call her (now) if he hadn't found it hard to talk on the phone this afternoon. Better wait until they are face to face.

Then, another phone call occurs to him. Why hadn't he thought of it earlier? Though he failed to attend the funeral, he can still find out about it. If he calls the Floral Gardens claiming to be on the magazine of the incredibly named Brotherhood of Maintenance of Way, he can inquire about Incardona's funeral without arousing any suspicions. And if he still wants to, it shouldn't be difficult to see the widow and the boy on some similar pretext.

Hello. Floral Gardens.

Diddy gives a fictitious name, identifies himself as a reporter for the union's magazine. "Got almost the whole Incardona story written," Diddy says cautiously, "but I need a little more information." The man on the other end said he'd help if he could. "Let's see. Oh, yes, I've got to know"—Diddy trying to ask something innocuous—"what cemetery the guy was buried in."

"You got it all wrong. He wasn't buried at all. He was cremated."

"Cremated! And where are . . . where have the ashes been deposited?"

"They were sent to his mother, who lives, let me see, in Texas. Yeah, that's it. Request of the deceased. It's all in the will."

Diddy so shocked at this news that he couldn't utter another word, let alone ask another question. Remaining silent, trying to force his sluggish mind to absorb what he's heard.

"Anything else you want to know, Mr. Douglas?"

"Oh, yes . . . yes," said Diddy. "I mean, no, I don't think so. No. . . . Yes, I just wondered if the . . . ashes had already been sent off."

"Shipped late this afternoon, first-class airmail, special delivery, registered and insured. I don't mind telling you Uncle Sam's post office collects a pretty penny on freight like this. Floral Gardens don't make nothing on it, except what we make on the actual cremation. That's not too expensive, though."

Diddy finds he simply cannot go on talking or listening, thanks the man. Hangs up.

Why does the fact that Incardona was cremated rather than buried so appall and alarm Diddy? Because it seems to throw the workman back again into the realm of phantoms. A corpse lowered into the earth and left to rot is a real thing. Still resembling what it once was: a dense, bulky animal body. That remains intact for a considerable time. Even a body as mutilated as Incardona's presumably was would be worth digging up for many months, even years to come; could still be submitted to an autopsy that would establish the fact of the murder. But cremation! Ashes are nothing at all. No body, no weight. Nothing to exhume. Nothing that can be linked to the living person, nothing to examine.

Diddy has let matters get out of hand. Something mysterious going on. Why should Incardona have wanted to be cremated? The man at Floral Gardens mentioned instructions that were in a will, but maybe he was misinformed. Wouldn't someone named Incardona be a Catholic, whose church prohibits cremation? Maybe the man at the funeral home—the undertaker's assistant?—was lying.

109

Or in ignorance of the truth. Perhaps it was the New York, Boston & Standard that wished the body disposed of in this irrevocable way. Or even Incardona's wife. Something they or she wanted to hide, which an extant corpse might reveal?

Suppose the telephone voice wasn't lying or misinformed. Still peculiar for a youngish laborer with only a high-school education to have drawn up a will. Unless Incardona had some presentiment of an early death. And cremation seems particularly implausible. Where would a lout like Incardona have gotten such an affected notion about the disposal of his body after death?

No doubt any longer in Diddy's baffled mind that he can't leave things as they stand, trusting telephone voices and misleadingly headlined newspaper stories. Diddy the Gullible will have to do some investigating of his own. See the widow, the railroad officials, the crew of the train, as many fellow passengers as can be traced. A number of interviews will be needed just to straighten out what happened, leaving Diddy still nowhere near the precise reckoning of guilt and innocence. But it's a beginning. Diddy's agitation starting to subside (now). A glimpse of the sense of mastery. Is it frustration that's making him feel more active, less inert?

What's sure is that Diddy does feel intensely frustrated by this latest news. For all his waverings about going to the police, he'd always expected that, eventually, an inquiry into Incardona's death would take place; for such an inquiry an intact body, or semblance thereof, is required. So assumed that Incardona's funeral would be the usual interment. Must be. The workman's body being stored away. Kept against future use, some use.

Some day, if not (now) or soon, they were bound to hold an autopsy. He'd always thought so; had imagined it clearly. The fecal smell of the autopsy room. A long steel table. Metal cabinets with glass shelves filled with rows of stoppered bottles, labeled in purple ink, containing remnants and trophies of tissue adrift in Formalin. The bullet-riddled organs of several notorious criminals cut down in gang wars. Body fragments from famous airplane crashes of the last decade. Rows of larynxes, cross-sectioned to reveal the gimmicks of death: a shrimp, a thumbtack, a piece of steak, a half dollar. Rows of embryos in every stage of development. Poisoned brains, narcotized nervous systems, tranquilized hearts, gassed lungs, ground-glass ruptured linings of stomachs.

Diddy is waiting. A Negro in white jacket and pants, reeking of vomit, brings in a body on a wheeled stretcher and pulls off the blanket. Four men are waiting, the Chief Medical Examiner and three deputies. The chief slips on his tight translucent brown rubber gloves, takes up a bright metal tool, makes one incision the length of Incardona's torso, from clavicle to pubis, and then another the whole width of his abdomen. (Now) he has put down the tool and stands with hands plunged in the cadaver's innards, gaze politely averted. The others watch attentively.

Any death which is sudden, unattended by a doctor or medically unsupervised; any death which is traumatic; any death which is at all suspicious, must be investigated by the coroner's office. Isn't that the law? Please continue the examination. Please look. Why don't you look? Don't rush to designate "no case." In New York City, Diddy knows, the coroner's office is also required to certify all requests for cremation. Had an autopsy already been performed on Incardona? But perhaps there's no such rule in this city. Just as in many cities a coroner doesn't even have to be an M.D.

An experienced public coroner, it's said, works intuitively. He can smell a homicide. Also a question of reasoning, correct reasoning. A coroner ought to be a skilled pathologist, backed up by six floors of laboratories: histology, chemistry, serology, X ray, microphysics, and toxicology. But there's so much evidence, more than one can handle. An autopsy may uncover several possible causes of death. Besides the damage done by Diddy's cowardly blow, besides being trampled by the Privateer, Incardona may have had a bad heart, cirrhosis of the liver, an undiagnosed ulcer, syphilis. Which one is responsible? Maybe the death looks like foul play, and wasn't. Or maybe it doesn't, and was. If someone is hit by a train, whose fault is it? Everyone agrees that one can't bring charges against the iron monster, which has only done its job, behaved exactly as it was designed to behave, speeding forward along the tracks on its lethal wheels. But then people often talk about themselves in a similar way, as if they were designed or made to order; their line of self-exoneration the same, too. Is the chief engineer in some remote way culpable? Or any member of the train's crew? And besides the vaguely-outlined question of naming, and then apprehending the murderer, if indeed the death is a murder, other issues are at stake. The amount of the insurance and the money from workmen's compensation going to the widow and fatherless boy will vary according to the manner of Incardona's death. Not to speak of a more general matter: the detection of any failure in the safety procedures set up by the railroad to protect its workers.

Murder stinks. That's the clue. Out of what inappropriate delicacy does the coroner avert his gaze? Isn't he thoroughly hardened to the horrors of his profession? If anyone is capable of fearless vision, it would be such a man.

But it hurts to look.

Incardona lies with his head thrown back. His body is split open, and all his organs carefully scooped out. The flesh of his torso hangs over the sides of the metal table in two brownish flaps, exposing his spinal column from neck to pelvis. The coroner wields his flashing knives. . . .

Late Wednesday afternoon, Diddy goes straight to Hester after leaving the plant. A brief visit before embarking upon his evening's sleuthing. He comes empty-handed. Being too impatient to buy anything but an unconsidered hasty bouquet at the florist's in the hospital lobby; not knowing what, other than flowers, to bring. Happily, Mrs. Nayburn's not there. As he comes in, Hester raises her head. Can she see anything from behind the dark glasses? And what manner of distasteful, impersonal tests have the doctors been subjecting her to? She seems all patience, but surely that's deceptive. Like him, she must be either vibrating with hope or stilled with despair.

He tosses his coat over the chair at the foot of the bed.

"Don't say. I know it's you," says Hester. She smiles. Diddy happy (now). Quickly comes over to embrace her; then sits close in the other chair, moving it against the frame of the bed. Clasps her left hand in his; with his right hand, reaches up to stroke her cheek. She brings his hand down to her mouth, kisses his fingers. He bends over to kiss her hair and mouth.

The dialogue of intimacy sustained, even when they begin to talk. Hester seems less guarded and enigmatic. Sitting upright (now); knees bent and drawn together, her spine curved like a bow. They are holding something like an ordinary conversation, the kind Diddy often finds insufferable, but which he finds soothing, reassuring (now). He sketches the history of Watkins & Company; outlines the company's present situation, borrowing from Jim's view as well as giving his own; describes the physical plant; conjures up the first three days of this week's conference, both text and sub-text, tedious round-table discussions and barely audible politicking. What could Hester find engrossing in the fumbling fortunes of the firm, in the genteel drudgery of Diddy's job?

In a controversial memorandum on standards of craftsmanship drawn up by industry spokesmen and circulated at this morning's meeting?

In the third-quarter statement?

In the antics of Gus Rike, the firm's lawyer?

In the new government contract jubilantly disclosed by Reager yesterday—the thought of which is haunting Diddy—for special instruments to be used in the Army's biological warfare laboratories?

In Watkins' latest feud with Reager?

In the mishandling of the sale of thirty Scope 21's to the University of Lima?

But even if Hester is only humoring him by listening so well, by acting interested, he's warmed by her graciousness. By her desire to please. Diddy wishes that what's scheduled for tonight after he leaves the hospital weren't happening tonight; because it's preventing him from being wholly present with Hester this afternoon. Open to her, nourished by her. Diddy trying to be in this room only, but he can't. He's already rehearsing in some remote bastion of his mind how he will enter the next space.

113

It's almost six.

"Did you come earlier because you have an appointment this evening?"

Diddy, found out. It seems impossible ever to conceal from Hester the diluting or vacating of his attention. "Yes," he said.

"Business?"

"No. A personal matter. It's someone I've never met before."

By giving such an answer, mysterious yet informative, doesn't Diddy invite Hester to question him further? Is that what he wants? Yes. Then is he disappointed when, quite firmly and noticeably, no more questions are asked?

Diddy starting to feel uncomfortable. The redundant white of the hospital room is imprisoning; stillness and immobility reside here, while Diddy knows himself to be free. He has permission to leave, doesn't he? A body suitably clothed to appear on the street, eyes to see where he is going. Whereas this room is static, a private cell, the arsenal of mortality. Monday's flowers know: they're beginning to languish. Can Hester sense his flowers' drooping, minuscule crawl toward death? When does death become perceptible? How far along toward death do flowers have to travel before their odor fades, their flesh stiffens and turns dark? Where's the boundary line?

Six o'clock. Hester must feel Diddy stirring restlessly in the white Leatherette chair, must understand the token plaint of his sweating palm in hers. But does she know exactly how edgy and upset he is? In all respects? Because she can't see him, she can't observe that his uncertainty about how to conduct himself later this evening is mirrored in an untypical confusion in his clothes. Diddy is wearing the wrong tie for that shirt, the wrong shirt for that jacket, the wrong shoes for those trousers. Except for mismatched socks, a sample of almost every conceivable sartorial error. Nothing felt right today.

Lonely as well as evidently attached to him (now), Hester wants him to stay on. Diddy doesn't mean to arouse further marks of affection on her part by his uncontrollable detachment tonight. Not the kind of man who'd try manipulating a woman he desires by playing cool. The attraction Diddy feels to Hester is something he'd

114

like to show. But this isn't the right time. Either that feeling is more potential than actual, or it's one that circumstances require deferring. Better to leave the hospital. Get on with it.

Diddy is walking along a narrow mean street, holding a slip of paper with the address he's copied from the newspaper clipping in his wallet; past rows of nearly identical two-story frame houses. Like the houses seen out of train windows that one rejects, interiors unseen, without ever inhabiting them. Stops before one of the houses, number 1836. The right house (now). A stocky buxom woman answers the doorbell. Wearing gold sandals, bell-bottom Op Art slacks, and a yellow sateen blouse; cigarette in hand.

"Mrs. Incardona?"

"Whatcha want?" The woman plainly on her guard. From the hallway visible behind her, a gust of stale smoke and the smells of frying.

"Myra Incardona?"

"What's it to ya?"

"I'm from the railroad." Diddy removes the wrong hat. "I'm sorry to bother you with more questions about . . . your late husband. . . ."

"Oh . . ." The woman's flabby cheeks swelled into a smile, flaunted a mouthful of bad teeth. "Come in." She seems pleased. How many investigators have preceded him? "Tommy!" she shouts in another, raucous voice. "Shut off the goddamn TV. A man from the railroad is here." Turning to Diddy: "Here, doncha want to take off your coat?" Diddy surrenders coat and hat, which she drapes over the bannister of the uncarpeted staircase leading up to a second floor; follows her into the overfurnished parlor. Clouded with smoke. The stench, identifiable as cigarettes, fish, and cooking oil, seems to trisect the air in layers. Across the room, down in the lower layer, fish, Diddy sees the boy kneeling before the dying image. If it's true, as the *Courier-Gazette* reported, that he's eleven, he seems small for his age. Certainly undersized, considering his parentage. "This is—"

"Mr. Dalton," said Diddy.

"Say hello, Tommy." The boy looks up briefly, then lowers his head without acknowledging Diddy, perhaps awaiting a sturdy

115

phantam image that will miraculously reappear on the small-screen TV. "He should be in bed by now or doin' his homework. You hear, Tommy?"

"Is the railroad going to give us some money, Mom?"

"My boy is very upset, Mr. Dalton. What with the funeral only yesterday. Don't pay no attention."

"No . . . please," says Diddy, flustered. The child doesn't resemble his father, at least not the man Diddy remembers. He's puny, fair-skinned, freckled, with a long V-face and glittering light-brown eyes. Incardona's build was thick; he had dark skin, a heavy squarish jaw, and black eyes and hair. His wife looks typically Scots-Irish and her eyes are light, though her hair, a garish copper hue, must be dyed; one can't determine its true color. Diddy looks around the squalid room, hoping to spot somewhere a photograph of the dead husband and father. Covering a patch of the flowered wallpaper? No. On the mantelpiece, with the souvenirs from the World's Fair? No. Not even on top of the TV, alongside the little plaster Child of Prague.

"You can stay if you keep your mouth shut," said the woman. She smiles at Diddy. "Sit down." She points, with a nicotine-stained forefinger, at the low table in front of Diddy. "Hey, how about some strawberry ice cream? I got some out in the icebox." Diddy shook his head. "Sure? All right. Now what can I do for ya?"

The woman's amiability is unnerving Diddy. He wants to turn and run. But there are questions to be asked. And Diddy, cautious Diddy, must be tactful.

"Well," he began. "As you know, we're completing our investigation. I'm afraid I have to ask you a few personal questions." Pauses, glances at the boy. The gross light of understanding widens the woman's face.

"Tommy, go to bed."

"Aw, Mom . . ."

"You heard me. Get."

The boy slouches out of the room, scuffling his feet and punching one of the chairs he passes.

"That boy!" Mrs. Incardona sits down heavily. "He'll be the death of me yet."

Diddy finding it hard to continue. Something in the woman's tone, voice, language is unpleasantly familiar. Could he have met her before?

"Mrs. Incardona, I know your husband had irregular hours and worked a good deal out of town. Did you see him often? I mean, when he wasn't working?" Why was Diddy asking this? To see if Incardona had really existed? A last absurd hope. Maybe this redhead only imagined she was married to a railroad worker named Incardona; in fact hadn't seen him in years.

"Well, Joe wasn't exactly what you'd call a homebody—"

Diddy interrupted, frantically. "Wait a minute! What did you call your husband?" Instant rebirth of hope. There's been a mistake. He's at the wrong house.

"What?"

"Your husband's name! You called him Joe. But I . . . our records have him listed as Angelo."

A mistake. A mistake in Diddy's favor? No.

"Oh, he never used that Eyetalian name. Only his ma calls him that. He said the boys razzed him bad enough as it was, 'cause it was on his punch card and his paycheck. We never called him nothin' but Joe. Kinda short for Angelo, I guess."

"I see," said Diddy, leaning back again, exhausted by his instant round trip of hope. "Excuse me for interrupting you. You were saying something before."

"What was I sayin', Mr. Dillon? I can't keep nothin' straight in my poor head these days."

"Dalton," said Diddy. "You were saying that your late husband wasn't, you said, much of a homebody."

"Oh, yeah. That's sure the truth. I guess no railroad man is. Else they wouldn't be workin' for the railroad. Right? Mr. uh . . ."

"Dalton." Diddy scowled. It was true. The woman was terribly muddled. Could one believe anything she said?

Mrs. Incardona was insisting. "Am I right? You tell me."

"I understand what you're saying." Diddy would not be bullied. "You asked me if he come home always when he wasn't workin'. I guess you know he didn't. Sure, I knew what was goin' on. Used to raise hell about it, too. But what can you do? A man's not like a woman. Know what I mean? No two ways about that."

Diddy sighed. Incardona was real, even under another name. "Thanks for being cooperative," he said.

"Now, why shouldn't I be? Tell me that, Mr. Dillon. Where would it get me? Joe's gone, there's no helpin' that. Oh, I cried. Lemme tell you. You shouldda seen me at the funeral yesterday. But then I dried my eyes, and I said, Myra, you just pull yourself together. There's no bringin' Joe back, I says to myself. And that's all there is to it."

Each time the woman said "Joe," Diddy flinched. Knew well enough that many people use a name other than what's on their birth certificate. Could the switch in this case be just that innocent, trite? And what about the eerie familiarity of the woman's voice and mannerisms, scarcely less of a shock than learning a new first name for Incardona?

"I cried," repeated the woman.

She was scrounging for a compliment. Weary Diddy would give it to her. "You have a great deal of courage," he said.

"That's what Father McGuire said to me. He's down at Immaculate Heart. Myra, he said to me, Myra, you're a brave woman."

"I'm glad," murmured Diddy, lost in something like thought. There was some very large woman far away or way back like Myra Incardona. But (now) very small.

"Well, what was I supposed to do, Mr. Dillon? I mean Dalton. Kill myself? Not me! I got a boy to raise . . . and, just between you and me and the lamppost, maybe it's a bit of a blessing, Joe's being taken from us like that. Though I hate to say it." She leaned toward Diddy confidentially. Diddy took out a cigarette, stuck it between his lips, and lit a match; his hand shook. Hoped the woman had failed to detect any trembling of the flame as it approached his jaw. "You know what I'm tryin' to say? He wasn't much of a husband. May God strike me dead if I'm not tellin' the truth. Just didn't seem to care about his family. Used to wallop the boy somethin' awful with one of them wooden hangers. It just broke my heart. But I couldn't stop him. Even when I tried."

Weary Diddy realized that he hadn't been listening to a word the woman uttered. His mind gone blank as a TV screen after the end of the broadcasting day: a flickering glassy gray-white wall, exuding a faint hum. He must force himself to replay the woman's last words inside his head, to use his mind, to make a connection. Think of what she's just said. Her admission that she'd disliked her husband. A motive perhaps; explaining why the workman had been cremated. Nobody hiding or concealing anything. A simple act of revenge. By the embittered wife. Just being dead isn't enough. To get rid of him really, once and for all. But Diddy, who indeed understands how she might have felt, doesn't know how to go about determining the truth of his newest supposition.

She'd been staring at him. It couldn't be at his clothes, could it? Why is Diddy finding it so hard (now) to talk?

"Sure you don't want some ice cream? It's awful good." Is she trying to put him at his ease? Make him feel more at home?

"No thanks." Diddy taking a deep drag on the cigarette. He'll fight this lethargy. "Mrs. Incardona"—Diddy has decided to move boldly—"I was wondering why your husband was cremated. That's a little unusual, isn't it?"

"Oh, Blessed Saint Peter and Paul!" The woman threw up her hands. "Mr. Dillon, don't remind me of that! Joe put it in his will, that's why. I didn't have nothin' to do with it. Can you see me gettin' mixed up with a fool stunt like that? No sir! And throwin' out good money for nothin'? I mean, where does all that fuss and fancy stuff get ya? Just showin' off, that's all. But when it's over you're still just as dead. Now I know when I go, I don't care what they do with me. Put me out on the street with the garbage, for all I care. Am I right?"

Is she telling the truth? Then what happens to Diddy's latest theory? "But your husband did have a preference," he said, trying to steer Myra Incardona back to the main line of thought. "He wanted to be cremated."

"Who knows what he wanted. You never could get a straight word out of Joe. Say one thing one minute, somethin' else the next. He'd do it just to get my goat. Then he'd laugh."

Diddy exasperated. "But cremation *was* mentioned in his will?"

119

"Sure! And you know what I said? I says to myself, it's just like Joe, I says. The man always was a damn fool, him *and* his brother. Why, he could of been buried real cheap in the Arlington National Cemetery, with a flag on his coffin and all. Joe had that comin' to him, you know. Bein' as he was a veteran."

What's this about a brother? Another railroad worker named Incardona? Dead or alive? But Diddy must resist getting sidetracked. If he's not careful, his mind will spill all over the place, like Myra Incardona's; seduced by every passing phrase and its associations. What was it she'd said (now)? Oh, yes. "Then why do you suppose your husband preferred to be cremated?" Diddy asked. "It seems odd."

"Are you tellin' me? Odd ain't the word for it. Plain crazy I call it. Why, when I heard what was in Joe's will, I just hit the ceiling. I tried to get 'em to change it, but they wouldn't. Said I couldn't go against the will, like it was sacred or somethin'. I think he put that in just to upset me. Spite, that's all it was. He knew it'd upset me because crematin' is against the Church." Looking at Diddy, as if she expected some answer (now). "But maybe you don't know about the faith. You ain't a Catholic, are ya, Mr. Dalton?"

"No," said Diddy, "Protestant."

"Well, that's all right," the woman said. "There's good and bad in all races, and I don't hold with lotsa people I know who think Catholics are the only good people and everybody else is goin' straight to hell. I wancha to know that."

"I'm glad," said Diddy. Loosened his tie, unbuttoning his collar.

"Say, it is kinda hot in here," said the woman. "How's about a drink? I sure could use one."

"Please go ahead," said Diddy. "But nothing for me."

The woman got up from the chair, and left the room. Returning in a minute with two cans of Rheingold, two glasses with naked mermaids on them, and an opener. Setting them down on the low, lacquered table. Diddy the Gentleman took over; opened one can. "What I was sayin' before," the woman spoke slowly, watching him pour half the can into a glass, "about un-Catholics goin' to hell. Seems kinda mean to say that, don't it? But I guess I do be-

120

lieve in it. I can't help it. That's the teaching of the Church. I learned it in school from the sisters and I never forgot it." Taking a large gulp of beer. "You know, I never forgot nothin' they taught me. They were strict, all right! But whatever they learned you, you learned good. And if you were a smart aleck and didn't do your lessons right or got caught passin' notes in class, then you really learned somethin'. Somethin' you never forgot. Why, I used to come home from school with my rear end red as fire!" She laughed. "Excuse me for talkin' this way, Mr. Dillon—" For a moment, chuckling too hard to go on. "Yeah, they could of used me for a bed warmer, that's how red and hot my little fanny was." More laughing. Then a sullen look. "But, you know, it ain't like that any more. Kids have it easy nowadays. Right? My Tommy goes to a school run by the sisters, but they never hit him and they don't give him half the homework they gave me. Last week he—"

"Mrs. Incardona, you were telling me about your husband's will and the cremation."

"Oh, sure, I'm getting' to it." Pouring the rest of the can into her glass. "Well, when they found Joe they took him to a place down near the train depot, but they told me I hadda make some other arrangement Monday morning. I went down there, but they wouldn't lemme see the body and I didn't wanna, see?" She paused. Diddy nodded. "It's my nerves, see. My nerves ain't so good sometimes."

Diddy waiting for her to go on. Is that the end of the story?

"Sure you don't wanna beer?"

Diddy shook his head.

"Well, I guess I can't let it go to waste." She grinned.

Diddy opened the other can, poured it. "What happened after they wouldn't let you see the body?"

"Well then I came back home and by this time, it was late Sunday night, there was a lotta people here, relatives of Joe and me and friends, drinkin' and cryin', mostly drinkin', and we opened the will. The minute I read it I knew damn well somethin' was wrong, so right away I hightailed it to the phone upstairs and called Father McGuire. That's what I did, even though it was past midnight and I had a bit of a load on myself, ya know, from

121

cryin' and feelin' so bad. Anyway, when I told Father McGuire about it he said I oughtta ignore the will and just get Joe to a proper Catholic funeral home like Donoghue's across from the church and he'd take care of the rest. But then Joe's brother Charlie, he's got one of those Eyetalian names but we call him Charlie, come bustin' in here about three in the morning. They just got a new Pontiac. And he drove all the way from Waltham Massachusetts which is where he lives. I'd called him around nine to tell him about Joe's accident, I mean I had to do that, but he never told me he was gonna come right away. But he has this big new car, see? Anyhow he came and he read the will and he has a real big thing against the Church, how the sisters hit him with a ruler all the time when he was a kid in school because he was a lefty and how the priests was always after him and upsettin' him and givin' him nightmares and what a lousy childhood he and Joe had."

The woman leaned back. Drinking up the beer; some of it dribbles down one corner of her mouth. Is this the end of the story? It's getting harder for Diddy to tell.

"Cigarette?" he said, extending the pack across the table.

"Thanks. Don't mind if I do." She leaned way across the table to get a light from Diddy; who'd also taken out a cigarette for himself. A good thing he hadn't drunk the beer, feeling as tired as he does. "Where was I?"

So there is more. "About the awful childhood your husband and his brother had."

"Aw, listen, I don't believe half a what Charlie says. He's just a big talker. Got a chip on his shoulder. Now take Joe, for instance. Joe was different. He didn't hold a grudge like that about the Church and he didn't go mopin' about what a miserable kid he was, and I bet he got hit just as much as Charlie. But Joe liked to always look on the bright side of things." She smiled broadly at Diddy; briefly, she looked graceful and almost generous. Twirling the long string of purple beads she wore over the yellow blouse, her eyes periodically resting on his.

Diddy felt the room getting smaller and smaller, and Myra Incardona commensurately larger. Despite a separation between them of some four feet, staked out by the low, oval table between the pair of identical high-backed easy chairs, he's as aware of her flesh as if she'd been sitting in his lap. Loose, thick, pungent flesh. For at least several minutes (now), parts of her body had acquired an almost hypnotic allure for him: her breasts, her pudgy hands, the gold fillings that showed every time she laughed, the dark brown roots of her copper hair.

Diddy the Disconcerted. Assaulted by disconnected sensations. As if there's something wrong with his eyes, his skin. He needs a buffer—a slab of hard, featureless, impersonal material to hold between himself and this oozing, prattling woman. Well, he doesn't have to look at her when he's talking. Only Diddy's losing the thread again. Must painstakingly reconstruct where they are (now) in this conversation. Myra Incardona may get lost, and not care. But Diddy cares. Imperative to stick to facts. A fact: Angelo—Joe—Incardona didn't mind having had an unhappy childhood. "But your husband's brother felt differently, is that right?" Diddy continued aloud.

"Charlie? I'll say! You should hear him, Mr. Dillon. He's got a wicked tongue. People sure think twice before they mess with him!"

"Then am I right in understanding, Mrs. Incardona, that you let your brother-in-law make the arrangements for the funeral? That after he arrived, he took care of everything?"

"Well, when Charlie come right out Sunday night and offers to pay for everythin' I couldn't argue, could I? I mean about the cremation. It was his money, see. Though I gotta admit I never thought he'd come through and offer. He and Joe wasn't all that close. I mean, seein' they was brothers. When he first said he'd do it, I razzed him for bein' an old souse. I guess I'd had a few myself. It was an awful long evenin'."

"You said your brother-in-law lives in Massachusetts. What kind of work does he do?" Diddy, suddenly aware that he sounds like prying, fatuous Mrs. Nayburn on the train; but it can't be helped. This is an emergency, and no time to be fastidious about whatever helps. As long as Diddy went on asking questions, Myra Incardona looked less mammoth in size. Empty words have their use after all.

"He's a bricklayer. They make good money, bricklayers, did

ya know that, Mr. Dillon? See, their union fixes it so that in cold weather they—"

Diddy intervened faster this time. "Then if it had been up to you, Mrs. Incardona, you would have had your husband buried in a casket, in consecrated ground, with all the rites of the Church. Is that right?" Diddy had to interrupt, because he is feeling faint. Didn't speak in order to know anything. To this question—and by (now), to many more—Diddy already knew what answer the woman would make. No solutions to his enigmas here. Each promising lead destined to be quickly overthrown.

"Say, what are you gettin' at?" said the woman. In an unpleasant tone that startles Diddy, who had been getting used to the inexhaustible flaccid genial one. "You tryin' to say that Joe couldn't of been buried proper, if he wanted to? I know what you're trying' to do. Put words in my mouth. It's because of that goddam newspaper story, where it says that somebody from your fuckin' railroad said that Joe mightta killed himself. Of all the nerve! There's a law against sayin' things like that, you know? I bet I could sue that paper for a hundred thousand bucks for slandering my poor dead Joe. And the railroad, too. My Joe was a good Catholic, so how the hell could he of done somethin' like that?"

Diddy had tried to interrupt this tirade several times, without success. The woman had stopped (now), set in her indignant look.

"Mrs. Incardona, you're just wasting your anger. I can understand your feelings about what was in the newspaper story, but that wasn't at all the point of my question. Honestly. All I'm trying to get straight is how your husband came to be cremated. So I asked you a simple, straight question. I asked whether, if it had been up to you, you would have preferred to have your husband buried, in the way Catholics ordinarily are."

But she still doesn't like that question. "Listen, Mr. Dillon!" The woman crossed her arms and looked peeved. "I got a feelin' you don't understand somethin'. Now I was educated by the sisters, God bless 'em, and I been a Catholic all my life and I'm gonna die a Catholic. And if my Tommy ever comes home and tells me he wants to marry an un-Catholic girl, I'll whale that kid within an inch of his life. He won't know what hit him when I—"

124

"Look," Diddy interrupted again, "I just need to know about the circumstances of your husband's funeral."

"Well, what d'you think I'm telling you," she exclaimed sourly. "Don't be in such a hurry. Where's the fire?"

"Mrs. Incardona, I appreciate your hospitality and your honesty. But I do have a job to do."

"I know, I know," she sighed. "You work for the railroad. Just wait a minute, I wanna get another beer. Sure you won't have one with me? Okay." Diddy leaned back in his chair while she was out of the room, closed his eyes. Myra Incardona's returning footsteps. "Listen," she said, settling in the chair again, "I wanna get something straight. You come in here and ask me a lotta questions and I don't act formal or anythin', and seein' as I got nothin' better to do I'm talkin' to you. But one thing I wancha t'know is that every word outa my mouth, every last word, is the God's honest truth, so help me God. Are you with me?" Diddy nodded sleepily. "About this whole goddamn cremation business, for instance, that you seem so interested in, though why the railroad should care what happened to what was left of poor Joe I'll be damned if I can figure out. You wanna know if I was for or against it. Or maybe why I didn't stop it. But I'm not tellin' you, though you're a perfect stranger to me, any different from what I told Father McGuire down at Immaculate Heart today. You know that man had the nerve to start bawlin' the daylights out of me, just this afternoon? And what for? I'll tell ya. For lettin' Joe be cremated. He told me that Joe's soul would rot in Purgatory forever and that he wouldn't be able to rise up at the Last Judgment and lotsa spooky stuff like that. Trying to make me feel bad. Like I done somethin' awful to Joe."

"I'm sorry," Diddy said. He really was.

Myra didn't even seem to hear Diddy's words, but sailed on. "And I told him, Father McGuire, I says, beggin' your pardon, Father, but you've got no right to talk to me like that. I didn't have no control over that funeral, I told him. Charlie's the one, and if you want to tell somebody off and make 'em feel bad, you get ahold of Charlie. Boy," she laughed, "would I like to see that! Charlie'd make mincemeat out of him. But Charlie's gone back to

125

Massachusetts already. So I had to handle him all by my lonesome. And I did. Father McGuire is a young priest, see, and when they haven't been long out of the seminary they get ideas. He's sort of serious, takes everything very hard, know what I mean? A little wet behind the ears. But I set him straight. He understands now."

Diddy sighed. Talking with this woman was like drowning. Just a bit more, then he'd leave and maybe go to the movies. But he hadn't got everything quite straight in his mind about Incardona and his family. For example, the situation between the brothers. Diddy sent up a probe. "How would you describe your husband's attitude toward the Church?"

"Say, can I have another cig? The brand I smoke is lousy. Thanks . . . Now what was that you said? . . . Oh, about Joe . . . Well, he had his gripes, you know. Like Charlie. Joe could go on somethin' awful when he wanted to. He was always talkin' against the Church, makin' fun of me and Tommy goin' to mass every Sunday regular as rain, while he lay around the house in his underwear swilling beer or gin, yellin', cursin', carryin' on."

There's the Incardona Diddy met. Things beginning to fall into place.

"Was he . . . Mr. Incardona . . . a very violent man?"

"Not what you call violent. But sort of mean, when the mood took him. I'm not talkin' about what he did to me. I can take care of myself if I have to. But Tommy is somethin' else. I told you that. Joe never did fancy kids much, though you'd think he'd like his own boy, wouldn't you? But he and Tommy never hit it off."

"Was Tommy afraid of him?"

"That little fellow? Not on your life. Stand right up to him, he did, big as life. How many times I seen it—Joe takin' off his belt to wallop the daylights out of Tommy for somethin'—the kid's got a lot of the devil in him, but he doesn't mean no harm. And Tommy, full of spunk, sayin', Go ahead, Pop. You dish it out and I can take it."

"Did he really say that?" said Diddy enviously.

"Well, not just those words. Tommy's got a temper, too. Takes after his dad, I guess. He'd call Joe some pretty dirty names. They made me laugh, but Joe didn't like 'em." She laughed, brought the beer can to her lips. "Oh . . ."

More vividly than before, Diddy envisaged the family in its squalid smoky nest. Grouped in a snapshot pose: the big brutal father, the sexy slob of a mother, the harum-scarum kid. All changed, because of him. But he's getting lost (now) in sentiment, in subjective guilt. That isn't why he came. It was to affix objective guilt and innocence if he could; and incidentally to find out what had prompted the cremation. Forget about that. The conversion of Angelo Incardona into ashes had, apparently, no more than a trivial significance for his family. Though, to Diddy, it seemed a terrible, frustrating judgment. Among other things, an invitation to amnesia. Diddy must not allow Incardona's reality to become flimsy, dubious. The workman existed and he was dead; even though the evidence of his body had been miniaturized and dissipated.

"Hey!" It was Myra Incardona waving her hand in Diddy's face. "Boy, you were really off on Cloud Nine that time. I thought you was in such a terrible hurry. Remember? When you couldn't wait to ask me questions?"

Is the woman starting to have doubts about who he is? "I am in sort of a hurry," Diddy said. "It's my job. I have to make one more call this evening, and then go home and write some reports before I can get to sleep."

Myra Incardona didn't seem to be listening to much of what Diddy was saying, either. Probably catches about one word in three, and makes up the rest in her own head. All she seemed to have heard of his generous florid lie was the bare word: job. "I know you got a job," she began, with a slack half-smile. "You work for the railroad."

Diddy nodded.

"But boy, I'll tell ya one thing. You sure don't look like anybody *I* ever seen who held down a job with the railroad. The clothes you got on are too smart. Your pants ain't cut wide, like the way railroad men wear 'em. And I never saw a railroad man wear a nifty tie like that. Now that I take a good look at you, you look to me like somethin' in an ad or somethin'. And your face. I can see you never had acne when you was a kid. Why, I can tell a lot just from the way a man shaves himself." She paused. "You're a real good-lookin' guy. Here's to you." The woman saluted Diddy with her beer can. "Good lookin'. D'you know that?"

Diddy shrugged his shoulders. Suddenly realizing what was going on: all that beer she's washed down beginning to take effect. He'd better clear out fast before the woman starts peeling off those slacks.

"Oh, Myra can tell." Her speech was becoming slurred, her head looked unsteady on her shoulders. "I'll bet lotsa girls have told you that. So it probably don't mean nothin' to you when an old bag that's pushin' forty tells you. Isn't that right?"

Diddy has decided not to answer. Concentrated on summoning the energy to rise from the chair, and get from there to the front door. Out of this house. But meanwhile Myra Incardona's wandering libido has settled, who knows for how long—a matter of seconds? months?—into friendlier, less pointedly seductive behavior. Endowed with more energy than Diddy. He's only thinking of getting up; she has already darted out of the room again. Getting still more to drink?

Probably from the kitchen, calling, "Say, what's your name? Your first name, I mean. I keep gettin' mixed up on your last one."

"Paul."

"Whad'ya say? Wait, I heard. That's a nice name." The voice (now) is further away, though Diddy can just make out the words. "I used t'know a Paul. Paul Follet, his name was. Big fella, real strong. Lived near here. Ever know him?"

"No."

"Too bad." Myra, with two more cans of beer, at the threshold of the parlor. "He was a swell guy. You might of liked him." She sat down. "No, come to think of it, you wouldn't." This time Diddy the Gentleman didn't take over. Myra using the opener herself; drinking straight from the can. "How old are you, Paul?"

"Thirty-three."

"Thirty-three?" She slapped her thigh. "You're kiddin' me! Gee, you don't look that old. You're gettin' gray, I can see that. But it's comin' in pretty even, and I always say gray hair looks sexy in a man. But your face ain't lined at all. You look, well, about twenty-eight." A rapid glance. "Yeah, I'd say twenty-eight." Putting the can of beer down; looked Diddy over slowly. "Hey," she grinned, "I got just the job for you. With them clothes and the way you talk and your face, you shouldn't be workin' for the railroad. They're a bunch of slobs. You should be in an insurance office or a bank. That's the best idea, a bank. Or maybe, if you wanted to earn more dough, you could go to school nights and study for a CPA."

Diddy puzzled. Is the woman becoming suspicious of him, or is this part of a seduction? Though his instincts tell him it's probably the former, he can't decide. Why can't he decide? Why does he just smile, inanely, affably; as if nothing's going on. Wait, something is happening. Diddy rescues Myra's lit cigarette which had toppled from the rim of the ashtray onto the coffee table. "Well, to tell the truth, Mrs. Incardona, I don't really work for the railroad—"

"You don't?" she yelled and was on her feet without Diddy having seen her stand up. Diddy alarmed and mystified. "Then what the hell are you doin' in my house? Is this a gag or somethin'? If it is, mister, you're gonna be right out on your ear before you can turn around!"

"Hey, hey, hey," said Diddy. "Calm down, Mrs. Incardona, you didn't let me finish my sentence. I was about to explain that I actually work for an insurance company that investigates accident claims for the New York, Boston & Standard. I was telling you," he smiled feebly, "because you said I didn't look like a railroad man. That's why. I'm not."

"Whew," said the woman. Falling back heavily into the chair. "It's a good thing I don't have a bad heart. You sure had me scared for a moment . . . Paul? Is that your name? I thought you was some creep, gettin' into my place under false pretenses. Like a burglar or what's his name, you know who I mean . . . the Boston Strangler."

Diddy laughed. For the first moment, enjoying himself in Incardona's house. All the lies he was telling had become so absurd and ironical they seemed on their way to becoming true. If only he weren't so uncontrollably sleepy.

At this moment, Myra Incardona is saying something about how she'd spotted him right away, just by his clothes. "It's that kooky tie," she said.

Diddy involuntarily glanced down at his tie. Something unusual about it? Looks to Diddy quite ordinary and conservative.

The woman was watching him. "Sure you don't want some strawberry ice cream? It's still sittin' out there in the ice box." Diddy shook his head. "Or I could fix you a whisky and soda. There's gin, too. And there's a couple of bottles of Dago red stashed in the broom closet. Joe liked that stuff, but I know I'm never gonna drink it up myself."

"No thanks. It's nice of you, but I'm just fine. I'll be going in a few minutes."

"Well I dunno," she said archly, leaning back in the chair and crossing her legs. "I never met a man yet who didn't like somethin' nice. And there's a lotta nice things around here." She looked at Diddy quizzically. "But I can see you're a very particular fella who ain't satisfied by the first thing that comes along. Am I right?"

Diddy suddenly very tired. A prodigious wave of fatigue that seems to have knocked him down; was pulling him under.

"Right?" she asked again.

"Right," said Diddy in a dull voice. Feeling faint, overpowered. As if he'd been drugged. Would it be a mistake, he was wondering, to ask Mrs. Incardona to let him lie down for a few minutes?

"You know," Diddy said, "I don't feel well all of a sudden. Would you mind if I took off my shoes and lay down over there on the sofa for a minute?"

She got to her feet. "Why sure, go right ahead. Maybe you ate somethin'." Diddy shook his head; still didn't get up himself. "Want me to get you an Alka-Seltzer?"

Again Diddy said no. "I just have to lie down for a minute. I don't want to put you to any trouble. Please don't let it worry you, because I'm sure it's nothing."

The woman alongside him as Diddy reached the couch. "I'm not worried. And you ain't puttin' me to no trouble. Listen, I got an idea. The springs in that couch are shot and it ain't really comfortable. Why doncha go upstairs to my room 'n lie down on the bed?" She put her hand on Diddy's sleeve as he sat on the edge of the couch; unlacing his shoes. "It's a whole lot quieter up there. You can rest for a while, long as you like. I'll see that Tommy gets to bed. Then I'll come see how you are and if there's anythin' I can do for you."

Diddy sitting; looked up at her enormous face. As with a magnifying glass saw the large pores in her nose, the badly applied rouge on her cheeks, the folds of flesh along her jaw, the creases on her neck. And the scary dead expression on her face—not at all the look of someone who wants to make love.

Although he's about to lie down (now), perhaps that's not what he wants. The feeling of faintness was passing; what Diddy started to feel (now) was nausea. Afraid he is going to throw up. And embarrassed that she would understand why. Perfectly true that the woman was atrocious. But she was also a human being; probably, like most people, perishing from lack of being touched and being able to touch. Diddy wished he didn't find her so unattractive and oppressive.

"I don't think I want to lie down after all," Diddy said firmly, and started lacing up his shoes again.

"Hey, what's the matter?"

"Nothing," said Diddy. "It's passed, that's all. I told you it wasn't anything. What I need now is fresh air." Didn't have the kind of metallic resolve that would permit him to look Myra Incardona in the face at this moment; a moment he knew she took to be one of rejection. Nor the hardness of heart to walk straight to the front door (now) and leave.

"Are you goin'?"

"In a few minutes. I'll have one more cigarette. Let's sit over there again."

Diddy suddenly angry with himself. For the last half hour he has almost forgotten why he's here. Why? Because Diddy has killed this woman's husband. And because Diddy has to know how and in what sense he, Diddy, is guilty.

Seated again in the pair of identical high-backed easy chairs. "I suppose there's still some information you want," said the woman sullenly. "But I don't know if I feel like answering any more questions. Maybe you better come back another time."

Was there really anything more to ask? Hadn't Myra Incardona told Diddy all that could be of use to him? True, she hasn't resolved Diddy's contradictory view of himself—as guilty and as innocent, as the aggressor and as the victim. But at least the information she's supplied has kept the possibility of choice alive; prevented it from being closed down for lack of evidence on the other side, and an unequivocal verdict of Guilty brought in on Diddy. In the light of the man's consistently brutal character as revealed by his widow, Diddy can spare himself in the future the thought that Incardona couldn't have meant him any real harm.

Is an even more weighty exoneration possible? Until this evening, Diddy had scarcely dared to think that possible. But perhaps he's been too quick at self-condemning. Given the right kind of reliable information about Incardona's character and habits, it's possible that Diddy's act could be construed as self-defense. Even without any witnesses to the act.

With a start, Diddy realizes he has been staring at his trousered knees, but without seeing a thing; has neither heard nor spoken a word. Looks up to find the woman's eyes upon him, an opaque gaze that he can't decipher. "Say, do you want to ask me any more questions or not? It's gettin' late and I ain't got all evening to waste."

Diddy knows she's bitter (now), but can think of nothing to say that won't make matters worse. His plan: to get Mr. Paul Dalton out of this smelly shabby house, reeking of staleness and brutality and self-deception, as quickly as he can. But, as long as he's still here, has to play out his role of sleuth and impersonator, to build a dossier for the attorney who will defend Mr. Dalton Harron at his trial.

"I believe there's only one more question I was supposed to ask you. I saved it for last, I guess, because I thought you might take it the wrong way. Did your husband drink?"

The woman's face changed, darkened. "Whad'ya mean?"

"I don't mean just a beer now and then. Did he get drunk?"

"Are you tryin' to prove that Joe was drunk on the job? That that's how he got killed? Of all the low-down—"

"Wait a minute, Mrs. Incardona." It was vital to stave off the woman's rage. If she gets angry, he won't be able to come back another time, if he thinks of any more questions. Diddy held out his hand. "I'm not trying to prove anything. I'm just asking you some routine questions."

"And I'm answerin' them, ain't I? I'm being cooperative, right? You said so yourself. You know, I could sue you people. I could probably collect a million dollars for Joe's death. I seen cases like this in the papers. Tommy and I would be sittin' pretty for the rest of our lives. I'd get the law on my side, and that crooked railroad of yours would just have to shell out, Mr. High and Mighty—"

"Mrs. Incardona, please!"

The woman stood up, marched over to the TV set and turned it on. A glare of hate. "What time is it?"

"Mrs. Incardona, no one is criticizing your husband. All I wanted—"

"Tommy!" The boy appeared instantly at the doorway. Could he have been just out of sight all along? "Yeah, Mom?"

"Come back in here and watch your TV. I know it's late. But Mr. Dillon don't have nothin' to say that you can't hear. Your dad was a fine man. I wancha to know that. I don't care who knows it, I'll stand up and tell the whole world."

The boy made a face at Diddy and strutted triumphantly across the creaking floorboards to his chair. When something that looked like Superman sprang to black-and-white life, Diddy's eyes kept wandering to the TV screen. It was hopeless with the woman. Diddy hasn't meant to offend her. But he had. And she, believing in this Mr. Dalton from the railroad with his unspecified investigator's powers, was probably regretting her indiscretions. Feeling rejected, anxious, and annoyed with herself; she'd then charged Diddy with saying something he should not have said. Understanding herself to be on the defensive, she'd decided to attack. Well, just because she wanted to be angry, Diddy doesn't have to get angry in return. Widow Incardona was coarse and stupid, like her loutish husband. But Diddy's sense of justice informs him that he is the stronger, even if he didn't feel strong; and she the underdog, irate and potent as she was. She had been injured by Diddy, though she didn't know it. And if, as seemed likely, she had reason to worry over her future, her husband's assassin had an obligation to assist her.

"Mrs. Incardona, one last question. Did your husband carry life insurance? Did he have any savings? What I want to know is whether you have funds for the future, besides what you'll get from the union."

"I know what you're up to, you son of a bitch," screamed the woman, flailing out with her hands and knocking the ashtray full of cigarette butts off the low table between them onto the floor. "Tryin' to make out as we don't need the rotten money we're goin' to collect from the railroad. Well, you listen, mister. My cousin's a lawyer, and a pretty good one, too. And he told me yesterday that it don't matter at all. Joe was killed in the line of duty, run over by one of your fuckin' trains. You people are gonna pay and pay plenny. You're gonna pay through the nose."

"We'd better stop. I've had enough of this," said Diddy, feeling claustrophobic and nauseated. How could he ever have been attracted . . . He stood up to go, stepping over the tiny gray dump of butts, used matches, and ashes. The woman had already bolted out of the parlor ahead of him. Diddy turned to the boy, longing to voice (now) some of the things he would have liked to have said to him. Such as: Are you the son of the man in the tunnel? Such as: I'm sorry. Such as: I want to give you and your mother some money. Diddy the Silent, looking. The boy stared back coolly, then reached to one of the dials of the TV and turned the volume way up.

Diddy joined the red-faced woman in the hallway. She pushed his coat and hat at him, pulled open the door. "You may be sorry you've acted this way, Mrs. Incardona."

"*You'll* be sorry, mister, before I'm through!"

Diddy was prepared for the slamming of the door behind him, but not for the emptiness in his gut when he reached the sidewalk. Dismayed that he had botched the meeting. He would have liked to have found a plausible pretext for offering the woman some money. Yet, from a purely selfish point of view, he'd done all right. Probably Diddy had learned all he could from the woman—assuming that she was as artless as she seemed; and was telling the truth. He'd found out, for instance, that Incardona's widow seemed to attach no special significance to the cremation. Yesterday evening, when he'd learned about it by phoning Floral Gardens, Diddy had instantly figured that this provision couldn't have been in the man's will. Someone, the railroad or the police or the widow, must be covering up something. (Now) all that may be, seems likely to be, just fancy. Though such a wish on the part of a workman of Incardona's background is eccentric, its authenticity can't be dismissed for that reason.

Confused Diddy must beware of seeing demons everywhere. That's almost as bad as not seeing anything. Maybe worse. If he's not careful, his brain will be fit for concocting only lurid hypotheses.

Remembering that there is a world of lucid, explainable, calmly proceeding events. Just as there is a world of the tunnel. A world of opaque, blind, high-speed events shrinking and distending, withering and swelling without any apparent logic.

But no, remember the first world. That's the one to think about (now), the clear one: furnished with low voltages and ordinary lighting; in which one can take at face value newspaper prose and shopping lists and sales figures; in which people speak, if not politely, at least when they're spoken to; in which one may expect apartments and houses to be either clean and orderly or dirty and messy.

Sure, there is some kind of portentous commentary on Diddy's deed expressed in the workman's cremation. But it's he, Diddy, who finds it there; having himself brought about Incardona's death and therefore the premature fulfillment of Incardona's whim.

More generally. As a result of the violently oppressive hour just spent with Incardona's widow, a sense of the reality of the entire situation has decidedly gained on Diddy. There seemed no cause, within the boundaries of reason, for Diddy to doubt the existence of the workman; and his role in the man's death. Nor hesitate to identify his workman with Incardona, whose existence seemed to derive posthumous credibility from the sour vexing impression made by his wife and child. So Diddy's visit has been a success after all. Unless he insists on learning something so unexpected that it confounds all his previous theories, throws his seasoned memories into disarray. Was that what Diddy wanted? A surprise? Confusion?

But if some objective had been achieved this evening, why isn't Diddy willing to return to his hotel? It's already eleven o'clock. And he has nowhere better to go. On Wednesday night in a small-ish city at this hour, the movies are about to let out, restaurants are closed, and the bars will be shutting down soon. He could stroll in the park, but that's located on the other side of town, near the Museum of Science and Industry and the college. And maybe the park closes at midnight.

Diddy might just walk back to the Rushland. It's several miles to the center of town from where he is (now); which ought to satisfy his desire to stay out longer. Although he came here by taxi, he expects to find his way without asking help from anyone; relying on his excellent sense of direction. Having walked about ten blocks (now). Hardly anyone is out on the street—a few teenagers, some old men. The houses end, and Maplewood Boulevard becomes a shopping district, whose facilities indicate the low average income of the neighborhood residents: clothing stores and grocery stores, pawnshops, candy stores, liquor stores, appliance outlets whose windows are papered with signs. "No credit." "No money down." Most of the stores are protected by heavy iron grilles. Practically everything is closed, and what remains open is almost deserted. Except for one place at the end of the block; red-and-green neon spells out SMALL'S PLACE in vertical lettering, with a neon drawing of a cocktail glass superimposed over the "S" and the "P." People going in and out. Diddy looks in the window, sees a bar that seems crowded for this neighborhood on a weekday evening at this hour.

Diddy sitting at the counter (now). Orders a double rye on the rocks. A thin blonde around thirty-five, wearing an earth-red sheath and matching shoes, is sitting on the stool next to him, chin cupped in the palm of her hand. She smiles at him over the polished tips of her nails, he smiles back mechanically. A few minutes later, staring into his drink, Diddy recalls her smile. Looks up to see if she's still there, wanting to play his smile over again, with more conviction. She moves her hand farther up her face, cradling her forehead.

"Anything wrong?"

She doesn't seem surprised that Diddy has spoken. "No, I'm tired. Maybe it's the jukebox. It gets on my nerves after a while."

"Have you been here long?"

She looks at Diddy differently (now). "What kind of question is that?"

"I don't know. Forget it. Let me buy you a drink."

The woman ordered a vodka martini. Diddy asked for a second rye. They aren't talking. Diddy because he can think of only one thing to say next. So sure is he of what the woman's response will be that he wants to think carefully, making sure he really wants to go off with her. Diddy silent, too, because the jukebox was playing something by the Beatles that he particularly likes.

"Now what?" said the woman, when he turned again to look at her.

"You're not a customer, are you? You work here, right?"

"You expect me to say yes to that?" she asked.

"Do I look like a cop?"

"Maybe. How do I know what a cop looks like?"

"Tell the truth." He offered her a cigarette.

"You could be a cop. Though, I don't know, you're dressed funny for a cop." She looked at all the wrong clothes. "You stick out in a crowd. Or, you could be just some poor misunderstood husband."

"I'm not that, either. . . . Well, actually, I'm an ex-husband. I was fired three years ago."

"Am I supposed to say I'm sorry?"

"No," said Diddy, putting his hand on her thigh. "Listen, are you free now?"

"Right now?"

"Yes, right now."

"I suppose you want to know if I have somewhere for us to go, right?"

"Do you?"

"I don't know." She took a compact from her bag—red satin, a lighter shade of red than the dress and shoes—and began powdering her nose.

"Listen," said Diddy, "I don't want you to do anything you don't feel like doing. Understand? I'm not drunk. You can say no, and I won't go away mad."

The woman closed her bag, swiveled on the stool. Putting her hands on her hips. "Okay. If you're on the level, I'll cut the comedy. There's a reason I've been sitting here so long tonight. The drinks are cheap, but I'm not."

"I figured that. Don't worry."

"Okay, lover. It's a deal."

"Sure you don't want another martini?"

"No thanks."

Diddy paid for their drinks, and when he slid off the bar stool and first felt the wooden floor under his feet became somewhat unsteady. Though he couldn't be drunk.

What's your name? "Doris." Mine's Dalton. "Oh."

"Coat?" said Diddy.

"Over there. The suède." Diddy retrieved the coat, helped her on with it. "So long, Angelo," she called to the bartender. Diddy's head felt swiftly unhinged at the jaw. Here was another Angelo, one who used his right name. No, better not look back at him; perhaps to see something he hadn't observed before.

Once in the street, Diddy's head clears a little. The woman slips her arm in his, and leads them four blocks down a side street to a three-story brownstone with a "Furnished Rooms" sign nailed to the door. "This what you expected?"

Diddy shrugged. "Come on, baby. Stop treating me like some kind of hick in reverse."

"You don't like being kidded, huh?" They were climbing the stairs (now).

"What do you mean?" said Diddy. "I love it. I'm just crazy about it." Puts his hand on Doris' behind and keeps it there the rest of the way up the stairs.

"Sure, sure. I can see what *you're* crazy about, lover."

"I'm crazy about a lot of things," said Diddy, grinning. Giving her ass a hearty squeeze.

Standing still. She was unlocking the door of a room on the third floor.

Inside the room. Shades down on the two windows, minimal furniture, walls of an indeterminate color. Years since they were last painted. "Well, here we are. What do you think of it? Some dump, huh?"

"I don't get you, baby," said Diddy. "Why are you always asking me what I think of things? What do you care *what* I think? I'm here, aren't I?"

The woman, taking off her coat. "Who says I care anything about what you think? You must be off your rocker."

"But you do, baby. Don't try to cover it up."

Diddy knowing he shouldn't pursue this line of talk. Doris isn't supposed to be a person. Get on with it. But he can't resist.

"I don't mean you care about me as me," Diddy says. "You don't know me. And maybe everything works better if you pretend not to notice the guy you're with, and if you think he's not really looking at you. But I do see you, I can't help it. In the bar I noticed how depressed you looked. And I noticed you seemed anxious as we were walking here, and that it got worse as we came up the stairs. And that's why you asked me a couple of dopey questions. Isn't that so?"

The woman looked at him. Incredulity. The softness in her face, the light in her eyes. A flash of genuine contact. Diddy smiled, without touching her.

Could that have been a mistake? A misreading. Because, right after, her face tightened again. And when she smiles back, it was a professional smile (now) that didn't address Diddy at all.

"Where do you come from?" said the woman. Diddy saw what happened. Saw it born, live, and die. In less than a minute. Back in the dead world (now).

Since Diddy didn't answer right away, she added, "I know you're not from around here. Are you from New York City?"

"Yes."

"I thought so." She was straightening the bed. "You're the quiet type. That's how I knew. There are a lot of quiet people in New York City."

Diddy laughed softly. Poor Doris, poor people. "Have you ever been to New York City?"

"A couple of visits. With an old boyfriend of mine. I never lived there."

"And you'd like to?"

"Like to? You bet! Jesus, would I ever like to get out of this dump! You wouldn't believe what comes into this room. A lot of pimply college boys begging you to make a man of them, and wop railroad workers who are so plastered they forget why they ever came up here."

"Then clear out of here. Why don't you move?"

"Maybe I'm scared of how I'd make out competing with big-city hookers."

Diddy, leaning against the chest of drawers, watching this Doris begin to undress, reached out and took her in his arms. "You'd do all right, Doris."

The woman turned out of his embrace. "Can we, uh . . ."

"Oh, settle about the money?"

"Yeah. You know how it is. I can trust you, lover, I can tell that. But I meet all kinds of men . . ."

Diddy covered her mouth with his hand. "Don't explain. Is thirty all right?"

"Is that all you have?"

"I could give you forty."

"Deal."

Takes the money out of his wallet and gives it to her.

They moved onto the large bed, and Diddy set about peacefully making love to her. "Hey, you're really ready, aren't you?" are the last words she said, and those right at the beginning. From then on, she did little, lying quite still in his embraces. Diddy wanted to ask if there were something which particularly gave her pleasure that she'd like him to do. But his experience with prostitutes had been slight, mostly in Europe on his vacations, and he didn't know whether she might take his insistence on pleasing her, as well as himself, as an impertinence or an imposition. Well then, Diddy will please himself. It's not that this Doris appears to mind, or even that she's unappreciative. Only that she seems very far away. Diddy must draw her as close as possible, making her the right size. He must be here, and not in his head. Doris is here. As long as Diddy doesn't let his mind stray to Hester's full body and eager way of taking her pleasure, it's enough. Even a kind of blessing.

After making love, Diddy has no intention of falling asleep. He was lying on his back. The woman on her left side, her head resting on his chest, her bent right leg thrown across his thighs. If stillness and even breathing mean sleep, Doris is asleep. To move would be to wake her up. The room is dark: no flashing sulphur-yellow light, and the bed fully as comfortable as the one in the Rushland. Diddy can take a quick nap. No hurry. Only a synthetic home awaits him, a room inimical to his true comfort. Since there's nowhere else he has to be, he might as well be here. A little longer.

Diddy hugs the damp, sleeping woman closer to him. Mumbling something. He tries to catch the words. "In the door," she says. "Don't wait."

"Doris?"

An odd noise, a kind of groan.

Diddy waits to hear more. Black silence (now) in the room. Feels something cool and wet on his chest, and realizes she must be drooling slightly between parted lips. As some people do when sleeping lightly. Joan and he often fell asleep like this after making love. Remembers that spot of wetness on his chest.

"Doris?"

Diddy closes his eyes. Soon after, he slept, deeper than he'd intended, and fell into a poorly lit, claustrophobic dream. One of those dreams in which scenes aren't clearly articulated. Not staged. At least, what the dreamer is left with upon awakening is not an adequate scenario which indicates movement in space and supplies dialogue; more a kind of summary. An unproduced dream.

The theme is Diddy making decisions, in dim light and in indistinct surroundings. It started with feelings, wishes, resolutions, all the fruits of the will. Then, in order to give Diddy's feelings the necessary lifelikeness, the background was hastily assembled or sketched in.

141

Decision first. Diddy had decided he would marry Myra Incardona and become Tommy's stepfather. Where had he proposed to the widow? In the front hallway of her small home, it seemed. But that wasn't clear. Maybe an afterthought.

Next came the wedding, which took place in a Catholic church. Officiating was someone who resembled the priest on the train Sunday afternoon. Standing with the buxom woman at the altar, head bowed, Diddy wonders if this is necessary. But before he has time to back out, the reconstituted family is installed in their house.

In what follows, the dream rapidly condenses a whole lifetime into a series of revulsions.

A life of shouting and screaming and whining: Myra's and the boy's.

A life of broken dishes and the stench of fried fish.

A life of ceramic ashtrays spilling over with cigarette butts,

dirty laundry piling up by the foot of the uncarpeted staircase,

TV that's never turned off,

a thousand filaments of copper hair embedded in the parlor carpet,

battered comic books wedged under the cushions of every chair in the parlor,

empty beer bottles in the back porch,

cockroaches in the coverless sugar bowl,

sour milk in the icebox,

ants in the cornflakes,

tubes of toothpaste squeezed askew and their caps misplaced,

corsets and brassières and stained underpants heaped on the closet floor,

hair curlers scattered between the infrequently changed sheets.

Doris?

Naked, thrashing about in bed with the bovine Myra, Diddy worries that someone hostile is watching. Even so, he can't stop. Brave Diddy, sturdier than he thought. The woman cries with pleasure, digs her fingernails into Diddy's lean shoulders. (Now) Diddy is on his back. The woman lying to his right on her side, her head, right arm, and right leg thrown across his body. How heavy she is. Diddy pushes her off, then rolls over on his left side, drenched in sweat. Who is watching?

Does he dare to try to fill Incardona's place as husband and father, compounding the criminal annulment of a life with the theft of an identity? Tommy doesn't seem to object. Diddy makes sure the scrawny boy has a plateful of strawberry ice cream at dinner most evenings, and tries to work up a stepfatherly interest in the Cub Scouts. But what about the murdered workman? Having lost his heavy body through the imprudent rite of cremation, Incardona can scarcely be tangible enough to make even a ghost. Yet the man is also too recently dead to be as faint, faded, and impotent as a ghost. Even boiled down into a little puddle of ashes, Incardona remains something more substantial. Still powerful. And pitiful. Like some sailor husband, given up as lost at sea, who steals back years later, unrecognized by his fellow townspeople because he's grown a beard and his hair has turned white, to stand shivering in the snow outside his shabby old house. Then to creep forward, to peer in through the icy window in order to witness his beloved wife, still youthful and unlined, contentedly embracing her new husband and their baby. Yet, even as a heartbroken or embittered Enoch Arden haunting this house, Incardona must appreciate that Diddy gains nothing by his new life. Nothing. Diddy only means to make restitution.

But dreams are never content to expound a single thought. Which is how dreams become entangled with conscious fantasy and accurate memory. Also, how dreams are exegetical, even didactic. Diddy's dream (now) proceeds to explain something he'd puzzled over, without success, during his interview that evening with Mrs. Incardona. For the woman in the dream isn't only Incardona's wife, at present Diddy's inheritance and lawful burden. She's also Mary, his nurse and Paul's. Oxlike, demented, vaguely pious, reliable Mary who had fed the brothers, bathed them, dressed them, spanked them, and installed them for sleep and turned off the lights in their common bedroom since they were born. Myra Incardona

143

(now) has Mary's straight short hair, a natural faded brown, instead of her bright copper curls. And (now) the widow's talk was identifiable as the same endless stream of inane wordy drivel that fell from the nurse's mouth. Talk as physical and inexpressive as the mashed potatoes on Thursday night or the oatmeal for Monday, Wednesday, and Friday breakfasts that Mary spooned into their mouths. Talk as unvarying as her wide waist or the funny smell that lived under her arms.

That talk! It was a wonder of repetition. Each evening Mary read aloud to the boys whatever gruesome accident, rape, or murder, preferably multiple, the newspaper had to offer. While vacuuming or dusting or cooking or canning or sewing on buttons, she retold the dozen stories about her eight sisters, all living, who were nuns and nurses and housewives, and her one brother, who had died falling down the kitchen stairs, an unmarried alcoholic cab driver. The same deck of reminiscences led to her late father and mother, formerly cook and coachman on a big estate in Pennsylvania. And to one superstory, consecrated by countless retellings: of the kindness of their lady and gentleman, who once summoned Mary, when she was eight, to come up to the Big House and play with their daughter for the afternoon. Unforgettable afternoon. "She was dressed so pretty. And they gave me dinner. And you should of seen my sisters' faces when I come home that evenin'. They didn't see why I was picked to go, and not them. I guess I was the prettiest. Oh, were they burned up!"

That talk! There were enigmatic battles with the milkman and the butcher and the grocer, apparently over whether they had the right to cheat Mary. Battles she always claimed to have won. "Told 'em where to get off, I did." And her faith, of which Paul and Diddy heard no end. The Church, or at least the idea of it, was nurse's solace. Father So-and-so said it was all right that she missed mass the last three Sundays, seeing as she had two boys to bring up practically by herself. Upon rising, there were the painstaking recitals of what they were going to eat that day for breakfast, lunch, and dinner. To Diddy and Paul, who took all their meals with Mary, the schedule of menus was all too well known. Without Mary's daily bulletin, all they had to know was the day, since long ago Mary had admitted the existence of exactly twenty-one possible meals and then closed the canon; and each triad was nailed forever to a particular, unvarying day of the week. And occasionally, Mary would have an unintelligible anecdote to relate about a date she'd had on her Wednesday off. One of the anonymous boyfriends, Diddy remembered, was a sailor. But nothing ever lasted long enough for Diddy and Paul to meet one of Mary's suitors at some street corner, unknown to their parents. When each new one came along, Mary's hopes rose fast, then waned even more rapidly. Disillusioned, she'd explain that this one had gotten fresh while walking her home. Or that the other one had tried to do dirty things to her in the balcony of a movie theatre, things that had something to do with the signals that old man in Moors Park was making behind the tree one Sunday morning when Mary hurried them away. "Of course, I know my boys won't be like that when they grow up." For many years Paul and Diddy didn't understand a word of all this. It didn't seem to matter, since when Mary was talking she never waited for an answer, never seemed to expect a response. Their mere physical presence sufficed. As long as Paul and Diddy could recall, they hadn't actually been listening to anything Mary said.

Paul was six years old and almost done with first grade when he bravely sought an audience with their mother to appeal for some independence from Mary's suffocating ministrations and inflexible routines. Diddy, finishing second grade, gained one more reason for admiring Paul and wishing to emulate him. Is Diddy the Bold about to be born? Not yet. Not done so easily. Usually, whatever Paul accomplished first became that much harder for Diddy to do. "Well, I lost one baby," said Mary, ostentatiously detouring around Paul's bed to come over to Diddy and tuck him in. "But I still got my other baby, don't I?" Leaning over, she hugged Diddy, partly pinned down by the sheets, to her huge bosom. Seven-year-old Diddy felt as sad as he did trapped, understanding how hurt Mary was. An irrepressible sympathy for her, like a sound to which one can't close one's ears. The sound meant he couldn't join Paul in his independence right away. Diddy was all that remained to Mary, the sole object of her already much-

145

confined lust to care. What a responsibility, to be someone's Last Pleasure! Mary would have to be very tactfully and patiently weaned, like a greedy oversized baby. The same project (now) with Myra Incardona. In the dream, Diddy knows he doesn't intend to remain married to her forever. It's just for a little while. Until she recovers from the shock of her husband's death. Then Diddy would be free.

Yet in the dream, Diddy thinks that it can't be right to have married his nurse. Mary must be so much older than he. Paul should be helping him, instead of lightheartedly claiming his liberty and then running off to enjoy it, leaving Diddy to mend the broken hearts and prop up the bruised egos of the adults. Were Paul to marry Incardona's widow, the recuperative process might go much faster. Paul neither as patient nor as sentimental as Diddy. With Paul, Myra Incardona would have to do her share of the job.

Has enough happened? Diddy watches Myra Incardona, who has kicked the top sheet to the foot of their double bed and sprawls, sleeping, with her nightgown rolled above her breasts. She seems happier (now). Diddy keeps to the edge of the bed. If he is to leave, he might do it best while she sleeps. Before she wakes and starts up that stream of whining babble that, surely, she can't expect him to listen to or take seriously. Language is sacred. As sacred as the body. Myra Incardona is one of the profaners of language, Mary's true disciple. With Mary, it had been a wonder that Diddy hadn't gone deaf. Beware of Myra. Diddy, although not as strong as he once was, doesn't intend to be so indulgent of others again.

The mattress is very soft. Diddy slips over the side to his knees, hoping that Myra isn't awakened by the creaking springs. If he can find his shoes. . . .

"Where you goin', doll?" says the woman sleepily.

Diddy realizes he's awake (now). Not dreaming. The space has changed again, and this woman is blond, small-breasted, and has a large black mole on her left shoulder.

"I can't stay the night. But I dozed off, and now," looking at his watch, "it's four o'clock."

"Suit yourself, lover," says the woman. Without switching on the light, Diddy gathers his clothes from the floor and dresses.

"Doris, I'm going now," he says softly.

"Sure thing. Maybe I'll see you again." She seems almost asleep.

Four-thirty. In the lobby of the Rushland, Diddy buys the "City" edition of the *Courier-Gazette* and then goes to the elevator; but once in his room merely glances through the paper before turning off the light. Before going up, Diddy has instructed the night clerk to wake him at nine o'clock. Doesn't even seem a victory of sorts not to rise at seven, as he's done every other morning this week, for the "Late Final." Why should Thursday's paper have something in it for him, if there's been nothing on Tuesday and Wednesday? Anyway, Diddy utterly exhausted. Even four hours more of sleep won't be enough. Skip breakfast, take a long hot bath. Then come down in time to get the car.

Just barely. Diddy is almost too late. Hurrying through the front door of the Rushland a minute after ten o'clock. Jim and the two others are already in our car, the Oriental chauffeur is softly revving the motor.

"You just made it, Dalt," said Jim. "We were going to leave without you."

"That would have been all right. I could have taken a taxi."

"What happened? Oversleep?"

"I slept later than usual."

"I bet you did. I dropped by your room about 2 a.m. to borrow your copy of the Butler memorandum, and you weren't in yet."

Diddy in the jump seat again; didn't answer. We are moving out of the central part of the city. A brilliant sunny morning. His eyes hurt him, after so little sleep.

Passing through the sedate residential streets. The three men are discussing a persistent rumor that the company may, at last, allow itself to be bought out by one of the giant firms that has made repeated offers in recent years.

147

"Reager will try to pass it off as something great," said Jim. "A merger. But you know what that means, don't you? Kaput."

"What do you think, Dalton?" Fred asks.

"Don't ask him anything," said Jim. "He's still asleep."

Diddy, who has glimpsed the blue and gold dome—the first tantalizing sight, quickly obscured—is not pondering the company's affairs. He wishes he could. Work would be an antidote to his obscure anxieties. But Diddy is without work. Only mysterious projects. The company's future, his own carefully tended job, are receding. Becoming intangible.

Already the fourth morning, leaving only one more day.

Through the gate, up the driveway. The dome shining with peculiarly vigorous brilliance. Our car had stopped. Diddy thinks of the blue and gold dome. Once again recalls its origins, dismisses its recent use. Diddy appreciated the fantasy the dome embodies; felt renewed, sometimes, by contemplating the eccentric energies of the man who'd insisted on this gaudy crown to his enterprise.

Diddy, going into the building. Up the elevator. Along the crowded hallway of the third floor. Into the long rectangular conference room. Most of us were already seated at the oval table. Diddy opening his briefcase, taking out his notes.

He admired people who loved their labor. Allowing themselves to be led by this love into extravagances, such as Amos Watkins' dome. Diddy's misfortune was to lack a vocation, some activity he could perform with love. Not to have gone into a profession, such as law or medicine or teaching, or into one of the arts. Instead, Diddy had only a job, which thus far he had valiantly aspired to like better than he actually did. Sad destructive choice. For which Diddy pays dearly. After the exasperating boredom of elementary school and high school, he'd enjoyed his pre-med studies at Dartmouth. Had been accepted at two high-ranking medical schools. What had prevented him? Meeting Joan in July, a month after graduation; getting married in August; by September acceding to her insistence on moving right away to New York? Only that? As simple, as merely erroneous as that? No. He refused to blame everything on Joan. If he'd truly wanted medical school, Diddy would have found an eloquence sufficient to persuade Joan to accompany him to Ithaca or Baltimore. Instead of letting her persuade him. Getting him to do what he really wanted to do. Not to do what he really didn't want to do. Diddy the Irresolute. Everyone gets the life he truly wants.

One of the scientists is presenting the budget for the proposed research on revamping the Micro-Recorderscope.

So he'd never had a vocation to love. And after a long, difficult time—eight years—he didn't have Joan either. That deficit must also be charged to his account. When she left she had said that he didn't love her. Though his feelings cried calumny, maybe she'd been right. Had he ever had anything beyond need and sexual attachment? Where was love? There was nothing stirring his energy to generate it. Genuine work would have fired his energy. Anything, from the most delicate problem-solving to gross labor. To love one's work is a way of loving oneself, and leaves one freer to love other people.

But beware the difference between loving one's work and being merely engrossed in it. This last Sunday afternoon, Angelo Incardona, totally absorbed in his work, had been anything but amiable. The workman had violently resented Diddy's intruding on the scene of his labor, distracting him. Became irascible, menacing. Had moved to destroy him. Whereas if Incardona were (now) to burst into this conference room, no chance of Diddy being too engrossed in his work to welcome him. Diddy would go over to him, grab his arm and then, apologizing for the interruption, introduce him to Reager, Watkins, and the others. To hell with their surprise at discovering Harron, who's "one of us," acquainted with a dirty, lower-class slob. If Diddy condescended to explain to those stuffed shirts, he could say the workman was a long-lost brother of his. Or perhaps someone brotherlike, such as the son of his old nurse. Incardona might be disarmed by such a reception. He could observe that Diddy entertained friendly feelings toward him, and most likely meant him no harm.

But Incardona isn't going to arrive. Neither mollified, entering after a quiet knock; nor cursing with outrage, battering open the door. Diddy tries to listen to what the others are saying. Time to vote on the new budget for the laboratory? Or has the vote already

149

taken place? Perhaps a few minutes ago Diddy raised his hand quite automatically, without knowing what he did.

Diddy catches Jim gazing his way. Is it possible that that little friendly mind has some deeply buried clue to what's preoccuping Diddy? Unlikely. Not the same wave length. Still, Jim is looking. Diddy tears off a sheet from his pad, scribbles a sentence on it, folds the paper; then asks Ayres, the head PR man, Diddy's neighbor to his right, to pass the note on to Allen. Jim spots the paper traveling toward him, reaches out for it, coughs. Unfolds it and reads. A perplexed look at Diddy. Then Jim, bowing his head, writes briefly on the same sheet, refolds it, has it passed back to Diddy. Furtively, Diddy opens the paper.

What he'd written was: "Jim, do you happen to know if there is a state law that makes an autopsy mandatory before someone is cremated?" And Jim had scrawled below. "Yes, I believe there is. Almost positive. Why?"

Diddy looks up; tries to fabricate an astute, friendly nod.

Jim is probably right. Still, what was performed Monday or Tuesday morning upon Incardona wasn't the autopsy Diddy wanted. The important thing for Diddy to remember is that if he wanted to check further, it was easy to find out for sure. Since Diddy tends to find any reliable piece of information soothing, why hasn't he already resolved this question? Could have called the *Courier-Gazette* or City Hall days ago to inquire about the existence of such a regulation.

He can do that later. (Now) must try to concentrate on what's at hand, Watkins & Company, the present. Diddy trying to behave as if the sole reason he is upstate, living for a week in this city, is business: he was picked—a flattering assignment—to attend the company conference. Trying to convince himself inwardly, while he lets the rote behavior of the competent junior executive persuade the others.

Diddy the Good was taking a business trip. Banish all private projects. Especially those two. Pursuing his investigation into the workman's death and his feelings about it. Visiting Hester in the hospital, and exploring his sentiments toward her. . . . Neither project is going well, a fact that's making him not so much uneasy as somewhat giddy and lightheaded. Does this lack of success make his projects more pure?

Watkins is delivering some evasive remarks about the merger. Reassuring everyone that the executive board merely has the matter under consideration. No final decisions have been made.

Finally, the vote. The scientists, leaders of the faction Diddy has supported, carry the day. One last go at improving Scope 21, pushing it back into first place, once more ahead of all competing models. Their motto: Don't give up! Diddy agrees. On Monday morning, he had found the arguments of both factions plausible. (Now), by Thursday, Diddy is amazed these policy issues are even a subject for general debate. Doesn't everyone here realize that some people just know more than other people. Don't the scientists know far more than Reager and Watkins do about Scope 21? Management just has to trust them. And as for the merger, maybe it's a good idea.

Eating in the cafeteria on the second floor. But not cafeteria style. Due to the presence of a guest speaker, lunch was more formal than it had been on the preceding two days. A director of the local television station outlined the projected half-hour panel discussion and interview program on which Watkins & Company will be featured as "Business of the Month."

"We need three volunteers for the panel discussion," said Reager after the speaker –his name began with H—sat down. "If you don't mind, I'll suggest a few candidates. Anyone named is of course perfectly free to refuse. And don't you others be envious if you're not chosen. I'm not"—he laughed hoarsely—"making a serious rating of my colleagues." Pause. "Comensky." A black-haired young biochemist at the end of the head table took a spoonful of fruit salad out of his mouth and nodded without expression. "Michaelson." Head of sales, West Coast. Another expressionless nod. "Harron." Though Diddy surely knew his own last name, he did wait a few seconds; then realized with embarrassment that he'd been wandering again. Waiting for someone else to say the yes for him? He nodded, too.

"Good," said Reager. "Now this won't take up too much of your time. We'll need you for a briefing tonight at the Channel 10 studio at nine-fifteen. Mr. Watkins and I will be there, of course."

"Just a quick run-through," said the TV producer, trying to be helpful.

Reager pretended to ignore the interruption. "And then we meet before the show, which is scheduled to go on, live, at 11 a.m. Saturday morning."

"That's right," chimed in the man from the television station, again without having been invited to speak. Reager frowned.

Coffee was being brought in. The head table, where Reager and Watkins sat, no longer solicited the attention of everyone else in the room. The noise level steadily rising. Having downed one cup of coffee, Diddy was already on his second when he felt a hand on his shoulder. Jim leaning over; hushed voice. "Why did you say yes to Reager, you dope? You could leave for New York Friday night. Now you're stuck here through Saturday."

"I don't mind," whispered Diddy. "I'd planned to hang around for the weekend anyway. A friend of mine has just checked into the Warren Institute here for an operation."

"Oh, sorry," said Jim. "But hey, before I forget, what the hell was that goofy note all about?"

"Oh, I just wanted to know. I was thinking about something."

Ernst Wildhaber, one of the scientists, who was seated on Diddy's left, got up; Jim slid into his seat. Smiled. "Sure is a strange thing to want to know in the middle of all—this." Jim waved his arm eloquently. "Unless there is a connection somewhere. Like you're all pissed off about the merger and planning to bump Reager off. Query. Will autopsy detect arsenic in the creamed chicken and peas, or won't it?"

"Something like that," said Diddy.

"Well, when you've got all your plans set up and your poisons operational, let me know. I might come in on it with you. Okay?"

"Promise," said Diddy. "But what I'm really hoping for is to make you my accomplice. From now on, I won't commit a murder without your advice."

"Just come up with something that leaves no traces," replied Jim. "And you can count me in. That is, unless I beat you to it and just shove one of those creeps out the window by tomorrow. I'm a pretty impulsive guy, you know."

Diddy, light in the head, aerated almost, wondering where this conversation was going to lead. What was the next sentence? The one after that? Was it possible that he's about to tell Jim about the undetected crime he's already committed? And after telling, to have yet one more incredulous auditor?

Sitting on the edge of his chair, Diddy sips his coffee. Waiting for the sticky strip of words to spurt from his mouth. Jim has turned away to talk to Denton of R&D, the man on his left. Anything might happen. The urgent blood in his head is spiraling down into his chest. Something hard, cubelike, rising in the back of his throat. He leans toward Jim. But just then Wildhaber returned to claim his seat; signaling the waitress for a fresh cup of coffee. This one's cold. I can't drink it. And Jim went back to his own table.

On the agenda for Thursday afternoon: a special tour of the plant, whose theme is the recently installed manufacturing equipment of which Watkins is so proud. For the benefit, mainly, of the representatives of the company's sales force present at the conference. One of Diddy's tasks in New York, before coming up for the week, had been to prepare and oversee the printing of a brochure explaining the new automated machines for the salesmen to take away with them. A mailing of this material was going out to the rest of the salesmen across the country.

Diddy decided he could skip the tour without anyone caring. At first, was going to phone Hester to say he was coming over immediately; instead of this evening. Then decides to arrive without giving prior notice, hoping that her aunt might wander out or have to leave early. But as Diddy comes down the corridor on Hester's floor, sees Mrs. Nayburn pacing outside her niece's room. As if she were expecting him. She doesn't waste a minute before beginning to fawn. Hester's pimp. He sees the woman gazing triumphantly at the flower's he's carrying.

"Any news from the doctor?" Diddy said mechanically.

Mrs. Nayburn announces that the tests have been completed. Assuming a suitable cornea is available from the Eye Bank, Hester's operation will take place tomorrow.

"And what does the doctor say?" Diddy feeling somehow that what he's heard must be bad news.

"Only that we shouldn't expect too much. My poor darling. She's being so brave."

"I'm going in now."

"You go right ahead and do that, Dalton dear. She'll be tickled pink to see you. And I think I'll just leave you two alone." An unexpected gift.

Entering the room, Diddy was shocked at the pallor of Hester's face behind the black glasses. She looked up. "It's me," he says.

"I know."

Diddy, feeling stupid, busies himself filling an empty vase with water and setting the flowers in it. Which he places on Hester's night table before he sits close beside her.

"Oh, roses. Thank you."

Pleased, Diddy takes her hand and kisses the palm. "How are you today?"

"Sad."

"Are you worried about tomorrow? Nervous?"

"Not really." She laughs gloomily. "I know the operation isn't going to be successful."

"Why are you so sure of that? Is it something the doctors said?"

"No. They try to keep up my morale. But I know."

Diddy gazes at Hester's face, which he has never seen register such misery. How could he have found that innocent, vulnerable face inexpressive? Her bed is disorderly, and the sheets crumpled. She must have slept badly last night.

"Look, Hester, it's true many corneal transplants aren't successful. But many are. Don't think of it as if it were like getting a skin graft from someone else or acquiring someone else's kidney. A graft in the eye will take, in a fairly large number of cases. The eye is special, not so adept as the rest of the body at rejecting foreign substances. You know, there aren't any blood vessels in the cornea.

And the eye in general has fewer antibodies than other organs. . . . But I'm sure your doctors have told you all that."

"How do you know so much?"

"My father was a doctor. And I was pre-med in college."

Diddy, hearing a replay of his last words inside his head, felt anew the grotesque intersection of their situations. Hester, unable to see with the naked watery eyes God had given her. Himself, engaged in publicizing the machine-eye that assumes the normal skills of unaided sight, and seeks to move beyond them. To a man wielding a microscope, his own seeing eyes are blind.

The girl seemed to be weighing what Diddy said. Then shook her head. Misery again stationed itself in her face. Could she be so naïve as to imagine that all she would need to be happy, always happy, is to recover her eyesight? If that's what she imagines, then think what Hester suffers, sure as she is that she's not going to see. Either not ever or never again? . . . Not only does the imagination dupe us, so we're always hankering after what we don't have, and in particular what we've lost; as if its possession or repossession would be our salvation. Diddy also thinks how the imagination localizes suffering. Creates and re-creates imaginary anatomies: exotic cavities, magic cartilage, organs of the secret life.

Yes, eyes are special. But besides the eyes of the flesh, which are mostly water, there are the secret eyes. That either see or do not see. This is the only consolation Diddy dares to offer Hester, since he must take seriously her premonition that the surgery will fail. Don't you know, he says, that you can really see? In a way most people with sight can't. And that most of what people are looking at with their eyes is just debris.

Gertrude, the nurse, comes through the door with the bare thermometer in hand to stick in Hester's mouth, and bustles about the room with a vaguely censorious air while waiting for the necessary time to elapse before taking it out. Leaves, after giving Hester a large white pill to swallow.

"How disagreeable that woman is," exclaims Diddy. They haven't spoken while she was in the room.

"Very."

Damn them all! But no, we were talking about something. "About what I said before, Hester. What do you say?"

The girl shifted in her bed; readjusting her pillows. Diddy hastened to assist her.

"What do you say, Hester?"

"That you overestimate me."

"Not at all."

"Yes. You think I have some special wisdom because I'm blind."

Because she is blind? Diddy hadn't thought he was making that connection. Only rediscovering the paradox of the wise person who happens to be blind as well. Diddy about to apologize for his tactless presumption, when the girl, in a timorous tone, went on. "Maybe you're right. Being blind does make one see better in a way. Nothing is either ugly or beautiful. When that's not of concern, an awful lot of scum is blown off the mind and the feelings."

Diddy, in his chair, feels her words as an immense blow. Though they take a few moments to traverse some unidentified distance. A good blow, like the harsh stroke of an osteopath knocking a dislocated shoulder into place. Not painful at first. The blow is moving out, in ever widening circles. (Now) Diddy feels—there's no other word for it—exact. Exactly where he is; being exactly where and how he wants to be. Can a few quiet words do that? Strip something away to permit this feeling, one he's never had before in his life? Not ever. Like being in the very center of something dense, surging, and resilient. In the center, but with no sense of being pressed in on all sides. A feeling of plenitude, instead. And of harrowing lucidity.

(Now) the blow, having rushed past him, already light years away, begins to ache. Tears rinse his eyes. Falling toward the mattress, the crown of his head against Hester's left thigh, Diddy comes undone. His shoulders bulge with sobs, which he cannot, dares not, try to control. But Hester doesn't lean forward to embrace him. Without sitting up, she extends one arm and rests her palm between his shuddering shoulder blades.

Diddy waits for her touch to become healing, to stanch the warm grief. It doesn't.

"Tell me," says the girl.

"I can't." But he can. Words have dropped the temperature, chilled his grief, begun to still its flow. Wiping his eyes. "I'm crying for many things. For you. For me. And over what you said just now. If you only knew how I suffer from my kind of seeing. How it hurts to see everything . . . almost everything as ugly."

"You mean yourself."

"Me, too. Sure." More words. Surely Hester knows what they're doing to him. She must want it to happen. Diddy dry-eyed (now). Dry withered grief.

"That's why you accuse yourself of crimes."

If only it were so! Diddy sighed. Hester knew so much, yet she knew nothing.

"I'm sorry. I said it wouldn't be good for us to talk about that, and now I'm breaking the rule. Dalton, tell me something else. Tell me who you like or love."

"I loved my wife. At least I thought I did. I guess I love my brother, too, in a way. But I don't see him often. I probably don't really love him; I'd just like to be him. . . . I think I don't really like anybody except you."

The girl was silent.

"I wish I could embrace you right now." Then realizing that, being only inches away from her, he could do exactly that; if he wanted. But it isn't a simple embrace Diddy wants, so he doesn't reach out at all. "I want to make love to you."

Since they're not touching, Diddy has to look up. Discovers it's come back, no trick of memory: that same inexpressive face that he had seen yesterday. A face like a dead animal, or an internal organ never meant to be seen. Throbbing, opaque, not addressed to him or to anyone else. Disconnected. Suddenly Diddy feels horribly restless. Has to stand up and pace about the room. Glancing intermittently at Hester as he stalked, pivoted, and stalked. Her head was tilted downward.

(Now) Diddy mistrusts his feeling for the girl. A kind of vertigo, which he's walking off. Diddy alarmed. What's he been getting into? There's some kind of strong positive feeling for her, yes. But maybe it's mainly pity; what he'd felt once for a maimed stray cat he took in and nursed. Not love.

Looks at his watch. Only four-thirty. Diddy ends the silence, starts making excuses to leave. Still striding up and down, tearing apart. Though he senses how disappointed she is at his early departure, the need to leave is beyond his control.

"Don't go, Dalton. The visiting hour isn't over yet."

But Diddy won't stay only because she wants him to. To be a shade kinder, he produces a lie. "I have a business meeting at five. You know, it was hard finding any time today to visit you." Not the first lie he's told Hester.

Of course, Hester isn't fully acquainted with Diddy the Liar. Or maybe she does know he's lying, and decides anyway that the lie is to count as the truth. She'll accede to his need to be outside, to breathe. Ungraciously, resentfully even, she agrees to his going.

"But wait." She pulls his arm as he stands by the bed to kiss her goodbye. "This will only take a moment. Please comb me. My aunt usually does it, but she pulls my hair. I want you to do it."

"I'll be late."

"It'll just take a minute. Please!"

"All right."

Diddy, anxious, distracted, takes the comb from the night-table drawer and sits on the edge of Hester's bed. His coat already on, buttoned. With his right hand, he pushes the comb into the thick center of the girl's long silky blond hair; with his left hand he holds the upper portion of the hair he's combing downward so that if the comb has to plow its way through a tangle he can grip the hair at a higher place and prevent it from being strained at its roots in the scalp.

"I knew you could do it like that, without hurting. It's nice."

Diddy, pleased that he can please her, instantly becomes one of the other Diddys again. He leans over for a moment to smell her hair and brush it with his lips.

"Don't you want to stay?" Hester has seized his hands.

Diddy's panic returns. His old panic, that of not understanding. His lips go dry; his head, the back of his neck, his armpits wet with sweat. Putting down the comb, his job unfinished.

"I have to go," he says obstinately. "I'm sorry because it's the day before your operation. . . ."

"That's all right. Please stop."

And Diddy flees.

Of course, he has nowhere to go (now). Since he's not due at the television studio until nine-fifteen. Best plan: hail a taxi and return to the Rushland. Once there, try to nap for a few hours.

But not yet. Not so quickly closed within another synthetic small space. Diddy wants to remain outdoors in the yellowish twilight. And, tired as he is, to stroll. Walking down routine streets, vaguely headed for the center of town. Diddy is probably going to walk all the way, though it's not necessary to decide that in advance.

The heavy emotions are what animate him (now). Which is why it's some help to keep moving his legs. As soon as he'd left the hospital building, his panic was replaced by shame. Diddy feels ashamed of himself. A heavy vitreous emotion, two-thirds of the way from water to something dense and viscous. Shame floods his body with phlegm. And in the yellowish twilight, sullen violet thoughts. Diddy has at his disposal only the shadows of energy with which to struggle up, hauling himself hand over hand, into a clear light. But he's trying manfully. Crawling when necessary. Scraping his palms and knees. Unwilling to admit defeat, or the presence of an insurmountable wall.

What's the matter with him? You'd think Diddy was trapped back there in the hospital in the same fashion that he was trapped, or thought he was, in the darkened train compartment Sunday afternoon. No one had him in a corner (now). A beautiful woman who was offering him love had aroused in him an unprecedented tenderness and longing. What could be more different from a trap? A liberation, rather. A blessing. A miracle.

Diddy is heading toward the center of town. As he walks, his bony nervous arms within the tweed jacket and the Chesterfield coat punching at the air below his waist. Diddy is enraged at himself for having fled his good. For having pained his new love. Ordinarily, Diddy was not indecisive. Rarely shy with women. If

159

he'd behaved so erratically and self-indulgently with Hester, it must be connected with other matters that have become unclear. According to an old rule of psychic contagion: that absence of clarity or outright confusion in one, just one specific, local matter will end by infecting the whole of one's judgment.

Diddy, like any animal, has two eyes. Let's suppose that one eye is diseased, or has been traumatized. That stands for Incardona's death, and its attendant enigmas. The other eye is a perfectly healthy organ. That one stands for his tie with Hester, and their deepening connection with each other. With this condition, how could he have been such a fool? Foolish enough to expect one's clear-sighted eye can remain uncontaminated by the diseased one. Man, a creature of binocular vision, uses both eyes to see; with both eyes moving conjointly, can perceive depth. But it is well known that if one eye has a severe inflammation or a serious infection, or even so grave a flaw as a detached retina, which comes about through a physical injury to that eye alone, the same condition eventually tends to appear in the other eye, the perfectly healthy one. A sympathetic reaction.

That sympathy for the damaged part of him was what was blurring his relations with Hester. If he doesn't take care, he will ruin everything. As he's always known: the two, Hester and Incardona, go together. In him their destinies are linked. Good eye and bad eye, beautiful vision and recurrent nightmare. To feel properly about one he must decide, once and for all, how he feels about both.

About the workman's death. Does Diddy feel guilty or doesn't he? Since he called on Myra Incardona last night—was it only last night? it seems ages behind him —he feels less. Less guilty. That's as it should be. Those people are really animals. One shouldn't waste emotion on their fate. It's people like the Incardonas who make life a nightmare. Diddy won't feel guilty. He can't. No room in his life for guilt. For if Diddy so much as admits guilt through the door, front door or back door, of his house, be it the most spacious of dwellings, the puffing swelling monster will end by dispossessing him entirely.

About the girl. What does he feel toward this delicate, troubled creature? Who's strong, perhaps, where he is weak, but surely weak in some ways in which he's strong. Here, his feelings are clearer. The stupidity of running away! (Now) Diddy believes he really loves her. And he longs for Hester to know of his love, if it will give her pleasure. To know before she's wheeled into the operating room tomorrow morning.

Footsore Diddy, his heart beating faster than usual, is nearing the downtown section of the city. (Now) is the time to acknowledge that he doesn't want a taxi. Noticing that the clock on a bank façade says it's already a quarter to six, he goes into a drugstore and asks the soda jerk if there's a post office nearby. Yes. Arriving at five minutes to six, stands at the sloping counter carpeted with tan blotting paper to write out his telegram.

Sharing the counter, to his left: an elderly Negro woman, wearing the clothes of the self-respecting poor, has crumpled up one yellow form with a sigh and started another. Probably a request for money. Or the announcement of a relative's death.

Diddy's telegram should be delivered to the Warren Institute in less than an hour. Who will read it to Hester? Hopefully, Mrs. Nayburn won't have returned yet. Then it would be the disagreeable Gertrude who brings the telegram to Hester's room. But if it should be the crass meddling aunt who recites his declaration, so what? Diddy has nothing to hide.

The woman on his left is still struggling to print the letters. That make up the words. That make up the news, probably bad; or the plea for assistance. Diddy, who always got A's in Penmanship, has his own reasons for printing on his telegram form almost as slowly as she. For bearing down as hard as he can on the fatigued ballpoint pen, one of two attached by slender chains to the frame of the writing counter. Diddy digs the blunt point into the paper, as if he thought it was this piece of paper that would be delivered to Hester. And wanted to make something Braille-like that she could decipher herself, by moving her fingertips along the indentations. Of course, he knows perfectly well that this isn't so. Telegrams come typed. And must be read aloud to the blind. Perhaps Diddy

161

is writing in this heavy fashion because he wants to engrave the words on himself.

I LOVE YOU. I AM WITH YOU TOMORROW MORNING. DALTON.

Diddy hasn't returned to the Rushland. Leaving the post office, he continued on foot toward the center of town. After sending the telegram, easier to walk. Except for being hungry, feels he could walk forever. Stopped off at a small Chinese restaurant and ordered a cup of wonton soup and a plate of barbecued spareribs, but the soup was water and the ribs burnt meatless. Diddy plays with the inedible food a few moments, then pays up and leaves. Still hungry. Better not to be so fastidious. Second stop: a pizzeria, where he downs without complain a doughy triangle smeared with tasteless cheese and tomato sauce, then another, then a third, then a fourth.

Since eight o'clock he's been wandering up and down a brightly lit street about fifteen blocks from the Rushland.

Diddy is looking. "Science has proved that 90% of all knowledge is acquired visually." What about the other ten percent? Do those who have to make do on that small fraction discover the ninety percent to be a distraction? Seeing an adulteration of genuine knowledge?

Or is seeing necessary? Is it like "Ninety percent of the eye is water"? The viscous medium needed to support and shelter the miniature organs, the bland sea needed to float the precious intricate devices of sight?

Diddy looking. Is that necessary?

On a brightly lit street on which are congregated a burlesque house, a movie theatre showing skin flicks, two penny arcades jammed with leather-jacketed motorcyclists and girls in miniskirts, and stores selling party records, scatological ashtrays, back-number magazines, devices for practical jokers, and sex books.

Diddy is looking.

Comparing the sizes of breasts in the stills displayed outside the

162

Casino Burlesque with those outside the Victory Theatre. Browsing in old issues of *National Geographic* and *Silver Screen* in one bookstore; the latest issues of *The Justice Weekly, The Spanker's Monthly,* and *The Ladder* in another. Diddy the Voyeur. What does he feel? Amused? Disgusted? Curious? Something, but not very much, of all three. Yet Diddy is trying to feel. Feels more in one of the novelty stores, examining rubber monster masks. When he tries on a limp cool mask of Frankenstein's monster; and sees his rectangular, stitched, pathetic Boris Karloff face in the mirror. The harsh, sad joke of Diddy the Monster. Dreamed by Diddy the Good. . . . All the looking has made him vaguely restless in a sexual way. As he's leaving the novelty store, Diddy stops before another mirror. Admired his de-Frankensteined profile. Turns to the mirror full-face, tenses his biceps, then approvingly feels the muscle he's made in his left arm with his right hand.

Diddy touring one of the arcades. (Now) dispensing quarters for the shooting gallery at the back. He's already weighed himself: eighteen pounds underweight. And read the fortune which the machine ejected. "You are about to take an important trip." Diddy laughs and sticks the white card into his wallet. Has already tested the strength of his handgrip. "Above average," if the machine is to be believed. Which is not bad for a man who's pale as the inmate of a maximum-security penitentiary, and lean as a mandrake root. He has also played six games on a pinball machine. And on another machine, tested his skill as a driver. "Good Insurance Risk." (Now) Diddy has been sufficiently expert with the breech-lock rifle, scoring with every one of the last ten ducks that bobbed across the target area, to have won a prize. "The panda bear, the cigarette lighter, or the set of six wine glasses, mister?" Diddy chooses the stuffed panda, a foot-tall thick creature with big round ears and festoons of red ribbon about its neck; carries his prize onto the street. Into a taxi, and gives the driver the address of the television studio.

Which turns out to be quite near, so Diddy finds he's the first to have arrived. Quarter to nine. The Channel 10 executive who'd been at the company lunch today greets him, asking Diddy if he'd prefer to wait in the reception area and watch TV, or come in and observe what's happening in the studios at this very moment.

"I'll come in," says Diddy. "Where can I put this?" The panda. No explanation.

"On the receptionist's desk?" replies the producer doubtfully. "Okay? She's gone home for the night."

Diddy wonders if he's about to be asked where he got the panda, or why he's carrying it. Puts down his prize. Then follows the man through a pair of swinging doors. "Silence." Down a corridor, to what Diddy's guide refers to as "our Studio A." At one end of a very large room, whose ceiling is two floors high and crisscrossed with lighting equipment, the local community theatre is taping their biggest success last spring, *Long Day's Journey into Night,* for NET; to be shown locally next month, says the man. Diddy peers through the huge window. Hard to get a good view of the actors or even of the set, because the cameramen are continually rolling their black machines in and out for close-ups. And since he's on the other side of a glass wall, Diddy is experiencing the play only as a soundless pantomime. Nevertheless, having seen the play on Broadway as well as the movie, he recognizes the passage the actors are performing. Remembering not only the sense of the scene, but even some of the lines. The play had moved Diddy greatly; and this scene in particular. The talented younger son, a portrait of the playwright himself, finally indicts his debauched older brother; confronts him with the failure of his life. With love, with compassion, with loathing. But that's almost simple, compared to the impasse between Diddy and his brother. Is it Diddy who should reproach Paul? Or Paul, Diddy?

On to our Studio B. A much smaller room. "We're taping part of the eleven o'clock news. Most of that goes out live, except for where we use some newsreel footage. They're timing that now." Is it the same man?

Yes. There in the spacious soundproofed cube, seated behind his desk, a map of the world at his left, a screen on his right, is the bland creature whose every word Diddy had strained to hear only four evenings ago. Last Sunday night that face was a blurred image on the glassy surface of the picture tube, its features built up out of tiny lines. (Now) it is the man's own face, his flesh, which Diddy sees. Glass does intervene. As a large rectangular wall that separates them, keeping Diddy outside and the newscaster inside; but at least it isn't the glass itself which renders the face.

"Is it possible to hear what he's saying?" Diddy whispers to the producer at his side.

Certainly. The man presses a red button next to the entrance to the studio.

Yes, there's the unctuous, denatured voice. For all the naturalness of the sound, Diddy might as well be watching the television in his room at the Rushland, lying on his bed. But maybe the quality of the sound reproduction in the corridor isn't to blame. Remember, this is the voice belonging to the man who reads the news who had no news, no information. Did he tonight? Not tonight, either. Just more about the unspeakable war, the one in which territory doesn't change hands and the sole measure of each victory is how many small-boned yellow bodies, with flesh charred by napalm or shattered by metal, huddle and sprawl on the ground after the battle. Waiting to be counted. The newscaster deploys the usual senseless numbers; repeats the well-worn gruesome tautologies of self-righteousness. With a broadly serious set to his face. Lies, but terrible smiling lies.

The producer has excused himself, and left Diddy lingering alone outside the viewing window of Studio B. Diddy presses his face against the glass; listening. If Diddy were given to tirades, he could deliver one (now) The words burning his throat. But against whom would it be aimed? There are so many targets for his revulsion, not least of which is himself. Diddy the Self-Denouncer. But he is scarcely the only thing that's wrong in this world.

The newscaster has stood up, and is jabbing a pointer against the map behind his desk.

There's no end to Diddy's rage; little economy in it, either. How can one slake the rage for self-correction? Provoked by the lies and inanities being disseminated by the newscaster, Diddy will once more try to embark on the endless mission of correcting his feelings.

The newscaster has some words to add to a still photograph,

projected on a screen to his left, which shows an American soldier interrogating a kneeling, blindfolded, teenage enemy prisoner of war. But Diddy isn't listening any more.

Reminded of the behavior of his own country, currently engaged in the cumbersome, drawn-out murder of a small defenseless nation —this being only the latest of the century's roll call of historical atrocities, of crimes that baffle the imagination—Diddy's own agonizing during the last four days over the death of merely one person shrank (now) to humiliating size. Considered as an action performed on this planet and in this decade, what Diddy has done is barely visible. Set Diddy's deed against the scale of reality, and it seems petty and amateurish. And his lacerating remorse little more than presumption, a kind of boastfulness; at best, the foolish endearing weakness of the overcivilized. Diddy the Demonic must learn the diminutive proportions of his misdeeds. By this, Diddy doesn't mean to excuse or to condone his inadvertent slaying of Incardona. Murder remains murder, a sluggish and putrid stain upon the feelings. As a death is still a death.

Dalton Harron is no longer Diddy the Good, if indeed he ever was. That may be conceded. Still, it's right to consider those far more vicious and ample murders being committed, ceaselessly, all over the world. With the assassins scarcely ever suffering the slightest ache of guilt. Why would they? When it's done for one's country, one is cheered for slaying a hundred Incardonas every hour: not only bashing in the skulls of the husbands, who may in some cases be able to defend themselves, but disemboweling the wives and throwing the children out of the window, too. It's the rare spirit, the exceptional murderer, who knows enough to feel guilty anyway—even though he's praised for his deed, and congratulated for doing his job. And the others, like Diddy, who haven't been licensed, who've stayed out of the arenas where killing is the respectable business of the day, have their corresponding, equally gullible role to enact. Diddy, too. Though he should know better.

For the questionable reward of being at peace with his neighbors, Diddy has swallowed the rotten bait.

Taken for his own truth the old lies about what makes an act good or bad.

It's not for an act of violence, resulting in a death, that Diddy flogs himself; and would, if he were caught by the law, be executed or at least shut away in prison. It's for not having the relevant job or identity, that of a hero or a professional killer. For not having a cause. For lacking a sanctifying public goal. For only killing, not overkilling.

Diddy, looking through the window at the bland newscaster, is glad to be reminded of the world. His own crime last Sunday appears in a saner perspective. And, which is more important, so does his ordeal of guilt.

Hadn't Diddy the Educated known all this for years? That the extravagant self-punishing moralism of essentially peaceful folk like himself serves no one but the mighty, consecrated killers of entire peoples. Confirming their authority. Making them more secure, more inviolate. Today no one has the right to be innocent about these matters, and Diddy is ashamed of his innocence. Over Incardona, what a waste of agony. Over Hester, what a risk of love.

A squeak of door hinges; enter heavy feet in a parody of tiptoeing across the carpet. James Watkins, Hubert's burly son, approaches. "Hello, Harron. See you got here early." Diddy shifted his legs mechanically, turned away from the smiling herald of absent-minded genocide on the far side of the large glass pane. Holding out his hand. "Hello, Mr. Watkins." Out into the reception area. Comensky had arrived, too, and was sprawled on a couch; thumbing through a tattered issue of *Life*. "The others will be along any moment, I guess," said Watkins, rubbing his dry reddish hands together. An old mannerism.

Diddy took out a cigarette and sat down. "Can I have one, too?" said Comensky. "I'm trying to stop, so I don't buy them any more." Diddy nodded, held out the pack. "Say, Harron, did you see my latest thing in the *Transactions of the American Microscopical Society?*" Diddy said he hadn't. "Hell, I'm glad I thought to bring a few offprints along with me tonight." Holding the unlit cigarette in his left hand and matches in his right. Comensky stuck

167

the cigarette in his mouth; began to dig one-handed into his inside jacket pocket. The wrong hand. Didn't Comensky remember he was, as he evidently was, right-handed? Eventually he has to put the matches somewhere, too, before he could pull out an offprint and shove it into Diddy's hand. "Thanks," said Diddy.

A few minutes later, Reager and Michaelson came through the door. (Now) we were ready, the group complete. Diddy guessed from the high spirits of the latecomers that they had both come from Reager's house; to which Michaelson had been invited for dinner, where he had put away one of those lavish meals with too many sauces, and himself been served up as the evening's morsel for Reager's ever less attractive, still unmarried daughter. They seemed to be talking about Evie as they entered. "Hey, Alex," Comensky called to Michaelson, "you didn't happen to see my piece in the summer issue of *Transactions,* did you?" Michaelson shook his head. "Wait, I brought you one. Just a minute. Don't go away. I have it here in my pocket."

Without giving the least encouragement to this gift, Michaelson slumped down on the left side of the long couch. Diddy (now) in the middle. Trying to keep clear of Comensky's elbow flailing out to his right. For again, Comensky has to dismiss, temporarily, the useful objects that seem naturally to encumber his hands. A paper cup of water drawn from the cooler in the hallway must be balanced on the narrow armrest of the couch, a copy of the *Courier-Gazette* set down on one knee, a barely smoked cigarette stubbed out in the free-standing metal ashtray next to the couch. Comensky plunges one hand inside his jacket, pulling at something. Almost as if he were, very awkwardly, trying to undress himself. Like a man with an urgent need to piss who discovers his pants have an unfamiliar button fly instead of the usual zipper.

Diddy is amused by Comensky's awkward zeal on his own behalf. The persistence of the born collector. Comensky, yet one more collector to have recently passed before Diddy's view, doesn't collect little objects or trophies. Like postage stamps, or seashells. This time, someone who collects his own ideas; then eagerly gives away, even to those who aren't interested, printed transcriptions of them. The items he purveys aren't the true prize, the original article of value, as is the case with stamp collectors trading real stamps. Or real shells. . . . More like souvenirs.

We were all sitting (now). The two senior men, Watkins and Reager, have commandeered the comfortable lounge chairs stationed in opposite corners, facing the long couch. On the couch, the three junior men. Michaelson had been handed his offprint and pocketed it. Comensky was looking at the paper again. Diddy, just being. Trying to be.

A very brief wait. Then the producer of "Your Community" enters the reception area through the swinging doors, his arm around the shoulder of the newscaster. "So try to work that in too, will you?"

"Roger," the newscaster said. "See you in an hour." And opened the front door.

"See you, Bud." The door closed behind the newscaster. The producer turns to the five men. "All here?" Beaming. "Good! Let's go into one of the rehearsal rooms, so we can start right away. . . ."

"I'd rather we began our discussion out here," said Reager, spacing out his phrases to allow for several puffs on his cigar. "There's someone joining us in a moment. Then we can move inside." He puffed some more on the cigar, as if to underscore how comfortable he found his chair and to demonstrate his body's unwillingness to move.

Diddy immediately guessed what mood Reager's in. He was going to give the producer a hard time and see how he responded.

How did the man respond? "Certainly, Mr. Reager." Well, that's that. The producer has lost. Reager, who was full of whims, scorned anyone who yielded to them without at least a token struggle. Which is what the producer had done. Changing his schedule to suit Reager, without so much as a question. Reager must want to fight. Doesn't he know he's already won?

But the producer has an ally. Watkins, who wasn't afraid of bickering and liked giving Reager a run for his money. "Now, Howard, why don't you tell us who's coming?" Watkins held an unlit pipe in his hand.

Reager turned on him coolly. "It's a surprise."

Who is coming, Diddy wondered? Has Reager added someone

169

to the program without telling anyone else? Some new young man, a rising star of the company, whom he wants to flatter? Or will it just be Reager's beloved Evie, carted along in the unquenchable hope that some day some young man will find her attractive?

Of course, the producer didn't know what was going on. Or how far matters had advanced. Still optimistic or merely insensitive, he was busily organizing our temporary work space. Intending by this shaping of space to assert his own authority. He'd gone out for a moment, then returned with a metal folding chair which he places in the center of the reception area. Then straddled the chair, with both arms hugging the back of the chair to his chest.

"Now." Looking from face to face. "As I'm sure you know, we want this show to be as informal as possible. 'Your Community' is a monthly public affairs show, sponsored by the Downtown Merchants Association, and designed to give people in the area served by Channel 10 a better understanding of the free enterprise system, and the problems and responsibilities of American businessmen. Your firm, being one of the oldest and most respected industries in this neck of the woods, is a natural for the show. In fact, I can't understand why we haven't had you folks on before."

Diddy knew. Until recently, the company's directors had simply not seen any benefit for sales in public relations addressed to the general public. That Watkins and Reager had (now) consented to "Your Community" doing a show on the company was more evidence of how much, in the last year, the serenity of the management had been shaken.

"Anyway, now we've got you," continued the producer. "And we're real pleased. But this show we're going to do on Saturday isn't like doing the White House Department Store, our last program's business-of-the-month. Everybody knows about department stores. Or they think they do. But microscopes are pretty technical stuff. Am I right?"

"Go on," said Reager. He looked at Diddy, who looked away. "Do you mean that you don't know much about microscopes?"

"Well, when it comes to science, all us laymen are pretty much in the same boat. My point is this, Mr. Reager, I'm afraid this isn't educational television. Though Lord knows, I wish it were."

"Listen, Harvey, why don't you tell me exactly what you're driving at?" said Reager, grimacing.

A first name or the man's last name? The producer, who was either First Name Harvey or Harvey Last Name, Diddy couldn't remember (now), shifted in his flat metal saddle. "It's really very simple, nothing to worry about. All I mean is that we *are* a sponsored show. And our sponsors want the viewers to have fun. You know." He smiled, as if demonstrating the exact quantity of viewers' pleasure he had in mind. "It's fine if people watching the show learn something. But they should be able to enjoy themselves watching us, too."

"Us?"

"Well, naturally, Mr. Reager, I have to include myself, since I'm privileged to act as your host on the show. And speaking of yours truly, this is as good a time as any for me to explain what I'm going to do. You gentlemen can get an idea of what you'll be doing."

"Fire away," said Watkins genially. Diddy had noticed that the old man usually made a point of being amiable whenever he noticed that Reager was annoyed at something.

And Reager was annoyed, unmistakably. Isn't it odd, thought Diddy, what irritates people? This Mr. Harvey or Harvey Something had given Reager no particular offense. Sure, he was an effusive fool. But so were most of the people with whom Reager came in contact. Why had this man been singled out? And what accounts for the instant unprovoked antipathy that sometimes arises between people? And does a person always know when—by his sheer existence or quality or smell or look, and not by anything particular he's done—he has unwittingly created that sort of feeling in someone? If one's instincts are in order, one should know. Something wrong with Diddy's instincts: that he hadn't recognized he had aroused such a feeling in Incardona, from the moment he'd broken in on the scene of his labor on the track. Likely, though, that Incardona's sensory apparatus was in good order. Likely that he knew he'd aroused the same kind of instant antipathy in Diddy. And, knowing it, started to react to it with anger and hostility—long before Diddy knew what he himself felt. Known it, how? Felt it? Smelled it?

Mr. Harvey or Harvey Something seemed to be receiving some of the vibrations of hostility from Reager, but wasn't ready to admit defeat. He paused, gazed from face to face. Diddy watched from behind his wall, observes him reflecting. Has Reager already made him lose his balance? Maybe. The producer seemed to realize that the time had arrived to make a stand. Now or never. If it wasn't too late. Without acknowledging the last words spoken, perhaps because Watkins seemed to be on his side without being asked, and without looking at Reager, he turned to the three junior men on the couch. "Mr. Michaelson, Mr. Harron, and Mr. Comensky, we haven't heard from you. Have any questions you'd like to ask?"

Diddy, knowing that this was a rebuke to Reager's cantankerousness. But doubting that this move to bring them into the conversation could work. For one thing, the two men on either side of Diddy hadn't been listening. Some minutes ago, Comensky had taken still another reprint of his article from the supply stashed in the inside of his jacket, placed it on top of the *Courier-Gazette* which still lay across his thighs, and had been, all this while, surreptitiously rereading it. Michaelson had a pad and pencil in his lap, ostensibly, to take notes; already has covered several pages with doodles of naked women and airplanes. That leaves Diddy, who had been listening. But, though listening, reluctant to say anything (now). Why should he bait this fool, since Reager seemed to have become, in a brief time, so devoted to that task? And why should he appease or mollify him, which was the role that had fallen to Watkins?

What could Diddy say? "Well . . . It's Mr. Harvey, isn't it?" A lucky guess. The producer nodded, affably. "How long have you been doing this show, Mr. Harvey?"

Diddy meant his words to be neutral. But they'd come out sounding like sarcasm, and Mr. Harvey flinched perceptibly at what he took to be a fresh rebuke from so unexpected a quarter.

From across the room, Reager waved one of his precious Cuban cigars, offering it to Diddy, welcoming him to the team of baiters.

Diddy the Depressed. How hard it is to say anything, just for itself. With the best will in the world, you find that you are saying it for someone. Someone, not you, whom you have no conscious desire to serve. Diddy wishing he could reroute his words.

Comensky went on reading his own article; Michaelson was still doodling. Diddy, who thought he might be blushing, imagines he is somewhere else.

"Okay, here goes," said the producer, flinging out his cheerful tone as if it were a net in which he might entrap the others. "We're all busy executives, right? So I'll make this as brief as I can." Reager yawned. Watkins finally lit his pipe. "Here's the format of the show. First, I'll give a little introductory material on microscopes. You know, background. Then I'll be commenting on some stills we'll project that show activities of the company from its beginnings, over the decades, down to the present day. Then the panel discussion in which Harron, Comensky, and Michaelson are participating, that I'll moderate. Then I'll introduce Mr. Watkins, who'll tell us, I hope, a little about his grandfather, his father, and himself. You know, the human interest aspect. After that, some remarks by Mr. Reager, your managing director. We'll follow with footage of the factory and offices as they look today, and close with some shots of the company picnic at Lake Canandaigua last May. All the visuals have been supplied by Mr. Wurst; and we've made a selection from what he gave us which I'll run off for you tonight."

Diddy looked over at Reager to see how he was taking it. Not too well, Diddy suspected. The producer apparently thought otherwise. So confident was Harvey that his adversary had at last calmed down that he thought he could afford to say something just to please Reager.

"Some of you may not know that these last photographs were loaned to us courtesy of Miss Evie Reager."

"A Bolex was what she used."

"Yes, indeed, Mr. Reager. They certainly are fine pictures."

"They should be! She's got an eye, that girl of mine. I've asked her to watch this evening and give us the benefit of her criticism. I'm sure we can all use it, Harvey. She should have been here by now. I don't know what's keeping her."

Diddy leaned back in the center of the couch, stretched his legs, lit another cigarette. It was going to be a hard evening.

After the run-through of Saturday's program, Reager and his daughter invited everyone back to their house for a nightcap. None of us really wanted to go. Watkins said no with the practiced brusque delivery of a man who's always been rather sparing with his yes. The junior men, for whom the invitation was in fact intended, hesitated a moment. Diddy, wary of his habit of humoring his employers, tried to keep his voice casual but decisive. Pleading fatigue, he begged off.

We left the television studio. Harvey's car was parked behind the station, so he left us immediately. Watkins' chauffeured Lincoln Continental was waiting at the curb to carry him away. Evie, explaining that she'd had to park two blocks down the street, led the way for what was left of the group. Comensky and Michaelson flanked her father. Diddy, intending to see them as far as the car, brought up the rear. Carrying his panda doll again.

"We'll drop you at your hotel, Harron," said Reager. To accept the ride would have been prudent: then they would have seen him going into the hotel, headed for rest. Whereas, if he took a cab, the suspicion was bound to cross at least Reager's wary mind that Diddy wasn't tired at all, but just had other, gayer plans for the evening.

But Diddy didn't want to ride with them. Anyway, Diddy is past prudence, or should be, after all he's gone through. "Thanks, Mr. Reager. I'll get a cab." To hell with the old buzzard. Let him think what he likes. "Evie, would you like to have this?" The stuffed panda. He put the large black and white creature in her arms.

Succeeded in finding a taxi almost immediately.

When he returned to the Rushland, it was already midnight. Passing the industrious student night clerk with a nod. And with not a thought of staying up until the "City Edition" of the *Courier-Gazette* was dumped at the hotel at two o'clock.

Diddy took another hot bath, gratefully pulled back the freshly changed sheets, and crawled into bed. Tired. But not, he thought, sleepy: assuming that his anxiety over Hester's operation tomorrow would keep him awake most of the night. He was wrong. Falling asleep turned out to be easy, since in his sleep Diddy could dream of Hester. And think thoughts even more fearful than those he allowed himself in his most anxious sleepless hours.

In Diddy's dream, he's visiting Hester at the hospital on the eve of her operation. Diddy enters the familiar white room, which in the dream is just as it really is. But Hester isn't wearing the same dark glasses. These frames are square, not oval. And hold lenses of a blacker hue than the ones she always wore; made of thick celluloid rather than glass. There's a tiny hole in the center of each lens.

Diddy sitting stiffly in the chair near the end of the bed. "New glasses?" he says stiffly.

"New treatment," Hester replies. "The doctors say I should have been wearing them ever since my condition was diagnosed."

There's some good news in these odd glasses, Diddy thinks. What is it? Of course! The tiny hole in each lens signifies that Hester retains some power of sight. She's not totally blind. But that's not the same as being able to see. Can she? Could she see all along? Then why didn't she see him leave the compartment last Sunday?

But then Diddy feels apprehensive. Because the new glasses also signify something wrong with Hester that he hasn't understood. He's heard of these glasses before. They're the kind prescribed for a detached retina. How did that happen to Hester? Through an injury? Or an infection? The similarity of the two lenses indicates that both retinas are detached. But that's serious. The element of time is crucial if she's not to become completely blind. As soon as this condition is diagnosed, the patient should be put in a hospital, kept in bed, not allowed to move. Any move might detach the retina further. Until the operation, Hester should be treated like a crate of raw eggs.

But if that's the care she needs, Hester has already undergone great and unnecessary risks. The train ride itself, its high-speed velocity, its rocking and swaying motion. The abrupt stop in the

175

tunnel. Diddy remembered how, when the train convulsively started up again, Hester had cried out. Then he'd thought that, being unable to see, she was afraid; he knew (now) it was because her eyes pained her, were coming further unstuck. And worst, and least necessary among all the risks, making love in the lavatory. Why didn't she tell Diddy she was so fragile? Had he known then what he (now) knows, he would never have gone with her to that small room. In her condition, that was nothing less than committing an act of assault. Is that what Hester had been trying to make him do? As Incardona had provoked him, until Diddy struck him with the crowbar. The two of them, accomplices? Hester trying to lead Diddy to injure her, or be the agent of her physical injury? To commit, involuntarily, still another crime?

Diddy cries out in his sleep with despair. Almost flings open his eyes, then falls back into the dream.

The scene changes to the hospital operating theatre. From the lamps overhead bright light flows down, drenching the covered figure on the table, the doctors and nurses in white, the instrument trays on their trolleys, the anaesthetist's equipment. Diddy above, in the gallery with many other spectators. But not just sitting and watching. He's standing in an aisle, holding something: a Bolex camera. Taking pictures of the operation. Diddy has some reason to be here among the medical students, though he's not one himself. And the reason isn't his personal relation with Hester. It's his job; he's a professional photographer. In the dream, Diddy is working for a studio that does legal and medical photography. Footage of operations, to be shown in medical schools for the instruction of students, and in hospitals for interns learning their art; still photographs of accidents and homicides, to be used as evidence in law suits and in murder trials. (Now), very carefully, he's photographing Hester's operation. The operation is delicate.

Until recently, the most advanced method used in such operations was cryo-surgery. A very slender tube containing extremely cold gas is carefully aimed, and the gas fired through the tube. If the surgeon's aim is accurate, the spike of high-speed gas pierces the front of the eyeball, passes through the water, and strikes the

176

rear wall of the eye at the exact spot where the retina is unhinged. The velocity and force of the gas are such that in seconds the loose ends of the retina are glued or welded together.

But Hester's doctor is trained in the newer technique, in which a laser beam is used. The same target, however. And the same principle: assault and puncture at a distance, without hard metal tools, but with gas and light instead. There's a murder weapon to confound the experts!

The doctor holds the miniature laser in his hands, pointing it like a toy machine gun at Hester's head. The gun gets closer. Her eyelids held widely apart with clamps. He fires. But there's no smell, not even that of burning flesh. Does she feel the tiny light burning through her eye? How can the surgeon be sure the light isn't traveling right past the eye, into the brain? She must be in pain. See how she's turning restlessly on the table. The doctors continue. Diddy would like to do something, but he's too far away. So he goes on photographing, his camera clicking.

(Now) Diddy is back in Hester's room, sitting by her bed, waiting for her to regain consciousness. Her whole face is swathed in bandages. Diddy wonders if this is necessary. How, when she wakes, will she be able to speak? To call his name, to ask for a glass of water? How can she breathe? And if Diddy can't see her face, not only can't he have a dialogue with her; he can't even be sure it's Hester. Already growing on Diddy that it's not she. That long form under the blankets doesn't look like Hester's body. Too tall, and built like a man, broad in the shoulders and narrow in the hips. Diddy suddenly has a horrible premonition that he's at the wrong bedside, keeping vigil over the wrong body. He knows whose body it is, too. But just for the moment, the name of the person eludes him. Someone he knows. Rather: knew. For this person is not breathing at all.

But then the dream changes, and the body beside whom Diddy sits is clearly Hester's. She has awakened and cries, "I can't see." Tries to claw the bandages off her face. Doctors and nurses come rushing through the door of her little room, crowd around the narrow iron bedstead, bend over her solicitously. Diddy is pushed aside. The medical personnel seem to be conferring. Diddy, squashed against the wall near the lavatory, wants to hear. But he's not allowed. Somehow, though, he knows anyway what the doctors and nurses are saying, without hearing. They've made the wrong diagnosis. Enraged, Diddy shouts: "But I told you so, you idiots! I told you that before." Paying no attention to Diddy, the doctors and nurses lift Hester's limp body on to a wheeled stretcher and take her out of the room. Diddy races after them, down long identical corridors. Sometimes the stretcher, with its precious burden and its white attendants, gets out of sight. This is when Diddy panics. He'll never be able to find Hester's operating room on his own. There are so many.

Where are they? He's lost them.

Down one more empty corridor, Diddy again catches sight of the ghostly party. Tall wooden doors, like those to Watkins' chapel at the factory, open to admit the medical team with their patient. Diddy wants to follow, but someone who resembles Comensky bars the way. "You can't go in, Harron," he shouts. "They're working on Top Secret Classified material in that laboratory."

Diddy pleads, "Damn you to hell, it's only an operating room!" Frantically trying to convince Comensky. The man is adamant. But after a while relents somewhat. Though Diddy still can't enter, he can peek through the keyhole. Kneeling, presses his left eye against the rectangular metal plate.

Like looking through a microscope. On the metal plate there are even some microscope-like devices that Diddy can adjust.

A large knurled wheel which supplies a coarse adjustment: the pinion head. This operates by a rack-and-pinion gear and changes the elevation of the tube.

Two smaller knobs, one on the right and one on the left, which supply the fine adjustment: the micrometer heads. On the right one a micrometer scale is inscribed so that the exact amount of vertical motion may be determined. This fine adjustment has definite upper and lower limits, and reaching either of which refuses to be turned farther. Movement ceases as soon as the objec-

178

tive touches the cover glass over the specimen, thus preventing damage to either object or lens.

Hester is the specimen beneath Diddy's eye. Turning the knobs very slowly, he moves the tube up and down gradually, seeking the most accurate focus.

There it is, clear as glass. The view Diddy wants. Hester lying again on the operating table, like a slide on the stage. But there are no students in this amphitheatre, as there were during the other operation. Has entry been barred to them as well? Apparently, Diddy thinks, these high-and-mighty doctors don't want their students to know when they've made a mistake.

The doctor is doing something with a scalpel to Hester's eyes. Diddy tries to see, because this must be the important part. But how small Hester looks! The rest are tiny figures, too. Diddy's view is slipping out of focus. He turns the pinion head, then the double micrometer head. Moves the knobs slowly at first, then rapidly. But can't seem to clear up the trouble. The image is shrinking, becoming indecipherable. "I think I have a defective instrument here," he says to no one in particular. But what Diddy is really thinking is that a microscope, any microscope, is inappropriate for this kind of scrutiny. And there isn't anyone to say that to. This is a world that loves the small.

From his kneeling position, Diddy looks up at Comensky, who is slouching to one side of the door, his arms loosely folded like a bored guard in some rarely visited museum. "Can't you tell me anything, you bastard?" Diddy snarls. "At least tell me what the doctors think it is."

"Corneal opacities, I think," replies Comensky in a lazy voice. Scratching his scalp.

Diddy scrambles to his feet, knocking over the microscope. "But I told them that! Those doctors had that diagnosis all along."

"Maybe they forgot," drawls Comensky.

"They've got no right to forget!" Diddy yells angrily. "It's sheer cruelty. Why do they make her suffer so?"

Comensky shrugs his shoulders. Now he, too, is going out of focus. A man with different hair, features, complexion, build. Looks like that Harvid, Harvid or something, from the television studio. A new resource. Diddy's microscope is broken, but other ways of seeing exist. Less diminutive in outlook. "Can I watch the operation on TV?" Harvid nods, points down the hall.

Diddy runs to the room Harvid had indicated, throws open the door, and finds himself in his own room at the Rushland. He switches on his set. All the channels are off. Blank. (Now) Diddy knows he's been tricked. But when he opens the door to leave, it's the corridor of the hotel he sees. Not the hospital. Really tricked! How will he ever get back to the Warren Institute, which is miles away? For suddenly Diddy knows Hester's in terrible danger. The anaesthetic already administered, her eyeballs slit open with a scalpel, the doctors must operate immediately. But a telegram has just been received in the operating room. Eye Bank regrets that it has no corneal transplants available today.

Wait! There's a possible solution. By a great stroke of luck, Diddy happens to know a suitable corpse. Someone recently dead; someone who was strong and healthy while alive, and is likely to possess a full complement of vigorous organs. If he could obtain Incardona's eyes and bring them in time to the hospital, Hester's sight could be saved. A lovely justice in this scheme; not just necessity. For them the workman's death wouldn't have been a complete waste. Diddy the Criminal not wholly culpable. Equipped with Incardona's eyes, Hester will see again. And through Hester, Incardona will go on living. Diddy will have them both.

Diddy rushes to the elevator on the fourth floor of the Rushland but it isn't in its right place. No time to look! Runs to the door marked "Exit," and hurtles down a long flight of stairs, taking two and three steps at a time. It's so dark. Diddy reminded of the tunnel. Childhood memories, too: steeling himself to venture alone into the cook's closet, the damp cellar, the dark pantry. But no, he mustn't go back there (now), to the house in Allentown. That's even farther from the hospital.

The bottom of the stairs. Light; a door; Diddy pushes it open. He's on the street level. But not the street scarred with trolley tracks in front of the Rushland. Is Diddy lost? Why doesn't he have a map? Diddy remembers how Paul, everyone, had always praised his sense of direction. He can't have lost that skill, which permits him to figure out fairly easily where he is, wherever he is, including situations where most people get lost. He just has to relax, breathe deeply, not fret or feel sorry for himself. It will come.

It does come. This street looks like Manhattan. Oh, Christ! Broadway and Forty-fourth Street. There's what's left of the Astor; and the dark shabby shell of the Paramount Theatre, closed and then opened and then closed and then opened and (now) closed for the last time. Its white, letterless marquee. An ignoble tombstone. Diddy is stranded among drunks and honking cars and whores and tourists. How will Diddy get back upstate, to the funeral parlor to find Incardona and rip the eyes out of the cadaver? Then to the hospital, to press the bleeding balls of flesh into the surgeon's waiting hands? A trip of many hours away. By the time Diddy arrives, the operation will have been called off. Hester dismissed. Returned, sightless forever, to her white room. But the surgeons mustn't give up. And Diddy urges himself not to lose heart either. If he just keeps moving, then he's getting closer. No motion without the abridgment of distance, some distance.

He'll have to catch a train. Perhaps if he runs to the station, the Privateer will be just about to leave. Diddy runs. His chest hurts. How out of condition he's gotten lately! Diddy, who won a medal in track at college, used to be able to run without tiring. Paul seems to be somewhere in this part of the dream. Maybe telling Diddy to run faster. But that's easy advice for sedentary Paul, who spends eight hours a day at the piano.

On time. The train, but not Diddy. Diddy is late. No time to purchase a ticket. Racing to find a helpful sign, something indicating the right gate or track number. Down a flight of stairs, like flying. The starting signal has been given. An official at the end of the long dirty platform waving a yellow signal light above his head. Diddy kneels down, gets into position, counts One-Two-Three under his breath, then leaps up and sprints down the platform. Past shouting conductors and train officials who want to intercept him, to detain him, to question him. How long it is. Diddy won't stop. They'll have to catch him. The train at the end is so small, so far away. His eyes darting back and forth from the platform to the trembling chain of coaches just starting up, Diddy runs down the endless platform toward the last car.

Sweating Diddy awoke with all his bedclothes fallen on the floor. His wristwatch curled up on the night table beside the bed: four-thirty. He could hardly catch his breath.

Diddy still tired. But apprehensive about falling back to sleep. Maybe the ugly dream would be resumed, like the second act of a play after a brief smoke in the lobby. Wiser, perhaps, to get up, take a shower to wipe the sweat and grime of his ordeal off his body, and do some work. Duva wanted a detailed report on the conference from him. Quite properly, Diddy had planned to write this after the conference had adjourned. Say, this Sunday. But what were the chances that anything of note was going to happen today, the last day? Slight. Diddy can just as well write it (now).

The first draft in longhand. By eight o'clock or so, he'll dare to use his Olivetti. Which is what Diddy did. Finishing only a few moments before it was time to go down for the limousine. Puts stamps on the envelope, leaves it at the reception desk to be mailed to New York.

Diddy finding it particularly hard to sit through Friday's meeting. Not only because it was the last; apparently set aside for redundant summings-up of what had already been decided, and for the usual tributes to leading participants and displays of company chauvinism. Also because Diddy has decided to be utterly silent. Having already written his report of the conference and formulated his recommendations, he had no intention of saying a word (now) that might provoke someone into making a new suggestion. Which might mean writing a postscript to his report. Nothing must happen at the plant. Everyone must be quite lifeless and speak only cardboard words, so that Diddy may escape intact to Hester.

He left the meeting as early as he could, arriving at the hospital at four-thirty. The operation was scheduled to begin at three o'clock, and to last for at least two hours. But as he approached the head nurse's office to inquire if the operation had started on time, he caught sight of the loathsome aunt hurrying down the hall toward him, her arms waving stiffly. Diddy knew instantly that things were already over, and had gone badly.

"Oh, Dalton dear! How glad I am to see you! Our poor darling is already back in her room, resting. She's still under the anaesthetic, and we won't be able to see her until this evening. Dr. Collins says there's nothing to worry about. She's a mighty healthy girl, he says. Only—" the woman faltered.

"I understand," said Diddy grimly.

"Do you?"

"Of course I do! You're telling me the operation was unsuccessful."

Mrs. Nayburn simply stared, opened her mouth as if to speak, then closed it again. She was taking a handkerchief from her purse to blot the tears in her eyes.

"I know the doctors always were a little pessimistic. Still, I was so sure they'd find a way. And then, after only an hour, Dr. Collins gave up. Only an hour!"

"What did he say?" said Diddy roughly.

"That there's nothing medical science knows at this time that can help her, and that she never had more than a fifty-fifty chance. Oh, why did we ever bother? Raising our hopes like that! It isn't fair."

Diddy refused to console the woman, who seemed far sorrier for herself than for Hester. Would save his sympathy for the person who deserved it.

"And the bills! Dalton, you have no idea how much this is costing her grandfather and me. And to think it was all for nothing!" Diddy was heading for the elevator, speechless with sorrow and rage. The woman scurrying along to keep up with his long strides. "The bills. . . ."

Well, it was easier to speak than to listen to this drivel, pretending to be a stone wall. At the elevator, Diddy turned on the aunt and looked at her sternly. "Mrs. Nayburn, I intend to help with Hester's hospital expenses. So please stop fretting about that."

"You do?" said the woman in an incredulous tone that was partly feigned, partly genuine. The small sharp eyes that Diddy hated, widening. "May I ask why?"

"You know perfectly well. Because I want to marry Hester, if she'll have me."

Diddy paused to let the woman play with her face and try on several different reactions. She started with "Why, Dalton!" Then quickly realized surprise was the wrong tack. Without transition, she switched to reassurance. "What do you mean, will she have you? Of course she will!" Diddy making his face as stern as he could, so Mrs. Nayburn would understand that approach was wrong, too. She settled, finally, for affectionate sagacity. "You know, I knew it all along. All along. Well, then, it *was* for a good purpose that the good Lord brought us here. He didn't choose to restore my baby's sight. But he did find her a wonderful husband."

The elevator opened. "I hope Hester thinks so. Please excuse me, I have to return to work. Tell her I'll be back." The woman's jaw dropped. Two desires. One, to follow Diddy into the elevator, to continue this extraordinary conversation. The other, to hurry to her niece's room, drag her by the hair out of her anaesthetized sleep, and pour out the news of Diddy's intentions. The result of Mrs. Nayburn's being torn between the two impulses was that she did nothing. Stilled ligaments, a bleached will. Couldn't take a step. Just stared at Diddy open-mouthed, as the elevator door closed. Stood, gaping, even after the car had started down the shaft.

Diddy, observing the spell he'd cast, was delighted to be rid of Mrs. Nayburn so easily. The outsized elevator car descended smoothly. The doors parted with a faint whirring of rubber. No familiar faces waiting for him in the lobby of the hospital. Diddy was free.

It was raining. Diddy began to feel chilled after walking several blocks. He wasn't free, he was just outside. And sorry (now) he'd spoken so bluntly and then left, since that meant Hester would first hear from her aunt of his impending proposal. Having let him get away, the woman would have no other thought but to return to Hester's bedside. Stationing herself there until the first vague stirring of the girl's body indicates that her mind was surfacing. Coming awake, awake enough to hear the news. If only Hester were deaf, like a snake. So she couldn't hear her aunt's raspy voice. Instead of blind, like those primitive species of fish that inhabit underground lakes in dark caves.

Wouldn't Mrs. Nayburn's crass enthusiasm contaminate his proposal in Hester's eyes? Bad tactics. Still, Diddy wasn't too worried about that. He had faith in the girl's independence of spirit. Hester was aware of her aunt's crassness and insincerity. Certainly, she must have known for some time how shamelessly eager Mrs. Nayburn was to get her off her hands. Diddy refused to consider that Hester might imagine that he, Diddy, was made of equally coarse cloth. That his proposal might be fired by emotions of the same venal quality, though different in aim and method than her aunt's.

What he thought most likely was that Hester would simply mistrust his intelligence. Thinking that he couldn't distinguish between pity or benevolence and love, she would try to save him from herself. He would try to save her for himself, more vehemently. Diddy has faith in the adequacy of his powers of persuasion, believed that he couldn't fail to convince Hester. Because (now) it was different. He had already convinced himself.

Still raining. Diddy, bareheaded, walking along a street near the Warren Institute. He could have returned to the conference, which had at least an hour to run. Should have gone back. The prudent thing to do. His abrupt departure, though covered by a plausible excuse, obviously had not sat well with his superiors. Diddy had always been a poor liar. Hated lying. When he attempted it, a combination of cowardice and pride always made him, somehow, transparent. They must have seen he wasn't really ill. Doesn't matter. What his bosses think of him was unimportant. The important thing was that, if only Hester will turn to him, a new life might begin.

Diddy the Daring will take the risk of the unknown. He clasps the idea of Hester to him.

Having no doubt that he loved her. And anything that might lead Hester to love him he would welcome. No scruples of pride there. If her knowing herself (now) to be permanently condemned to blindness enhanced his suit, so much the better. How lucky he is that she had so few choices. For if the choice was between living with him and living with her aunt, he had little doubt what she would choose.

But if Diddy hadn't been thinking at this moment how Hester's blindness and her consequent need for a reliable and loving protector favored his courtship, would he then have regretted her being blind? On her behalf, yes. The truth is, Diddy doesn't really think of Hester as being blind. In the sense that the world is divided into two camps: the fortunate majority with normal eyesight, and the tiny minority of the blind. The world is not so simple. Diddy saw eyes everywhere. Everyone has some kind of eyes. There are the squinty-eyed, the fish-eyed, the dragon-eyed, the piercing-eyed, the wolf-eyed. And the no-eyed and the all-eyed. The no-eyed not to be confused with the blind. And besides their number and qualities and uses, eyes may be distinguished by their composition. Some people's eyes are made of water; others of vapor; and others of crystalline splinters. Diddy thought his own eyes might be made of paper; at best, a tough parchment. Whereas Hester's eyes were made of the same soft flesh as her sex. For him, she had seeing eyes, and always had. All over her body. Like those animals such as the frog and the guinea pig and the rat, whose skin is rich in the pigment melanin; making the entire surface of their bodies responsive to light. Like that Russian girl with extra-ocular vision recently discovered by scientists, who can read—slowly—with her elbow.

Were it within Diddy's powers to make Hester see, he would. But he could also be grateful that the operation this afternoon changed nothing. Leaving her sight and the rest of her health exactly as they were before.

Leave everything as it is. Just walk in the rain. So Diddy will not go back to the conference. He will stroll and daydream for an hour. Afterwards, get some coffee. And then return to the hospital.

As soon as she gets out of the hospital, they would return to New York. After that move, communication with Mrs. Nayburn would become extremely infrequent and casual—at least Diddy hoped Hester would agree to that, hoped she wanted to be free of her aunt's supervision. When would they marry? So deep was

Diddy's feeling for Hester (now), and so powerful his wish to secure the tie between the girl and himself as strongly as possible, that he would like nothing better than to have the ceremony performed in the hospital. This week. Or downtown, at City Hall, the day she was discharged. For that speed, he'd even put up with having Mrs. Nayburn as godmother and witness. But perhaps Hester wouldn't want to be rushed. Don't! Diddy would count himself blessed if she consented to live with him on a trial basis.

So Mrs. Nayburn would be packed off, and Diddy and Hester would live together, marry legally whenever Hester was willing. But where would they live in New York? His apartment was too small. Not an apartment. Diddy would try to borrow money for the down payment on a house: a brownstone on the West Side, or perhaps, even cheaper, an old frame house on the fringe of Chinatown such as one he'd once gotten a rental agent to show him. Hester would know every inch of that house. Without having to extend her arms to keep from colliding with doors and walls and furniture. She would never bruise herself.

More rain. Diddy is getting drenched. There's hardly anyone on the street (now). Does Hester like to walk in the rain? Diddy doesn't know yet.

He stops in a phone booth to call the hospital. Gertrude, the head nurse on the floor, who knows Diddy by (now), tells him Miss Nayburn is still unconscious. She should be awake by eight. He can come for just a few minutes' visit then.

It's only six o'clock now. Time for more walking, and cups of coffee, two cheeseburgers, a slice of pie, another cheeseburger. By seven-thirty, Diddy is almost lost somewhere in the neighborhood. The sky is starting to clear, the rain is fading. Seven-thirty already. Perhaps she's regained consciousness already. He hurries back to the hospital.

No one stops him at the nurse's desk. Diddy races down the hall, then stops before the room. His heart is thumping loudly. And softly opens the door. Hester is awake, though lying flat on her back without any pillows. Mrs. Nayburn is by the bedside whispering. As Diddy comes in, he's aghast at the pallor of that half of her face not masked by the thick white bandages. He rushes to the far side of the bed, leans over, and touches her cheek with his lips. "How do you feel?" She smiles wistfully. "Does it hurt?" She motions no with her hand. "Can you talk?"

"Yes."

Diddy, burning, leans across the bed. "Mrs. Nayburn, would you please leave us alone for a few minutes?"

"Why?" the girl whispers.

"Hester!" Diddy pleads.

The aunt glances haughtily at both of them. "I'll do whatever you say, lovey. I certainly never meant to be in anyone's way." Diddy's no longer to be humored. His proposal blurted out, he's already to be taken for granted.

"Hester!"

The girl strokes her aunt's hand. "Yes. For just a few minutes." Mrs. Nayburn rises with a sigh. "Don't get her overexcited, Dalton," she says as she leaves the room.

Diddy waits to hear the footsteps growing fainter as she moves down the corridor. Hears nothing. So she's just outside. Still, there's a door between.

"Hester, am I being very selfish? Was I cruel just now? It's just that I had to be with you alone."

She reaches up to touch his hand. "It's raining, and you've been walking. For a long time?"

"Hours. Ever since I came at four-thirty, and they wouldn't let me see you."

"You could have stayed, and seen me earlier. When I woke up about a half hour ago, Aunt Jessie was right outside the door."

"Hester, don't reproach me. You're right. But the thought of spending several hours in that woman's company, while I was waiting for you, was intolerable. I had to go out."

"I feel sorry for her," the girl says in a strange weak voice Diddy has never heard before.

"For God's sake, Hester, stop thinking about her for a moment. Tell me how you feel. Are you in physical pain?"

"I ache all over, I guess from the anaesthetic. Otherwise, I don't know. No, I don't think I'm in pain."

"What about your . . . face. Your eyes."

"No. I feel nothing there."

"And how do you feel inside?"

"I don't know."

"Well, are you very sad?"

"I've been sad all along. You know that I knew the operation wouldn't work."

"One more thing. Very important. Did your aunt tell you anything about what I said to her when I came this afternoon?"

"Yes, she told me you want to marry me."

Diddy straightened up slightly from the uncomfortable position he'd adopted, in which he is leaning over Hester, his head above hers, his elbows and forearms resting on the mattress on either side of her head, the upper half of his body close but careful not to press on hers. She'd spoken (now) of what was most important to him, their future together; but in such an odd, remote way. Maybe he should never have brought the matter up. Saved it for tomorrow, when she would be stronger. Still, he couldn't bear to pull away altogether. Without knowing more of what she felt or, at least, could feel (now).

"Were you surprised?" A stupid question. Take it back. No.

"Well, your telegram last night. . . ." Hester's voice faded out.

Diddy should stop asking questions. Oh, please! Only one more. "Are you glad?"

"I'm not sure."

Diddy's limbs stiffen. "Not sure of what? Not sure you can be happy with me?"

"Oh," the girl says wearily. "I can be happy with almost anyone, I think. It depends on me, whether I'm happy within myself."

"But you weren't happy living with your aunt? Yes or no?"

"No, I wasn't happy."

"Will you leave her and live with me?"

"I'll try." Diddy, speechless with joy, lowers his face and kisses Hester's cheek. Is that all, really all? Is there no special eloquence needed? Nothing more he has to say? Not really. But Diddy about to say something anyway. When he notices Hester moving her pale cracked lips; her voice so low he has to strain to hear it.

"What, my love?"

"Can we call Aunt Jessie back now? She must be waiting outside."

Are those the words that follow? Diddy can't help feeling hurt. "Don't you want to be alone with me, Hester? For just a few minutes?"

"I can't be alone with anyone right now. I'm too tired, and I feel as if I've been sliced into a thousand pieces. Don't you see, Dalton, there isn't one person here for you to be alone with? So you mustn't be jealous of my aunt."

"I'll try not to be." He's been clumsy, overbearing with his tenderness. Who is Diddy to insist that he's better for Hester than her aunt?

He held the door open for Mrs. Nayburn. The woman walked stiffly to her niece's bedside; began whispering to the girl. Diddy stands contritely at the window, graciously allowing the two women to ignore him.

The door opens again, to admit just the head of one of the nurses. "Visiting hours are over. Come back tomorrow." Diddy stepped over to the bed, brought Hester's right hand to his lips, said a husky good night to Mrs. Nayburn, and stepped rapidly into the hallway corridor.

Once out in the street, Diddy looks at his watch. Five minutes after eight. He's missed most of the cocktail party from seven to nine o'clock at the Green Room of the Congress Hotel: biggest hotel in the city and four blocks from the Rushland. But has (now) really no excuse for not turning up at the company's banquet to celebrate the end of the conference. Nine o'clock in the Terrace Room of the Congress. No point in offending Reager and Watkins, with whom he'll have to spend tomorrow morning doing the television program. Diddy gets in a cab, returns to the Rushland, shaves again and changes his suit, and arrives at the Congress a few minutes before the hour.

Pretending not to notice Jim, signaling him from one of the long tables that he's saved Diddy a seat. Diddy finds a seat near some men in the production department whom he scarcely knows, and managed to eat most of his dinner without speaking either to his neighbor on the right or to his neighbor on the left. Diddy, hungry, entertains the fantasy that he's eating for Hester, who's probably on liquid nourishment; as well as for himself. He'll be strong for both of them tonight.

Saturday noon, after "Your Community," Diddy is outside the two-story building that houses Channel 10. Shaking hands with Watkins, Reager, and the others. Receiving their compliments on his performance at the conference, particularly his contributions during the early sessions. And their wishes for a pleasant trip back to New York. Diddy forces himself to be silent.

"Taking the plane or a train, Harron?" asks Watkins.

"Train."

"Take the Privateer," said Reager. "That's the crack train between here and New York. No train does that trip as fast. It leaves here at two-forty, so you should have plenty of time to make it."

"I know the train," said Diddy. Feeling bold. "I came up on it."

The temptation to talk about the events at the beginning of the week has subsided. It's not the story of Incardona which swells up in Diddy's throat, rises, then thrusts itself behind his teeth. Pushing to come out. The words that want to spill through Diddy's mouth (now) concern the future. We all look rather genial this morning. Diddy feels his soul is lacquered with milk. It would be a pleasure to tell his bosses and colleagues what he really intends.

Don't. What use would that be?

Diddy returns to the Rushland, and first stops off at the desk. Instructs the clerk to prepare his bill. Then he goes up to his room, and packs his suitcase.

Of course, he's not going to the station to catch the Privateer. Is he insane? No. Diddy carries his suitcase downstairs, pays his bill, goes outside the hotel, and has a cab hailed. Once inside, he tells the driver to drive to the Warren Institute. "What I really mean is around the Institute." Asks if he can recommend a decent hotel in that neighborhood.

"I'd try the Canada," says the driver. "Unless you're looking for something real cheap."

Fine, says Diddy. Let's go.

Passing Monroe Park, high afternoon, Saturday, November (now), the day after a rain. Yesterday's rain and wind have practically swept the remaining autumn leaves from the trees.

Single with shower and bath?

In less than an hour Diddy unpacked and installed. One bed, and a larger room than he had at the Rushland. Pleasanter, too, than the other hotel, because (now) he's out of the center of town. From his window, a good view of the park. And beyond the park, Diddy can see two towers of cream-colored stone, the principal buildings of the Warren Institute.

Two-thirty. Diddy calls the hospital, is told he can visit Hester briefly around six o'clock. Time for a two-hour nap. Leaving time enough to accomplish one more piece of business. At five-fifteen Diddy sits at the small glass-topped desk opposite the foot of his bed; writes another letter to Duva, requesting a sick leave. During the week of the conference, Diddy explains, he has undergone a series of tests at the Warren Institute to try to learn more about his old virus infection which had laid him low again just a month ago. This morning has gotten the reports on the tests; and the doctors have prescribed a course of treatment to effect a permanent cure of the recurring infection, for which approximately ten days' hospitalization is required. Diddy will need to remain upstate for at least another two weeks.

Downstairs. Diddy buys a stamp from a machine and puts the letter in the mailbox in the lobby. Has a sandwich at the drugstore on the corner. Walks across the park. The sun has already set, and the park is practically empty. Notices two little girls, about eight and ten, on the swings. Bright, strong, fleshy, seeing children such as he and Hester will have one day.

As he enters Hester's room, Mrs. Nayburn starts up awkwardly. "Be back in a few minutes, lovey." And darts out of the room.

Diddy standing near Hester's bed, ill at ease. "How are you?"

"Stronger." She's propped up again on the pillows.

Good.

He sits next to the bed, in the chair which the aunt has just hastily vacated; still warm from her body. Hester doesn't say anything more. Nor, when Diddy takes her hand, does her flesh seem very alive. He fears she's angry with him for Mrs. Nayburn's departure. "Darling, I'm sorry for what happened now. Sorry, I mean, if it's upset you. Or if I've made your aunt unhappy."

Hester turns toward Diddy. The thick white bandages cover so much more of her face than the dark glasses did. He's vaguely alarmed that (now) he can't read her expression at all.

"But you do understand how I feel, don't you?" Diddy continues. "I'm so eager for us to be alone."

"I'm afraid we'll be too much alone when we live together. You may hate that."

"Never," Diddy says ardently. "Try me."

"I will," said the girl, "try."

"That's all I ask."

"But you must remember that I warned you."

"I promise to remember." Diddy wanted to hold her, but she looked so thin and fragile. He senses something wrong. A different sadness from yesterday. "What's the matter, darling?"

"Did you come to say goodbye?"

Diddy laughed joyously. "No! No! What are you talking about?"

"Aren't you going back to New York now? Isn't the conference over?"

"Sure, the conference is over. The last thing I had to do was this morning. But that doesn't mean I'm going. You don't know me, Hester. I'm staying right here. So I can see you every day. In fact, I've moved out of my hotel downtown this afternoon and taken a room nearby. I can even see the hospital buildings from my window."

"How long can you stay on?"

"I'm staying until you leave. Until you leave this room and go down that elevator, and we walk out of here together. Which reminds me. After they kick me out of here this afternoon, I want to go and find your doctor and see how long he wants you to remain in the hospital. Has anyone given you a date yet?"

"Two or three weeks, Dr. Collins said."

193

"Good. Then, after you're discharged, whenever you feel strong enough to travel, we'll go back to New York."

"But how can you stay up here?" Hester exclaims plaintively. It sounded like tears, filling those poor wounded eyes behind the thick bandages. "You'll lose your job, Dalton."

"Leave it to me," said Diddy soothingly. "I've thought of a good excuse already. After eleven years, I'm not going to be fired for taking a couple of weeks' leave of absence."

"But then, when we get to New York, you'll go back to your job? Right?"

"Honestly, I don't know." Which is the truth. Already, Diddy not sure he ever intends to return to Watkins & Company. The prospect of leaving Hester alone in the apartment each day while he goes to an office seems unthinkable. Her physical safety, for one thing. And Diddy's sheer possessiveness, and incipient jealousy of the whole world. No, don't underestimate that.

Not having any private income, he will need to work to support them both. There must be some job he could do at home. But all that can be settled later. No need to rush to a decision. While he and Hester get settled in New York, he may need his old job. Hence, his letter of this afternoon. This decision is the decision to stall.

"You've never lived in New York, have you?"

The girl shook her head.

"You might not like it. The air is filthy, strangers are rude, even nasty, there's a lot of noise. But the city may please you or interest you anyway. And if it doesn't, we'll move elsewhere. To another city, or to a small town. Or out of the country altogether."

"Can you do that? Are you rich?"

"No," said Diddy. "But I can always manage. When I want to be, I'm a very practical guy."

Knocking on the door. And the aunt's voice, asking querulously if she should come in (now). "One more minute, Mrs. Nayburn."

"Dalton, you shouldn't do that. Let her in." But this time Hester was smiling slightly.

Diddy took heart. "Darling, I will. But you must promise to urge your aunt to go home within a few days. I want to be the one to take care of you, understand. I've already told Mrs. Nayburn that I would contribute as much as I could to your hospital bills. I wish I could pay for the whole thing. So, please tell her soon to go. Promise me that."

"I promise." Hester lifts her mouth for Diddy's kiss.

Then Diddy went to the door, and opened it. Mrs. Nayburn, red-eyed, weeping, her gray hair untidier than ever, was swaying on the other side of the threshold. Suddenly, Diddy was overcome with remorse. How unjust he'd been to the woman, and how petty he'd been in himself. She was never a person to him, just a creature. Something looked at under a microscope. Not seeing that she really loved Hester, truly suffered over her. Why had he been so spiteful? So possessive since the first moment he saw Hester? Already on the train, from the beginning, he'd aimed to take complete possession of the girl. Which required caricaturing the aunt, and trying to discredit her with Hester.

"Forgive me!" The tears he should have wept yesterday, after the failure of Hester's operation, flooded Diddy's eyes. Opening his arms to the elderly woman, he embraced her. "Forgive me."

The relief and exaltation of tears wept in concert. Like the joys of common interests. Diddy wishes Hester could see them next to her bed, he with his arm around Mrs. Nayburn's shoulder. But drowsy as she is, she must know what's happening.

Minutes later, iron-voiced Gertrude enters Hester's room. Making the expected announcement that our patient's too weak to have any more visiting that evening. Diddy, leaning over Hester's bed to kiss her goodbye, whispers that he will take Mrs. Nayburn out to dinner and devote the rest of the evening to her. Hester nods. Suddenly she does seem too tired even to speak.

When they leave the hospital, Diddy is busy looking for a cab. Doesn't notice that the aunt is crying again. When he does, the words sound wrong. "Please don't. We mustn't be any less brave than Hester is."

"I know," wailed the woman. "I just can't help myself."

In the cab, Diddy gives the address of a steak house downtown. "You haven't really seen the city yet, have you, Mrs. Nayburn?"

"No," she whimpers. "I just go back and forth from the hospital to the rooming house."

Diddy accepted the reproach graciously. "That's going to change now, you'll see." Putting his arm around her shoulder. "You know, I'd like to call you Jessie. It would help me feel closer to you."

"That's nice, Dalton. Or you could call me Aunt Jessie."

"Maybe I will some day. I don't have any living aunts. I had one once, though, whom I liked very much. She was my father's sister, Anne, but I didn't even know her name until I was grown up. From the way I heard the adults pronounce it, I'd always thought her name was Aunt Dan."

Mrs. Nayburn's face was clearer (now). "What happened to her?"

"Ran away to California with a married high-school teacher in our town when I was nine. My father and mother never mentioned her again, and later I heard that she'd died."

"Families are a wonderful thing," sighed Mrs. Nayburn.

"Well," said Diddy almost laughing, "I wouldn't go so far as to say that." When Mrs. Nayburn didn't make the conventional protest, and even smiled faintly at what he'd said, Diddy felt immensely relieved. If he hadn't actually misjudged her, she wasn't as simple and predictable as he'd thought.

In front of Cavanaugh's. "I think you'll like this place, Jessie."

"I'm not very hungry."

"You will be, you'll see." Appetite comes with eating, doesn't it? Diddy will set the good example.

Clam chowder, a sirloin done medium for Mrs. Nayburn and rare for Diddy, salad with Roquefort dressing, hot apple pie, and coffee. That's not exactly not being hungry. Mrs. Nayburn is a greedy eater. But if the woman's mouth is busy with food most of the time, Diddy, habitually slow and fastidious at the table, has the advantage. Can do most of the talking himself this meal.

"Goodness, I didn't know I was so hungry." Between mouthfuls, brushing a strand of gray hair from the corner of her mouth.

"I told you so. Now you'll start feeling better." Diddy, remembering Mrs. Nayburn's bulging bags of food on the train, senses something unpleasant in his stomach. Which he strives to fight down.

"Aren't you hungry, Dalton? It's a shame to waste such a good meal."

"Don't worry about me. I always dawdle over my food." He took a forkful of salad. "My mother used to say I was the slowest eater she'd ever seen." Why this impulse to bring up his family at the slightest pretext?

"Your mother is dead, isn't she, Dalton dear?" Another mouthful.

"Yes. She died when I was in college. But we were never very close. I really liked my father much better."

He must stop talking about himself. Idle chatter: a facile way of putting this woman, with whom he was about to contract a family sort of relation, at her ease. Mrs. Nayburn is cutting up large chunks of steak two at a time, each demanding a good deal of earnest chewing. Here's Diddy's opportunity to ask his questions, not just volunteer random information or answer Mrs. Nayburn's queries. Serious questions, about Hester. Engrossed by the excellent meal, wearied by her recent expenditure of emotion, the naturally talkative woman is quieter. Subdued, stripped of some of her exasperating mannerisms. Even when she speaks, it's with more gravity. Seems (now) almost capable of the truth.

What Diddy is most eager to know about is Hester's parents. All he's been told is that Mrs. Nayburn is the widow of her father's brother, and that Hester's father left his family when she was twelve. Became a uranium prospector in New Mexico, disappeared from sight years ago. But what about her mother? Whom neither Hester nor her aunt had ever mentioned.

Diddy asked. Then saw that he'd trespassed on something painful. Mrs. Nayburn halted the motions of her jaws. Looked at him in a strange, imploring way. Was the mother dead?

"No, not dead." Began chewing again, more slowly.

"Where is she? Does Hester ever see her?" How impossible to drop that word.

Mrs. Nayburn took up her fork and knife to cut into the steak, then set them down. "Hester hasn't seen her mother in many years."

"Where does she live?"

"Dalton, I don't think I want any more. Would you like to finish this piece?"

Diddy stopped eating, too. "Jessie, where is Hester's mother?"

"This steak is tough."

"Jessie, where is Hester's mother?" In his sternest voice. Reluctant people must sometimes be forced to divulge their secrets.

Mrs. Nayburn lowered her eyes. "In a hospital."

"A mental hospital, you mean." The woman nodded. "For how long?"

"I think I want my coffee now, Dalton."

"I'll get it." Signaling the waiter. "When was Hester's mother put away?"

"A long time ago."

Diddy told the waiter to bring them their coffee (now). "Wait," said the woman fretfully, as soon as he'd left. "Change the order. Coffee will keep me awake."

"Tea?" Diddy trying to catch the waiter's eye again, without slackening the heavy stare he was imposing on Mrs. Nayburn.

"Oh, I don't know. Maybe I won't have anything."

"The lady is changing her order to tea. I'm still having coffee." Now, his full gaze upon her again. "Jessie, I won't let you put me off. I have a right to know about what concerns Hester. Now, stop stalling and tell me how long she's been in an asylum?"

"Since Hester was fourteen." The woman looked away, apprehensively. Something dark surged forth in Diddy's mind.

"And Hester became blind when she was fourteen, isn't that right? You told me that the other day."

"Yes. . . . Dalton, let's change the subject."

"Then there's a connection." Diddy the Persistent. "Between her mother and Hester's blindness. You've just admitted it."

"That's something I don't want to talk about." The woman's face took on a hostile, childish look. As much as declaring, in the words of childhood's chant, That's for me to know and you to find out? Or registering something truly serious?

"But I must know! If you don't tell me, I'm afraid I won't be able to keep from questioning Hester. And if it's painful for you to speak of the past, imagine how much more painful it will be for her. Tell me now, and I promise never to bring it up again."

The woman was spooning four lumps of sugar into her tea. "What do you imagine it is?"

"For God's sake, Jessie!" cried Diddy, in anguish. "Don't play games at a moment like this. How do I know?"

"Well, think!" Bitterly. "What's the most horrible thing you can think of?"

Diddy can't help realizing how ironic is that command to put his imagination to work. Doesn't he do little else these days but summon up the most horrible things he can think of? What could the awful story be? One possibility: when the mother had become insane, Hester had succumbed to a fit of mad adolescent guilt; either deliberately or inadvertently, had blinded herself.

He said it very slowly.

Mrs. Nayburn shook her head. "No, not that. Something even worse."

Then Diddy knew. The mother had blinded her.

"How horrible." Was there anything else to say? "But why did she do such a thing?" Diddy feeling very remote from his words. "Did she just suddenly go mad?" Insensitive sentinels of his thought.

Mrs. Nayburn shook her head. "I suppose we all should have seen it coming. She was so unhappy after Hester's father left her. Then everybody was saying that Stella was crazy. But we didn't mean it. And the idea of her harming the child never crossed anyone's mind. She seemed to adore Hester. Always kissing and hugging her, calling the child her beautiful angel. That was the main reason we were sure things would stay on an even keel with Stella. She acted so devoted to Hester, and seemed so responsible. Overdid it, actually. Worrying about her all the time. About the littlest scratch or cut. Or when Hester would be a few minutes late from school. And then, it was when my husband and I had left for a week to visit relatives in Denver, one day . . . she did it. Just like that. With lye. And she seemed to know afterwards just what she did, mentioned it often, and didn't seem a bit sorry. The state's

199

attorney talked about a trial, but finally they just put her away."

Diddy had hardly touched his coffee. He could hear Mrs. Nayburn talking. He could even decode the words, and encode some of his own. For instance: "Where was Hester all this time?"

But all the while there is this terrible iron pain speeding toward him.

"Oh, Dalton, that was heartbreaking, too. Hester was in the Children's Hospital for a whole month. With those awful bandages on her eyes. Being so brave. Just like now. . . . And every day, when my husband and I would visit her, she'd plead with us to go to the police and tell them she didn't mind what her mother had done. Just so they wouldn't keep Stella locked up. Worrying and worrying about her mother, not herself."

Diddy was silent for several moments. Submerged, grappling with a curious absence of mind. Seeing a smaller version of the Hester he knows (now), lying helpless in that other hospital bed. Fighting off the dreadful Gothic scenario projecting itself inside his head. The woman with disheveled clothes, hair streaming about her face, the light of madness in her eyes. Advancing toward her daughter, bottle of vile chemical in her hand. Hester, asleep in her bed. Or, with her back to her mother, at the kitchen table doing her homework.

The Advance.
The Assault.
The Screams.
The Police.
The Jail.
The Hospital.

Whenever he thinks he's understood and registered all the cruelty of living, all the horrors of which people are capable, there are more. Too much to digest.

Diddy, still silent, struggling to say something. "You said it happened when you and your husband were on a trip. Do you mean that Hester and her mother were living with you then?"

"That's right. In the same house, for about two years. After George left for New Mexico, my husband and I had taken them both in." She began to cry again, and put down her cup of tea.

"Oh, Dalton, I shouldn't say my husband and I." Took a handkerchief from her bag, and blew her reddened nose. "I don't deserve any of the credit, not one bit. It was my husband's idea, God rest his soul. He . . . he never liked George very much, always disapproved of the way he lived. Maybe he just wanted to show his brother up to the world for the kind of man he really was. And that's why he took on the responsibility for the wife and child George had abandoned."

"You don't really think that's all there was to your husband's decision, Mrs. Nayburn," said Diddy gently. "I can hear in your voice that you think of your husband as a good, generous man."

"He was," said the woman, sighing. "I guess it's awful of me to say he helped them out for that reason. But I did think so then, at the time. I was against the whole scheme. Fought and begged and cried. I suppose I was a little jealous of Stella, too, because she was so . . . beautiful. Yes, I was jealous. I used to imagine my husband was interested in her, and maybe had always been waiting for George to clear out so he could make a play for George's wife. . . . Then there was little Hester, too. I had lots of bad feelings inside me because of not having any children of my own. Maybe I would have welcomed a baby, a little thing that I could mother. But Hester was already twelve when she came to us, and so stuck on her mother she didn't have any use for me. Though maybe that was my fault, too. She really was a very loving child. Exceptionally so. But I'd hardened my heart against children. When the two of them came to live with us, I didn't see anything special in Hester at first. I used to tell my husband that all the time. I didn't even think she was pretty. But my husband was crazy about her. So was Stella, of course. At least we thought so. So was everybody. Everybody loved that child. So after a while I came to love her just as much as the others."

Diddy didn't know what to say. "And she's lived with you ever since?"

"Except for when she was in a special school for the blind in Chicago. That was, let's see, just the last two years of high school. She graduated at eighteen and then came home to me."

Diddy wondering if in that boarding school Hester first made

201

love. With other students or with her teachers? Or with some of both? And what pleasures did she provide for herself after returning to live with her aunt? A blind girl couldn't stroll on the streets late at night, when her aunt was in bed. But that wasn't necessary. Mrs. Nayburn, who worked at the Public Library, left Hester alone every day. During the day, Hester could make assignations by phone, and receive her paramours in her own house. Certainly, the girl was experienced sexually. Suggesting not only promiscuity, which Diddy wouldn't mind if it were exclusively a thing of the past. Suggesting, too, that Hester might have a very detached temperament, affectionate but not loyal. Because of her blindness incapable of settling down with one man: renouncing chance adventures and the touch of others. Because she was blind, Diddy felt awkward even speculating to himself about her erotic life. Would be tongue-tied if it came to questioning her directly about it. Blindness a kind of coercion of others; obliging Diddy to be blind, too.

For all Diddy knew, she could have been carrying on this week with Dr. Collins or one of the interns. Diddy, not usually a morbidly suspicious lover, imagining himself ringed by invisible rivals. But different (now). A girl as willful and spontaneous as Hester, who had made love with him only minutes after they'd begun to talk, would surely be capable of something like that. The attentive touch of a physician during an examination could easily become a prelude to bed. Hester need only sigh, or make one brief voluptuous movement. What healthy man, even if engaged in his professional duties, could resist such an invitation? He would hardly need the extra stimulus of panic and guilt, and the anguished need to reach out for another person, as Diddy had last Sunday afternoon on the Privateer.

Diddy wanted to become Hester's protector, not her jailer. And not, God knows, her dupe.

Diddy sipped his cold coffee, signaled the waiter to refill their glasses of water. Really because he still didn't know how to continue the conversation. Something about a school in Chicago. Nothing to add to that. But he couldn't keep silent, because of the danger that his face was betraying him to Mrs. Nayburn's anxious gaze. That he looked (now) as unhappy as he felt.

"I wonder if Hester can be happy with me." As close as Diddy dared approach the thought poisoning him. Delivered in what he rated a casual, musing tone. But immediately Diddy saw he'd made a tactical error. His remark didn't reassure, though it wasn't honest either. Mrs. Nayburn looking anxious, as if she feared Diddy was backing off from his marriage proposal.

"Oh, but she's the sweetest-tempered girl in the world, Dalton. Everyone says that, and how pretty she is. But you—" she paused.

"What?"

"You aren't getting any silly ideas about what I told you before? You remember that I didn't want to tell you, but you made me. Of course, I don't believe in lying, either. Heavens, not to someone who's about to become a member of the family. That was my problem. But about Hester's mother. . . . I mean, Dalton, no one else in Hester's family, either on her mother or her father's side, has ever been crazy. I swear it."

"Jessie, believe me, I'm not thinking of that." Patting the woman's hand reassuringly. "I spoke awkwardly just now. It's only that Hester is a very complicated person, as I'm sure you know. She keeps a great deal within herself—"

The waiter brought the glasses of water. Diddy ordered another coffee, another tea.

The woman impatient to get Diddy's attention again. "Heavens, that's true enough. Why, sometimes the child hardly says a word to me for days. But she's not sulking or cross then, believe me. Just quiet."

"Sugar, Jessie?"

"Thank you, dear . . . Dalton, tell me what you're thinking."

"Jessie, nobody could think better of Hester than I do. Don't defend her—as if I were criticizing her, or about to. I'm not. I'm just trying to understand her."

What particularly preoccupied Diddy was Hester's mistrust. Easy to understand, in the light of the hideous assault her aunt has just conjured up for him. A child is supposed to trust his parents,

203

right? Suppose you're a normal, trusting child. Then one parent abandons you, and the other flings acid in your eyes. Could anyone who endured such betrayal ever trust another person again? Remember, there are people who do put themselves entirely in other people's hands without ever trusting them. Would Hester ever trust Diddy? Or was she merely consigning herself, fatalistically, to him? As she'd agreed to undergo the operation. Knowing it was the correct thing to do, but all the while without hope?

Diddy knew he couldn't talk further. His closeness with Mrs. Nayburn ebbing, wanting to salvage what remained. They're both exhausted. Among the effects of this exhaustion: Mrs. Nayburn drifting back to her old coy, presumptuous manner; and Diddy becoming very stiff, upset. Diddy asks for the bill, pays; they leave. Hails a taxi and will take her home.

"But it's out of your way, dear. I can take the taxi myself."

"No, it's not. I moved this afternoon to the Canada."

At this most reassuring news, Mrs. Nayburn took a deep, comfortable breath. "That big hotel on the other side of the park? Why, that's wonderful, Dalton dear. Hester will be so pleased. Did you tell her yet?"

Rather than say yes, Diddy nodded. Important to keep Mrs. Nayburn from talking too much, making him shrink further into himself and become incapable of seeing anything human in her.

Diddy let the taxi go in front of Mrs. Nayburn's rooming house. At their final good nights, the newfound tenderness for the woman flared up again. But quickly, quickly. "See you tomorrow, dear. And thanks for the lovely dinner." Faster. Diddy walks past the Institute. Looks up at what he counts off to be Hester's room; dark, naturally. Then across the park, and back to his hotel room.

The gloomy mood settling in. Maybe he hadn't let himself feel all the horror of Hester's blinding. Feel it (now). Get in bed, under the covers; turn off the light. What's the matter? Diddy can't see Hester any more. She's a story he heard, not a real woman whom he loves. Maybe that's because until the present he's never made a blunt, energetic effort to comprehend her. Diddy the Selfish has been busy thinking of himself.

Think of Hester. With a catastrophe of such dimensions behind her, a wound of such depth incised upon her as she was just emerging from childhood. Enduring such a betrayal.

Think of Hester, only setting aside what he can merely guess at, never estimate: how much she suffers from the usual pathology of survivors. Feeling always, somewhere, that they too should have perished. To survive is to be guilty. Because unpunished.

> Someone who survives his death sentence through accident, last-minute rescue, or mere luck rather than through his own strenuous efforts knows that, really, he should be dead. Knows that he has no true title to his life. He cannot be identical with his life when, after being on the threshold of death and even resigned to it, his life is incoherently and arbitrarily and at the last minute returned to him. However unjust the verdict which sought to deprive him of his life, it has in retrospect more meaning and coherence than his survival. To live, therefore, is to remain convicted and under sentence. But to have evaded, somehow, the execution of the sentence. To be alive, then, is chiefly a negative condition. Judged, one has escaped judgment. Sentenced, one remains mysteriously unpunished.

Is Diddy thinking of Hester? Think of her, damn it. Neglecting only these most general feelings she might harbor for having survived her mother's death sentence. Apart from this common pathology of the Survivor, what is Hester really like?

It's like having to conjure up a whole row of dolls on an imaginary shelf. They are all tall, full-bodied, fair-skinned, with long fine hair and sunglasses. But each has a different repertoire of actions. Diddy in bed; lying in near darkness, having turned off all the lights except the one in the bathroom, closes his eyes. The Hester-dolls begin to move, gesticulate. Even quarrel with each other.

Which doll is the real Hester? And to whom does the real one belong?

One doll is screaming and shaking her fist. Another doll, seated at the end of a long bench set against one wall of a large empty room, cringes. Another smiles ceaselessly, mechanically. Another,

205

who wears a nasty expression on her tiny mouth, rushes to the doll on the bench and begins throttling her; then slaps the smiling doll across the face. She seems to have a gun in the pocket of her white linen dress. Or is it a bottle of acid?

What could Hester really be like? She could be bitter. Or stupefied. Or defensively superficial and ingratiating. Or vicious, seeking to inflict upon someone else what was done to her.

She was none of these, Diddy knew.

Call it perversity or what you will, Hester's character is not so ordinary. Sweep those dolls off the dream shelf; and consider the life-size mannequin that Diddy imagines sitting on the windowsill in his hotel room at this very moment. The figure looking at nothing in particular. Listening, perhaps. And gravely receiving Diddy's vibrations. That's the Hester who belongs to Diddy. At least, the Hester he has claimed. Diddy opens his eyes for a moment, looks toward the window. Shade up, curtain not drawn. Half looking for the creature spawned by his imagination; and, because he knows she isn't there, half looking at the full moon through the leaf-stripped trees. Diddy sighs; leaves bed to get a drink of water from the bathroom. Yes, she could conceivably be bitter; or stupid; or superficially ingratiating; or vicious. But she wasn't, wasn't those dolls.

Or, she could need to be a saint. Because her mother was wicked.

These were Hester's choices. For them Diddy has opened his heart. Loves her for what he (now) dares to describe as her sanctity; though it doesn't manifest itself in the usual good deeds. And for her sanity, which shows itself, among other ways, in the girl's strength and firmness of character.

Diddy stares at his face, less haggard and bony than last week, in the mirror above the bathroom sink. Then turns off that light too, and finds his way back to bed by moonlight.

This election of the right Hester from among the impostors and pretenders still gives Diddy no clue as to how Hester feels (now), as distinct from what she is. How happy or unhappy; how much and how actively she suffers. And if she suffers terribly, from what? Is it mainly grief? Despair? The impotence enforced by blindness? Unexpressed rage? Guilt? Sheer loneliness? Or longing for her mother? No way of questioning the apparition on the windowsill about that.

Perhaps Hester is too intelligent to suffer a great deal. Doesn't the capacity to suffer depend on a kind of superior stupidity? So thinks Diddy. With his eyes closed, becoming drowsier. A talent for suffering is to be found only among people of middling intelligence, those neither stupid nor wise, people with minds such as the one Diddy the Despairer has been endowed with or inherited or settled for. Especially during the last three years.

Until the age of thirty, Diddy was even duller mentally. Hard to believe, but true. Before then, which was all his life, Diddy's mind used to be even worse. Too stupid to suffer. Those were the years of sub-suffering, everyday misery, a complacent dull pain. And the belief that everything would turn out all right. When Joan left, Diddy became wiser. And so on. Wiser and wiser. He hadn't been watching the wrong play for thirty years. But he'd been watching it without understanding the theory behind its staging—assuming naturalism of script and staging. In retrospect, a naïve error. The script is intricate, and charged with obscure references; and the presentation concocted by the director, set designer, and lighting technicians is fanciful and stylized. Take, for instance, the lighting effects. It had occurred to Diddy, from his comfortable seat in the orchestra front center, that the lighting on the stage was rather dim. But after a moment, he banished any question about it; plainly, that was just the way this play was lit. Then, three years ago, he realized that the stage was and had always been much more brightly lit than his eye could see. And that he was (now) about to see it. Wiser and wiser. The scrim was raised. The gauzy light became, suddenly, knife-sharp. Almost gouged out his heart. Wiser. And suffering, for the first time. But not truly wise, wise enough to transcend suffering; and never likely to be.

Except if Hester will teach him.

Monday. Two days after the unsuccessful operation, Hester was moved to the fifth floor for the balance of her recuperation period. The new room looks out onto a courtyard, rather than onto Monroe Park. And, though barely twice the size of the one she had upstairs, contains three beds.

In the bed nearest the window, a college girl who had smashed her ankle in a bicycle accident. After being set and put in a cast, the ankle had failed to mend. Had to be broken again, reset and pinned together by surgery, put in a new cast; it was (now) suspended in a traction sling.

In the middle bed lies the wife of a state senator who, during the middle of one night last week, had almost hemorrhaged to death from a previously undiagnosed ulcer. She'd just had half her stomach removed.

Since Hester is sharing this room with two other patients, even when Mrs. Nayburn is absent, they're never alone. Still, all things taken into account, Diddy prefers her new accommodation to the private room on the seventh floor. Finds he's able to spend much more time with Hester, during the next fifteen days, than he had before. On this floor, there's less supervision of the comings and goings of visitors; their irregular presence in the patients' rooms is treated casually. Diddy's gotten away with an occasional morning visit, without trouble. The evening seven-to-nine sloppily enforced. And Diddy usually has at least three hours of the afternoon, sometimes more, before a nurse thinks to take the temperature of one of the three patients. Happens to come in. "My goodness, are you people still here? You have to go now." A new nurse—Gertrude doesn't work on this floor—obviously unused to giving orders and having them obeyed.

Hester requires little medical attention (now). The girl is checked by Dr. Collins each morning; and slowly, systematically, the bandages over her eyes are thinned out. When Diddy arrives for the afternoon on the eighth day after the operation, he finds Hester down to disk-shaped bandages cupping each eye. Slim enough to put the dark glasses over them. Which she is wearing today. To Diddy another sign of recovery.

Hester, who's in the bed nearest the door, appears to enjoy the company of her roommates: Diddy often finds her in conversation when he arrives. But the state senator's wife sleeps a lot. And the college student gets lengthy noisy visits from her parents on most days. For Hester's additional diversion, Diddy has bought her a transistor radio with an earbug.

Since visiting Hester has become an event absolutely relied on by both of them, Diddy wishes to give it more weight. But they have so little privacy. Diddy fearing the consequences of the kind of conversations to which they're restricted. Only talk which could be overheard by the two other patients and their visitors, as well as by Mrs. Nayburn. Determined that nothing between him and Hester must be allowed to get mechanical and flat, Diddy seeks a means for reducing conversation without losing contact with the girl. Already lacking images, words cannot be sacrificed altogether. Only replaced. The habitual polite words. But what to put in their place? For Diddy is not willing to play Diddy the Docile, much less Diddy the Silent. Letting the garrulous Mrs. Nayburn chatter away without hindrance. Yet the only words Diddy wants to speak to Hester can't be uttered here; must wait until they are finally alone.

Other words must be found (now), which are not his words. Other words, which Diddy will deliver. Cutting off Mrs. Nayburn's flow.

Taking his cue from Hester's remark that she liked her aunt reading to her, Diddy expresses his eagerness to perform the same service. Mrs. Nayburn had probably already thought of volunteering for that task herself; but, thinking over the meaning of Diddy's presence, dismissed the idea. Diddy is bound by no such reciprocal scruples toward Hester's aunt.

"I'd love it," Hester exclaims. "What will you read?"

Diddy asks her to allow him to make his choice a surprise; promises to bring a book that evening.

From the beginning, more of a success than Diddy had anticipated. His selfish goal instantly achieved. (Now) he need not bring out so many of those limp words, crafted for such a compromised function: to be acceptable to Hester, but also to be heard by ears other than hers. He reads an hour the first evening. Hester's ordinarily pallid face gleams; undergoes a kind of fading when he stops.

Begs him the next afternoon to read for a longer time, unless it tires his voice. Diddy is delighted to comply, and from then on reads for a substantial period of each day's visits, so that he finished *Pride and Prejudice* in eleven days; and by the end of the post-operative period of seventeen days that Hester spends in the hospital is well into *Emma*.

Unexpectedly, Hester's aunt seems to derive nourishment from Diddy's reading, too. More than anything else, this reading seems to certify Diddy's competence as Hester's future guardian; and to convey in the least painful way to Mrs. Nayburn that her attendance on the girl, gratefully acknowledged and, in this very act of Diddy's, being paid token homage by imitation, is (now) superfluous. Mrs. Nayburn has been replaced, but Hester's in good hands. Diddy's expressive baritone voice and his educated pronunciation bespeak an authority and compel a respect that Diddy the Whole, speaking his own words, is not always able to command. As do the abstract certainties about pleasure and discord proposed in the novels Diddy has chosen to read. Chosen for no better reason than that he liked them—but Diddy, an enthusiastic devourer of printed words, likes many books—and that these were the only acceptable choices among the paperbacks available on the revolving rack in the drugstore near the Canada. An arbitrary choice, perhaps. But, whether Diddy knows it or not, a favorable one.

Mrs. Nayburn, Diddy, and perhaps even Hester, calmed by Jane Austen's authoritative prose well pronounced and energetically delivered in Diddy's pleasant baritone. The trio inspired by that unflagging intelligence, neither modest nor self-deprecatory. Intelligence, good will, and reasonableness all seem possible. Indeed, inevitable. A few pages before the ball at Netherfield takes place, Hester and her two caretakers, the elder teetering on the verge of abdication and the younger barely more than an upstart pretender, unite in an unspoken alliance expressly designed to denigrate nobody. A treaty, out of tact never exactly spelled out but nonetheless binding, is concluded. Which regards everybody's interests as having equal weight and dignity.

First article of the treaty: the aunt will be present during the afternoon visit. Most of which is filled by a new installment of Jane Austen's lucid narrative; the remainder, with watery old conversation led by the aunt and with Diddy's vaporish musings.

Second article: Diddy and Mrs. Nayburn will eat dinner together.

Third article: the evening visiting hours are reserved for Diddy alone. With the aunt either returning to the rooming house to watch TV in the parlor or to chat in the kitchen with the friendly landlady, a widow about Mrs. Nayburn's age; or going to a movie that Diddy usually selects and to which he escorts her after they leave the restaurant. When Diddy returns to the hospital, usually reads to Hester for a full two hours. Occasionally whispering an endearment. An expression of his solicitude and yearning.

Diddy aware each evening, from the moment he enters the restaurant with Mrs. Nayburn and all the while he's seated at a table with her, and also whenever he takes her up to the box office of a movie theatre, usually located downtown, that he risks running into Watkins or the Reagers or one of his other colleagues at the plant. Slightly apprehensive. But doesn't want to hide. Sooner or later, they're bound to find out what he's been doing these weeks anyway.

Although Diddy awaits Hester's release impatiently, he finds this period enjoyable. Time passes lightly. Something comforting in the regularity of his actions. A routine has been set. And things are in their places, where you'd expect them to be. His room at the Canada always looking the same. Maid service irreproachable: each day the bathroom is mopped down, the bed remade with fresh sheets, his shoes shined, the desk replenished with flowers. And Hester always where he thinks she is: in the hospital. Diddy's fantasies that she's having a romance with her doctor have subsided. And Mrs. Nayburn always on hand. Her unfailing presence also, in its way (now), part of the reassuring stability of things, ever since she's come to annoy Diddy so much less. Ever since she divulged the truth about Hester's blindness, on the day after her niece's operation, Diddy has continued to feel warmly toward Mrs. Nayburn. The feeling of mild affectionate esteem doesn't grow, but still holds its own. Not tolerance, exactly; Diddy is too divided in his real feelings. A kind of meta-tolerance.

How absurd it seems (now) that Diddy once found Mrs. Nayburn not only an exasperating trial to his patience and good manners, but a menace, too. He scarcely minds the dinners they (now) take together each night. Even though the conversations conducted then are invariably shallow. One topic that recurs again and again: the hospital bills. But even Mrs. Nayburn seems shy about asking Diddy straight out how much he's willing to contribute. Finally, one evening, he tells her. And makes out a check. Being not that intimate that either cares to talk about himself, they talk mostly about other people. Two other people. And about the past. Mrs. Nayburn tells stories about Hester as a child—all stories, it's understood though never stated, taking place before the girl was fourteen. In exchange, Diddy talks about Paul's childhood, about what it's like to be a child prodigy so far as a mere brother can understand what Paul felt. And accounts of Paul's later glory: the scholarship to Paris, the first appearance with the New York Philharmonic when he was fifteen, the international piano competition won at the age of nineteen which made him world-famous. Mrs. Nayburn's pleasure in his stories is so artless, Diddy can hardly take offense. Nor be depressed, even though in all these conversations there's no reversion to the intimate soundings of that first dinner. Diddy able to remember he's not sitting across from a witch; or a reincarnation of Mary; or a faceless occupant of a train compartment with two bulging paper bags, like dead dogs, at her feet. Across from him in a booth or at a table in the Olympia Restaurant, the Greenleaf Diner, Cavanaugh's Steak Joint, or any of the other restaurants they try, is Jessie Nayburn. A decent, well-meaning, lonely woman. After Diddy, the person most devoted to Hester in the whole world. Nurtured and cared for Diddy's beloved all those years before Diddy found her. He calls her Jessie with pleasure, though still Mrs. Nayburn in his head. But in his head, he isn't calculating exactly when Mrs. Nayburn will or must return to the empty house in Indiana. Since she appears to grasp the situation and to accept it, Diddy assumes she will leave shortly. As far as he's concerned (now), she can stay until Hester leaves the hospital, since the two of them can't be alone until after then.

What does Diddy do before his visits to Hester and the nightly dinner with Mrs. Nayburn? Nothing. Which isn't odd, when you consider where he is and what engages his attention. But odd, perhaps, that he doesn't mind it. At least, a little. A man who's had virtually no time to himself in many years, except for the four days at the beginning of October—actually, six counting the weekend—following his release from the hospital. A man holding down a five-day-a-week job for so many years, who devoted his annual two- and then three-week vacations, usually spent in Europe, to the kind of strenuous traveling which allows less leisure than the same number of ordinary weeks of work. Odd, then, for a man so inured to work to take so naturally to his present leisure.

Doesn't feel the lack of occupation (now). Neither bored nor restless.

Maybe Diddy wasn't such a compulsive worker, after all. It's amazing how much he sleeps, too. Nine or ten hours, usually dreamless, each night. Hasn't slept so long since he was in grade school, when Mary was so strict about the boys "keeping a schedule." Throughout his childhood—more precisely until he was fourteen, when Mary either left the household of her own accord or was fired by his mother—Mary monitored the bedtime hour of both boys. And by a standard that was distinctly Victorian. Bedtime was advanced thirty minutes each year, but the hour remained too early; always a time when most of his neighborhood pals were still up and playing. So Diddy had good reason to hate going to bed, to grumble loudly when the light was turned off and Mary left the room. But found, nevertheless, that he rarely could hold out against sleep for more than a few minutes in the dark, or almost dark. Even though agitated with admiration and envy of Paul, in the other bed, who could remain awake for hours; studying scores by flashlight under a tent made with his blanket, so his light wouldn't shine on the floor and be detected by someone passing outside the bedroom. In imitation, Diddy got a flashlight of his own, and sometimes tried to read a novel in his own tent. But all too soon, sleep vanquished him; vanquished pride, too.

The sleepless nights came many years later. And (now) Diddy is sleeping again. Voluptuous, generous amounts. Rarely waking before ten or eleven o'clock. If showered, shaved, dressed and down by eleven, he can still make breakfast in the hotel coffee shop. If later than that, the drugstore on the corner is equally good. Of course, he picks up a copy of the *Courier-Gazette* first thing when he comes down to the lobby, as a matter of duty. Conscientiously reads it through at breakfast, to prove to himself that he's not afraid of finding what, in fact, he doesn't find. Then, if it's not too cold, a stroll about the park in what's left of the morning. Occasionally, he turns up at the hospital and sneaks up to Hester's room for a good-morning hug; though visiting at this hour is forbidden. With or without the illicit extra visit, it's soon time for lunch, which Diddy usually takes in the dining room of the Canada, except for Wednesday, when the Lions hold their weekly luncheon, and Friday, the day for the Junior Chamber of Commerce; on which days he eats at the drugstore. A brief nap after lunch, sometimes no more than fifteen minutes. But always easy to slip into and arise from. Time for his legitimate visit. Diddy usually leaves around two o'clock, walking across the park again. His evening meal with Mrs. Nayburn starts at six o'clock, sometimes even five-thirty; so he can rejoin Hester promptly at seven. After leaving the hospital at nine, or as late as the nurse's negligence permits, Diddy usually walks straight back to the Canada; though sometimes the longer way, around the park. Buys one or two sandwiches and a container of Coke at the drugstore, and weighs himself. Also, a paperback book or a magazine, either at the drugstore or at the newsstand in the hotel lobby. To his room. Gets in bed with snack and reading matter. Rarely turning on the television; he might get interested in the movie, and push himself to stay awake longer than he would have otherwise. This way works better. Eats and, rather quickly, reads himself to sleep.

Lacking exercise, apart from his three or four walks each day across the park to and from the hospital, and eating three full meals and snacks in between, no wonder Diddy is putting on weight. By the end of the seventeen days, he's close to gaining back the whole twenty pounds lost to despair and shame and death. Throughout his twenties, he'd kept pretty much the weight he had in college; the normal weight for a man of his height and relatively slender frame. Started to lose, very slowly, three years ago. And then, a month ago, shedding twenty pounds within a few days. Has he gained it all back? He hasn't been enterprising enough to seek out one of the hundreds of scales that must be distributed in examination rooms throughout the hospital, accuracy guaranteed by their site. Instead, Diddy feeds a penny into the undoubtedly inaccurate scale at the back of the drugstore every evening. No matter. If used frequently enough, it appears, an inaccurate machine is just as useful as an accurate one. And Diddy goes on weighing himself daily on the drugstore's scale. The base figure which the inaccurate machine gives may be wrong, but from then on it will tell Diddy exactly how much, if anything, he's gaining each day.

A few fluctuations, of course. One evening, Diddy found he had lost two pounds. Then remembered that yesterday there had been a slight estrangement, veiled but still bruising, between himself and Hester. And that he'd been so upset he had skipped the late evening snack, as well as lunch today.

Mostly, Diddy's weight is going up steadily. Clothes don't fit well (now). Notices in the shower a slight paunchiness about the waist. A different notch in his belt. But Hester doesn't object. She must notice—blind people would be especially perceptive about these things—the new fullness of his face when she strokes his cheek. Diddy likes this bigger, more robust body. Taking up more space in the world. Feels pride when he's added enough flesh to his fragile left wrist to warrant readjusting the buckle on his watch strap. Enjoying the slightly cramped situation of his body inside his clothes, which is such that he's no longer comfortable keeping anything thick, especially any metal object, in his trousers pockets. To repeat: Hester, who must notice, doesn't mind. At least, hasn't commented on it. But should Hester suggest that he lose some of this new weight, Diddy would accede without complaint or resentment. Partly feeling she's right, and that he's indulging himself. Partly out of the desire to please.

215

On the twelfth afternoon following the operation, Mrs. Nayburn announced that she was leaving tomorrow. Has her bags packed. And a train ticket for home in her purse, bought that morning.

Isn't that awfully abrupt, announcing her proposed departure only a day in advance? Is she angry? Hard to tell. Mrs. Nayburn's manner with her niece is affectionate but matter-of-fact. Hester seems genuinely sorry at the news; at least the suddenness of it. Asks her aunt several times if she's really sure. Seems to accept Mrs. Nayburn's firm yes at face value, and not unhappily. To Diddy's relief, didn't plead with her aunt to stay on a bit longer.

Yet, Diddy thinks, Hester must be anxious. Isn't it plausible that she's wondering whether Mrs. Nayburn has told the whole truth about her decision? Doesn't Hester worry that, because she can't study the woman's face, she's missing some clue to her aunt's feelings and intentions?

Diddy studies the woman's face for her. Decidedly more impassive than usual. Could she just be attempting to be dignified? All the while holding back her real feelings: wounded dignity, sense of loss. But if Diddy had to judge, he'd say that the kind of pride that prompts people to make such successfully expressionless masks of their faces isn't part of Mrs. Nayburn's character. Diddy's guess is that the woman doesn't mean to leave tomorrow at all. It's because she's not actually going that she's not really sad.

Hoping he's made clear that his resentments have entirely dissolved, Diddy tells Mrs. Nayburn that, as far as he's concerned, he'd prefer that she didn't go. Unless she genuinely wants to. "Anyway, you'll be visiting us soon in New York." A surprising thing for Diddy to say when, probably out of consideration for his clamorous wish to have Hester to himself, neither of the two women has yet spoken of a future visit; though it must have, many times, crossed their minds. Odd that it should turn out that if anyone is faintly coaxing Mrs. Nayburn to stay, it's not Hester but Diddy.

But Diddy is wrong. Mrs. Nayburn isn't bluffing; is truly bent on going. And when he realizes that the aunt's plans are genuine, Diddy begins to feel an unexpected elation. Hadn't thought it mattered to him, one way or the other. Apparently, it did. The old spiteful feelings seep back. Mrs. Nayburn is, after all, a kind of barrier to the union between Hester and himself; a formidable vestige of the past. But when she goes, the only hurdle left to surmount is Hester's discharge from the hospital. Diddy, allowing a shade too much of the jubilation he feels to show. (Now) Mrs. Nayburn, with more sensitivity than Diddy had given her credit for having, immediately picks up the subtle change in his manner; and correctly interprets it. Becomes more distant to both of them, vaguely reproachful. Aiming a diminutive sour barb at Diddy. "Hester, if I stay here any longer, lolling about, just sitting and eating and watching movies, I'll start getting fat like Dalton." Hester smiles. Diddy feeling a wonderful solidarity with her, despite the fact that they can't exchange those light, ironic glances that any other young couple would at such a moment, while dealing indulgently with the whining petulance of their elders. Of those who've outlived their chance for happiness.

However disagreeable Mrs. Nayburn might be to him this afternoon or evening, Diddy's not offended. Feels sorry for the elderly woman about to return, alone, to the place she called home. Leaving behind the person closest to her, virtually her daughter. Returning to no loved ones. A widow and childless for the rest of her days. Even though, as Hester has assured Diddy, Aunt Jessie's prospects back in Terre Haute are not that sad. Has her job at the Public Library until she turns sixty-five, and has many friends her own age whom she's known all her life.

When, over their last dinner together, Mrs. Nayburn argumentatively brings up the question of when he and Hester are going to marry, Diddy was tempted to speak the truth. To tell the woman that the decision rested entirely with her niece. That he, for his part, was ready to marry Hester any time. Tomorrow, if she wanted. But then reconsidered, thinking that the truth might sound ominously complicated to Mrs. Nayburn, though it really was quite simple. Wavering, not knowing exactly what to say.

"You know, Dalton," the woman continued plaintively, "I've been pretty broad-minded about you and Hester. I've never suggested you come back and have a church wedding and all that. I know how young people feel these days. And Hester is so strong-

217

minded, I wouldn't even dare propose it to her. But you're more levelheaded than she is. You're a reasonable, well-brought-up young man, I can see that. I saw it right away, from the beginning. On the train. So make Aunt Jessie happy, will you? There's been enough scandal in our family already. . . . I know I can't make you do anything you don't want to do. Hester's of age; so are you, of course. Still, I'm asking you anyway. Give me your promise that you'll marry as soon as Hester leaves the hospital. I don't care if it's a civil ceremony; you can make it as simple as you like. Just so you're married, not living together like animals. Please promise, Dalton."

Genuinely moved, Diddy gave Mrs. Nayburn the promise she wanted. Half rising out of his seat, leaned across the restaurant table, took her head with the untidy gray hair in his two hands. And gravely kissed her on both cheeks.

The next afternoon Diddy took Mrs. Nayburn to the station to see her off; she wouldn't have to change trains once to get back to Terre Haute. His first time in the station since his arrival almost three weeks ago. On adjacent tracks, the New York, Boston & Standard trains were operating. Indeed, he read from the information board that the Privateer itself, on its daily run from Buffalo to New York City, was due in forty-three minutes. Diddy shaken by a slight surprise to have evidence that the train was still running. A foolish surprise. Could he have thought there were no other Privateers after his, after the one that made the northbound run on October 27th?

Diddy wondering what had happened to his feelings. Dead? Or just muffled under his new flesh? How was it possible for Incardona's murder to recede so far from his mind as it had these two weeks? Diddy must be living in some dream. Or suffering from amnesia. Or undergoing the disintegration of his character.

That's why, boarding the train carrying Mrs. Nayburn's suitcase and some of her brown-paper bundles, helping her to locate her roomette and get settled in, Diddy didn't think he would be particularly upset. Wrong, again. He was. The train-world brought back all the familiar constrictions, recharged the old nightmare. Within moments, he'd begun to panic. Desperately fearful that the train would start up before he could get off, and carry him away from Hester.

"Thought I heard the whistle," muttered Diddy anxiously.

"The conductor said the train stops here for twenty minutes. I'm sure you have time. . . . Dalton, reach me down that suitcase again from the rack, please. I want to take out my bedroom slippers."

"No, I'm sure I heard something." Terrified of being trapped on the train, Diddy grabbed upward at the suitcase, in his haste pulling at it clumsily and knocking himself on the head with it as he brought it down.

"Oh, you've hurt yourself! Let me look at it. Dear me! Wait a minute, I have some Band-Aids in the suitcase."

"Don't fuss, Jessie. It's nothing."

"But you're bleeding, Dalton. Don't you have a handkerchief? Here, use mine." The woman began rummaging in her purse. Diddy thought he heard the train whistle again. Convinced that if he is bleeding slightly near his hairline, it was because the blood was pounding so hard in his head. His skull felt as if it was about to split open.

Waving aside the handkerchief that Mrs. Nayburn withdrew from her purse, Diddy leaned over, touched her soft powdery cheek with his lips, and delivered her a curt goodbye.

Once on the platform, he felt very foolish. Plenty of passengers were still boarding the train; some strolling down the platform, seeming in no rush at all. The train was supposed to leave at three minutes after two. His watch said ten minutes to two; so did the platform clock. Of course he stayed, waving at the woman and directing smiles at her through the dirty window. After what seems an interminable time, the whistle did sound. Men along the platform made their signals. Was there someone on the track right in front of the train, a workman just (now) clambering to safety? Diddy couldn't see ahead of the long straight train. Slowly, the train started up. Diddy ran alongside it for a few yards, maintaining his pantomime of waving and smiling. The train picked up speed. Diddy stops.

If only he can get out of the station without mishap. Who

knows, Capt. Mallory may be lurking around, still pursuing his investigation, though it's not recorded in the papers. Capt. Mallory, having studied a list of the passengers who were on the Privateer on Sunday, October 27th, somehow, through an occult hunch, recognizing Diddy and stopping him to ask questions. Or Myra Incardona, down to complain about why she hasn't received the dough she thinks is owed her by the railroad, emerging red-faced through some office door with puny Thomas Francis in tow. Or even the stamp dealer or the plump cleric, either of whom may live in this city or have business which brings him here regularly from New York.

If Diddy really means to turn his back upon the past, that means not just Joan but all of the past; all. Even the most recent. Even the most terrifying. Supreme courage is needed to refuse the past, a courage far greater than that required in situations of acute physical danger. Diddy not all that brave. The past draws. Like a wind tunnel, with Diddy the ingenious scale model of some new experimental airplane that's being thrust into the tunnel, fiercely buffeted. And while perhaps not simply, rudely, shattering in pieces, the model visibly trembles; sags; buckles under the tunnel's stresses. Is too fragile to meet the normal standards of performance and safety. With rethinking and more work in the laboratories, the structural faults of the new plane may be mended. So it is urged. But is it worth it? The plane has had its chance, been put to the test. Energy is better spent working on something new, an object without the stigma of failure. So the company decides to invest no more money or time in research on the plane; cancels plans to put it into production.

Diddy feels the sucking of the wind. Feels himself swaying, as he might if he were still excessively thin. But no, he's not that thin any more; though not fat either. And it's only the bitter wind of winter; for Diddy's farther north, where the climate is colder than he's used to. Added to the violent air currents set up by the thunderous entrances and exits of the trains. But that's not enough to account for Diddy's having trouble standing erect. He's not that fragile.

True. And not that strong either; or particularly brave. But then, he doesn't have to be (now), since he's no longer alone. If the past draws, here's a counterpull from the present. That is, the future.

Diddy still in the station, but heading away from the site of train traffic. Heading (now) toward the exit. Past may not be directly converted into future, but the problem admits of a more round-about solution. Treat time as space. Once time is converted into space, then one space may be exchanged for another. For example: Diddy's case. The past is here. Here where the guilt surges up. So he will go elsewhere. And he has a place to go to, the hospital where his future is being born. Diddy has Hester and the space she inhabits, which he will share with her. And when she shares with him the space he inhabits, when he draws her into it, it will become a different space. Transformed and disinfected.

Diddy in a taxi, his panic and tumult pacified, getting closer and closer to the hospital and his afternoon hours with Hester. Is Diddy being complacent? Perhaps. Thus far, Hester is a very smooth stone in his consciousness. Not that he's complacent about the girl; his feeling for her has all the energy of romantic passion. But he's not obsessed with her. She's too exclusively a release from, or neutralization of, his obsessions.

How well does he understand Hester apart from himself? Not very well, it would seem. Admittedly, she doesn't make understanding easy. But is Diddy trying as hard as he might? The sum of all his recent efforts.

Perhaps, to understand Hester, he'll have to do more than love her and be in love with her. Perhaps, if their union is to succeed and their life together genuinely flourish, he will have to become obsessed with her. But is one ever obsessed with anything except what is, in some way, destructive? No. Then perhaps Diddy will have to locate the element of destructiveness lodged deep in Hester. Seems absurd, doesn't it? But perhaps not. There aren't any saints on this earth, are there?

Take Hester's attitude to her mother. Can't be that her daughter simply forgives Stella Nayburn for what she did when Hester was fourteen. Can't be that Hester simply loves and misses her mother. What happened to the rage of the betrayed child? She could only

221

suppress it, which means it's still there: coming out, inverted, as goodness. With dark and bitter fluids seething underneath. Maybe Hester doesn't know how else to be; except to be good. But, if that's the case, she's murderously good. Cannot expunge her dark, demonic side. Only keep it hidden. Diddy must look at her more carefully. Without getting too close. Without inviting Hester to turn a comparable look on him.

The taxi is pulling up in front of the Warren Institute. Diddy pays, gets out. Lying in his pocket, the paperback edition of *Emma*. He stops off at the coffee shop in the hospital lobby; orders an egg salad sandwich on toast and a coffee to go. Hester, a light eater, will already have had her lunch; but Diddy, who gobbled down a club sandwich with Mrs. Nayburn at the station an hour ago, is hungry again. As he rides up the elevator, with his small paper bag in his hand, the inside of his mouth begins to get moist. Its stimulus: being hungry and knowing he's about to be fed. Another stimulus: a wave of tenderness toward Hester. Anticipation of the intense pleasure of just seeing her, sharing this afternoon with her, however restricted their situation. But it's improving all the time. Today Mrs. Nayburn left. No more talking for courtesy's sake. And Hester herself is more active. Ever since she's been allowed out of bed—a week already—they may choose either to stay in her room or to settle in the patients' lounge at the end of the corridor. And on the horizon, only two days away, the largest choice of all: the whole world from which to carve out their space.

His thoughts in the taxi seem (now) very foolish to Diddy. His plans to scrutinize the girl in the hope of unmasking her perfections, something perverse and mean-spirited. If Hester discloses flaws of character, as who does not, he will be the tactful lover. Like Mr. Knightly, waiting patiently, his true sentiments undeclared, until the moment when Emma perceives her follies, feels shame over them, and repudiates them. Then, because it's finally wanted, Mr. Knightly can offer the healing balm of his generous love.

Presumptuous Diddy! Far more likely to be Hester who will discover the flaws, his flaws. Hester who will need much patience to put up with him. But can't that painful process be circumvented? If Diddy already knows what he does that's foolish and stupid, why can't he become wise? Act wisely. For, oh, Diddy has perceived his follies countless times. Is heartily ashamed of them, strenuously repudiates them. It's only that he doesn't understand. Not really. A hopeless, bumbling tourist in the somber labyrinth of his own consciousness.

> The punitive labyrinth.
> The initiatory labyrinth.
> The architectonic labyrinth.

The girl with the oval sunglasses, sure-footed in the dark, will lead him out.

"Hester?" Not in her room. Diddy wants to know from the college student and the wife of the state senator where she's gone.

Probably in the lounge.

Diddy races down the corridor. To the room at the end, a room with a wall of windows like a sun porch. Yes! At the sight of her, Diddy's heart breaks open; for somewhere he's never rid of the fear that Hester doesn't exist. Or will vanish, as Incardona has. Be withdrawn, like the newspaper account of Incardona's death. Diddy troubled by the diminished substantiality of this death, the fact that he's (now) so much less powerfully obsessed by it.

Hester, stretched out on a leather reclining chair, wrapped in her yellow bathrobe, holds her face to the sun. Her long blond hair hangs over the sides of the chair; looking as if it had been freshly washed. This morning? How pale she is. So much in need of sun, pure air, exercise, food that whets the appetite, and the body of an ardent lover. But Hester has, at least, found the sun. Which starts, glintingly, off her dark glasses. As Hester is the sun that Diddy's found, the black sun.

Wednesday morning, three days later. Hester scheduled to leave the hospital at ten o'clock.

On the slight chance that she might be sent down earlier, Diddy arrived at nine. Is Diddy's early arrival the precaution of Diddy the

223

Overexcited? Not exactly. Arrived a whole hour early because of the pleasure he took in being extra-considerate on Hester's behalf, the most vigilant lover and protector imaginable. Preferring to wait for her rather than run the slightest risk of keeping her waiting for him. And also, a less happy reason. Because he senses that Hester is suspicious of him. Something more than the natural mistrust of the blind and dependent of those to whose care they are, without recourse, committed. It was a mistrust of him, Diddy. Who has (now) to prove himself to his bride.

At exactly ten, Hester comes out of an elevator into the lobby. A nurse is holding her arm, carrying her suitcase. Diddy stubs out his cigarette in a free-standing metal ashtray, jumps up from the bench where he's been restlessly chain-smoking and thumbing through magazines, rushes across the marble floor to embrace the girl. And to grasp her arm and the suitcase. As they're walking out the imposing main door, Diddy notices that Hester's pretty face seems puffy. Has she been weeping? Her eyes, of course, are concealed by the large oval dark glasses, so he can't tell without asking. But doesn't want to ask. If Diddy can make Hester happy starting from today, it won't matter. And he can. Feels full of energy. Enough for both of them.

"Let's walk a little," he says. "The sun is so good."

An unseasonably warm day for late November. Diddy helps Hester take off the light brown camel's hair coat she's wearing, and folds it over his left arm.

Diddy steering, they walk the three blocks leading directly to Monroe Park. Diddy, exhilarated, wanting to think only of her, can't help noticing with displeasure how many men stop, turn around, leer grossly at her soft body in the slight, clinging dress. Like the one she wore on the train, a dress intended to be touched more than to be seen. Ordinarily, Diddy would be pleased to notice other men envying him his woman, coveting her. When men had stared in the street at Joan, Diddy liked it. Different with Hester. Joan could see the men staring at her, could look at the men themselves; appraise them, reject them, reaffirm Diddy. But Hester, who can't see anyone, can't make many choices. Take, for example, what's happening at this very moment. That bastard in the blue jeans who just strutted by. And stared, then mouthed and tongued at her obscenely. Maybe, if she could see, Hester would choose to go with him. Maybe she'd prefer him to Diddy.

Even though the sun is shining. Even though Hester is truly his for the first time: they're outside in the world, just the two of them; he has her entirely to himself. Still Diddy continues to think of the world. As well as of Hester. Diddy, not exactly glad she doesn't see, is glad she'll never see how ugly everything is. A potent ignorance. Perhaps, hopefully, contagious. If Hester can't see the ugliness, it's possible that, after a while, he'll be unable to see it, too. How fine that would be. Simply not to see. Garbage trucks, bums, neon signs, gutters, plastic toys, parking lots, unhappy children, Automats, old women on the benches of the traffic islands on upper Broadway.

He can't imagine ever, in Hester's company, being frightened of Incardona. Because she could never share his terror. How fortunate (now) for Diddy that Hester doesn't believe in what happened in the tunnel. Extra insulation from his fears, besides the fact that blind people can't see ghosts, any more than they can see palpable people. They can't be haunted. Can be, at worst, only bewildered. Diddy's not frightened of Incardona (now). Because he no longer has to think only, or even mainly, of himself. Hester is here, interposed between Diddy and himself. Unable to see. Refusing to see. Refusing to acknowledge the doubling of the self in dreams.

They're approaching the park. It had rained yesterday, and Diddy is dizzy with pleasure at the keen smell of the air this morning. "Smell it, darling," he exclaims. His right arm, the arm he has encircling her waist, pulling her even more strongly against his right side. "Do you feel the sun?"

Yes.

"We're passing a pond with . . . let me see . . . seven white and brown ducks. A boy is trying to launch a metal model of a PT boat in the pond . . . But it's sinking. Listen, he's crying. Now his mother is picking him up. . . ."

Past the duck pond. "Do you want an ice-cream cone? A Popsicle? An Eskimo Pie?"

Yes. A vanilla thing on a stick with coconut icing. Diddy buys two of them.

A little farther, out of the vendor's sight. Diddy chooses a sunny piece of ground under a tree, lays their coats to one side. "Feel the bark of the tree, darling. Here, give me your hand. . . ." He sits beneath the tree, leans his back against the trunk; Hester stretches out perpendicular to him, rests her head on his thighs.

"You've gained weight." Nuzzling her head against his belly. "You needed to. It's much nicer now."

Diddy throws back his head against the trunk, looking up into the sky. If he could just have this moment always inside his head. No words are conceivable. She must understand. What Diddy feels for Hester is rooted more deeply than anything ever felt for Joan, or for any other woman. His love is the signature of his life.

"Are you comfortable, Dalton? Never mind my head, if you want to change your position."

"I am. I won't." He strokes her hair, then grasps her head, and pulls it over the pulsing sex inside his trousers; against his belly. "Try to sleep."

Hester seems to breathe more slowly and deeply. Is she asleep (now)? Diddy could push back her glasses to see whether her eyes are closed, but that might wake her. For one thing, because the sun is strong and he doesn't know whether her eyes still retain some sensitivity to light.

No, she's moving slightly. Passing her hand across her forehead.

"Were you crying this morning before you came down?" asks Diddy softly and after a longish silence. The girl nods. "Why? Will you tell me?" Maybe Hester was grieving for her mother. Had this operation succeeded in restoring her sight, her mother's crime would have been repealed. Stella Nayburn, though still guilty, would somehow be made less guilty. As Diddy's guilt would diminish, though never disappear altogether, if Incardona could rise from the dead.

"Why?" Diddy repeats.

"Because I still have so many tears inside me. And I don't believe in miracles."

Diddy suspects that something bad is happening. But wants to allow it, not deflect it. "By a miracle, do you mean us? Our coming together. You don't believe in . . . that?"

"Yes," said Hester.

"I see. No, maybe I don't see . . . Tell me, is believing in it so very important?"

"No. At least I don't think so . . ." Diddy gasped. Was it all right then? He could understand the words. Hester reaches up to touch his cheek. "Am I upsetting you? I'm sorry. I don't want to."

"Don't worry about me," Diddy said hoarsely.

"But I do," Hester says. "You know I do. Everything's more difficult for you than it is for me, I think. You have a truth that's different from mine. Granted mine is painful. But yours is even harder to endure. Don't you know I know that?"

"I don't understand what you're saying."

"Don't you? I don't know how to explain any better. . . . Look, Dalton, I understand what you feel about me. But it isn't as simple as you think. You're so pious, darling." Diddy smiled at the endearment. "That's where the business of truth comes in. You want to annihilate your truth, and be like me. I don't think you can do that, Dalton. And even if you can, you shouldn't want to. You have to respect my limits. And yours. You mustn't be too eager to change yourself."

Mainly, what Diddy heard were the sweet tones of Hester's voice. But does understand a little; knew that he was being rebuked. Tenderly. And, therefore, found the rebuke acceptable. As long as Hester wasn't taking back her love. Which, already, had become almost unthinkable. Suppose, one day, she declares in her quiet way, I don't love you. If what Hester would be saying was that she'd never loved him, never, he felt (now) he would die. However, if what Hester would mean was that she didn't love him any more, then Diddy could try to make her love him again. Putting his life as the forfeit. Of course, couldn't literally force Hester to love him. He'd have to convince her. But by what means? What signs, tokens, evidence of his love could he give to a blind person?

"I love you so much." Is it wrong for Diddy to say that (now)? As his only reply to what she's just said? Words cannot compel the unconditional movements of the heart.

"You know I love you, Dalton. I just hope my love is good for you."

Diddy, bending over to find Hester's mouth, her tongue. If she only knew.

Diddy satisfied. He has his treasure, has banished his swarthy demon with the flame of love. His blond, sightless angel will heal him, will redeem him. Which she's already begun to do. And he, in return, will protect her from the world. Which is partitioned off with walls, made of wood and brick and stone and cement; which is stocked with sharp pointed objects that cut the flesh; which is charged with dead looks and inhumane caresses that bruise the spirit. Diddy will devote himself entirely to taking care of her.

Goody Did aware of the selfish gratifications in all this. Attached to his pledge of absolute devotion and care, there's one stipulation. Hester is to depend on him, and on no one else. To see the world through him only, not through the eyes of any other. That much is fixed. Diddy won't share Hester with anyone. Does she know how fanatically possessive of her he's going to be? Will she hate that?

Gratified apart from the need to possess. . . . In contemplating all the arduous responsibilities and practical tasks about to be his, Diddy has, correctly, no sense that he's making a sacrifice. For he himself will be a co-beneficiary of his humblest daily services for Hester. If Hester will benefit from his faithful attendance in a practical sense, he gains more. Gains in a spiritual way.

That benefit consisting in the fact that, when he will be charged with narrating the visible world to Hester and negotiating for her all her transactions with palpable things, he'll have a chance to see the whole world with fresh eyes.

Diddy will tell Hester about old sunsets, and the sun will be seen to fall behind the horizon for the first time. Seeing a child being beaten will not make him weep blood for days after. The literature about the Nazi concentration camps will no longer seem the only real truth about man. The death of a gnat will become something trivial: the death of a gnat. The muck of large cities will not so easily leap from its crevasses and ledges, and adhere to him. The loud, rude, metallic voices won't collect like silt inside his head.

And all the imaginary and swiftly imagined lives of bedraggled passers-by in subways, in buses, in auditoriums, on beaches, in parks, in offices, and on the street will seem less mortally horrifying.

Though his job is to protect Hester from the world, Diddy will try to view the world more generously. Not only as an arena of contamination, but also as a space to be continually reinvented and reexamined. If only he weren't so fearful of being touched. Convinced in advance as he is that it's bound to be wounding, not soothing. So fearful of touching. Convinced in advance as he is that he's bound to be repulsed.

Undoubtedly, Diddy's fears would be modified if he couldn't see. Sight permits him to reach conclusions at a distance, before he's come close enough to touch and be touched. Sight encourages abstractions—a luxury of sighted persons. While for Hester, as for all blind persons, judgment must wait until she closes, in specific contact, with something particular. When nothing has a look, there are no general categories. When nothing has a look, everything becomes concrete, palpable, touchable.

It occurs to Diddy that perhaps all his terrors derive from the mixed blessing of being able to see. Because he can see, he can perceive the world abstractly. At a distance. That's what Diddy has to unlearn. Disband his imagination, which is glued with incredulity upon past images and gazes with apprehension into the tube of the future. That imagination which depletes his vitality, consigning everything to the rack of time. To be in the present; to be without imagination, unable to anticipate anything; to be.

Of course, he can't get rid of his eyes. Not the right sort of guilt. Diddy's is the harder task: with the fleshy globes—ninety percent water—still lodged in his skull and functioning normally. Must unlearn the old ways of seeing. If it's not too late.

Immediately upon his return with Hester to New York, Diddy submitted his resignation to Watkins & Company. "Reasons of health." The refund of what he'd paid into the company pension plan, proceeds from some stock, which the company was eager to buy back, and three years' savings add up to enough to keep himself and Hester going for at least a year and maintain the payments to Joan. Diddy vaguely thinks of some kind of job he might do at home before the money starts to run out. Such as translating technical books; Diddy's good at languages, knows German and Russian. Or free-lance editing for a publishing house that specializes in scientific and medical literature; he's qualified for such work and through his former job has many contacts in the scientific-journal and book-publishing worlds. But hasn't yet done anything toward lining up such a job. Or about going down to City Hall and getting a license. Or started looking for a new apartment.

In the opening days of an unseasonably warm December, Diddy and Hester spend most waking hours outdoors and, so far as the word applies, sightseeing. Hester, though made nervous by the roaring, screeching, and honking of heavy oncoming traffic, seems to crave variety and the sense of movement. At first Diddy conducts long excursions: the Bronx Zoo for the animals' sounds and smells; the lake in Central Park to get away from cars; the Battery and the Staten Island ferry for the stench of the sea, tar, and creosote, and for the rocking and dipping of the boat. As they roam about Coney Island, Diddy conjures up with words the ravaged skeletons of last summer's contraptions for amusement; after sneaking in to poke amid the rat-infested ruins of the World's Fair, Diddy keeps up two hours of the same kind of animated verbal picturing. Diddy can be a lively talker when he wants to please someone. Then a silent day: wandering hand in hand along the wintry deserted beach at Montauk.

Piece by piece, reentering the world. But hasn't Diddy mistaken this enterprise, and drawn the map of too big a world? Isn't his reach too long? Remember who is his companion (now). Hester is not only blind but entirely unfamiliar with this city and its environs. But maybe being blind is all that counts. To her, all places and all distances must be virtually the same. Unable to surmise what relation one place has to another, how can she ever know, at any given moment, where she is?

While awaiting further insight into the topography of the blind, Diddy decides to rein in his explorations with Hester. Closer to home. Manhattan: where the distance is counted in blocks, and blocks can be measured in feet. But this doesn't mean that Diddy will be bored or become restless. Though a resident for over a decade, Diddy is far from knowing his adopted city well. Even neighborhoods of downtown Manhattan, the locations of both his apartments, contain sights he finds fresh.

In the second week, then, a smaller scale. Forgoing public transportation; they venture only as far as they can walk. Diddy describes the buildings, the cars, the billboards, the people they pass on the street. While speaking, tries to sift the nightmare out of his vision, to disinfect his words of disgust. To be neutral, vivid, even humorous. The strange thing is that once Diddy has decided for Hester's sake to suppress his morbid reactions and to cultivate his sense of humor, it's not difficult at all. Everything just as funny (now) as before it was appalling. The signs on the stores and warehouses and trucks in the neighborhood, for instance. Haven't they always been there? Diddy must have seen them before, hundreds of times, marketing or picking up his laundry or walking Xan or passing in a taxi. Then why, as he reads them off to Hester, do they seem so exotic and arbitrary (now)?

> Congo Tire Company
> Manhattan Auto Radio and Repair Company
> Welcome Fulton Tenants Meat Market
> Pena Pharmacy
> Automated Flowers
> Eagle Paper and Twine Company
> L & S Dairy
> Murtha's Bar and Restaurant
> Gothic Color Company, Inc.
> Hercules Flooring Company
> Brause & Brause Dog Training School
> Eureka Stamps and Coins
> Jacob Rice Glass Company

Troiano Trucking
Good Heart Restaurant
Universal Japanning Company, Inc.
Peper Painting Supplies
Reliable Coated Fabrics Company
Uneeda Printing
Mensch Mill & Lumber Company
Century Composition Service Inc.
Gallant-Roth Blouses
New Chelsea Reform Democratic Club
Adele Delivery Company
Johnny's Hot & Cold Heros
Rentways, Inc.
Kaplan Rigid Set-Up Sales Packaging
Ecco Knives
Accurate Steel Partition Company, Inc.
Country Custom Cleaners
Ben Gentry & Son, Pork Butchers
Spectronic Plating Company
La Muralla China

Usually, after Diddy has called off several of the names, they both break into a paroxysm of giggling.

Squatting near the entrance to the West Side Highway is an old-fashioned diner, railroad-car style, with a long blue neon sign running almost the length of the roof: OLD DUTCH COFFEE. At the beginning of their daily walk Diddy and Hester usually stop here for a sandwich and coffee, play the jukebox, eavesdrop on the banter between the truck drivers and longshoremen and the waitresses. Most days during the second week, they continue on foot as far as the Forties, where they shop in the odorous Greek, Italian, and Spanish grocery stores; then, as laden with brown shopping bags as ever Aunt Jessie was, take a cab downtown. Xan is brought along on these expeditions at first. But the dog was an encumbrance, too much for Diddy to manage. Who didn't want to divide his attention. And, to his surprise, Hester seemed entirely uninterested in the dog.

In the third week, the weather turns sharply. One day of light snow, several of rain, another of heavy snow and sleet. The daily walk gets shorter, and is usually confined to an area close to home. On the coldest days, they avoid the river, where the wind is stronger and crueler; walking east instead. A dreary part of the city, except for the flower market. On one walk, Diddy, not very hopefully, tries to evoke and bring to life for Hester the Christmas statues on the façade of Macy's; after which they huddle for ten minutes in the store entrance to get warm, and are driven out by the crush of shoppers. Of the strolls Hester and Diddy take together (now), that was the longest. But it seems less necessary to walk about at all. Food, not as tasty or as varied as what they bought on Ninth Avenue, can be ordered by telephone from the nearest supermarket. Some days it's only Diddy who goes out, three times, to walk the dog. Which he tries to do as quickly as possible, feeling apprehensive about leaving Hester for even a few minutes. Xan is becoming an absolute nuisance.

Cutting out the daily walk leaves that much more time for activities at home. Hester won't hear of having a maid; insists on doing the cleaning herself. But first Diddy must bring Hester to every object in the apartment, so she can touch it and learn its location. While her hands are engaged in sensuous study of the object, Diddy usually relates where he bought it and anything memorable in his past connected with it. The home as museum, a meditation on one's past, a miniature mausoleum. Diddy comes to tell Hester a good deal about his bleak passionate marriage in this way, though until recently he'd shied away from even referring to Joan. Assuming Hester would prove to be as possessive and pained over his past as he would have been, had she been married before.

Hester listens to Diddy's anecdotes attentively, but always appears satisfied by as much or as little as he tells her. The truth, somewhat painful to Diddy, is that she seems barely curious about that former life of his. Perhaps it's simply not real to her. The only point at which she sometimes questions Diddy closely is when the object, whether a roasting pan or a lithograph or a lamp, is identified as something Joan herself had selected. But hadn't taken with her when she left.

"Do you keep that for a reason? Does it remind you of her?"

It didn't. Thank God, not any more. But Diddy savored this evidence that Hester, for all her ostensible calm on the subject of Joan, might be a shade jealous after all. Relished, too, Hester's apparent freedom from any romance with objects. Was that freedom one of the dividends of blindness? No matter. Not for Diddy to know. Whatever the reason, an enviable trait. Diddy, all his life helplessly loyal to his past, however ungratifying, and plagued by useless attachments to souvenirs and vestiges of the past, found Hester's indifference an inspiration.

For Diddy to feel liberated, disburdened, Hester needn't insult or snub his objects. And didn't. She simply has to turn on them the innocent neutrality of her sightless appraisal. It's for Diddy, then, to scour his all-too-retentive vision. Which he does, with scarcely any sense of strain. In introducing Hester to each object, guiding her hand over its surface, relating its history, Diddy comes to see his possessions with a fresh eye. Sometimes discovers that he doesn't at all like something he owns. For example, the pair of blue-green vases with a spider-web design in relief, circa 1900, he'd bought in the Flea Market in Paris two summers ago. At least, no longer likes them (now).

The eye as window;
The eye as lamp;
The eye as jewel.
But what is more discriminating and peremptory than the white hymen of the eyeball?

Thus, apart from the pleasure all intimacy between them affords, making an inventory of his world for Hester brings Diddy several minor, private pleasures. Among them, the pleasure of throwing out intact, handsome, satisfactorily functioning things. After putting the Art Nouveau vases out with the trash one Friday evening, Diddy's impulse is not to mention it at all. Except that he must. Hester's navigational chart must be kept scrupulously up to date. These are, or were, two less objects for her to steer clear of.

December is almost used up. Just before Christmas, a bitterly cold week. They discuss whether to get a tree. Even though Xan, who's so refractory to discipline lately, will probably make a shambles of it, why not? Something good to smell. Hester smiles and puts her arms around Diddy in an unfamiliar way, almost shyly. Diddy has a fleeting glimpse of the little girl Hester once was or could have been, and rejoices. He bundles her up, fussing over her, insisting on ski socks and his windbreaker under her winter coat, as well as a muffler and mittens; then, perhaps unconsciously, under-dresses himself. They go down, the first time they've been out to-gether that week. Giddy with happiness, Diddy decides to buy two bulky firs, each seven feet tall; one for the living room and one for the bedroom; and breathlessly—why does he get so easily out of breath?—lugs them, one at a time, up the four flights. Decides it's hardly worthwhile to put up the bulbs, strings of lights, and tinsel for himself alone. The trees seem more vigorous for being nude. Their pungent odor is like a little spill of life into the quiet apart-ment. Smell this one! Now smell this one, darling! Isn't there a slight difference? Yes? Can you tell? Now I want to smell you. And be-fore Diddy sets to work installing the trees in the flimsy red and green stands purchased at Woolworth's, he leads Hester to their bed to make love.

Love is beautiful and strong. So are the trees. And so is food.

Diddy had almost forgotten the less glamorous but no less re-warding satisfactions of marital domesticity. Having someone to eat all his meals with, for instance. Though currently supplied with only the canned and frozen fare delivered from the supermarket, their meals are attractive. Diddy, reasonably skilled in the kitchen, has been doing all the cooking throughout this first month. While Hester keeps him company in the small kitchen, perched on a skinny stool next to the refrigerator, and afterwards helps with the dishes. One evening, just as Diddy is rolling up his sleeves to begin dinner, she claims his job. "Please, Dalton!" Diddy afraid she'll burn herself. But Hester assures him that she's memorized the site and operation of every kitchen appliance; knows the contents of each cabinet; can put her hands in a moment on the canned goods, the dishes, the pots, the pot-holder, the spices, the silverware. To bolster her credentials, reminds Diddy that from the age of eighteen it was she who did most of the cooking for her aunt and herself. Of course, doting Diddy shrinks from refusing Hester anything she wants. But can a blind person be the best judge of her own safety? Diddy hears himself sounding much more like an anxious parent than a lover, and dreads Hester so interpreting his tone and resenting it. But she doesn't seem to. Just laughingly orders him out of the kitchen while she goes to work. Diddy slumped in the bentwood rocker in the living room, sweating with apprehension. Gets up to pour himself a shot of rye; then another. Meanwhile, Hester opens a can of gazpacho, heats up a package of frozen spinach, fries two slices of liver in butter, and brews the coffee. Other than bringing in the soup can and package of vegetables for Diddy to verify that they're what she thinks they are, manages everything without his aid. Not making a single mistake. Sugar is sugar, not salt. And, thank heaven, no burns or bruises.

Diddy insists, nervously, on at least setting the table in the dining area.

No, not that either.

Hester puts down a fresh linen tablecloth, and hands Diddy a bottle of sangría for him to uncork. They haven't eaten so ceremoniously in several weeks. Most meals have been spread on the floor in the living room or taken into bed. And tonight's food, Diddy has to admit, is as tasty as anything he's prepared. Still, he finds it hard to eat. What's happening to Diddy's appetite?

"Let's have some brandy," Hester said, when they settled in the living room. Diddy, always a reluctant drinker—liquor usually made him feel dull and depressed; never, even initially, euphoric —agreed. Should have told Hester he'd had two shots while she was in the kitchen, but didn't want to spoil the festive character of the evening. Maybe it was the sequence of whisky, wine, and brandy: more than Diddy could stomach without feeling done in. He went to bed early.

From then on, Hester cooked the dinner. The next night there was a new cloth on the table, and the wine was Pouilly-Fumé. The third night, the same cloth and a bottle of Pommard. On the fourth night, Diddy refuses to drink any wine. It couldn't be only the wine, but he's noticed that he gets drowsy (now) very early each evening. Wineless meals are good, too. Gradually, they took to eating more sloppily again. To accompany the meals on the living-

236

room floor, Diddy usually builds a wood fire, even though the apartment is, if anything, overheated during the winter months. The fire smells so good; and these days he's hearing more acutely, finding the sound of flames as vivid and satisfying as their turbulent color.

Diddy balks at putting music on during the dinner. Because he wants Hester's attention all for himself. Whether or not they talk through the meal—often, long silences arise between them that Diddy finds either narcotically soothing or mortifying—he wants to leave untrammeled the possibility of talk. After eating, though, Diddy was content to let the time be furnished by something other than his love. By music then. And discovers a small lump of tension between them. Hester really likes only string trios, quartets, quintets, and their improbable enlargements. Diddy the Eclectic loves his Papa Haydn, too. But life proposes more than one set of loyalties. Undertakes with zeal to convert Hester to his fondness for blues, rock 'n roll, and folk rock. Tries out everything from Dylan to Billie Holiday to the Beatles, whom he eulogized, for Hester's benefit, as the collective Mozart of recent pop music. Even attempted to teach her to frug, as Joan had taught him. But Hester remains unmoved. Diddy, by this time, has given up. No more struggling awake bleary-eyed at 8 a.m. to WOR. Goodbye Top Forty. Following dinner, Diddy is perfectly willing to stack the chamber music LP's high on the long spindle of the hi-fi, or keep the dial roving among the FM classical-music stations until Hester hears what she likes.

Most evenings, soon after their meal, Diddy reads aloud. Almost done with *Sense and Sensibility*. But Hester doesn't seem to find Jane Austen as delightful as she did in the hospital. When he finishes this one, perhaps they shouldn't pass on to *Mansfield Park* right away. Choose another writer. Or, in case it's his reading she is tired of, not read at all.

Starting at the end of the second week, Diddy gets into the habit of not turning on the lights after sunset. Unless it's decided he will read aloud. Man and wife, one flesh: Diddy doesn't need electric light in the evening any more than Hester does. Finds he can

237

manage quite as well in the dark. It's never wholly dark anyway, thanks to the street lamps outside. But what Diddy wants doesn't require even that dim light. He wants to touch.

Idling. Becalmed. Like a pair of moist happy ducks.

Partly undressed, entangled together, silent, in near darkness. Lying full-length on the living-room couch one evening after midnight, some four weeks after returning to New York. The flatulent buzzer that announces a visitor downstairs. A guilty commotion in Diddy's heart. Paul? Incardona? No, take that back. Don't be a fool.

What is Diddy to do? In a way, he's safe. No one can just walk in on him; no one else has the key. If he doesn't buzz back, Paul can't ever know he wasn't out. Or, if there, in the darkened apartment, so deeply asleep that he can't hear the buzzer.

"It must be my brother." No answer from Hester. Diddy sits up, pulls on his shirt. "Hester, are you asleep? Did you hear me before?"

"Yes, darling, I heard you. But you must do what you want." She's awake. But still prone; has made no move to dress herself.

What kind of reply is that? Who is Diddy the Indecisive that he should do what he wants? Presumptuous enterprise! But wait, think of it this way. Whatever he does (now), he won't, strictly speaking, be doing what he wants. Since it's Hester who has given the master order, instructing him to do-what-he-wants.

Diddy gets up, goes into the hall, and buzzes back. Returns to the living room; kneels by the couch.

He'll be right up.

Gazes at Hester, wishing ardently that she could see. That she could mutely signal him with only her eyes what she advised him to do. The fluttering double pledge of love.

A knock at the front door. "You remember," he whispered. "I've told you. He never lets me know when he's coming. I never even know when he's in town."

The doorbell, pressed down impatiently. "Hey, Diddy!" Xan has darted into the small foyer, is barking and scratching at the door.

"Hester, do you want to meet my brother?" His voice faltered.

While the dog barks and Paul shouts, Diddy realizes, the thread linking Hester and himself has snapped. Another level of sound, another kind of energy is surging on both sides of that paneled door. Inimical to their contact.

"Are you there, Diddy? Wake up! Hey!"

"What's he calling you, Dalton?"

Too complicated to explain (now). Anyway, it's too noisy. Without answering, Diddy gets up. He's suddenly become afraid.

Afraid of Paul: of what will happen if he lets him in. Of what his brother will think of Hester. Will he see right away that she's blind? And of what he'll say to her. Maybe something coarse or enigmatic that will make Hester regard Diddy in a new, less favorable way. Or maybe he'll be rude to Hester, and wound her feelings.

Afraid of Hester: that she doesn't want to meet Paul but won't tell him that plainly. But Diddy can't read her mind, can he? Maybe he's wrong. Perhaps she does want to meet his brother; but considers it's for Diddy to make this decision and to take the responsibility.

"Paul?"

"For Christ's sake, Diddy, let me in."

Wait a minute!

Diddy grabs his keys and shoves them in the back pocket of the unpressed chinos he's wearing. Then opens the door slightly, as far as it can go with the chain latch still on. Blinking at the brightness of the hall light, and at Paul's eager, sharply illuminated face, at the long blond mustache and the brilliant black of his tuxedo. "Hi, Diddy! What's the matter? Were you asleep? Oh, I bet you've got a girl with you."

"Yes. And I can't let you in. But I'll come out."

Unlatches the door; opens it quickly so Xan can't escape, too; slips out into the hallway; closes it behind him.

It takes a while for Diddy to get accustomed to the blow of light. His eyes smart, and he can't stop blinking. Meanwhile, Paul's talking.

"I'm sorry to barge in on you like this. But couldn't I come in? I've really got a load on, and I'd give anything to lie down and sleep it off. I won't bother you."

Though his eyes are somewhat better (now), hurt much less, Diddy still glad he has other senses to work for him. That with his nose, for example, he could smell the alcohol on Paul's breath. As well as, with his sight, see. Notice Paul's swollen bleary eyes, and the slight disarray of his clothes. "I wish you could, Paulie. It's too complicated to explain, but I just can't let you stay tonight."

"Why, is she someone I know? It isn't Joan, for Christ's sake, is it?"

What a thought! "God, no."

"Oh, I bet I know. It's that actress you had around when I came up last August. She lives on this floor, doesn't she? What was her name?"

"Paul, listen. You don't know this girl at all. But I do want you to meet her. It's serious. We've been living together for about three weeks, and I'm hoping we can get married soon."

Paul, looking angry (now), started to unfasten his black bow tie. "Now, I really don't get it at all. It's not some married woman, right? Not a piece of jailbait. And not someone I know who doesn't want me to know that she's—" Paul's speech becoming slurred, indistinct; he grabbed Diddy's collar, then let go—"with you. Right?" Liquor always made Paul prattle. "In short, not just a lay, but the real thing. . . . So, I ask you, why can't you let me in right now? This is as good a time as any to meet her."

Diddy shrugged his shoulders. Paul straightened up, suddenly seeming almost sober. Not so drunk after all. Was he pretending? Oh, Paul was a clever one. Knows more games than Diddy had ever been able to figure out. (Now) seemed quite lucid and casual. He'd removed the tie; stuffed it in his pocket. "Um, I get it. You've been having a fight. Well, guess it's just my tough luck tonight." Or was that pretending, too?

"I'd like to explain, Paulie. But I need a little more time."

"Okay, okay. No hard feelings. I'll come by again soon." Paul, heading for the stairs, but then turning back. A deeper tone in his voice. "Listen, Diddy, is everything all right? You know, you look terrible. How come you've lost so much weight? Are you sick or something?"

Diddy, wary of some new gambit of Paul's. But the posture of wariness is hard to maintain, since he's genuinely startled by what Paul has just said. When had he started to lose weight again? Since Hester had taken over the cooking? And didn't notice because he hasn't put on a suit in weeks. Wears only chinos or loose-fitting corduroys, a T shirt or denim shirt or a sweater.

"I'm not sick. Don't worry about me."

"But you look awful," Paul insisted from one step down. "And you didn't go to work today looking like that, did you? I bet you haven't shaved for five days."

"It's been weeks since I've been to work."

"That's what I told you. You're sick."

"No. I quit my job."

Paul stepped up to the top of the landing again. "What in hell did you go and do that for?"

"Don't shout, Paul!" Diddy whispering. "I told you, I can't explain now. But it's all right."

Paul leaned against the wall, near Diddy. He was having a little trouble standing erect; at least, standing still. Out of courtesy and embarrassment, Diddy bore his blurred gaze for a while.

"Diddy, are you taking any stuff? You know what I mean?"

Diddy laughed. "You mean drugs? Don't be an ass."

"Honest? You can tell me."

"I've told you." Is Paul going to fall down?

"Well, then, do you need some bread? You know I make piles when I'm on tour. My own brother's got as much right to it as the government or my agent or those chicks I've been balling."

"When I need you to support me, Paulie, I'll let you know."

"Okay, okay, don't get mad. I'm just trying to be helpful. . . . Besides, if I unload some of the money on you, I'll have less for booze." He started giggling. "That's funny, huh?" Began to bend over, swaying, holding his stomach. "Because, you know," he said with a silly grin, "I'm a little tight right now. . . ."

Diddy remembering the pretty, off-Broadway actress in the apartment across the hall. Left the doorway and came over to Paul. "Listen, I'll walk you down. We're going to wake up everybody in the building."

Follows Paul downstairs, out on the street. A blast of icy air pregnant with snow. Suddenly, Diddy feels dizzy. Had to grab a railing, then sit on the stoop. Paul leans over him. "You *are* sick, Diddy-doo. You've got to call a doctor."

"Cut it out, Paul. I'm not sick. I just forgot to eat today, so I was feeling a little faint. And right now I'm freezing my ass off, sitting here. So you get going now. Find yourself a cab, and go sleep it off at one of your girlfriends' apartments. And call me tomorrow, don't forget. Maybe I'll have figured things out by then and you can meet Hester and I'll explain everything."

"Hester?"

"Yes, that's her name."

"How long have you known her?"

"Long enough, Paul. Mind your own business. Why don't you tell me where you think you're heading now, and how long you'll be in town." Diddy stood up.

"I'm worried about you, Diddy-doo. Maybe you ought to let me come upstairs." He belched. " 'Scuse me."

"Look, there's a cab. Run for it."

"He's got his off-duty sign on."

"Come on, you know that doesn't mean anything. Go ask the nice man if he'll take Paulie where he wants to go."

"Okay. I guess I'd better. I'm ready to drop." From across the street, as Paul got into the cab: "Call you tomorrow!"

Shivering, Diddy climbed back up the stairs. Two flights up, remembered he hadn't commented on the new mustache. When had he grown it? Not exactly flattering, but it made him look ten years older and that's to the good. Even Paul must have tired of being a boy genius forever.

On the fourth floor. Diddy let himself into his apartment. In what seemed to him (now) utter darkness, felt his way to the couch. Which Hester had vacated. Then, with his hands probing and groping outward, to their bedroom. She must be there. And she is. Already in bed, the covers drawn just above her waist. Diddy leaned over her, felt her arms reaching up to encircle his neck, pulling him down upon her naked breasts. Lay down on top of her. In a moment he would get up and undress himself. Not yet. (Now) annealed to Hester from head to foot, even though their flesh is sundered by the blanket and Diddy's clothes, he relayed to her, at first wordlessly, the sorrows of his fraternal condition. How, whenever he asked him to be a brother and a real friend, Paul was never there. But when Diddy had learned his lesson and pulled away, it wasn't long before Paul would come round, ebullient but mutely reproachful; intimating that Diddy had neglected him, laying gross claim on Diddy's thwarted need to bestow affection. Until Diddy was again persuaded he'd misjudged Paul; believed he could depend on him after all. Returned to Paul the solicitous love he had nowhere else to put. Whereupon Paul would vanish again.

"Paul is a lousy human being."

"You may be right," she says. "I don't know."

"The hell of it is that I don't know either whether he's really good or bad," Diddy continues. "And it's eating away at me. If only I could just hate the bastard and be done with it."

"But you want to make Paul into a thing instead of a person. A thing whose measurements you can take once and for all."

"Oh, darling, please! Don't start that. It sounds awful, sure. But I just can't spend my whole life being perpetually astonished by people, by the way they behave, by how mean and rotten they are. And feeling all the time like a prize dope." He hesitated, struck by the self-pitying ring of his last words.

"Dalton darling, don't make everything too simple. It's all wrong. You're leaving too much out."

"Well, it *is* simple," he says doggedly. "People make things seem complicated when they're stalling. When they don't want to make up their minds. They're damned good at it, too."

Hester sighed. Does Diddy believe a word of what he's saying?

"Maybe I'm just dumb," he continued, "but then dumb people

also have a right to take measures in their own self-defense. And that's all I'm doing with Paul. Jesus, I'm not setting myself up as his judge. Anyway, doesn't everyone say that the few people like him in each generation, people with such extraordinary gifts, aren't to be judged by the same standards as everyone else? I don't like that idea myself, but it doesn't matter. *I* know how special Paul is, and I wish him well, and all that crap. But I'm tired, baby. And full of unattractive old wounds."

"So you don't judge him. What then?"

"Not much, I guess," Diddy replies. "Except that I know nothing Paul could do now or in the future would make me trust him. Ever again. I don't trust Paul." He rubbed his cheek back and forth across her naked shoulder. "I don't trust anybody except you."

"I don't trust someone who doesn't trust anybody."

Is Hester angry? What a strange thing for her to say.

Diddy raises himself on his elbows. "Hey! Just a minute ago, you were talking me out of judging Paul. But look at you now, sitting in judgment on *me*." He wishes he could see her face. But the tone was familiar and unmistakable: reeking of certitude. Diddy (now) angry that he has apparently been dealt out another one of Hester's irrefutable, crushing chunks of wisdom. Which don't seem to leave Diddy room to breathe. However right she is. Diddy angrier still. If she doesn't defend herself, he'll go on. "You're being highhanded and unkind, Hester."

"Maybe I am. But sometimes your despair wearies me."

Diddy stung by the harshness of her rebuke. "My despair!" he murmurs, rolling over on his side next to her, but keeping one bent leg over her thighs. "Why don't we ever talk about *your* despair? You're just as miserable as I am; only you're more stoical. I'm fed up with stoicism. I'm not too proud to complain and curse the people who've betrayed me."

"And *I* am? Is that it, Dalton? Is that what you're saying?"

"Yes."

Hester has pulled her body from under Diddy's leg; is sitting (now) on the edge of the bed, her bare feet on the floor. Pulling down her yellow blouse, which hangs more or less permanently on one of the bedposts; putting it on and buttoning it. For just a moment, Diddy isn't thinking of anything other than her breasts, gleaming by the light of the street lamp. Does Diddy know what's happening? Their first full-blooded quarrel, the honeymoon's end.

"You might as well go on. Say what you mean," the girl says in a rough toneless voice. Then she went into the bathroom for a moment, leaving the door open. Diddy could hear her urinating. Waited, choking on pent-up words; until she came out again and stood at the foot of the bed. Something ugly is beginning. But Diddy's too disappointed at Hester's initial withholding of sympathy for him, and too angry at this novel, unprecedented streak of viciousness she's just disclosed, to stop.

"You know very well what I mean! Don't tell me you haven't suspected that I'd learned from Aunt Jessie about your mother. And about how you became blind."

"Yes," Hester said, "I did assume you knew. Aunt Jessie was bound to tell you. So what? I don't understand what you're reproaching me for now."

Diddy, who knows what he wants to say, says it. "I'm reproaching you for creating a certain kind of atmosphere that's strangling me. I must be just the dope, maybe the only one in the world, who could adapt to it."

"I still don't understand," Hester says. "You mean my blindness? That I use my blindness to get you to treat me in a certain way that you wouldn't, if I could see? I make you feel sorry for me? I demand that you coddle me?"

"No! That's exactly what I *don't* mean. If it were that, I could understand and condone and overlook what you do. But you don't play on your blindness. To get sympathy, or special treatment, or anything else. God knows, that would be a very human weakness. What you do is worse."

"What?" cried the girl, impatiently. "Tell me, Dalton. Have some guts."

"I will," Diddy says. "It's what you do about your unhappiness. And I don't think that would necessarily be any different if you could see. You have a line—there's no other word for what you do. And I fell for it. Your unhappiness became something hidden,

245

sacred, unmentionable. While mine was farting and prancing and swooning and howling all over the landscape. Until now, you know, I was never consciously bothered by the difference. If I noticed it, I considered it still more evidence of your superiority. You were too marvelous to be just unhappy, grossly unhappy. Like ordinary people. Like me. And, having fallen for your line, my own freedom of discourse and mood was terribly limited. I could never even let you know that I knew how you became blind. I never wanted to bring it up, because I imagined the subject must be so painful to you. As if you were too elegant to suffer. But I'll be damned if I'll go on tiptoeing around your horrors any longer!"

"Dalton, you're a fool!"

"Good! That's the way I like to hear you talk. Off your pedestal. Just like any other ordinary, ball-breaking American wife. It does my heart good to hear you."

"Don't protest too much," said Hester.

"God damn you," cries Diddy. "I won't let you one-up me or climb back on that pedestal. Why don't you stop acting so god-damned morally superior to me, Hester? Remember how all this started? Do you? I made a simple and, as it happens, entirely justifiable complaint about my brother. To that I added a declaration—I admit it's sentimental, but so what?—of my faith in you. And what do you do? You jump on me, and berate me for being a coward and a cop-out. A life-diminisher, as someone would say."

"Aren't you?" said Hester, coldly.

Yes, something awful is happening. "Well, if I am," Diddy yells, "you're no better than I am. I, at least, trust one person—you. Though maybe I should put that in the past tense. . . . But you don't trust anyone. Certainly not me."

"Maybe I trust myself," said Hester slowly. She is standing next to the bed. "And maybe that's enough."

(Now) she's putting on her skirt; bending over to buckle the straps of her sandals. Why is she doing that? She isn't going to leave, is she?

From the bed Diddy was jabbing his skinny finger in the air inches from her breast, as if she could see his gesture and might involuntarily flinch from it. "I don't believe you. Oh hell, why do

246

you make me say these things? . . . But you asked for it, Hester . . . I meant that. I don't believe you. I don't believe you trust yourself. You can't, because you don't know yourself. I'm not saying something inane like 'I know better than you do.' I don't. But I do know about some things that you *must* be feeling, and don't seem to be aware of at all."

"For example."

"For example, you must feel betrayed, unlovable, insubstantial. You must, after what your mother did to you when you were fourteen. And even apart from that unspeakable betrayal, you must. Simply because you're blind. Because, for whatever reason, you can't and never will see yourself or me or other people. You just make up the world as you go along, and you think it's all right. You decide to love your mother, instead of hating her as would any normal victim of such mad cruelty. You agree to come to New York and share my life, when you don't understand me, you don't trust me. . . ."

"Go on," said Hester. "Why are you stopping? Don't stop now."

"I guess I don't want to go on." Diddy sighing bitterly. "It's all too ugly."

"Please," says Hester sarcastically. "Don't stop now."

"All right, I won't." New energy. Diddy sits up again in bed, throws the covers down to his knees. "Now, why don't you be honest, damn you? Tell what you really feel about your mother. About being blind. About me."

"You know, Dalton, you could have asked me all that any time you wanted."

"Sure, sure. I know," he says bitterly. "And I've been free all along to ask you how many men you've fucked, too. And if you've slept with anyone since we met. . . ." Hurried on, because he didn't really want these questions answered. At least, not first. "I could ask you a lot of things. And for answers, you could serve up that gnomic crap I've fallen for. That you have your so-called truth and I have mine. . . . You're hardly the most confiding or approachable of women, Miss Nayburn. Though I imagine that your unshakable esteem for yourself and your cult of honesty tell you that you are."

247

"I'll answer any questions you ask, Dalton." A dare.

"All right." Which question? There are so many. Like throbbing boils in Diddy's flesh. Might as well start at the beginning. "Tell me how you feel about your mother."

"I hate her."

"Since when?"

"From the time I understood what she'd done."

Diddy, poised on the verge of a scathing long-winded reply, suddenly took a deep breath. Well, go on. "Is that all?" he says, tauntingly. "Not a big tablespoon of saintly love, forgiveness, and compassion along with it?"

"Dalton, I swear to you that I loathe my mother. Loathing and disgust are all I feel toward her."

Not what Diddy expected to hear. "All right, I'll believe you for the time being. Now tell me how you feel about being blind."

"Oh, God! What do you think?" Hester cries. "Idiot!" By light from the window, Diddy can see her face twisting with the effort to hold back tears.

"Hester! Hester, I'm sorry. I don't know what I'm saying. Let's stop." Reaches out to touch her. She pulls away sharply.

"I don't want to stop," Hester said shrilly. "You want honesty, you stupid fool. You're going to have it. Don't flinch. I'm doing most of the work. And if I can take it, you can."

Diddy streaked with pain by her words. "You're damned right I can take it. And I'll ask you again. You can call me idiot, fool, or anything you damn please, but it's true, I *don't* know how you feel about being blind. I mean, you don't seem to hate and feel bitterness when you have the reasons I've always understood make anyone hate and feel bitter. You do something else. You back away. You dissolve. It's as if you don't exist any more. Then you fade in, come back, very serene. But it doesn't seem to have much to do with the other person at all. And each time there's a little less generosity in you, as if that were being used up gradually by whatever you do to yourself inside. I used to love you for that serenity. But now I think there's mostly vanity in it. And all this I connect, though I can't prove it, with your blindness. So much so that I think you almost *like* being blind."

"Maybe that's how you'd be," says Hester coldly, "if you were blind. Speak for yourself."

"Hester, tell me straight out what you feel. About being blind."

"I hate being blind so much that most of my waking hours I wish I were dead."

Move quickly. "And about me?" Diddy delivers the words so fast he hardly had time to envisage the blunt, agonizing blow he was inviting.

"It's so complicated. . . . At times, I love you deeply. I hate you sometimes; maybe most of the time. And then I pity you, and I'd like to help you. But whenever I think of what it would mean to help you, I become frightened. You have a powerful desire to destroy yourself. I'm afraid that if I really held out my hand to you, you'd pull me under, too."

Diddy shocked. But quite unwilling altogether to let what had been an exposure of Hester turn upon him (now). "Okay, you've leveled with me. I'm grateful. But let's not change the subject. We were talking about you, Hester. What about *your* destructive needs?"

The girl didn't answer for a moment. A sigh? Then she sat down in the wicker rocking chair near the window. "My destructive needs? . . . Believe me, Dalton, I don't want to evade your question. It's just that it's hard to answer, since I'm not sure I've even begun to express those needs. But I'm not trying to suggest they don't exist, or that they're only puny desires that are largely dormant. I don't know what their size is. The only thing I'm fairly certain of is their direction. . . . It would be to destroy someone else, rather than myself."

"Logged any victims yet?" Diddy says bitterly. The energy for quarreling beginning to fade. Hester had returned to the bed (now); if only to sit on it. The heat and moist odors flowing off her body had begun to suffuse Diddy's mind, blurring his thoughts, interposing a dense vapor between his ability to reason and the crystalline word-blocks stacked in his mouth and ready to be fired off. "Who have you done in so far?"

"You . . . maybe."

"Me?" Diddy's voice becoming hoarse. "Don't flatter yourself, baby. I'm perfectly capable of destroying myself without your subtle assistance. All by myself."

"Maybe you're right."

"Are you being sarcastic now?" Diddy says scornfully.

"No. I'm thinking. Wondering whether what you said is really true. . . . Listen, Dalton, however much you hate me right now, or think I hate you, you must believe that I don't *want* you to go under. And whatever you're bent on doing, *I* don't want to be the means of destroying you. And maybe I'm not. And couldn't be. Maybe you're doing it all by yourself, as you just said. God, how I'd like to believe I'm not part of it! . . . But I can't. What I think is that you do want to be destroyed, but aren't strong enough to do it. You *do* need me to help you. And I don't want to—at least I think I don't. . . ."

"Hester—"

"Yes, maybe I do. I'm not a saint. And you're tempting me, Dalton, it's the most depraved kind of seduction. I don't want to destroy you. But deep down I feel that's just what you're begging me to do."

Could Hester be right? Suddenly, for a brief flash of light, Diddy the Deceived saw the truth illuminated. Saw the vast extent of the dark, fatal labyrinth in which he was toiling. Perceived how alone in it he was. Either there was no one to lead him out, or Diddy's false Ariadne had dropped the thread.

But maybe matters aren't that hopeless. Maybe their pain could be explained in terms less absolute. A psychological explanation, if you will. Diddy, not really alive, had a life. An unfortunate example for a person like Hester, someone younger and essentially innocent. She (now) was beginning to see the monsters, half brute and half human, that Diddy saw. Perhaps being blind, without literal vision of her own, makes her even more susceptible to his black visions. His commitment to suffering was infecting Hester. Her own precious ration of vitality, preserved through such excruciating trials, leaking away. Once Hester, really alive, was her life. Didn't merely have a life. Sharing Diddy's provisional existence was adulterating her vitality. The longer she lived with him, the more fully she partook of his suffering and morbidity.

Hence, her tirade tonight.

"I'm going to think long and hard about what you've said," Diddy murmured. "I think it's all wrong, absolutely crazy. *I* know what the trouble is."

"Do you?"

No, to tell the truth, Diddy doesn't. And Diddy the Truth-teller says so. "Okay, maybe there is something right in what you're saying, too."

Diddy extremely sad. Not angry any more. Sad that Hester should fear him. As if he were someone risen from the dead, to be honored at a distance for his extraordinary feat; not loved at close range. But her instinct may be sound. If indeed he is a post-humous creature whose very touch was withering.

A final flaring-up of resistance to Hester's verdict, even as she is visibly softening toward him. "But goddamn it," Diddy cried, "you can't be right all the time!"

"Why not?" said Hester.

"Why not?" Diddy repeated incredulously.

"What do you think, Dalton? That being right is something democratic? A guarantee that you can be right half the time and I can be right the other half? Darling, it isn't like that—except when it is. And with us, it isn't."

Diddy turning restlessly in the bed, not knowing what to answer.

"You were about to tell me something," Hester continued. "You were saying you thought I was at least partly right in what I said. What's right?"

"Maybe . . . that I am a kind of Lazarus. I feel like one. Especially since I tried . . . to kill myself."

"And what's wrong in what I said?" Hester was unbuttoning her blouse.

Diddy grimaces; reaches out to put his hand on her breast. "What's wrong, at least what I pray will turn out to be wrong, is that living with Lazarus is dangerous for you."

"But you know, Dalton," she said, slipping under the covers, "I was saying just as strongly that I'm dangerous for you. If you're Lazarus, maybe I'm Medusa with the snaky hair turning you to stone."

Diddy had forgotten about the stone. Wait, think a moment. But his body feels as different from a stone (now) as a swallow is from a hammer. Should he trust what his body exuberantly urges? Or should he heed the garish premonitions that swell inside his mind? No choice. The choice is already made. Diddy clasped the girl in his arms. "Take the damn skirt off," he murmurs. "Why have you worn your skirt into bed?"

"Have we stopped quarreling?" she asks.

"Hell, I don't know. I can't think any more. My mind's a blank." Diddy waited for Hester to say something. But at least she was pulling off the rest of her clothing and throwing it on the floor. "You don't want to fight any more, do you?"

"No. I'm worn out."

"But you must promise me that tomorrow we'll talk about Paul."

"Why?"

"Because it's important to me. Even more important now. This whole nightmare tonight started, remember, because I said I didn't trust Paul. And you took that to mean something about me, not about my brother. Now, all the more, I insist that you meet him and see for yourself what he's like."

Diddy confident he would be vindicated; at least on this particular issue. If, to Hester's ears, he sounded spiteful and unloving, she could have no inkling of Paul's shallowness, his flair for exploiting those who loved him, his vanity, his self-deceptions. But she should be able to guess how much, once, Diddy had loved Paul.

"You must meet him this time," Diddy repeated. "Then you can judge for yourself." That seems a good idea. But perhaps not. Why is Diddy so confident Hester will see through Paul? See the whole Paul. She might see just part of what Diddy sees. The graceful Paul who can, when he chooses, make anyone smile; can make it easier for anyone to like himself a little more. Maybe she'll find him attractive. More attractive than Diddy. "Tomorrow . . ."

"Dalton, please don't talk about tomorrow. Where are you? I want you closer to me."

"He said he'd call us tomorrow. I don't know for how long he's in town this time, but I want to know if you'll meet him."

Hester thrust her body against Diddy's in the way that always arouses him. The shuddering, almost painful knotting of his groin, the hard flowering of his sex. Hester has slipped farther down under the covers; is taking his sex in her mouth. Diddy groans, throws back the blanket, presses on the back of her head with his hand. She's devouring him, taking him inside her, pulling him toward her. Dragging him away from thinking, from memory, from words, from Paul. Let all that go, then. It doesn't matter. No, it does. But can wait until tomorrow.

But Paul never phoned the next day; though Diddy and Hester didn't go out. Nor on any of the days following.

In the first days after their quarrel, Diddy and Hester seemed to move about more quietly, for the most part in silence. Both in a state of shock, as Diddy thought. Reluctant for any kind of contact other than the sexual one. But gradually the rhythm of their days became less haunted, took on renewed vigor. Although still extremely quiet. Passing days on end indoors. Since the daily walk was abandoned, seldom leave the apartment.

Whether this was originally Hester's desire or Diddy's—he isn't sure—both wish it (now). Diddy doesn't even have the one morning and two evening strolls with Xan any more, having turned the dog over to the ASPCA. Far from subsiding, as Diddy had expected, Hester's antipathy to the animal worsened. Xan began to react. Shrank under the couch when Hester entered the living room; became servile and overagitated when Diddy fed or combed him or got out the leash for their walks. If Diddy thought he might have been able to resurrect the old Xan, lively and spirited, he would never have given his pet up. But he didn't. Accepted the dog's transformation as irrevocable. He didn't like Xan any more.

Though he's not aware of actively missing the creature on whom he'd lavished so much balked affection for the last two years, possibly some vacuum (now) does exist in Diddy's heart. Of which he's unaware. Some yearning for the kind of loving dialogue possible only with an animal; at least only with someone who doesn't speak. And this may be the reason—if a reason is needed—why he was thinking all last weekend of something he'd once written. In his sophomore year in college, Diddy had started a novel, and worked on it fairly diligently for a year. Called *The Story of the Wolf-Boy*. And written in the first person, for Diddy couldn't imagine the story being narrated by anyone except the hero himself. He never dared show his effort to anyone, teacher or friend. Sure that he'd then realize he had no talent for writing. And since abandoning it, when he became serious about his pre-med courses, never again attempted any fiction. But he must have valued it. While never rereading a single page, he'd kept the manuscript all these years. Both the first draft, written into three loose-leaf notebooks with a Parker pen, his mother's gift when he graduated from high school; and the second draft, which he'd typed. (Now) he'd like to read his "novel" aloud to Hester and to himself.

Knows exactly where it is. In that heavy cardboard box, the one never opened, on the shelf in the front hall closet. In which are stored, among other things:

report cards from grammar school;

four high-school yearbooks and twenty-five issues of the weekly school paper from his senior year when he was Managing Editor;

his diplomas;

long manila envelopes stuffed with photographs of himself and Paul as children;

the crude slingshot he'd made when he was eight;

his "Catholic" diaries, from the age of twelve to fifteen;

his letters in track and basketball;

an album pasted full of clippings from newspapers and magazines about Paul, concert programs, and other miscellaneous souvenirs of his brother's career, up to 1960 only;

the watercolor portrait of Pasteur he did when he was ten;

some Stevenson campaign buttons;

a bulky package tied up with string that holds all the

letters, as many as three a day, the notes, and the telegrams Joan and he exchanged during the first two
months after they'd met.

Takes down the box. But it's not there. Neither the written nor the
typed version. How is that possible? Look again! Diddy sure
there's no way in which it could have been gotten lost or been
thrown out without his knowledge. Diddy the Methodical rum-
mages in other likely places. Eventually, going through all the
closets, drawers, and boxes in the apartment. The manuscript nowhere to be found.

One other thing is missing from the cardboard box. The gold
medal Paul got when he won the Chopin Prize at the age of
eighteen. "You keep it for me, Diddy," Paul had said negligently,
when he came back from Warsaw. Putting it on Diddy's dinner
plate, grinning. Diddy could never decide whether it meant Paul
was more fond of him than he'd supposed or cared less than he
supposed about the unexpected victory and becoming famous overnight. On the balance, Paul's surprising present felt more like a hex
than a fraternal blessing. Thinking that Paul might ask for it back
one day, Diddy had never had the nerve to chuck it into the trash
bin. But when, after dumping the contents of the cardboard box on
the hall floor to make sure his manuscript wasn't there, he noticed,
almost in passing, that the medal in its handsome leather and vel-
vet case was also gone, he felt a distinct relief.

But the disappearance of *The Story of the Wolf-Boy* was something else.

Diddy trying not to be too depressed by the inexplicable loss of
his manuscript. Reminding himself it wasn't anything more than
adolescent junk. Couldn't have been really good. So, not a true
loss. But painful anyway. He had so looked forward to reading it
to Hester. To bestow a part of him never shared with anyone,
something he'd kept secret from even Joan. And he'd gotten an
intimation that the story might in some way have eased the barely
perceptible ache he suffers from giving up Xan. Nothing as strong
as solace. Still, the themes connect.

Hester has come from the living room; is standing near him.
"What are you doing, Dalton? Are you looking for something?"

Oh, just sorting out some old junk. Getting rid of things.

About the best that Diddy can do is to resurrect, in a recurrent dream, a parody or fragment of the bizarre story set down in his lost manuscript. This, just about the only dream he has (now), arrives as a welcome change from the dreams—unrememberable nightmares, rather—plaguing him for the last month. Dreams that had laid Diddy low; awakening most mornings with the sensation that a huge flat stone is lying on his chest. But from this dream and its variants, Diddy often awakens pleasantly, feeling lighter, somewhat purged.

Dreamed, *The Story of the Wolf-Boy* retains something of its origins, the "literary" qualities Diddy might have admired when he was a novel-reading college sophomore. Grave, slowly paced, somewhat overembellished with naturalistic detail. While recurring over a period of several weeks, the dream kept pretty close to the original plot. The only significant variations were in the ending.

In its standard form, the dream begins with a prologue. Diddy meeting the Wolf-Boy, who is crying. Although there are times during the dream when the Wolf-Boy looks thoroughly human, as ordinary-human as anyone could wish, he's really an animal. Diddy knows it. The Wolf-Boy knows it. In fact, this is why he's crying. Because he's an animal, and because he aspires to be something better. What is better? End of prologue.

The dream proper divides into two parts.

In Part I, the Wolf-Boy recounts the history of his life; beginning with his birth. Diddy listens, with the reaction so common in dreams. Being surprised by what he hears, following it with suspense. And simultaneously feeling that it's an old story he has heard many times, but is nonetheless glad to hear through once again.

The Wolf-Boy's story. Tells Diddy that he was born into a respectable circus family, the Shaws; an only child; and christened Hiawatha after his paternal grandfather, a full-blooded Cherokee. His father was an acrobat who worked on the high wire, his mother a lion tamer originally from Budapest. Both aristocrats among circus performers, for possessing skills that are rare but not freakish and for not being physically deformed. Passed a happy and fairly

256

adventurous childhood on the road with his parents until they were both killed in an automobile accident. In North Platte, Nebraska, where the circus had been performing for almost a week at a fair. Young Hiawatha was just fourteen.

The orphan was quickly adopted by the person his parents had considered their best friend in the troupe. Lyndon the sword swallower, a man already treated by Hiawatha as a favorite uncle; whom he'd known as long as he could remember and always liked. But, as a step-parent, this man disclosed a fund of meanness the boy had never suspected. Neglect, which was decorated by sarcasm, which was enhanced by all sorts of petty indignities. Until the final, most cruel of wounds. One day, in a totally unjustified rage at the boy, the sword swallower told him icily that his dead parents hadn't really been his parents. "Now you think you're a foundling, huh? Maybe you even think that's exciting. Something classy. Like you might be really the son of a prince or a movie star. Wait! Don't get your hopes up, kiddo. There's more." Lyndon punched himself in the head to stop laughing. Then settled back, snapping his suspenders. "This is a good story. Not with one of your sissy milksop happy endings."

Hiawatha Shaw not only not the son of the Shaws; but of no one like them, either. What he was, in fact, was the offspring of two giant apes who had been with the circus many years ago as part of an African act. A mutant, a freak birth, a sport of nature without medical precedent. Of course, the pink hairless human infant was taken away from its animal progenitors immediately. Minutes after his birth on the straw of the apes' cage. And claimed by the amiable, childless couple who had raised him.

"Does everyone in the circus know about it?" Hiawatha asked, trying to stifle his sobs.

"Yeah, everyone," said the sword swallower. "They were plenty shocked, too, when you dropped out of that big gorilla's twat, though it takes a lot to shock circus people. Wanted to shoot you, right off the bat. Not even register your birth. Doing you a favor. An act of mercy. Nobody could have gotten into trouble for it. Who would have believed you even existed? I know I was for doing it. The manager, too. Said you were an insult to Providence or something, that the Almighty would want you to be dead. Now, I didn't hold no truck with that religious stuff, but I was on his side."

"What happened?" whispered the heartbroken boy.

"Oh, in the end, he chickened out. A bunch of softies got their way. But since some of the boys was so riled up and wanted to do something, we passed the hat, so we could shut the manager up with some dough afterward, and shot your big hairy old man and old lady instead."

This was the story the Wolf-Boy, crying as if there were no end to his tears, related to Diddy. Blew his nose. Then went on.

Shortly after this unspeakable revelation, Hiawatha ran away from Lyndon the sword swallower, from the circus, from everything. Started by leading a tramp's life, riding the rails. But found that too sociable. Gradually mastered the regimen of a precocious hermit. Found shelter in isolated caves, ditches, mountain ravines, and abandoned shacks outside small farming and ranching communities—in Nebraska at first, in Colorado later, finally in Arizona. A life that proved more to his taste.

What an unutterably sad fate, Diddy thinks in the dream. And feels the tears streaming into his eyes, too. Only for the Wolf-Boy? Or for his own dishonorable isolation as well?

But the Wolf-Boy's tale has an even more terrifying sequel. It began after more than a year of wandering, when Hiawatha was just sixteen. And concerned his appearance; and all the depths—historical, biological, psychological, spiritual—with which appearances connect. Up to his early teens, had looked like any other American boy. Shorter than most boys his age, but the doctor who traveled with the circus had allayed Hiawatha's fears. Delayed maturity, an uncommon but by no means unnatural condition: though rare, it's entirely normal biologically for boys to reach puberty as late as the age of eighteen. Nothing to worry over. Indeed, something he might be grateful for one day: the odds were that he'd be a very tall man. Understandable that when, at sixteen, he noticed hair had begun growing on his face, the boy was elated. Even though he hadn't added so much as an inch to his height in the last three years. Hiawatha was living at this time in an abandoned miner's shack in northern Arizona; his subsistence mainly wild berries and small game that he had learned to trap and, sometimes, managed to catch with his bare hands. Immediately after joyfully examining his face, as well as his chest, armpits, arms, back, groin, and legs, the boy set out for the nearest highway and thumbed a ride into Flagstaff, the nearest town. Where he stood on a corner by the entrance to a movie theatre until he'd panhandled enough money in nickels and dimes to buy a razor and blades at a drugstore. Then hitchhiked out of town and returned to his shack. And shaved himself.

It was after shaving that first time, the Wolf-Boy explained to Diddy, that he realized something was wrong. Discovered his face to have a tough hirsute layer underneath the finer hair he'd razored off, all of which grew back within an hour anyway. Hair not only in the ordinary places—lower cheeks, the chin, above the upper lip—but all over his face. On his forehead, for instance. On his upper cheeks. And on the sides of his neck, below his ears. Not to speak of the thick furry tufts sprouting all over his body. Only his palms, the back of his knees, and the instep of both feet were spared.

In short, Hiawatha Shaw was turning into the Wolf-Boy. Nothing he could do to halt the process. An irreversible, if delayed, metamorphosis. Already—ever since Lyndon the sword swallower's cruel and gratuitous revelations—afraid of people, of their masks, of their unlimited capacity for betrayal, (now) nature's sequel to little Hiawatha Shaw had the very strongest reasons to shun all human company. Though he'd always been a light sleeper, he trained himself to sleep during the day and go out only at night. To run away whenever he heard the sound of a human voice.

Thus he has lived, he told Diddy, until this day. Four years. And was (now) just twenty years old. Diddy was glad to be told the Wolf-Boy's age; he couldn't have guessed it from his appearance. Although extremely short, just under five feet tall, the Wolf-Boy had powerful thick arms and legs. Usually dressed in cast-off clothes that he recovered from trash cans or found abandoned along the highway; on Sundays wore his better clothes, what he'd been able to steal from the laundry lines of small ranches. His belly filled with food stolen from the kitchens of ranches and with picnic leftovers. It was the leavings of picnics—generous and varied fare, the Wolf-Boy told Diddy—that had been keeping him alive for the past year.

His latest home, for over a year: a cave, once occupied by a mountain lion but abandoned (now), in Sabino Canyon, which lies in the foothills of the Catalina Mountains just outside of Tucson. The canyon, a spectacular site even in natural surroundings that are rarely less than beautiful, was a favorite weekend picnicking place for families and couples from the town. From his deep niche in the face of a seventy-foot cliff, the Wolf-Boy would look down on them; listen to their laughing and joking, their transistor radios. Watch how, after putting away a huge lunch, grandparents doze in the shade and couples go off by the stream to neck and high-school boys toss a football around. The Wolf-Boy both longing for, and recoiling in dread from, that kind of easy human fellowship which he, too, had once known. Sometimes people would set up their feast at the very base of his cliff, so that he could look directly down on them, a distance of about fifty feet. And, thanks to the canyon's remarkable acoustics, could hear every word they said. There was little danger he'd ever be discovered. The sheer rock face of the cliff offers only slim, widely spaced footholds. The climb dangerous enough to discourage amateurs, but not so high or really dangerous to intrigue the professionals.

Only once in the year he'd been living in the cave did one of the picnickers seriously attempt the cliff. She was a tall, skinny girl about twelve or thirteen years old with long black hair; wearing sneakers, blue jeans, a red checked shirt, and a fringed leather jacket probably bought at the tourist store on the Pima Indians reservation south of Tucson. From a thong around her neck hung an aluminum whistle, which the Wolf-Boy had observed her using that hot afternoon to summon her dog, a terrier whom she called Lassie. The girl couldn't have any inkling of the dangers of the ascent; obvious to the Wolf-Boy, anxiously peering down, that she was neither an experienced climber nor even particularly well coordinated. But she doesn't fall. Ignorance, pluck, self-love, and a total absence of height phobia were bringing her safely up the side, panting and grunting. She's scaled the first twenty feet. Takes a wretchedly uncomfortable pause; the spiky rock she's grabbed for support is bruising her palm, drawing blood. Then resumes her climb. The Wolf-Boy held his breath. For she was, quite sensibly, making directly for his cave. A natural resting place, nearly three-fourths of the way to the top, and the only one on her entire route.

Diddy is getting restless, just listening. How will this story end, happily or sadly? Doesn't want to be forced to imagine a body lying, broken, smashed, on the rocky floor of the canyon. The Wolf-Boy tugs at Diddy's sleeve, trying to reclaim his attention. When has he had such a listener before? Listen.

Diddy sucking in his breath, as the Wolf-Boy continues his reminiscences.

The girl's still scrambling upward, hand over hand. Drawing closer to the Wolf-Boy's lair. He's begun to panic. What would he do when she gained the slanting ledge of rock at the threshold of the cave and hauled herself up, when she actually saw him, saw what he looked like? As she would in several minutes. Could he imitate the roar of the absent mountain lion, scaring her away before she actually reached the cave? Probably. But if he frightened her too badly, she might lose her precarious balance and tumble all the way down to the base of the cliff fifty feet below.

Closer and closer. The Wolf-Boy's hairy integument streaked with sweat, from his small forehead to the soles of his moccasined feet; the furry sheath for his small alert head flattened down, parted in many places, by the rivulets of sweat. Indecision, one of the last surviving endowments of his waning humanity, collided with terror. Squatting on the cave floor, the Wolf-Boy chewed at his upper lip with his neat tiny fangs, then compressed his lips tightly. Torn between humanlike compassion for the girl's probable doom and the healthy animal's mandate that he look after himself.

The Wolf-Boy doesn't want to be an animal. Envies the superior suffering of human beings. Diddy had noticed him earlier, while he talked, delicately, nonchalantly, crossing his hairy knees. What a child he is, Diddy thinks. A pretend-child. Like a big floppy doll.

Doesn't want to be an animal, but he has no choice. Terror so buffets his smallish body the Wolf-Boy fears he'll burst, his hairy seams split open. Then let out the beast (now), of his own accord. Instead of having it ripped from him. As a casualty of nature, he's nothing. But as a real animal, the Wolf-Boy may even yet become the Wolf-Man.

His good angel mortified, the Wolf-Boy prepares to kill. Accepts the imminent death of the youthful intruder who means him no harm. But just at the last moment, when, jaw already agape and with humanlike tears seeping down his hairy cheeks, the Wolf-Boy was about to spring to the mouth of his cave and deliver a ferocious lion's roar, he was saved. Both were saved. Probably thanks to Lassie, who'd been barking unhappily for the last ten minutes, the girl's parents had just raised their heads from the wicker food basket, looked around them, then looked up and noticed where their youngster had gone to. Hastily rose to their feet. Began shouting, crying, begging her to come down this instant and not to do this to them. Frightening them to death! How could she? A reprieve for the Wolf-Boy. No one wants to be a murderer, if he possibly can help it, right? Diddy's not so sure.

But is the girl going to obey her parents? Will it occur to her to be disobedient, to place her own self-esteem over her parents' self-pitying anxiety for her safety? Yes to the first, no to the second. She's only a child, too. Children all. The climb is called off; and also the danger. As he shrank back into his cave, the Wolf-Boy hears the girl's labored breathing only a few feet beneath him. Hears her sigh, which was for her ears alone; her childish alto muttering, "Oh, hell!" and then the loud voice fired down at her parents, "Okay! Okay! Wait a minute! I'm coming." The Wolf-Boy's jaw went slack; and the mountain lion's roar, the shout of the future Wolf-Man, fell backward, unheard, into his gut. Knees like grass.

Diddy confused. Forget about the girl. What course of events would have been in the Wolf-Boy's best interests? No one should be burdened with inventing his own nature from scratch. No one should be asked to decide whether he's good or bad.

Later, in attendance at a florid desert sunset, the Wolf-Boy invited Diddy to share a pipeful of some dried weed that grows all over the Catalina foothills. The Wolf-Boy unburdened himself some more. Diddy could hardly believe it, but the Wolf-Boy swore to him that this incident with the black-haired girl, whom he'd seen only once and not talked to, who had never seen him, was an almost unbearably intimate experience. Hadn't been so close to another human being for years. (Now) a memory he treasured, fed from. For months afterward, used to conduct long conversations with her in his head about sorrow and joy. Usually while he is just falling asleep in the cave. But sometimes when he ventured down into the canyon, after midnight and everyone had long gone. To forage in the wire trash bins for discarded food. To sing to himself and revel in the canyon's echo. To bathe in and drink from the stream. Or when, waking early, just before dawn, he descended the cliff and went for a walk in the foothills outside the canyon. To be able to run, to turn cartwheels, to howl at the moon, to surprise small gray ground-moles in their dwellings and rip them apart with his precise white teeth.

"The closest I've been to anyone in years," repeated the Wolf-Boy mournfully. Diddy and he are sitting cross-legged on splintery bare rock at the mouth of his cave. "I mean, until you came along."

Diddy so strongly moved by the boy it's like a physical pain. How can one bear such suffering? Unendurable just to know that sorrow on this scale exists—much less, to suffer it. Is there anything he can do for the Wolf-Boy? thinks Diddy in the dream.

Then, either because he feels embarrassed at his show of feeling or just suddenly mindful of his duties as a host, the Wolf-Boy excuses himself and goes into his cave for a moment, a little way, returning with two cactus pears for their dinner. "It's all I have," he says simply. "Try one. They're good. I didn't like the taste at first myself. But you get used to it after a while."

Diddy accepting the heavy green globe, still studded with tiny thorns, from the creature's outstretched hand. "Don't stick yourself," says the Wolf-Boy. "Here, give it back for a minute. I should have cut those things off first."

(Now) the Wolf-Boy has gone to get a knife to peel the cactus pear for Diddy. But he—a handicapped waif—shouldn't be waiting on me, Diddy thinks. I should be helping him.

But maybe Diddy isn't filled with generous compassionate feelings only. Maybe he's also wondering what creature, animal or human, and if animal, what sort of animal, will be returning in a moment. With a knife.

Everything becomes dark (now). But that's all right. A natural interval, since what comes next would properly be titled Part II of the dream. In the first part, the Wolf-Boy and his personal history occupy the center of the stage. Diddy merely a sympathetic auditor; hardly convinced sometimes that he's present in the dream at all. The dream more like a movie he was watching, or a story he'd read once he was remembering. But in the second part, Diddy has taken up firm residence in the dream. His feelings lodged at the center. The Wolf-Boy becomes in his turn an even more silent, shadowy, and finally indeterminate figure. Diddy can't tell if that's because the Wolf-Boy's shape is continually altering. Or for another reason.

For he recalls this part less well. All Diddy usually retains from the second half of the dream are fragments of acts. And a sequence of his own tormented thoughts.

At one moment in this part, the Wolf-Boy seems incredibly hairy. Is that because it's the first time Diddy is looking at him clearly? Or is the Wolf-Boy really changing? The process of reversion to the brute accelerating, so that he's becoming more animal-like right before Diddy's eyes? But Diddy doesn't try to figure everything out. What he's most aware of is that the Wolf-Boy's profuse and exceedingly long hair is not only dirty but very matted. When night falls, they should descend to the stream, Diddy thinks; there, he'll wash the creature's hair for him. For the time being, perched in their eyrie, he can at least comb it out. Which Diddy knows how to do without hurting. Having done this service for Xan many times.

Begins gently combing the vicious snarls and knots out of the mane that falls down on three sides of the Wolf-Boy's head. Then, with the fine teeth of the comb, sifts through the brown curls on his forehead, the beardlike tufts that grow out from his cheeks, and the more delicate blondish hair protecting his neck. What's this cool hard object buried in the fine hair just below his throat? On a slim silver chain. A kind of talisman. Somewhat resembling the medal Paul won at Warsaw. Diddy fingers the ornate disc for a moment; about to ask the Wolf-Boy where he got it and what kind of good fortune or protection it's associated with. When he notices the creature's polished teeth drawn slightly back, and an anxious vexed look veiling his handsome brown eyes. Don't bother with questions (now). Don't spoil his pleasure. Gently replacing the medal under the Wolf-Boy's tattered khaki shirt, Diddy returns to deftly combing his hair. Notices, approvingly, the warm open look returning to the Wolf-Boy's eyes. Who is squatting at Diddy's feet (now), resting his head on Diddy's knees. Even when Diddy fears that he's inadvertently yanked the creature's hair and hurt him, the body leaning against his legs doesn't tense or flinch. No matter what Diddy does, the Wolf-Boy seems to be enjoying all of it. The sheer fact of Diddy's paying so much attention to him as well as the physical sensations themselves. Making purring noises; sometimes yawning, tensing his pectorals, then relaxing. More strange noises, not like a cat's. Indeed, from this point in the dream forward, apparently to the dream's end, the Wolf-Boy doesn't utter another word. He who seemed so at home in human speech, even boyishly loquacious when relating the story of his life, doesn't seem (now) to know how to talk. Mute, as animals are.

Diddy finishes his combing of the creature's hair. The Wolf-Boy seems to be shrinking (now). Child-size and something like a child. Small enough to be carried. That's what Diddy does. Picks him up and carries him toward the rear of the cave. Which extends much farther back than Diddy had imagined. The Wolf-Boy behaving as if he doesn't ever want to be put down: lying in Diddy's arms all curled up, his face buried in Diddy's chest. So Diddy carries him for a long while, deeper into the tunnel-like recesses of the lion's cave.

Diddy still walking. And gradually, becoming afraid. Old superstitions have risen up to frighten him. A fear of contagion. In the same spirit in which he'd believed, when he was eight, despite his parents' derision, that warts come from handling frogs, he (now) worries what he will catch from handling the Wolf-Boy. Will Diddy become an animal, too? Dwindle to less than five feet? Grow hair over the whole surface of his body? Diddy looks at his hands, clasped around the Wolf-Boy's torso; takes one hand away to feel his neck, ears, and forehead. No unwanted hair or any other changes that he can detect. But this doesn't hold true for the Wolf-Boy. Only a moment has elapsed since the last solicitous look— Diddy must occasionally interrupt his gaze to check his footing —but when he turns back (now) the creature has in the meantime sprouted more hair on his face and on each unclothed part of his body. Not only is his hair still growing, but at such an astonishing rate that growth can be seen, even by the most impatient spectator. The Wolf-Boy himself is visibly bigger than he was a few minutes ago; more heavily muscled, vastly stronger, more imposing-looking in a coarse way. Though still no heavier for Diddy to carry.

A narrow passageway in the dark interior of the cave. "I'm going to put you down here," Diddy says quietly. Half wants to, and half doesn't. Gently sets down his grunting, squirming burden. The Wolf-Boy doesn't seem to mind too much. Crouches on the cold floor of the cave or tunnel, and stares up appealingly at his benefactor.

Diddy realizing something important. He has misunderstood the animal; wrongly feared it. Kneels down next to the Wolf-Boy. Hugs him. Awkwardly, for he can't estimate how much affection and sheer physical contact the Wolf-Boy can bear. Wants to pull him on his lap, rock him back and forth. But only if that doesn't offend the bereft creature's pride or undermine his strength of character, purchased at great cost through pitiless solitude.

It's at this moment, for some reason, that Incardona breaks into the dream. Not as an actual physical presence, but the thought of him. While Diddy is gazing affectionately at the Wolf-Boy, trying to say with his face what he knows he can't clothe in words, he can simultaneously conceive that there exists, somehow, a hope of making restitution in the matter of the slain workman. He wants to make this restitution. Not to a single person, Incardona, a stranger. Rather to what Diddy had despised and feared in Incardona— animal vigor, for instance. Diddy feels (now) that he's not haunted by Incardona any more. Is capable of affirming him.

An exorcism: although disembodied, the most satisfying part of the dream. Perhaps it's this part alone which propels Diddy up from sleep feeling somewhat lighter, purged; not the long story accumulated from the beginning of the dream. It works best if he's lucky enough to wake exactly at this point, instead of going farther into the dream, as he sometimes forces himself to do. Where he became completely lost. One foot in front of the other, into the trap. One-way ticket. Diddy the Damned.

Diddy has put the bad ending aside. If he could only maintain that good feeling—which comes from going far, but not too far—whenever he has it, however infrequently. Not embalm it in amber. Instead, plant it. Get it to take root, to grow. But some acid secreted by his own character always dissolves the good feeling; or some force from outside weights it with lead, then drags Diddy back to his own fettered consciousness.

The ending remains uncertain. That's why, although he would gladly have read Hester the manuscript of the unfinished "novel" which inspired this recurrent dream, Diddy finds it impossible to recount the dream itself. Not because Incardona figures in it, and he's never forced her to accept the truth about Incardona; which he might well be able to accomplish just by reading her the clipping. Though Hester's ignorance *might* create a problem, were all other obstacles to his telling the dream cleared away, the other obstacles do exist. The dream seems such an intimate part of himself. Everything's bound up in it. His relation to his parents, to Mary, to Paul, to Joan. Above all, to himself. The arbitrary and swift yet indelible drama with Incardona. And his love for Hester.

Diddy, who feels obscurely that he has dreamed out his very soul. Would like, in principle, to share that event with Hester. As he's yearned to deposit everything with her, keep nothing back. Maybe he's just afraid. Since that bitter row after Paul's unannounced visit, doesn't altogether trust Hester; never will, in the old way, again. God knows, he wants to. But can't. Her words have scored him. Like the light that scored his eyes on the night Paul came, when Diddy first opened the door and peered into the hall.

As the loss of Xan has damaged him, too. Though it was Diddy, not Hester, who suggested getting rid of the dog. Renouncing Xan has only reconfirmed this punishing vision of himself and of a world at large in which it's lunacy to trust anyone or anything. But what if Diddy weren't Diddy the Damaged but another person? The kind of person capable of reclaiming Xan; who could have restored that hysterical, frightened animal to itself? To its better self. And what if Diddy weren't Diddy the Damaged but another person? The deft vital person he obstinately thinks he should be?

Wanting to be Diddy the Good. And consistently living, morally, beyond his emotional means.

In that case, shouldn't Diddy settle for something less?

These are the questions Diddy can't face. Because he isn't outstandingly intelligent? Or simply not strong enough? Or just defective from the start in vitality and force of character? Diddy has never tackled these questions, either. Or even tried. As always, he tries to force his way through the terrible questions to some endurable, stoical vantage point. Expunge the glittering agony. Find a cool quiet place where he can sit in safety. The battering ram of the will. Using his will, Diddy tries to will his way through. Emulating blindness.

> Actually, there are two kinds of blindness.
>
> Noble blindness. As in the Greek statues. Because they're eyeless, these figures seem that much more alive, more centered in their bodies, more present. Making us, when we contemplate them, feel more present in ourselves.
>
> Ignoble blindness: the blindness of impacted rage and despair. Something passive. A thing of absence. As in the negative statuary of death. When someone drowns, the eyes are the first element of the body to disintegrate or rot; it's through the vacant eye sockets of a freshly drowned corpse that eels swim.

Diddy would like to be blind in the noble way, like the Greek statues. Would that he knew how!

He doesn't. Instead resumes, in this even more dangerously condensed and concentrated arena of his new life with Hester, the old habits of not being fully present. Not being in his life. Once, coming out into the kitchen for an apple while Hester is preparing lunch, he finds her in a spasm of raw, bleak tears. It's only the second time he's seen her weep, isn't it? The first being toward the end of their quarrel on the night of Paul's visit. And the first time Diddy's ever discovered her crying; for no particular reason that he knows. Though she once told him—he will never forget the telling and its circumstances—that she cried often. Apparently, then, she either no longer cries: something remarkable, worth understanding. Or else she still cries stanchlessly, but conceals it from Diddy: also worth understanding, if that's the case.

Shouldn't Diddy have grasped how precious this moment in the kitchen was? Another turning point, possibly. And been able to reach out for a three-dimensional Hester, to find her in a way he's never done before.

But Diddy, once again, fails to seize the moment. Tangled in the labyrinthine skein of his own inner life, he merely takes Hester in his arms. Praying silently that she is not unhappy because of him, or over anything he's done.

And when, after a few minutes, Hester dries her eyes and smiles at him, takes that at face value, too.

Diddy and Hester have been living for more than six weeks on West Twenty-first Street. Since Xan was disposed of, a few days after Paul's abortive visit, no living being shares the apartment with them.

The awful quarrel seems almost forgotten. At least, as far as Diddy is concerned. And Hester never alludes to it, or makes remarks to Diddy which remind him of her devastating accusations that night. The fact that Paul has, quite typically, disappeared again, Diddy assumes, has convinced Hester he wasn't being unfair about his brother. But he can only infer that she must be persuaded. They haven't actually discussed Paul since. Hester not only seems far from quarreling, but lately has said very little at all. Though unfailingly loving to Diddy. And seeking to become useful to him in all sorts of charming, unexpected ways. For instance, she can cut his nails and hair. When she first implored him to let her try, Diddy doubted she could possibly do a decent job, or fail to cut either herself or him in the process. He was wrong, as with the cooking. Hester didn't have one mishap with the nail scissors. And Diddy's prematurely graying hair, when he examines it afterwards with two mirrors, has been given as even a trim as any skilled home barber could give.

Is this the paradise Diddy anticipated? Yes and no.

Has exclusive possession (now) of his love, whose physical beauty and laconic speech afford him inexhaustible pleasures. Yet, also aware that some of his own newfound strength, on which he'd counted so much, is ebbing away. A curious symptom. At times, Diddy starts to say something to Hester after a long silence. Of course, she hears the unspoken buds of sound trembling at the back of his throat and pressing forward into his mouth. Looks up, waits. But then Diddy can't think of what he was about to say. This might be written off as a nervous tic, nothing alarming. What's important is that Diddy and Hester aren't quarrelsome. Seem pledged to avoid any more battles like that awful one. Even if they talk a good deal less, what words they do exchange are loving. And isn't it usually so, that lovers who share their daily lives with each other gradually find they need to put very little into words? Once it was Hester who set the example with her terse habits of speech. (Now) Diddy even more sparing with words than she. There seems less to say; good reason, often, not to talk at all.

So far, so good. But there's more. Occasionally, but with increasing frequency, Diddy imagines that he's losing the power to speak.

At times, the fantasy repels and upsets him. It has occurred to him that the craving to be mute must mean that there's something very important to say, something he wants to say and is not saying. Diddy the Coward. If mute, he'd have no choice. Couldn't say it, whatever it was—even if he wanted to. Other times, he views the fantasy in a more indulgent light. As part of his love, a passionate metaphor. Were Diddy unable to talk at all, it would establish a rough party between himself and Hester. The girl being blind, justice demands that Diddy subtract a comparable faculty. So considered, the fantasy of being mute pleases him.

Still, something has definitely gone wrong. The two of them becoming closed in. Which was not at all Diddy's intention, his original scheme. Planned for himself and Hester to inhabit a bigger space. And one that's fresh for Diddy; not encrusted with the immortal dirt of the past and the habits of faltering vitality. But they haven't moved; Diddy hasn't even looked at the *Times* ads or phoned a real-estate broker. Remaining where they are, where Diddy has lived for three years. This apartment was compact; which means comfort and security to a blind person. But Diddy has needs of his own to satisfy. However suitable for Hester, the apartment is too small for him. Too familiar. The space divided into three rooms, that Hester (now) knows as well as he, seems to be shrinking. Becoming almost as cramped and overcharged with use as their compartment on the Privateer.

In still another way, as far as cleanliness and order go, the apartment increasingly resembles the ill-maintained train. The condition of the floors, strewn with cigarette butts and dirty plates and LP's not put back in their sleeves and clothing discarded in the haste of making love. Hester's no longer doing the cleaning each day. Look at the windows. In such a filthy city, windows are the first to show the results of inattention. A thin layer of soot forms on the outside of the windowpanes. Perspiration on the inside of the windowpanes of the overheated apartment mixes with the subtler grime that collects on indoor glass in New York. Together, weakening the already faint winter light that enters the apartment during the day; imparting to the light inside a deader quality. Filtering out the clarity and detail in Diddy's view of the street and neighboring buildings. Less and less view. Not so much organized looking. Instead, organized screening out.

> Of course, unlike the view from a train window, the one from an apartment scarcely changes. Except in particulars.
> Who is on the stoop across the street? The grocer's boy.
> There's a red Volkswagen parked by the fire hydrant.

That man has been standing in front of the Mexican restaurant for hours.

The woman across the street on the third floor is walking around naked. No, there she goes. She's pulling down the shade.

And so forth. Despite particulars, still remaining essentially the same.

After the fourth week, less tempting to move about. It's approaching full winter (now). These are the shortest days of the year, supplying the least light. It seems natural for Hester and Diddy, like the animals, to spend more time in bed.

Usually they fall asleep at the same time, but Hester habitually sleeps several hours longer than Diddy. From the beginning Diddy chose to remain by her side until she opened her eyes, around noon, smiled, reached for her dark glasses on the night-table, and rose up naked, putting her bare feet on the floor. At first, it was from the desire to keep her company that Diddy stayed in bed, awake, through the long morning. As well as from the delight of remaining close to her warm, soft body. Lately, he's found it hard to get up even when Hester does. Often staying in bed while she takes a shower, brushes her hair, dresses, and then moves into the living room to play records or into the kitchen to prepare some food. By this time, it's usually about one o'clock. Hester brings the food into the bedroom; they eat. If he succeeds in dissuading her from then returning to do the dishes, she will often get back in bed. If she insisted on returning to the kitchen, within fifteen minutes Diddy is calling from the bed; telling her to come back.

When she does return, they make love. Which is, more and more, the unifying theme of their relationship. At first somewhat inhibited and, since Joan's tirades, holding a modest opinion of his talents in bed, Diddy amazed to find himself graceful and almost tireless with Hester. A miracle. And, another miracle, this lust does not feed on deprivation and rejection. Seems to be fully returned. She, no less enthusiastic, inventive, and eager than he. After a month, they're making love even more frequently than they did at first. Three, four times a day. Diddy suspects he's inspired by more

272

than sheer erotic need. Could the same be true of Hester, who seems equally hungry for their sexual union and takes the initiative as often as he does?

The vertigo of sex. The miniature frontal lobotomy that follows orgasm. Diddy drifting off, but not exactly into sleep. And sometimes wishing he dared to propose to Hester, Let's die together. Let's kill ourselves (now). While we're united and really happy.

Sometimes Diddy thinks they must have a long talk. Not to quarrel. Not to propose a suicide pact. To clear the air, drag whatever it is that neither of them understands out in the open. Right. Start (now). But just at these moments his mind grinds to a halt, goes blank and hums faintly and senselessly like a television screen when all the channels are off. Diddy possessing no idea, not even the vestige of an idea, of what he thought he wanted to say. Tries to summon the fugitive idea. But he feels so heavy in his flesh. Is it the effort of trying to think, and not succeeding? An overwhelming lassitude. If he's not already in bed, wants to rush beneath the covers. If he is in bed but Hester's not beside him, wants to summon her immediately. To linger there together. To sleep with every part of his body embracing Hester's, his chest against her mobile back, his arm folded around her supple, full waist and tucked in under her side. To wake, to kiss, to rub, to make love. To dream, not to wake fully, to make love.

Perhaps what he wishes to say concerns Incardona. Since Diddy doesn't doubt the reality of his crime, it seems a painful blemish on the unity and openness of his connection with Hester that she won't believe, or ignores, what he knows he's done. That Hester shouldn't be allowed to remain in ignorance of what her lover is capable. Yet he's reluctant to recite the story. To close the fissure of truth. Positively fearful. Truth's all very well, but what one does with it or how one responds to it can't be guaranteed in advance. With the truth, Diddy would just have to take his chances. Hester might become afraid of him. As, during their quarrel, she'd suggested she already was. And, whether because she's frightened of him or not, might think he ought to do something. Hester is very persuasive; but Diddy doesn't want to be persuaded. Might urge him to go to the police. But no burden of guilt or remorse, Diddy felt, could

273

justify his doing that (now), thereby separating Hester and himself. Not if he'd slain a thousand Incardonas. Diddy has no intention of doing anything about Incardona's murder. He can't expiate it. He's not willing to be punished for it. And he can't excuse it, either.

Telling Hester would seem to be mere self-indulgence. Its only result: to make her sad; perhaps a worse feeling. A selfish move on Diddy's part. What good is a confession of guilt which, apart from burdening the hearer, carries no consequences?

Diddy stands alone, then. Waits for Incardona to shrink some more. Prepared to bear the vertigo and nausea associated with that receding knowledge. But Diddy has braced himself in vain. The painful consciousness of Diddy's secret doesn't diminish any further than it already has. (Now) it congeals. Establishing an unbridgeable distance between him and Hester. For Diddy knows that, whatever genuine love flourishes between them, their being together is founded upon his concealment of the truth and her willingness to be deceived. The very energy of their initial meeting on the train was surplus energy, left over from his encounter with Incardona.

Perhaps that's why Diddy finds it hard (now) ever to leave the apartment. With the best of intentions, and the best possible will to work on the world and transform it in the light of his alliance with Hester, Diddy has discovered the world to be made of more intractable stuff than he'd envisaged. Thinking to dissolve its recalcitrant ugliness with the acids of his regeneration; at least, to make of the world a palimpsest, to etch his benign fantasy upon it. (Now) finds the world closing in on him, untransformed and unequivocally menacing. Hard and heartless as a stainless-steel mirror. Quite simply, every person he knows—from Paul to the merest acquaintance—speaks to him of Incardona. All people, by virtue of their human estate, however slight and token the form in which they manifest their humanity, address him on Incardona's behalf. Without knowing it, every person seems to be Incardona's deputy; howling mutely for Diddy's blood. Hester alone stands outside this magic world of infinite duplication. Hester, Incardona's foil, reminds Diddy only of herself.

274

There's finally a point when Diddy can't get out of bed at all. Diddy in despair. He was to be the strong partner, nourishing and protecting Hester. To be her eyes, as she was to become his soul. He's doing nothing for her (now). She navigates entirely by herself about the apartment. Occasionally mopping, sweeping, dusting, darning socks. Playing records. Typing a letter to her aunt. Cooking, of course. She washes Diddy, shaves him, serves him meals in bed, and every few hours joins him under the covers.

Diddy waking up drowsy from a nap one early afternoon in mid-January. Neuralgic pains in his forehead. Short of breath. Sweating heavily. But all these are familiar sensations (now). How did it happen? By imperceptible stages? Anyway, without being aware that it was happening, it has. He's become entirely bedridden and debilitated, and Hester is his nurse. His body is failing. Except to use the toilet, he doesn't get up at all. And always dizzy when he did. Sometimes has to lean on Hester.

How dark it is outdoors. What day is it? Diddy presses his hands first to his face, and then to his chest. Obvious that he's continued to lose weight. His cheekbones, ribs, elbows, knees, pelvic bones protrude painfully. Somehow, so confident of life and hopeful for the renewal of feeling, has made a wrong turning. Realizes, with frozen baffled clarity, that he's on the road to his death.

Quick! Something must be done, if it's not already too late. Hester's not in bed beside him; naked, against him. Oh God, she couldn't have gone out, could she? Diddy has made her swear she wouldn't go anywhere without him. But he was sleeping just (now). For how long? He calls anxiously, and she's at the door almost instantly. Wearing an old blue shirt of Diddy's, a velour skirt, and sneakers. Holding a broom in her hand, which she props against the doorway. Entering the bedroom with a firm step, her right hand slightly extended to warn her if she's about to bump into anything. Of course, she doesn't.

Scarcely any likelihood of that happening (now).

Every inch of this space is as familiar to her as her own body. And all the objects in it: the dishes in the cupboard, the towels in the linen closet, the records in the cabinet which Diddy relabeled for Hester in relief letters.

Just as Diddy, for weeks, has been walking from bed to bathroom at night in total darkness without ever miscalculating a step, knowing exactly by touch and the memory of locations where everything is. Able to reach out without faltering for the aspirin bottle in the medicine cabinet, the roll of paper next to the toilet, the faucets, the doorknobs. The light switch it's no longer necessary to turn on.

Hester at the side of their bed. By this time Diddy is wracked with dizziness. Takes her hand, tugging her into a sitting position beside him.

"Want me to lie down?"

"Darling, we have to talk."

"Why?"

Why! Diddy's shouting inside his head. Doesn't she know? "Because there's something wrong. I'm not well. I'm not taking care of you; you're taking care of me."

"I enjoy caring for you. What else have I got to do?"

"But I shouldn't need to be taken care of! And there are many, many other things you could do. That we could do together . . . Darling, remember how strong I was a month ago? Now, no matter how much I eat and sleep, I get thinner and weaker every day."

"Let's call a doctor."

"Hester, I'm not sick physically!"

"How do you know that?"

"I just do. I know what's wrong, why I'm sick."

"Why?"

Did he want to say it? Yes. "I think I'm sick because I'm afraid."

An abrupt movement. Diddy's hand released. "Wait a minute, I hear the coffee boiling over." Hester left the bedroom. Seeing her from behind, Diddy thought, no one would ever suspect she was blind. How proud of her sureness of movement he was. At the same time, how envious.

Hester returning with two mugs of coffee. "Here, Dalton. Tell me if it needs more sugar. I put in just one lump." Sat down again on the bed.

Diddy took the mug from her hand, sipped it tentatively. "Too hot," he says morosely.

"Silly! Of course it's hot. Wait a minute till it cools."

Suddenly Diddy felt tears coating his eyes. "Hester, I can't stand this any more!"

"The coffee?"

"Oh for God's sake, listen to me! Look at me." Diddy beyond himself (now). "Look at me!" Yes, wanted Hester to look at him; even if she didn't see. To stare at him until his face hurt, until he was forced to lower his own eyes. But all Hester does is turn her head to him. When, after a brief moment, she lowered it to drink from her mug of coffee, Diddy gripped by a convulsion of rage so unexpected that, without being aware of first-thinking-then-doing, he flung his own mug against the far wall. A loud crash.

"What did you break beside the mug?" Hester asks calmly. "Was it the photograph of Garbo?"

"Yes, God damn you. As you know perfectly well. You can tell from the sound of it, can't you?" He began to weep and laugh at the same time. "Even though . . . even though you haven't the faintest idea what Garbo looks like."

"Dalton, please calm down. Tell me what's the matter." Setting her mug down on the floor, Hester grasped his shoulders, and pushed him back on the pillow. Put her hand under the sheet, and begins stroking his chest. Diddy shoved her hand away, sat up violently.

"For God's sake, Hester! Stop treating me like a child having a tantrum."

"Isn't that what you are?" She stood up and walked to the foot of the bed.

Diddy calmer (now). "All right, maybe I am. But I still have a shred of my adulthood left, and it's that grownup man I want you to listen to. It's the grownup you've been ignoring. . . . Do you understand?"

"I'm listening."

She's so far away. "First, come back here. Next to me. On the bed."

Hester sitting on the edge of the bed again. "I'm listening, Dalton."

Can anything be done? Diddy will try. Balancing rage, frustration, and despair.

"I said, I'm listening."

"Yes, I hear you . . . It's hard. I'm very angry. Yet somewhere I know what I'm angry about isn't your fault at all."

"Oh Dalton, be angry. I beg you. Stop fussing with yourself. If you're worrying about me, don't. I can take it."

"Do you remember what I was saying before you had to interrupt me and rush out to get the coffee? Do you remember, Hester?"

"Perfectly. You said you thought you weren't sick for a physical reason but because you were afraid."

"That's right. Now, do you know what you were then supposed to ask me with affectionate concern? Your next line?" A sullen impacted look settled on Hester's face. Diddy snapped his fingers. "Quick! Quick!"

"Say your line again," said Hester.

Diddy almost laughed. No point in browbeating her. Try to be patient. "Okay. My line was 'I'm afraid.' "

"Afraid of what?"

"Bravo!"

"I don't like this game."

"God damn it, it's not a game, Hester!"

"Yes, it is. But let's play . . . I'll play. I want to play. Look." She's doing something to her face, just as sighted people do: pushing away the loose strands of hair from her forehead, settling her glasses further up on the bridge of her nose, smoothing out the frown. "Afraid of what?" Hester trying to sweeten her tone, Diddy could hear it. Still something metallic in her voice she couldn't disguise. Why was she so angry? Natural for a woman to want strength in a man. And natural for Hester, condemned to blindness, to need exceptional strength and competence. Yet, despite her handicap, she's strong, too. How unfair of her to resent so deeply his confession of weakness. Isn't she capable of sympathy for him?

"Afraid of what?" Hester says again.

Diddy longs to kick aside the warm sheets, vault out of bed, pull up the foul window and let in the icy air. Go for a walk, if only by the warehouses and docks along the contaminated waters of the Hudson. Board a train and leave the city; get on a boat and clear out of the country. For good. . . . But that would be a lie. And Diddy's body won't lie (now), won't transport him anywhere. Even to the window.

Once again: "Afraid of what?"

Diddy had almost forgotten. Startled, he blurts out, "I don't know. The truth, I guess. . . . Isn't that the only thing anyone is afraid of?"

"I don't understand, Dalton."

"Yes, you do! Why do you say that?" Is this the opaque side of Hester he'd always dreaded? Her destructive energy made manifest? A wall. "I know you understand me as well as I do myself. If not better." Diddy felt as if he were the blind one, utterly dependent on another's good will. Despises himself for begging, but he's so frightened. "Hester, don't shut me out."

"But I don't understand, Dalton. Truly. And you mustn't expect me to. I know you detest my saying this, but I have to. Remember what I told you the day I left the hospital, when we were in the park? I said your truth was different from mine. And that hasn't changed."

"Of course I remember," Diddy cries impatiently. "And sometimes I think I even understand. But other times, I really don't. Then, I absolutely hate you for having said that; and for sticking to it . . . But listen, we mustn't quarrel now. I'm willing to believe what you said. Even assuming it's as you say, you can still help me. One real difference between us in this is that you're not afraid of your truth. And I am," he groaned. "Absolutely terrified of mine."

She leaned her head on his chest. Why won't she say anything?

"Help me, Hester!"

"What are you afraid of?"

"I guess. . . . I guess, I'm afraid that I'll have to do something,

279

something I'm not doing," Diddy stammered. "Something I'm languishing in this goddamned bed to avoid doing."

"Well, then, get up and do it."

"Will you come with me?"

Hester said yes.

On time. At ten-fifteen in the morning, the Cherry Valley Local exited, racing, from the northern mouth of the tunnel. A slim, puny, rackety train; conveying an impression of considerably less force than the Privateer. When one recalls the sealed-off reticence of the Privateer's powerful diesel, the very smoke spewed out from the funnel crowning the engine of this train seemed an emblem of weakness.

Standing on the sloping field, a few feet above the track, Diddy watches and listens, Hester listens. The last rumbling of the train fades beneath their feet. (Now) the ground is still again. It had snowed yesterday. The fields are lightly dusted with snow; covering the crossties and rails of the two tracks, a strip of thin white icing. But Diddy and Hester aren't cold. The sun is shining; the temperature must be in the fifties—unusual for late January.

Figuring from the railroad timetables that Diddy had consulted and was this moment pulling out of his pocket to check for the last time, the next train using this tunnel in either direction on Thursday enters at twelve minutes after eleven. In exactly fifty-seven minutes. Diddy calculated that it should take them no more than fifteen minutes to reach the site where the Privateer had stalled. Allowing another fifteen minutes to get out, they would have plenty of time. Diddy didn't plan to linger. A few minutes, he expected, would suffice.

Diddy entering the tunnel with Hester, their arms linked. They proceed cautiously, leaving the late morning light behind them. Though Diddy has brought along a heavy 6-volt torch, it's still hard to see. The powerful, wide beam does not repel the blackness. No more than did the slim, feeble beam of the pocket flashlight he'd carried before. The tunnel remains, essentially, unilluminable. In addition, Diddy has in the past months developed a more complex, suspicious relation to light. Perhaps the torch's ineffectuality is connected with the fact that it's only for him. No light can assist Hester to see better; with or without a flashlight, the tunnel is equally dark for her. But so profound is their sympathy that Diddy can no longer distinguish himself from her in such matters. What's dark for Hester is equally dark for Diddy. This tunnel, for example. Though he oughtn't to forget that the bright wintry fields outside, .stretching away from both sides of the track, are dark for Hester, too.

The tunnel is cool but humid, thick with the smell of oil and damp rock. They continue walking, Diddy slightly in the lead. "Don't worry, darling. I can see exactly where we're going." But he *is* worried. Feels they're the two children from the fairy tale, wandering hand in hand through the enchanted forest. Lost. Being the boy, he's obliged to be the braver and the stronger. Reassuring his little sister who weeps in fright; supporting and tending her. But in the end, Diddy recalls, the girl proves to be the more level-headed and effective. While her brother is captured by the witch, jailed, readied for eating, the resourceful girl still contrives to preserve a portion of her liberty—through guile rather than strength. It's she who manages to rescue him.

Diddy trying to be strong and guileful.

But the tunnel is not only a site of terror and threat. This time, it's also reassuringly familiar. The advantages of doing something more than once. The tunnel is like home.

As is the darkness. Several months living with Hester have made Diddy feel king of all dark places. Darkness a familar element. He could make his way in the tunnel equally well without a light. Deciding to test his prowess, switches off the torch for a minute. Indeed, it does seem to make hardly any difference. Didn't Diddy always have an excellent sense of direction? But then, feeling that he's showing off, behavior inappropriate to the gravity of the occasion, turns the light on again.

Trudging (now) through a chain of puddles. Doesn't faze Diddy, because he's wearing heavy cleated boots; not street shoes of soft leather. But Hester's feet must be getting wet. "Darling, let me carry you. You aren't dressed right for this. You should be wearing flat shoes and slacks. How stupid of us not to think of that!"

"I'm all right."

"Sure?"

"Yes. But I hate the smell in here."

"It's diesel oil, I think."

"No, something else besides that," she says. "Can't you smell it?" Diddy does smell something else, which he can't identify.

"Are you cold?" Diddy the Concerned. Beginning himself to feel chilled. Realizing that Hester is wearing only a thin linen dress under her coat.

"No, I don't mind the cold."

Diddy about to say something else that's solicitous, when he tunes into a sound other than their footsteps. Not, thank God, the roar of an approaching train. A low, tapping noise. "Hester, do you hear that?" Grips her hand.

"I hear something." Don't whisper, darling. They have to talk above Diddy's heart thundering in his chest. Both begin listening (now), while trying to walk as noiselessly as possible and not to slacken their pace. "Dalton, I'm afraid." He clasps her hand more tightly. "Really. I want to go back."

Diddy not knowing which alarms him more. The indecipherable noise ahead, getting slightly louder (now) and more distinct. Or Hester's anxiety; and its possible consequences. That she might compel him to turn back with her. Or that she might desert him, leaving him to continue without her.

"Darling, don't make me go back with you now. You know I can't let you turn back alone, and I don't want to go on by myself. Trust me. Stay with me."

Hester doesn't reply. But doesn't pause, either; keeps walking, not even slowing down. Oh, let her silence and the steadiness of her step signify that she's willing to continue with him. But she could change at any moment. Fear may win. And once Hester decides to turn back, she will. Diddy won't be able to dissuade her;

or stop her, except by force. Knows she's afraid. The difficulty is that he's frightened, too.

There's no doubt that the tapping sound is getting louder. Whatever or whoever is making the sound must be only a short distance ahead. (Now) the tunnel no longer seems familiar, known, even knowable. Diddy doubts that he's ever been here before. How could he have been? In this tunnel? All Diddy perceives are features common to every railroad tunnel: the long enclosed space, the damp cool air, the darkness, the bed of hard earth, the empty track along which they're walking. And, as in every tunnel, all sounds are deadened; almost an echo effect.

Only one idiosyncratic feature: the track is curving. As did the track last time. Yet, although no long jointed iron train languishes alongside to supply an index of the degree of curvature, Diddy is convinced that this track's curve is more pronounced than the other one.

(Now) Diddy sees light ahead. Not a direct source of light, but an aura seeping from beyond the curve of the track. To make sure, extinguishes his torch for a moment. "Light ahead," he whispers to Hester. She doesn't answer. Diddy switches his light on once more. Then turns it off for good, and hooks it on his belt.

After walking another minute, the new light and the person who performs some task under its glare both spring into Diddy's view. The light comes down from a huge fixture which hangs from the ceiling of the tunnel, made of irregular strips of black wrought iron and harboring at least a dozen naked bulbs. Under the light, a tall swarthy workman is engaged in some kind of repair of the track. At a distance, Diddy observes that the man has on work clothes that closely resemble Incardona's. Boots, overalls, and undershirt. The main difference is in the accessories: unlike Incardona, this man wears a knee-length brown leather apron that covers the front of his shirt and ties around his neck.

"I see someone just ahead," mutters Diddy.

"Have we found the trackman?"

Hester's question stalks Diddy, reaches him, leans on him like a huge flat stone. Startling, heavy, oppressive. Diddy appalled by the possibility of such a misconception. As if Hester thought the

283

man they were approaching is the same one Diddy described yesterday, before they set out; when he'd presented her with the whole truth, including the newspaper report and his interview with Incardona's widow. As if he still hadn't been understood. Or more likely, still wasn't believed.

"Another man," Diddy, not trusting himself to speak further.

(Now) they're almost upon him. In face and form, Diddy sees, this man does resemble Incardona. And, what's more upsetting, he too is working at dismantling what appears to be a kind of barrier across the track. But this barrier is built of different material from the first. Rectangular gray-white blocks—whether of quarried stone or concrete, Diddy can't tell yet. A good portion of the job already done.

Holding Hester tightly around the waist, Diddy halts about ten feet from where the man is energetically at work with a chisel and hammer, chopping away at the cement filling between the blocks. Diddy's head begins to thicken. Much as he longs to deny it, the resemblance between this man and Incardona is uncannily close. Both about the same age, build, height, and complexion; both have similar, rather ordinary gross features. Could they possibly be brothers? A slightly younger or older Incardona, who works for the railroad. Named Charlie. Being brothers is at least one step away from being the same. But no, that's absurd. Look again. Diddy trying to hang on to the differences. Once again: there's no lamp strapped to his brow; this man is wearing a leather apron. And it isn't of a miner hacking at the under-earth that Diddy is reminded. This man suggests, partly by his appearance and partly by his style of work, a tanner. Or a smith at his forge. Or, somewhat remotely, a gravedigger.

"What do you see?" Hester whispers.

Diddy aghast at Hester's having taken the liberty of speaking at this moment, even in a whisper. Intent on his work, the man apparently hasn't heard them approaching. Why else would he not have looked in their direction or acknowledged them? But since Hester has ended the silence, the workman's self-absorbed behavior takes on another, less innocent meaning. He must have heard Hester's voice just then. Aware (now), if not before, of the man and woman standing close by. So if he still doesn't speak or even look up, he's deliberately ignoring them.

Diddy panicking. Has had the mad idea that if they didn't speak they wouldn't be seen. Since Hester has spoken, they are discovered, exposed.

But to what? To a situation that's unpleasant, even dangerous? All depends on whom they're dealing with.

Is Diddy prepared to admit that the surly laborer near them is none other than Incardona? Yes, as much as anyone is ever prepared to admit something that doesn't make sense. Something of which no account can ever be convincing, ever appease the obvious doubts. Diddy not only prepared. Has arrived at the rim of belief, actually. In fact, already there. In the crater. Settled, in residence, among impossibles. Doing the circuit which connects an album of sites wherein those impossibilities are housed.

To put Diddy's capacity for credence in a less extreme form: he believes two incompatible things. That Incardona died and that Incardona lives. Not all that different from, or significantly harder than, believing that he, Diddy, died; and also, that he lived.

Here is Diddy's view, in the least extreme form. It *is* the same man, he (now) both believes and cannot believe.

With so many refinements of belief and assertion, it's hard to give a simple, straight answer to Hester's question. Better to watch and wait.

Grunting with apparent satisfaction, the workman has stopped knocking and chipping at the cement. He squats beside a canvas pouch lying on the ground and extracts another tool, a huge hammer. Comes to a standing position, rises on the balls of his feet, raises the hammer straight above his head, brings it down; delivering a powerful blow to one of the blocks making up what's (now) the top tier of the barrier. Recoiling at the brutal sound, Hester screams faintly. Diddy covered her mouth with his hand.

Another block has yielded, and the man works it loose with the aid of the crowbar. Whistling tunelessly as he seizes the conquered chunk of matter, carries it over to the pile of already dislodged blocks heaped up inside a niche in the tunnel wall. On his way back to the barrier, he glances directly, very coolly at Diddy and Hester. Continues whistling, but says nothing.

Diddy, ashamed of his cowardice, removes his hand from Hester's mouth. "Forgive me, darling," he whispers. "I'm trying to think for both of us. But if you give in to fear, I get confused. I can't think at all."

The trackman at work again. Perhaps overheard what Diddy said, because when he looks up for a moment this time, he laughs. He smells like an animal, breathes like an animal.

"Why is he laughing?" Hester has been leaning against Diddy's left side, even after he's taken his hand from her mouth. When she straightens up, finds that the heel of one shoe is jammed between a segment of the rail and a huge bolt; in working it free, almost loses her footing.

Diddy grabs her. "Watch out!"

"I'm all right." She wants to stand by herself. "Dalton, why is he laughing?"

"I don't know," says Diddy. "Or maybe I do. He's playing bully. He's trying to intimidate us."

"How far away is he?" Although whispered into Diddy's ear, it's possible that the workman overheard.

"Just hold on to me," Diddy whispers.

"Just hold on to me!" says the workman in a harsh, husky voice.

At last! Diddy relieved to be getting on with it. "So you've decided to start talking, have you?"

"I don't know if I'm talking to *you,* man," says the workman. "But the lady, well," he grins, "that's something else. Yessiree, something else."

"Dalton!"

"Dalton!" mimicks the trackman.

Diddy enraged. The man being insolent again, more insolent than before. Crudely menacing. But this time, since Diddy's not alone, everything's different. Incardona doesn't appear to be paying much attention to Diddy. Has dismissed him as an adversary of no account whatever; is hardly looking at him. This time he's after Hester. Not contempt, like the other time, that Diddy sees (now) distorting the workman's heavy features. It's lust. Which, of course, Hester doesn't and can't see. Diddy must see for both of them. Protect her, even above himself, against the beasts that overrun this world. Diddy as St. George.

He's coming closer. With one arm, Diddy grips Hester tightly. Looking about for his weapon.

Incardona has underestimated his adversary. This time it's an experienced Diddy, his hands already baptized in blood, who stands. Tense with hatred, ready for combat. Diddy lets go of Hester.

Incardona still coming on, so confident of his physical superiority to frail bedridden Diddy that he isn't even holding an ax in his hands. But Diddy, straining with fury and loathing, is not going to play the gentleman. Even though this is something of a duel of honor. Having thrust the trembling Hester behind him, he picks up the crowbar again and stands ready. "Oh, want to play games, huh?" sneers the man, nodding in the direction of Diddy's weapon.

"Just come one step nearer," Diddy shouts, "and you'll see what game I'm playing." Diddy feeling strong, invincible. Feels he is made of stone.

"All's fair in love and war!" Incardona sneers, and feints dodging to Diddy's left, as Diddy brings his crowbar down in the empty air. The force of the unsuccessful blow makes Diddy almost lose his balance; he just avoids smashing himself in the shins with the crowbar. No, stop! Hester moans. Incardona has pawed at her breast, but then darts away, dancing about like a boxer. "Hester!" Diddy shouts. Doesn't dare look at her again, because he'd have to take his eyes off Incardona. But he has to know. "Hester!" Meaning: Are you all right? Did he hurt you?

"Dalton, don't kill him!"

But it wasn't possible for Diddy to hear what Hester has just cried out, much less to understand it. Seems to be mixed up with many other muddleheaded exclamations and exhortations and assertions such as, "Wake up!" and "Hey!" and "Try the oxygen!"

Outraged Diddy means to kill. There is no going back on that. You must kill what you hate absolutely; unless you're willing to let it kill you.

Although Incardona is weaponless, Diddy's task isn't easy.

287

Diddy has figured out that he will never get at Incardona by running at him head on; even without a weapon, the large, powerfully muscled workman is too agile. Diddy will have to use guile. Still numb-fingered from his previous blow, he grasps the iron tool with both hands as firmly as he can. At the same moment, shouts: "Hester, lie down!" Incardona stops leaping about, looks away for a moment from Diddy to Hester. Which is when, exactly when, Diddy brings the crowbar down on the man's head.

With an ugly yell, Incardona throws his hands up to his head, sways, pivots, his knees bending; then collapses to the ground. Lying there, huddled. His shattered head pours forth blood, brains, bits of bone, and something that looks like dirty water. There's no doubt this time. Diddy has killed him. No need for a train to finish the job. This was a frontal blow, as well as a more energetic and well-aimed one. Diddy looks down at the man crumpled on the tunnel bed, meaning to gloat. And even finding himself able to muster that brutal emotion, overriding his helpless twitchings of horror and disgust. Diddy triumphant.

At last, Diddy thinks. He's really dead (now). Because I was halfhearted the first time, I had to come back and do it again.

He hears Hester behind him, whimpering; turns. She's squatting on the ground, head lowered; stained with grease, mud, and blood spattered by Incardona's gashed skull. Dropping the crowbar, Diddy kneels beside her and embraces her tightly. Has forgotten entirely what he took to be her outcry of panic, of fear for his safety: "Dalton, don't kill him!" Can only assume that Hester realizes the duel is over. And that Diddy, unscathed, is the victor. Kissing her cheeks, her mouth, her neck, "Now you saw me," he murmurs. "You saw me this time."

But Hester appears not to understand. Doesn't share Diddy's euphoria, his obstinate exultation. On the contrary. Hester seems (now) even more charged with obscure grief. She pulls away from Diddy's embrace. Stands, rebuffing his attempts to aid her. Fiercely brushing at her clothes, stamping the mud from her shoes.

Diddy, baffled, stands up, too. "What's the matter, darling? Why are you angry? Everything's all right now. You saw what happened."

"No, I didn't see," she says bitterly, "and you know that." Pause. "But if this will satisfy you, I *do* believe you."

"There's something more you're thinking." Diddy says agitatedly. "That you're not telling me."

"It's all over," said Hester. "And it doesn't matter, it couldn't have been otherwise. You had to do what you had to do."

"I just don't understand you," shouts Diddy. "We're not talking about the same thing."

"Yes, we are. I've said it already. I do believe you."

Diddy can't understand why Hester's become cold and severe. What reason she has for refusing him his long-deferred vindication. "That's not enough," he insists, sullenly. "You must *see* me." What good is such a defective, distracted witness? None, none at all. Must I kill him again?

"But I can't," she cries hysterically. "You know I can't."

Diddy throbbing with anger at Hester. He has saved her life, he has saved his own. And, most important of all, he's brought their truths together, yoked them; made them coincide, even though it had to be by force. And in response to this feat, what does Hester do? Hurls at him the arbitrary technicality of her blindness. Diddy will not have it. "I want to be seen!" he shouts.

With that cry, something in Diddy yields. Maybe it's his anger. He felt the taut struts of his body loosen, stiffened fibers begin to dissolve, tense nerves dilate. The air seems to lighten, become less putrid-smelling. And much warmer. Diddy afraid to look at Hester; glances again at the crumpled man, a little spill of watery muck still draining from inside his skull. Finds what he perceives neither terrifying nor sickening. Such reactions presuppose that Diddy understands what he sees, and what he's done. And would then be able to marshal the old, tired reactions.

But it's different (now), everything is different. Waves of newness are flowing over the surface of this event.

Yet, how can that be? When this isn't the first but the second time?

Diddy knows the answer. It lies not in an idea, but in a deed. He wants to make love to Hester. Here, at this moment. For that love-making is the supplementary act. To all his murders, the sequel. The two somehow go together. But not in the way he'd understood before. Before, he had thought of union with Hester as the pardon that followed his guilty deed; or even the reward. (Now) Diddy wonders if, perhaps, he doesn't kill the trackman each time only in order to renew his ability to make love. The touch of violence being merely the necessary prelude which makes the other, the touch of love, possible. If this is true, love would be Diddy's goal, not his anodyne. Violence, demoted, only clears the ground? . . . But why must Diddy proceed in so roundabout a way?

After spreading his windbreaker and sweater on the strip of ground between the pair of tracks, a few feet from Incardona's body, and unlacing and taking off his boots, he makes Hester lie down with him. Takes her in his arms—quite inert at first, not responding at all. But Diddy feels so elated, so confident in his desire, that he didn't doubt he can arouse Hester and make her join him. Begins to caress her breasts; then puts one hand between her legs while, with the other, lifting up her dress to her waist. Diddy lost in the sweet, wet flesh. Yes, she is beginning to love him again, in spite of herself. After slipping down his trousers and shorts as far as his knees, Diddy moves his body on top of hers. She is beginning to move, too; though her head is turned curiously far to one side, so Diddy has trouble kissing her face. Their movements begin to braid together. Without ever breaking their rhythm, Diddy unfastens her brassière from behind and lifts her dress even higher; kicked his pants completely off, and puts himself deep inside her. It is only the beginning, and already Diddy's pleasure is more acute and imperious than at any time they have made love, including the first. It must be true for Hester, too. For (now) she's with him in everything, though still with her face, guarded by the sunglasses, turned sharply away. They come once, but it's not enough. Each must offer every part of his body to the other—to genitals, mouth, hands, knees, hair, feet. Both crying, crooning, groaning, laughing, hissing, chanting obscenities—an arrangement of urgent sounds that Diddy has never heard from either of them. Diddy and Hester, like two wild creatures who have never coupled before. Trying to stay on top of Diddy's sweater and windbreaker, but eventually rolling off, tearing any clothes they've still kept on, smearing themselves with

290

filth, scraping their skin. All part of the same magma of sensation, in which pleasure and pain are one. They come together again. (Now) truly, Diddy feels forgiven. He is rising out of his lean weak body, like a sea creature out of its shell.

Hester fell back from his arms. Can she have fainted? Anxiously, he puts his cheek to her breast and listens to her breathing: the slow, regular inhalation and exhalation of someone deeply exhausted, who's mercifully fallen into a vast, much needed sleep. Asleep, then. Let her rest. Diddy draws Hester's nylon underpants back up her legs and around her hips, pulls her torn dress down to her knees; stuffs her cotton bra into her coat pocket; pushes her limp arms through the sleeves of her coat, and buttons it. Then, grasping Hester in his arms, he carries her several feet to the nearby shelter. Just inside; at the very mouth of the shelter, sets her down in a sitting position. Propped against the wall, near the heap of stone blocks that had once been part of the barrier.

Occurred to Diddy that it could be dangerous to leave Hester here. Safer, surely, to carry her out of the tunnel altogether, and lay her on the slope by the track. After depositing her there, Diddy could return to the tunnel again.

But he was afraid to leave the tunnel, even for a few minutes. He might not want, or not be able, to return. And it's only for a little while that Hester must lie here. A little farther that he must explore; while curiosity, the sensations of physical well-being, and the mood of orgiastic fulfillment still run at high tide in him.

Should he move Incardona, too? Hell, no. Let the bastard lie there in his filth.

Diddy should dress himself (now) before proceeding any further. But feels an aversion to putting back on those creased and ripped garments; like Hester's, spattered with Incardona's brain juices and blood; further stained with mud, grease, dirt, sweat, and sex. Of course, he would have put them on if he'd felt cold. But he's not, as it happens. Not only not cold, but feeling somewhat flushed and overheated. Perhaps Diddy has a fever. No matter. All that matters is that, for the present, he lacks all desire to dress.

Then thinks of a better use for his clothes. Hester's head, which he'd set against the shelter wall, has already slumped down in an awkward-looking position that must be uncomfortable. And the hard wall must hurt her spine. She'll ache when she wakes up. Folding his boots, trousers, shirt, and sweater into one bundle, Diddy pulls the unconscious girl forward for a moment, then arranges the bundle pillow-fashion behind her; after leaning her back again, drapes his windbreaker over her torso as a blanket. Much better (now).

Why keep anything on? Diddy stoops down, removes his socks and then his T shirt. Placing these just beside Hester.

(Now) he's free to go.

Diddy lifts one naked leg, then the other, over the incompletely dismantled barrier. Of course. Just as he'd secretly suspected all along. What lies beyond it isn't just a tame continuation of the tunnel and its two tracks. The tracks end only a little farther ahead, some twenty yards beyond the barricade. After that, the walls widened. (Now) widening still farther.

Why not? "There is another world but it is inside this one." Diddy no longer walking in a tunnel but, rather, through a long, wide, damp gallery. Once again, reminded of a mine. Except that this chamber is powerfully lit. By naked bulbs, set in fixtures on windowless walls at fairly close intervals. The lighting even powerful enough, perhaps, to produce a perceptible increase in the temperature. How else can one explain why Diddy, walking about naked in late January, isn't chilled? Can't be simply the odd climate of the gallery, the curious heat-producing dampness, can it? But whatever the cause, Diddy is (now) never less than warm. And occasionally close to sweltering; he could wish it a good deal colder.

Diddy, naked, with his seamless sense of well-being. The narrow toes of his highly arched feet grip the dirty stone flooring as he walks. His testicles, drooping in the warm air, fall pleasantly against the inside of his thighs. His arms swing freely at his sides. His shoulders are relaxed, not tensed; his head held erect. And the entire surface of his skin seems coated with an effulgent smoothness, as if rinsed in sleep.

The harsh, almost brutal lighting leaves Diddy in no doubt about the details of the enclosed space through which he's walking. And about its marked difference from the space of the tunnel. In contrast with the hard-packed earthen bed of the tunnel, here was a genuine floor. Paved with dark-gray stone; perforated at intervals of thirty feet or so by square drains, covered by heavy iron grilles. The walls were of the same dark-gray stone.

Diddy half expected, at any moment, to come upon an elderly guard dozing on a cane chair, from whom he could ask directions and thereby begin to orient himself. Imagined this functionary so clearly. An unkempt man about sixty, with sagging cheeks and a wen on his forehead, who hadn't shaved for at least two days. Who wore a shiny blue-serge uniform with frayed cuffs peeping out of the sleeves of his jacket; whose pockets were littered with old gum wrappers, canceled stamps, torn ticket stubs, and dirty Kleenexes. Who had a paunch, and suffered from bursitis. Who went home each night to a furnished room where he slept on a horsehair mattress with a picture of his dead wife above his bed. . . . Diddy wanted to ask this old guard, tilted back against the wall on his chair: Where am I? The man would make some lazy reply. It would suffice. For Diddy doesn't expect much information. Grateful for what he can get. But, despite the modesty of his projected demands, doesn't find even a decrepit custodian—either at the start of the long gallery or stationed anywhere throughout. Only finds on the floor, washed to the edge of one of the drains, a straw hat, size 7¾, which might have belonged to such a man.

The long gallery through which Diddy is walking, naked, is virtually empty. Except for numerous odd, nearly valueless items, which Diddy discovers at widely spaced intervals and which seem lost in the grandiose dimensions of this space. Objects that are abandoned? Lost? Hidden? Arranged here in sequence to convey some cryptic message?

First, the straw hat already mentioned.

Some yards farther down the gallery, along the wall, a Zenith radio circa 1930. All of whose tubes proved, upon examination, to be burnt out.

Still farther down, a large stack of 78 rpm records. Diddy stooped down for a moment, with the thought of rapidly sifting through them. But the records, all opera arias, were so dusty; and after looking at ten records, and dirtying the tips of his fingers, he had still to recognize the name of a single singer.

Farther, a crate of coconuts. Diddy picked one up, and shook it to listen for the sloshing sound of the milk. Felt thirsty. If only he had a small screwdriver, he could open one and take a drink. Such a small screwdriver— on his Swiss Army knife—lies in the pocket of the pants he left back in the tunnel.

Farther yet, a box of cigars. The Cuban kind that Reager liked. It might be fun to smoke one (now), if they aren't too dried out. Unfortunately, the box doesn't contain any matches.

Still farther, along the spigotless wall, a long length of orange plastic garden hose plus three different kinds of nozzles.

And still farther: a pair of rusted garden shears; a chamber pot decorated with a green, brown, and white curvilinear pattern and with the words "Minton" and "N° 12" stamped on the underside; a bale of magazines, mainly *Popular Mechanics* and *Science & Mechanics;* a legal-size envelope containing a dozen stills from Mexican movies of the 1950's featuring Dolores del Rio; a worn-out automobile tire; a tattered Barbie doll, with no Ken in sight; a spool of brown thread; a neat small pile of autumn-colored leaves; a wooden hanger labeled "Hotel Luna"; an empty fifth of Smirnoff's Vodka; a tube of dentifrice used for cleaning false teeth; and an incomplete deck of plastic playing cards. Diddy counts forty-nine.

Diddy appears to have stumbled into a world of things. A few, maybe, can count as collector's items; if somewhere there exists a taste odd enough to want to collect things like these. But granted that things are all that's native to this world, and even restricting things to objects of such a marginal or out-of-date character, what's also remarkable is how widely distributed the things are. An uncommon problem for Diddy: that of too much space. What would be clutter if dumped into most rooms, apartments, or houses is barely visible when spread about in a space as lavish as this.

Therefore, also a world of the absence of things. Apart from the aforementioned items, of a nature less plausibly described as "contents" than as "litter" or "debris," the gallery is devoid of furnishings. Bare.

Excepting, of course, what's on the walls. For what this extremely long, relatively narrow space lacked in the way of objects to fill it was partly made up for by the quantity of messages posted on both walls. A lengthy, unremitting pageant of quotations and mottoes.

For the first several hundred feet of the gallery, these were posted at irregular intervals and heights, rather casually. Sometimes simply painted or chalked on the stone wall. Or crudely lettered on cardboard, acoustic board, or plyboard; and then taped up or nailed on the wall. But the farther Diddy walks, the more densely they proliferate; and the more costly the means of mounting them. Some were printed on placards; and of these, many had elaborate multicolored initial letters and border designs. Some were incised on metal plates. Still, one couldn't discern among the styles of typography, printing, and metalwork represented—whether primitive or naïve—any unifying or even dominant tendency or period. A wholly eclectic assortment of graphic styles and plastic standards.

Something similar might be said of the texts themselves, all relating loosely to the theme of death. A hodgepodge of lines from poems, of homiletic quotations, a few intact but most of them a truncated sentence or phrase, and of popular wisdom. There seemed to be no ethical, temperamental, or cultural consistency in these messages and mottoes. As if many randomly chosen people had been invited to contribute their favorite bit of wisdom, and done so. With no thought to the harmony of the whole.

> "It is better never to have been born at all" was set alongside "The wages of sin are death." Which follows "Order, calm, and silence." Which was followed by "Gather ye rosebuds."
>
> Others that Diddy noticed, among which are a few he

might even have jotted down, if he'd carried a pad and pencil:

"I despise the dust of which I am composed and which speaks to you. I give it to you."

" 'The world has not promised anything to anyone.' Moroccan proverb."

"Easy come, easy go."

"O grave where is thy victory?"

"E dietro le venìa sì lunga tratta/ di gente ch'io non averei creduto/ che morte tanta n'avesse disfatta."

"Out of sight, out of mind."

"Et in Arcadia ego."

" 'The question is, is there a life before death?' Hungarian saying."

"That tossed the dog/ That worried the cat/ That killed the rat."

"Death and taxes."

"Enkidu, my friend, whom I loved so dearly/ Who underwent with me all hardships/ Him has overtaken the fate of mankind!/ Six days and seven nights I wept over him/ Until the worm fell out of his nose."

"When you gotta go, you gotta go."

"Because I could not stop for Death — He kindly stopped for me—"

"Ashes to ashes, dust to dust."

"My only regret is that I have but one life to give for my country."

"Wir Geretteten/ Aus deren hohlem Gebein der Tod schon seine Flöten schnitt/ An deren Sehnen der Tod schon seinen Bogen strich."

"What doesn't kill me makes me stronger."

"I am that which was, which is, and which shall be. And no man hath lifted my veil."

"Better Red than dead."

"And death shall have no dominion."

"Où sont les neiges d'antan?"

"Dead men tell no tales."

"This thought is as a death which cannot choose/
But weep to have that which it fears to lose."

"I went down to the Saint James Infirmary."

"Or discendiamo omai a maggior pièta;/ già ogni
stella cade che saliva/ quand' io mi mossi, e 'l troppo
star si vieta."

"And death comes as the end."

"In the palace of the troll king."

Passing from inscription to inscription. A surfeit of wisdom: harmless or blunt or antiquated or tactless. Interchangeable wisdom. Carrion wisdom. The plaques on the wall are thinning out (now). Before one of the last, two lines from a Donne sermon, Diddy pauses; almost tired. Lays his flushed cheek against the cold stone for a moment. His strength quickly returning, continued on his way. Diddy's nostrils suffused with the odor of lava, the stench of the sea. And just one layer beneath these, something unpleasant that smelled like vomit. His fingertips brushing the grimy granite walls, as Diddy walked slowly. The slurred sounds of his steps echoed in his lonely skull.

Then Diddy saw a spacious vaulted archway. Beyond which a room, four times as wide though less long than the gallery in which he'd been walking. Antechamber, rather. Of the room he (now) approaches. And at the end of this room, was there still another doorway? Perhaps. Diddy's view, from here, too obstructed to permit him to see. Nevertheless, has already occurred to him that both the long gallery and the room he's about to enter are only the start of a series of connecting, underground chambers.

Through the doorway, Diddy passing into a vast squarish basementlike space with a high vaulted ceiling. A room, except that it was windowless, eminently suitable as the interior of a church. A church in some poor, pious Balkan country.

But worship wasn't the use to which this space had been put. Diddy has entered something like a huge burial crypt. One which is extravagantly ill-kept. Although the central aisle in which Diddy walked was fairly clear, everywhere else coffins are lying about in the most careless profusion. Hundreds, perhaps more than a thousand of them. Aslant; or tilted on one end; or turned over on

297

their sides; or precariously piled up, six or seven high, like logs for a fire. Looking as if they'd been heaped, tossed, thrown by someone in a state of exasperation and rage; or, maybe, fallen into the room. Rather than having been placed or even stacked. Nowhere giving the impression of any care or forethought. Too many of them, surely, even for this large space. But thus haphazardly disposed, disregarding every rule for the economical use of a limited space, the room appears far more crowded than it need have.

Maybe this wasn't a burial crypt in the ordinary sense, a place in which the dead were reverently placed, and periodically visited by grieving relatives and friends. Rather, a storage place for surplus bodies. Which would explain the shameless flouting of minimal standards of upkeep; as well as the absence of flowers, fresh or wax, and any of the other tributes that customarily decorate the resting places of the dead. Most of the coffins lack even a small plaque giving the name and birth and death dates of the deceased. Impossible to imagine this place being visited by anyone. How distressed any memory-burdened survivor would be to see the remains of someone he loved so ill-used, so negligently housed.

For it wasn't only the manner in which the coffins had been disposed. The coffins themselves in great disrepair. Diddy could see that fairly good wood had been used for some of them. But whether mahogany or oak or cheap pine, the wood was usually scratched, scarred, chipped. Even gouged—a peculiar, fairly uniform chunk about the size of a half dollar taken out. On the side of some coffins, the scratches were deeply incised and continuous, suggesting cursive writing. Nothing that Diddy could read, though. Illegible graffiti. And where wood had been painted rather than left in its natural state or simply varnished, the paint was peeling and discolored. In some cases, the very frame of the casket was coming apart; boards separating off from each other. Diddy, walking about in nothing but his tender flesh, has to keep an eye out for protruding rusty nails. Also, stay alert for the occasional warped board or partly loose lid jutting into the aisle that could scrape his ankle or shin or thigh. And since the lids of many coffins had been completely pried off, and then, sometimes, laid diagonally across the open coffins, Diddy had to be careful not to bump into one of these. Especially when he left the aisle, as he did several times, to clamber among the dense forest of death chests on either side. If he didn't watch his step, he'd quickly be spotted with blue and yellow bruises. Must also watch out for his bare feet. The danger of nails on the floor. And of wooden splinters from some of the coffin lids that had been ripped off and, neither placed diagonally across the coffin itself nor simply carried away, had fallen on the floor.

One selfish advantage in the deplorable condition of the coffins, though. Diddy could see inside. The entire contents of those without lids, just by looking down. And many of those coffins whose lids remained in place, firmly nailed down or fastened with bronze hasps, featured a small square window in the lid. Just by bending over and, when necessary, pushing some debris off the top, Diddy could see inside these coffins as well. Faces, at least.

The corpses he examined were of both sexes and all ages. Fully and rather formally dressed. And remarkably well preserved. Often, the face and hands—all that was visible of flesh itself—had a full sheath of dry parchmentlike skin. These faces were clearly human, mostly belonging to the white race, and, in many cases, recognizably American. Though overexpressive. Often badly distorted. Shrinkage of the skin, as it dried out under what was evidently a very superior embalming process, produced some painful grimaces and smiles. And not only was the skin mostly intact. Frequently, a full head of hair as well—in a color recognizably analogous to the original brown, blond, black, gray, or white as the case had been. And on about half of the men, beards and mustaches.

At first, this frequency of beards and mustaches puzzles Diddy, who recalls how few American men, either in his generation or in his father's, grew them. Until he realized that most of the bodies were much older than he'd assumed. All were decades, some even centuries, old. Diddy wouldn't have been able to guess their age simply from the color of the preserved skin, a strong sallow brown. But there were other clues.

Often, dress identified the period in which the dead person had lived. The woman in a coffin at the top of an unstable heap on the left, for instance, clad in a long, high-necked dress of the 1890's, with padded bosom. The man in the powdered wig and

Colonial shirt and breeches. But it was one particular coffin that gave Diddy what he considered virtually conclusive evidence for the considerable age of most of the bodies. This was a coffin in much better state than most, of highly polished oak, barely scratched, whose firmly secured lid had an almost full-length window. Diddy looking. The body of a little girl wearing a pink frock, white socks, and pink ankle-strap shoes of patent leather; according to the plaque on one side of the coffin, Martha Elizabeth Templeton, 1922–1933. But the child doesn't show any signs of decay that Diddy can detect through the glass. She looks alive. Just sleeping. Perhaps a little jaundiced, that's all. (Now) add to this striking sight the fact that, among the other coffins bearing names and dates, Diddy found, in an admittedly rapid, cursory search, no date as recent as 1933. And no body in as fresh and wholesome-looking a condition. So concludes that the others must go back in time, much further back.

Martha Elizabeth Templeton's coffin was sealed. But the temptation to touch was irresistible. Where touch was possible. Diddy reached out gingerly to several of the open coffins and stroked the withered, dusty faces. Most of the coffins containing, of course, only a single body. Sometimes accompanied by an object. Beloved or merely necessary, totem or tool. Beside one man in a full dress suit, a bassoon. A pair of crutches lay alongside a man in a brown tweed overcoat and cream-colored scarf; a man not visibly crippled; but perhaps the deformity would be visible if one rolled up his trouser legs, which Diddy started to do, but then stopped. He had glimpsed a piece of the white shinbone. What's rather touching, though, is the neat-looking old woman with gray hair who is still wearing her large pink plastic hearing aid.

In just a few of the coffins, Diddy found two people together. Because, having loved each other so much, they couldn't bear to rot separately; had rejected the idea of decaying anywhere except in each other's arms. Or because their families saw how much money they could save if they bought a single coffin? Peering through the pane of glass set in the top of one coffin, Diddy sees a withered youthful couple, the man on his left side and the woman on her right, embracing. Stretched out on her back in one of the

300

lidless coffins, a woman in a long white lace dress has clamped an infant—also wearing a white dress, a tiny replica of hers—to her breast. Diddy reached down and stroked the baby's cheek. Its skin looks fairly fresh to the eye. But feels soft like newspaper, not skin, to the fingers; as dried out as that of the oldest person he's touched here.

On the far side of some coffins which had tumbled into the long aisle and which he has to shove aside with his bare feet, then grapple and haul with his hands, Diddy has sighted an impressive doorway. He paused for a moment, indecisively. Wipes the sweat off his face with his forearm. Another moment of reflection. Chews at his lips with his teeth.

The answer to the unvoiced question is no. Not yet. Necessary for Diddy the Disciplined to proceed systematically, or he'll get lost. There's a system of priorities here, as anywhere else, that Diddy might be wise to observe. One thing at a time. (Now) the time to restrain mere curiosity. Diddy isn't ready for something new, since he has yet to explore with thoroughness the area in this room on both sides of the long aisle. That's why he turns back into the aisle, continuing for a distance of some fifty feet.

Diddy has ventured again into the intricate crowded space. Finding miniature pathways for his naked body between the heaped-up coffins when possible; more agile climbing over the coffins when necessary. Diddy's score: only one near fall, plus a scrape on his right knee. And, as he expected, his efforts have yielded results. Diddy does uncover an exit in each of the walls parallel to the aisle. So, besides the room straight ahead, there's another room branching off to the left, still another to the right. Diddy has much to see.

These rooms, also crammed with coffins, are far smaller than the main crypt; with flat ceilings about ten feet high. And warmer, Diddy sweating. Making him feel even dustier and dirtier. Wipes away moisture from his palms, forehead, upper lip, the back of his neck. Anything to be done for him? One could hardly hope to find a thermostat in rooms as unsentimental, bare, and purely functional as these; Diddy is already fortunate to have this much good light, furnished by the naked bulbs jutting out of iron wall fixtures

301

in all the rooms. Still wishes it weren't so warm. Perhaps the temperature of the place has to be kept high; part of the method by which the dead bodies are preserved. For them it may be just the right temperature. But not, altogether, for Diddy: lone subject in a world of objects. Think, though, that he could be worse off than he is. What a lucky whim that was long ago, when he decided to discard all his clothes.

Nakedness may mitigate heat, but it doesn't redeem the squalor of these rooms. Which continues to dishearten Diddy. None of the rooms are infested with either vermin or rats—as far as he's noticed, anyway. Still, everything is appallingly dirty. Not grime and soot. Nor blood, excrement, grease, semen. Not the dirt of animal secretions and excretions. Not industrial wastes, either. The dirt of time. Immortal dirt. Thick, thick dust.

Which Diddy is getting used to (now). Being naked may not render his surroundings less squalid, but at least it minimizes some of the penalties for being here rather than somewhere else. Diddy may dislike the contact of his own flesh with what's dirty or soiled or rotten or slimy. But doesn't, in addition, have to endure the indignity of getting his clothes dirty as well.

Becoming more accustomed to this new space and its stringent topography. Learning how to manage obstacles. The common case of new skills arriving just when they're needed, no sooner. Diddy the Vulnerable stands in acute need of being transformed into Diddy the Intrepid. Precisely at this moment. For Diddy had never suspected the tunnel to be this vast, so complex. And (now) he's eager to explore all of it.

Trying, in turn, each of the new rooms.

Finds, in every one of these smaller rooms, more coffins. Lying about in a foul disarray—that resembles, on a smaller scale, that of the large vaulted chamber. And the coffins themselves as poorly cared for. Individual caskets are coming apart; and some of them, perhaps once neatly stacked, have toppled over, broken open, and spilled out an arm or leg. Watch out! Don't trip over one of those. Several skulls that have gotten separated from their families, the bones below. Skulls like shells.

These rooms give on to still more rooms. Diddy the Naked

passes through them very rapidly (now), his brisk walk sometimes breaking into a loose-limbed run. No need to gaze at everything closely, when everything looks more or less alike. Diddy the Surveyor just checking, to see if the general idea remains the same. But to do this, he must at least glance in every room. Usually possible. But not always. Diddy exasperated when, as happens several times, disorder mounts and clutter becomes so dense that there's not space enough to enable even a single person to pass through. To keep moving. One solution would be for Diddy to set to work and clear a narrow passageway for himself. But he doesn't. Not that he lacks the physical strength. It's a question of prudence and the best use of his time. At the entrance to one room, a rickety wall of coffins rises almost to the ceiling; ignorant of what lay on the far side of the doorway, Diddy thought it hardly prudent to undertake the strenuous labor of dismantling the improvised wall and hauling the coffins away, one by one. Similar decisions made on two other occasions when, exploring a new corridor, his route was halted by what looks like the aftermath of an avalanche of coffins.

Then what happens when the massive wooden casket boxes are piled so thickly as to obstruct Diddy's passage, preventing him altogether from getting by? Only one alternative. Diddy is reluctantly forced, several times, to retrace his steps. To regain the big chamber. Then to move forward again in a straight line. Keeping to the central sequence.

Diddy is reconnoitering the future. Diddy is exploring his death. Cautiously, thoughtfully, diligently. He wills to know, he will know all the rooms in this place; even if it's the house of death.

Thought a moment ago he hears the throbbing of a fast train charging along the tracks. Coming closer (now). If that's what the sound is, he's safe. Diddy could hardly be in a safer place. No train can follow him here; no tracks have been laid on these stone floors, or possibly would be. Then let it come on as fast as it likes. Aren't there speeds so great they obtain immobility?

(Now) Diddy has entered another large chamber, fully as wide as the first and even longer. Only the ceiling isn't as high; and not vaulted. Still, it's more than twice the height of the ceilings in the small rooms. As before, the room is harshly lit by a plentiful number of naked bulbs. But for all the light, it's definitely cooler; for which Diddy, gleaming with sweat, was grateful.

Diddy in what could be called the second grand crypt. A room whose contents or furniture differ from those in the room he's already explored—the first large chamber and its dependencies. Here, not even a halfhearted sloppy attempt is made to enclose the dead in coffins. The dead (now) are simply in an upright posture, side by side. In three rows, using up all the space on all four walls from floor to ceiling. Each body is secured in place by two long heavy ropes: one wound once around the chest, passing out on either side under the armpits; and the other wound once tightly around each pair of knees. Both upper and lower ropes run from body to body; continuing unbroken, not even knotted once, the entire length of each wall.

If these three rows of bodies had been all, the second chamber would have had a remarkably uncluttered, spacious look. But, as before, the genius of disorder and overpopulation that governed this place had been at work here, too. Though every foot of the long walls was taken up with bodies, there were apparently more candidates for these spaces than could possibly have been accommodated. These surplus bodies lie, three and four high, at the base of the gray stone walls. And while the bodies suspended on the walls are arranged quite neatly—initially, at least, a good deal of care must have gone into their installation—those stacked on the floor lie in all sorts of awkward positions. About the only idea of order that appears to have been acknowledged at all is one concerning direction. Keep their heads to the wall, their feet pointing toward the center of the room. Needless to say, that rule had been violated or ignored a good many times.

In short: Diddy notices here the same lack of careful maintenance as in the rooms with the broken and heaped-up coffins. And, with better care, who knows how much more intact and lifelike these nonetheless remarkably preserved bodies might have been? A wider range on that matter, here. Some of these bodies seem better preserved than any he saw in the rooms with the coffins. Some are in far worse condition. So far as Diddy can deter-

304

mine—given that, as before, all the bodies are clothed—fewer here have an envelope of skin that is relatively intact. But the skin itself seems tougher, more durable. A very dark leathery skin, rather than the frailer parchment on the bodies laid out in the coffins. All too frequently, though, the leathery skin is falling away, and the bones sticking through. And some figures on the walls are virtually without any of this metamorphosed flesh. But even those that are merely skeletons are never bare skeletons. Always at least some patch of leathery skin adhering to the bones. As was the case with the coffined bodies, most of the faces here are very distorted. Because the shrinkage of the flesh has twisted the leather mask into grotesque expressions. Or—this additional reason, a penalty, no doubt, of upright posture—because the jawbone has fallen off. Producing the effect of a grotesque scream. But almost all the toothless skulls with their empty eye sockets retain some of their hair, if nothing else. A full head of perfectly preserved hair, like a wig, may lie above a face whose flesh has entirely dropped away. Some with only shreds of flesh sport thick chunks of scalp hair. Diddy noticed one skull with no flesh at all, except what could be presumed to lie under its flourishing beard and mustache.

Again, it's by the clothing that Diddy could always tell the sex of the body, usually the period in which the person lived, and often his or her occupation. The condition and color of the hair also give some evidence, though hardly conclusive, of the person's age at the time of death. Some of the guesses Diddy makes may be farfetched, but they are better than nothing. For, in this new chamber or zone of the space he's exploring, none of the bodies is labeled with name and dates of birth and death. Perhaps there is a book, somewhere. A huge, moldy, fascinating catalogue in which everyone is identified.

As if he were wandering through a warehouse, Diddy began taking stock. What are the contents, in more detail? This large chamber seemed to contain a random collection of bodies. Of both sexes, all ages, who lived in widely different periods. The earliest specimen Diddy could find belonged to the seventeenth century: a Pilgrim with a broad-brimmed hat, round stiff collar, breeches, and buckled shoes. But nearby, many modern types. A banker in a top hat and striped pants and cutaway coat. A boy in his Cub Scout uniform. A registered nurse. A policeman, one of New York's Finest. For this room, bodies seem to have been supplied right up to the present day. Many figures on the walls who postdate the unhappily brief span of Martha Elizabeth Templeton, *d.* 1933. For instance, a GI in the battle dress of the 1960's with a Silver Star pinned to his left breast pocket. But not one body, however recent, was as fresh, as nearly well preserved as that of Martha Elizabeth Templeton. Maybe she was just an exception to all the rules.

Passing on to some of the succeeding, small rooms, Diddy has to admit that a good deal of care has been taken here. At least, at the time the bodies were installed. For most of these small rooms were specialized. Bodies had had to be sorted out, and then the subgroupings of bodies assembled.

A whole room, for instance, given over to young children. Just as many rows, three, of bodies less than five feet tall could be mounted on all the walls; even though the ceiling here is considerably lower than that of the large chamber. This room is the first on his tour to make Diddy feel sad. At least if the children had been put in coffins, they could lie hugging a favorite doll or some other toy. But hanging here, they look so abandoned and unloved. Each completely unrelated to all the others, as if they'd been captured and strung up while still alive; dying, not of starvation or physical mistreatment, but of loneliness. Look at that little girl in the second row near the corner, the one wearing her white communion dress. The splendor of children is never, really, more than pathos.

In another room, only firemen. Decked out in their uniforms, with rubber boots to the tops of their thighs. Many with the huge, red, oval-brimmed hat that's their trademark. Cocked on their skull; not so much rakishly as awkwardly, since the head, with or without meat and hair on it, tends to slump forward. (Now) the mood is quite different. Adult splendors are either satisfying or comic. Diddy feels these men are quite pleased with themselves. And that they know why they're here.

In another room, nothing but priests. Diddy looks about the

walls for "his" priest, the plump smooth-voiced man with the breviary. But how can he tell any more? Any one of these grinning black-suited bodies might be that man. No point in not looking, though. Diddy came closer. Until he realized that these priests, especially those in purple and white ceremonial robes, have a bulk that cannot be genuine. Faking? Alas, yes. Even here. As Diddy discovers, most of the bodies—or rather, skeletons—have been stuffed with straw to give shape to their imposing clothes. Sometimes, when the trick fails, the effect is almost funny. As it must fail, of course, when the body has no skin left. For instance, with that very rotund priest wearing the black vestment for a Solemn High Requiem Mass. With bits of straw peeping out of his wide sleeve, above the few skinny bones which are all that remain of his wrist and hand.

And an entire room of figures wearing Civil War uniforms, both blue and gray. This room, on closer inspection, seems to be even more specialized than that description would indicate. Reserved not simply for men who had fought in the Civil War but, judging from their white hair and generally small stature, for aged veterans only. Many, perhaps, who hadn't died until quite recently. At a hundred years or more. A funerary parade for the Republic.

In another room, men and boys in the uniforms of various sports. After the experience of the roomful of stuffed priests, Diddy more suspicious (now). Could one be buried or interred—or whatever this is—in a uniform to which one has, properly, no title? After all, not everyone can be glamorous. But so many people want to be, or at least think they do. Is he genuine, that football player by the doorway whose massive shoulder pads come up, on either side, almost to the top of his bare, small skull? Even when fleshed and alive and running, must have had a small head. Over there, a catcher for the San Francisco Giants—if one can trust the evidence of the uniform and the mask whose metal bars cover the dead man's lean, contorted, well-preserved face. Diddy in a mood to be pigheaded, to take nothing on faith. But why should the dead pretend to be other than they are? And even if such was their dying wish, why should the survivors indulge it? Are there many among the living who would go to the trouble of masquerading these bodies to satisfy a vulgar vain fantasy that expired with the deceased's last heartbeat? Diddy scraps his policy of suspiciousness. Resolving to meet the evidence halfway or more; to give the corpses the benefit of the doubt. For instance, it's hardly likely that any of the figures dressed as basketball players are phonies, impersonators. Because of their height. The tallest of those assembled here being a seven foot seven skeleton in the uniform of the Cincinnati Royals, an impressive figure with his knee guards still clinging to his bare patellae.

In another room, figures in denim overalls and workshirts or similar tough, shapeless clothing. No pretensions here. Farmers and farmhands, Diddy supposed. Many types of blue-collar workers are probably represented, too: riveters and welders from automobile factories, sewing machine operators, ditchdiggers, telephone-line repairmen, janitors, bricklayers, longshoremen, garage mechanics, and so forth. Is this where Incardona would be assigned a place? Here? Strung on one of the walls of this very low-ceilinged airless room? As if he were in fact the admissions officer charged with making the decision, Diddy hesitates. Diddy behaving as if he has found some fault in the way Incardona's application has been filled out, as if he seeks some bureaucratic technicality that would bar the workman. Why? Because he thinks that Incardona deserves better accommodations than these, or because he wants to bar Incardona from the kingdom he has already come to regard as his own? Diddy is being tiresome. Whether it's the first, a misplaced solicitude, or the second, a burst of spite, he should stop. Stop stalling. Why not Incardona? Why not here, for God's sake? Or anywhere else. Surely Diddy can't take very seriously this *ad hoc,* amateurish system of filing the bodies? And if what moves him is not a habit of inane deliberateness when confronted with any organized system, then Diddy is being not only vindictive but snobbish. Where does he think he is? It's hardly an exclusive club. A candidate doesn't need to have a good character, or meet any other standards that might be applied to his life. The only prerequisite is being dead. Diddy the Reluctant Democrat. Well then, let's bury him. Diddy takes a step backwards, glancing over his shoulder at the doorway through which he has just come. But Diddy doesn't want to retrace his steps; would rather do almost anything than go back out into the tunnel. Someone else is there besides Incardona. But a stranger might go in Diddy's place. Voluntarily perform the arduous errand. As a favor. Or an act of charity.

Isn't there anyone else around to drag that heavy body in here, and hoist it on the wall and secure it with the ropes? Assuming, of course, that there's room. That a place can be made for him.

Indeed, space seemed to be rapidly becoming more of a problem. As Diddy ventured farther, quitting the room that was Incardona's prospective resting place for new rooms, noticed how much more crowded they are getting. Also that most of the bodies he saw (now) had scarcely begun to decay, which suggested that it was the population of the recently dead rising to unmanageable numbers? Strange. Doesn't the casualty rate remain fairly constant? Maybe not. Whatever the explanation, the density of the bodies is definitely increasing. The ones hanging on the walls more closely packed together, and sometimes in double rows; those on the floor, stacked higher and higher and also farther toward the center. One room succeeds another. The unachievable goal being, eventually, to leave no empty space at all. Let the vacuum be filled. The house properly ordered. A plenum of death.

What does Diddy feel as he reconnoiters the future, taking note of the inexhaustible contents of this charnel house? Except for being too warm, he's not physically uncomfortable; and dusty old-fashioned blade fans suspended from the ceiling in some of the rooms are slowly turning, circulating the musty air a little. His state of mind and heart not too uncomfortable, either. You might imagine he's overcome, some or all of the time, by disgust. But that's not so. Then is he at least depressed by what he sees? Not that either. Frightened? Which would seem to be natural. Again, no. As it happens, none of these emotions are the ones appropriate to this labyrinthine interior and its displays. Which, however somber, generate in Diddy a mood that's somehow light. Despite the squalor and overcrowding that had at first so upset Diddy, the effect of this place upon him is curiously soothing. Inducing a state that's almost emotionless.

Bathed in this dull iridescent state of feeling, Diddy continues walking. But gradually slowing down. Such his compromise between the urge to run and the insidious desire to dally along the way. Another barely perceptible conflict headed off.

Sometimes he visits the same room twice. Which isn't particularly his intention.

Yet Diddy is not just wandering, trying to pretend he isn't lost. Rather than feeling like a tourist bravely attempting to master an exotic town who lacks both guide and an adequate itinerary or agenda, he feels like a pilgrim who has been briefed thoroughly by his predecessors. If becalmed, then with the concentration of devoutness. What remains to be done has been done before many times, by many others. Diddy not in possession of all the details. Yet how could he feel so confident, so at home; why should everything novel he sees also look familiar? The explanation is easy. What has been happening thus far has constituted an order. Why shouldn't it so continue? Diddy can't be lost. Even though, at this point, in this place, has stumbled into a new medium. Entering a new phase. What phase? From one point of view, this space is a panoramic stage set, a kind of theatrical display. And Diddy may be invited to give his opinion of it. Unless he's got matters wrong, and he's not the judge at all. Maybe, if this space is a theatre of judgment, Diddy's task is to find another person, a judge. Who will examine and render a verdict on him.

From another view, of course, nothing could be less relevant here than judgment. That's what death is about. They're all collected here, the guilty and the innocent, those who tried and those who didn't. Which thought makes Diddy laugh aloud. Absolved from the duty of classifying himself or appraising his surroundings.

What Diddy sees is, at the very least, never less than interesting. Death = an encyclopedia of life.

Is this place Diddy's nightmare? Or the resolution of his nightmare?

A false question, since there are in fact two nightmares. Distinct, if not contradictory. The nightmare that there are *two* worlds. The nightmare that there is only *one* world. This one.

Wait. Perhaps he has the answer to that desperate thought about the world. Life = the world. Death = being completely inside

310

one's own head. Do those new equations refute the puzzle of the two nightmares?

Diddy pondering so intently about these matters that for long intervals he completely forgets where he is. Where and in what state is his body. Even (now), his thoughts bully him. Wouldn't you think he would have discarded them, along with his clothes, when he entered this place? But they're still with him, preserved in their own amber.

As though Diddy were living at last in his eyes, only in his eyes. The outward eye that names and itemizes, the inward eye that throbs with thought.

But he's not always so solemn. Sometimes almost gay. "Gather ye rosebuds." This is when, while perfectly able to see, he is not just a pair of wet vulnerable eyes lying in their sockets like molluscs in their shells. Swarms with the happiness of being in his body, and feels his nakedness as a delicious blessing. His alert head; the strength of his supple feet traversing the cool stone flooring; the easy hang of his shoulders and the bunched muscles of his calves; his sensitive capacious chest; the hard wall of his lean belly; the tender sex brushing the top of his thighs. Astonishing, isn't it, that any infant human being ever surrenders such pleasures. And consents to put on clothes.

Other moments, though, he can't help tensing his shoulders, raising them; his breathing becomes shallower and his step sags. Feels a sickening edge of something that resembles fear. A particular hush. A rancid smell. He may be about to ask himself what he has done. Whether all this is a dishonorable isolation, a useless ordeal. But Diddy knows how to cope with such vexing moments that threaten to subvert his courage. He dreams that he will find Hester at the end of his tour. That at this moment she is in some distant room or gallery, placidly awaiting him. Her role a perfectly clear one, and well within her powers. To save him, like the princess in some fairy tale. Love's power sweeping him up from the kingdom of death. "Death and the maiden."

All he has to do is keep walking. Put one foot in front of the other. Whether Hester is waiting or not.

More rooms. More deaths.

Has Diddy reached his destination?

Dying is overwork.

Again Diddy hears the sound of a train, and faint shouts. A dog barking.

A trim, youngish Negro wearing white jacket and pants wheels a cart to his bed. Reeking of vomit. Who is? Diddy. Diddy the Soiled.

More rooms. Diddy walks on, looking for his death. Diddy has made his final chart; drawn up his last map. Diddy has perceived the inventory of the world.